**"Thank you for your kindness to my sister,"
Joseph told her softly. "I have never seen
her so happy."**

Nugget broke free and skipped ahead. Annabelle
didn't have the heart to stop her.

"I'm glad to have given her something to be happy
about." She smiled. Joseph wasn't too bad. Cleaned
up the way he was, it was almost easy to pretend he
was just a normal man.

Annabelle stumbled slightly. Joseph wasn't a normal
man. And it wouldn't do for her to entertain feelings
when she knew she couldn't count on a miner to
stick around. Not that she had any intention of
entertaining feelings about any man.

At least not here in Leadville. The town was full
of shiftless drifters, and the one time she'd let her
guard down to trust in someone, he'd betrayed
her. Something she'd do well to remember in the
presence of this man.

Especially with the way Joseph's sparkling smile
made her tingle all the way down to her toes.

Danica Favorite
and
Jessica Nelson

Rocky Mountain Dreams
&
Family on the Range

LOVE INSPIRED
INSPIRATIONAL ROMANCE

LOVE INSPIRED®

INSPIRATIONAL ROMANCE

Recycling programs
for this product may
not exist in your area.

ISBN-13: 978-1-335-44874-3

Rocky Mountain Dreams & Family on the Range

Copyright © 2021 by Harlequin Books S.A.

Rocky Mountain Dreams
First published in 2014. This edition published in 2021.
Copyright © 2014 by Danica Favorite

Family on the Range
First published in 2014. This edition published in 2021.
Copyright © 2014 by Jessica Nelson

This edition published by arrangement with Harlequin Books S.A.

For questions and comments about the quality of this book,
please contact us at CustomerService@Harlequin.com.

Love Inspired
22 Adelaide St. West, 40th Floor
Toronto, Ontario M5H 4E3, Canada
www.Harlequin.com

Printed in U.S.A.

CONTENTS

Danica Favorite loves the adventure of living a creative life. She loves to explore the depths of human nature and follow people on the journey to happily-ever-after. Though the journey is often bumpy, those bumps refine imperfect characters as they live the life God created them for. Oops, that just spoiled the ending of Danica's stories. Then again, getting there is all the fun. Find her at danicafavorite.com.

Visit the Author Profile page
at Harlequin.com for more titles.

ROCKY MOUNTAIN DREAMS

Danica Favorite

You intended to harm me, but God intended it for good to accomplish what is now being done, the saving of many lives.

—*Genesis* 50:20

An author's first book often comes from years of support from friends and family. This book is no different. It would take an entire book to thank all those who've supported me through the years, so here is my general thank-you to all those who deserve it. You know who you are. Thank you.

For those who didn't get to see this dream come true before their passing—Theresa and Pat, you guys get the first nod. Your love and support meant a lot, and I wish you could have seen this come true.

Randy, Army Girl, Accountant, Cowgirl and Princess, thanks for putting up with crazy writer mommy.

Chip, I guess you told me so. Thanks.

Everyone else, I'll catch you in future books.

Much love to all,

Danica

Chapter One

❧

1881

The soft breeze floating off the Mosquito Range made the air feel more like midsummer than early June in Leadville. Which meant Annabelle Lassiter could almost declare mud season officially over. Though today's walk to the post office hadn't resulted in a letter from her aunt Celeste, surely she could escape this town and its painful reminders soon.

She paused as the parsonage came into view. A man waited on the porch. Annabelle sighed. Her father's mission to care for the miners in Leadville was wonderful, but these days, they had more hungry people showing up on their doorstep than she knew what to do with. They had food aplenty, but Annabelle's heart didn't have the strength to keep working when it seemed like every day held a new heartbreak.

Annabelle pasted a smile on her face as she walked up the steps of the parsonage to greet the man so covered in grime she couldn't make out his features. Probably a younger man, considering his hair was still dark.

This place had a way of aging a person so that appearances could be deceiving. Two white eyes blinked at her.

"Supper's not 'til seven." She'd learned not to be too friendly, too welcoming, lest her words be misconstrued. Besides, her face was too weighed down by her heart to find it in her to give this stranger a smile.

Those eyes continued staring at her. She'd seen dozens of men just like him. Miners willing to spend everything they owned to strike the big one, and when they ran out of options, they arrived on the Lassiters' doorstep.

As she got closer, she noticed a small child huddled next to him. So he was one of those. Bad enough to waste your life on a fool's errand, but to take a child with you...

"Of course, if you'll come around back, I'm sure I can find something for your little...girl." At least she hoped that's what the child was. Underneath all that filth, it was hard to tell. Whatever kindness Annabelle had left in her remained reserved for the children. Innocent victims of their parents' selfish dreams for riches that most who came to Leadville never found. Or when they did, they squandered their money in the many saloons in town. The Colorado mountains were tough on anybody, but especially on the little ones.

"I need to see the preacher." The man's voice came out raspy, like he'd spent too many days underground working the mines.

Annabelle tried not to sigh. Her father held more grubstakes and pieces of paper promising repayment when the mine finally paid out than she could count. If they had a penny for every paper they held, they'd be richer than these miners ever thought they could be. But, if she turned this one away, and her father got wind of it, he'd be upset.

"Come around back, then." Maddie would have her hide if she brought them through the front parlor. The last thing she needed was to be at the other end of Maddie's tongue for more bootprints on the carpets.

The man stood, and the little girl buried her head further into his side. At this angle, Annabelle could see sloppy braids cascading down the girl's back. Poor child.

"It's all right, sweetheart." Annabelle knelt in front of her. "My name's Annabelle, and my father is the preacher. We'll help with whatever you need."

Round eyes with dark centers blinked at her. The little girl let loose of her hold on the man's filthy pants enough for them to walk down the steps and around the path to the backyard. Knowing her father, he was puttering in the garden, hoping to coax their spindly plants into doing something they were never designed to do at this elevation and these temperatures.

But he had faith that if Jesus could feed the masses with His loaves and His fish, then their tiny plants could keep their community fed. Annabelle shook her head. Too bad that faith hadn't yet panned out.

"Father?" Annabelle spied him plucking at a half-dead tomato plant.

His straw hat bobbed as he looked up at her. "Who've you got there?"

He didn't wait for an answer but stood and started toward them, brushing his hands on his pants.

"Joseph Stone, sir. I need a moment of your time." The man glanced at Annabelle like whatever he had to say wasn't meant for a female's delicate ears. There wasn't much Annabelle's delicate ears hadn't heard. Such was the life of a preacher's daughter in a mining town. Her family had come here to make the miners' lives better, and that meant dwelling in the deepest muck found in the human heart.

But just as working in the mines had a way of prematurely aging a man, helping the miners had a way of tearing at a person's heart. She wanted to love and care for people like this man and his little girl, but her heart felt like it had been wrung out so completely that there was nothing left to give. Surely if she left this place, her heart would finally have room to heal.

"I'll go put on some tea." She glanced at the man. "Or would you prefer coffee?"

He stared at her. "Nothing, thank you."

No, he probably just wanted Father's money. Some might say it was wrong of her to judge so quickly, but enough miners had come to their home that she no longer had to guess what they wanted.

Annabelle smiled at the girl, pulling on her heart's last reserves. "Want to come help me in the kitchen? I baked a whole mess of cookies earlier, and if you don't help me eat them, my father and I are going to have to do it ourselves. You don't want us to get bellyaches, do you?"

The little girl smiled, which would have been a pretty sight if those baby teeth of hers weren't almost all rotten. How could a man be so selfish in his pursuit of riches that he'd let this sweet thing have such a rough life? Not her business. As sweet as this little girl was, Annabelle couldn't let her heart get too involved.

"Can I?" She looked up at her father with such hopeful eyes.

"Annabelle will take good care of her. She has a way with youngsters," her father said quietly. He, too, had a heart for the children.

The man, Joseph, nodded. Annabelle held out her

hand. "Come along now. We'll get you washed up at the pump, then go inside for some treats."

The little girl looked at Annabelle's hand, then took it. "Nugget."

"I beg your pardon?" Annabelle looked at her.

"My name is Nugget," the girl said softly.

Annabelle suppressed a sigh. Her father was one of those. So enraptured with the idea of getting rich, he even named his child after the evil silver.

"That's a nice name." It wasn't the girl's fault. From the way her face lit up at Annabelle's compliment, she'd probably gotten more than her share of teasing for such a ridiculous name.

Once she helped Nugget wash up, they went into the house.

The little girl looked around, then ran her hands along the lace tablecloth adorning their kitchen table. "This is pretty, like at Miss Betty's place."

What had they gotten themselves into? Miss Betty was one of the town's notorious madams. Her father had helped plenty of women escape that profession. Still, Annabelle had never been inside one of those places, and for a child to know…was simply unfathomable.

How unfair that someone so young had seen the inside of a brothel. Worse, that if something wasn't done to help her, the little girl probably would end up working there someday. One of the harsh realities Annabelle faced daily.

Which was why Annabelle had to get out of Leadville. Though her father would tell her she should not grow weary of doing good, she was weary. Weary of helping people like this little girl and her father only to have it end badly. Perhaps they helped some people, but these days, all Annabelle could recall were the great losses.

Annabelle put a kettle on the stove for tea, then got out a plate of cookies. "Do you like snickerdoodles? They were my late mother's favorite recipe."

"You don't got no mama, neither?"

Annabelle closed her eyes, trying to push the memories away before looking at Nugget. "She died of a fever last winter."

Her father's faith hadn't done them much good then, either. Their prayers hadn't worked for her mother, or Susannah, or her brothers Peter, Mark and John, or anyone else for that matter. Half of their congregation had died from the same fever that had killed Catherine Lassiter. Even the two miners she'd worked so hard to nurse back to health. Though the fever hadn't taken them. No, they'd lived only to find death in a drunken brawl in one of the saloons.

No wonder her heart was so weary.

But bitterness wouldn't help this child, and she at least could offer the little girl kindness.

Annabelle gave Nugget a small squeeze. "I'm sorry for your loss."

"My mama had the pox."

Ears burning, Annabelle forced herself to focus on being compassionate rather than frustrated at a world that would let a little girl like Nugget know about the pox. Times like this, it was difficult to understand why her father chose this life. No matter how many people they helped, they continued to encounter more tragic situations every day.

"You poor thing." Annabelle wrapped her arms around the girl, knowing that one hug wouldn't make up for anything. But her heart ached for this child, and she couldn't help but give what little she had to comfort the girl.

The back door banged open, and Nugget jerked away. Annabelle looked up to see their housekeeper returning from her errands.

"We have a visitor," Annabelle said.

Maddie looked the little girl up and down, then gave Annabelle a knowing glance. She liked the invasion of her household even less, but the tenderness in her eyes reminded Annabelle that she wasn't the only one with a soft spot for children.

"How about some tea to go with those cookies?" Annabelle gave Nugget a little pat, then busied herself with fixing the tea. She stole a glance at Nugget, who nibbled at a cookie.

Well, she wasn't starving. The hungry ones wolfed down the whole plate at once, and Annabelle always felt compelled to send them away with sandwiches. But this little girl...

At least her father kept her fed. Maybe she shouldn't have judged him when she'd first encountered them. She knew nothing of their story. Once upon a time, Annabelle would have wanted to hear that story and see what she could to do to help. But it seemed like too many of the stories Annabelle participated in only ended in heartache.

The only thing Annabelle could let herself help with was making sure this family didn't go hungry. Still, there were hungers that went deeper than the need for food. Of those, Annabelle knew. She might not have ever gone to bed wondering where the next meal was coming from, but she always went to bed wanting. Someday, she would have a life outside of a hopeless ministry that only broke her heart more and more each day.

Surely her aunt Celeste would send for her soon. Then Annabelle could move back East, where people's lives weren't filled with empty dreams of riches. Maybe there, she could meet a man who wasn't blinded by tales of the mother lode. The search for silver brought too much heartache to a body, and Annabelle was ready to leave this life behind.

The little girl tugged at Annabelle's skirts, reminding her of the steaming kettle, and that as easy as it was to dream of a new life, there was still so much work to be done here.

Joseph Stone followed the preacher into the church, watching as Annabelle escorted his sister into the house. Though she hadn't seemed very warm toward him, Annabelle had treated his sister with more kindness than the other ladies they'd encountered in town.

Most of the pretty girls he knew wouldn't have taken the time to be nice to a young child, let alone someone as ill-kept as Nugget. Not that he had much experience with pretty girls. The only woman who'd paid him any notice, Margaret Anderson, had thrown him over for Walter Blankenship because, in her words, "Walter didn't have any brats to care for." Probably for the best. If Margaret hadn't been able to stomach the idea of helping him care for the siblings he had back home, how could he have expected her to have anything to do with a child of Nugget's background?

Not that he'd put Miss Annabelle Lassiter in the same category. Sure, they were both pretty, but Annabelle's blue eyes were more like the sky on a cloudless day, unlike Margaret's—

He had no business thinking about any girl's eyes, especially not a preacher's daughter's. And especially not when he had a family to provide for and a father to find.

The preacher didn't speak until they were seated at

a desk in his office. Joseph respected that. The other miners had told him that Preacher Lassiter was a good man who treated all with respect.

"What can I do for you, son?"

Son. Not in a condescending way, but in a way that sounded like he actually cared. In a way that made him wish his own father was more…fatherly. And not a low-down snake who'd put him in this predicament.

Joseph swallowed the lump in his throat. "I need help. My father, William Earl Stone, came here several years ago in search of silver. I need to find him."

His chest burned with the humiliation of what he'd encountered searching for his pa. "When I made inquiries about him, I was directed to Miss Betty's." Hopefully his face wasn't too red at the mention of the place, especially in front of a man of the cloth. But Preacher Lassiter didn't look like the mention of a house of ill repute bothered him.

"When I got there, they gave me Nugget. Said she was my pa's, and to give her to him because her ma was dead."

It still rankled to know his pa had reduced himself to visiting those women. At least his ma wasn't around to witness his pa's betrayal. Joseph swallowed the bile that rose up every time he thought about his poor ma, waiting for news of a man who had to have betrayed her the minute he arrived in town. Oh, he didn't doubt that Nugget was his sister. She had the look of his sister Mary, waiting back at home for a pa not worthy of her regard.

Preacher Lassiter leaned forward on his desk. "What do you want me to do? Find a home for the little girl?"

"No!" The word burst out of his mouth. Much as he hated to admit it, Nugget was kin, and she was an innocent child who didn't deserve the life she had.

Joseph leaned back against the chair. "I don't know what to do. Ma died nearly four months ago. Pa stopped sending money shortly before her death, and I just know Ma died of a broken heart because the bank told her they were going to take the farm."

No expression crossed the preacher's face; at least none Joseph could discern. "I've got five sisters and a brother staying with an aunt in Ohio. We've got no place to go. Aunt Ina is threatening to send them all to an orphanage. I've been working hard to make up for what Pa used to send, but it's not enough. When Ma got sick, the doctor was so expensive. I couldn't afford it all and we lost the farm."

Joseph's gut ached at having to share so much of his personal business with this man.

He looked the preacher in the eye, straightening in his chair. "I'm not asking for me. I know how to make it on my own. I've been doing it since I was a boy. But I've got to do better for my brother and sisters. I need to find my pa and get the money he's been denying us so I can keep them out of an orphanage."

The last word squeaked out of him—a painful reality he didn't want to face. Especially now that he had another sister to consider. How could he be responsible for sending seven kids to an orphanage?

"The boardinghouse wouldn't let me keep Nugget there with me. Called it improper. I can't afford the hotel. We've been staying in a tent outside of camp, but it's no place for a little girl. I've been working in the mines to send money to my aunt so she'll keep the others a little longer."

And, from the letter he'd just received, probably not much longer if Daniel didn't stop his antics. It wasn't

Daniel's fault, not really. But living with all those girls, and not having a man's guidance...

Joseph let out a deep breath. "Sir, I know you get all sorts of people on your doorstep, but I need to find my father. You're my last hope of finding him. People say there isn't a miner in these parts you don't know."

The preacher rubbed his stubbled jaw. "What'd you say his name was?"

"William Earl Stone." He exhaled, then said, "The lady at Miss Betty's called him Bad Billy." He wasn't sure he wanted to know the reason for his pa's moniker, not with the way the woman had winked when she'd called him that. One more reason to hate the man.

The preacher closed his eyes for a moment, then sighed. "I didn't recognize the full name, but at mention of Bad Billy, I know who you're talking about."

What kind of man had his pa become, that even the preacher had that disgusted look in his eyes?

Joseph swallowed. "Can you tell me where to find him?"

"I'm sorry, son. Your father died nearly six months ago."

Dead. So Joseph had spent everything he had on a fool's errand. He should be comforted to know that the reason the money had stopped was that his pa had died. But comfort wouldn't feed his family or keep them out of the orphanage.

Chapter Two

Joseph stood and extended his hand. "Thank you, sir, for your time. I appreciate your assistance."

The preacher didn't take it. He looked up at him with cornflower-blue eyes that inappropriately reminded Joseph of Annabelle.

"Sit back down, young man. You have a problem, and informing you of the sad news of your father's passing doesn't solve it. I can't in good conscience let you leave until we've got a better solution for your family."

A man who'd spent years caring for a family in place of an absent father didn't weep. But in the face of the past few weeks, combined with the news that it had all been for nothing, this man's kindness made him want to do so.

Preacher Lassiter stood. "It seems to me that as your father's son, you'd be next of kin. Therefore, I think it fitting that I give you some papers your father entrusted me with. I recognize you from a picture he showed me."

Hopefully those papers would lead to the source of the money his pa had been sending. It hadn't been much, but maybe, just maybe, it would be a start. One of the men he'd sat next to on the train had talked about places out West that still needed settling. He could take advantage of the Homestead Act. Sure, it wouldn't be the farm they'd lost, but it would be enough. Farming was good, honest work, and certainly more rewarding than all the time Joseph had spent in the mines.

For the first time since coming out here, Joseph felt hopeful that maybe things would finally be all right.

"I appreciate that, Preacher. Anything you can do is a blessing."

The preacher smiled at him. "Call me Frank." He pulled a key out of his pocket and walked past him. "I've got his things in a safe I keep in the other room, so I'll be right back."

It had to be a good sign that his pa's papers were important enough to be kept in a safe. Maybe his snake of a father had done right by his family after all.

Joseph looked up to see a portrait of Jesus staring him down. He gave a long sigh. It had been wrong of him to be so disrespectful of his pa. Someday, he'd be able to ask forgiveness for it. Right now, though, he couldn't be sorry. Not with all the mouths he had to provide for. And the fact that his pa was the very reason they were in this predicament.

Was it wrong to reserve his forgiveness and apologies until after he knew his family was safe?

Probably so. But it had been a long time since Joseph had been to church. Not since his pa left and one of the women in their old church had said something to his ma about her husband never coming back. After that, Ma hadn't wanted to be around the mean, spiteful women, and Joseph had too much work to do to argue.

The door opened again, and Frank returned, carrying

a stack of papers. "Your father had interests in a number of mines. I grubstaked him on a few of his projects."

It didn't seem very pastorly for a man of God to give out money for prospecting. "Why?"

He smiled, again reminding Joseph of Annabelle. "Because a man has a certain level of pride. It's easier to ask for money if you think you're giving someone something in return. So I give the miners what they need, and they give me a ten percent ownership in their mines. It eases their pride knowing that they're not taking a handout."

Frank's grin turned a bit mischievous. "I've never had a single mine pan out, but boy, wouldn't that be something."

"It sounds like gambling." On one hand, it was nice that the preacher was willing to give money to miners in need, but how was he helping those men? How many of the men taking money from the preacher had families back home who could've used that money?

"Now you sound like my daughter." Frank sat back in his chair. "I see it as an investment in these men's dreams. When I was a boy, I wanted nothing more than to be a preacher. But my family came from money, and such things weren't done. So I followed their plan and found myself rich and miserable. When I told my wife I was leaving the family firm to become a preacher, she asked me what had taken so long."

The peace flitting across Frank's face stirred envy unlike any Joseph had ever experienced. What would it be like to give everything up to follow your dreams? Of course, it had been so long since Joseph had dared dream anything, he wasn't sure what that would be.

"So here I am, spreading God's word in an ungodly

town. And if I find a man whose dreams I can encourage, I do. I call it an investment. I suppose the difference between my investments and gambling is that I don't expect a return. At least not here on earth."

So nonchalant about being able to give it all away. "Doesn't the church object to you spending their money on such a foolish endeavor?"

Another grin. "I don't use the church's money. The money I invest comes straight out of my personal income. It irks poor Annabelle to no end that I help the miners, but they've got to have someone who believes in them."

Maybe. But he'd have to agree with Annabelle that he'd be better off not funding such schemes. "How much was Pa in to you for?"

Frank chuckled. "Again, it was not a loan. I gave him money freely. But that's not the right question. The question is, how much will you be able to get from his mines?"

With that, Frank sorted through the papers. "I have here papers for five different mining claims. As far as I know, not one has panned out." He looked up at Joseph. "However, about a week before he died, your father was anxious about the Mary May. He came to me and asked if I could keep his papers safe."

"Did someone kill him?"

Frank shrugged. "Hard to tell. He fell down a ravine. Did he fall or was he pushed? No one knows. And no one really cared enough to find out."

Joseph supposed he should care, but honestly, if his pa wasn't already dead, he might have to kill him himself. "Why would someone kill him for holdings that aren't very valuable?"

Frank looked around, slowly. "Every now and again, I'd find bits of silver in the offering. I never knew where they came from. I figured it was a miner's way of giving back but not wanting to call attention to himself. One day, I noticed your father slipping silver into the offering when he thought no one was looking."

He leaned forward and lowered his voice. "Now I ask you. Why would a man hide having so much silver?"

With what Joseph was learning about his pa, he had a pretty good idea. "So he wouldn't have to give your share to you? Only he felt guilty about not giving something to the church, so he put in a portion?"

Frank leaned back and gave another shrug. "Or maybe he'd found the big one and was trying to go about securing it before making the big announcement. Like I said, he'd been talking about the Mary May last time I saw him."

At least his pa had some loyalty, naming the mine after one of the daughters he'd abandoned back home. Not that it would give her any comfort at all.

Joseph riffled through the crumbled, dirty papers. Each of his sisters had a mine named after them. Maybe he'd give each of his siblings the papers to their mines. Probably worthless, but at least something to remember their pa.

"You think I should check out the Mary May?"

"Wouldn't hurt. He had a cabin up that way. Maybe you'll find some of his personal belongings or something that can help your quest."

Joseph sighed. The preacher was right. It wouldn't hurt. Maybe this cabin would be a safer place to keep Nugget. "I'll check it out. See if the cabin is livable."

Frank pointed at the shadows in the window. "Not tonight, you won't. It's going to be too dark to head up there now, and having been to the cabin once, I can tell you that Billy did a real nice job of making it hard to find."

Somehow, his pa's cleverness at making a hidden cabin didn't bring the same kind of twinkle to his mind as it did to the preacher's eyes. Maybe he'd once had that kind of fondness for his pa, but after cleaning up so much of his pa's mess, he wasn't so kindly inclined.

"Thank you, Preacher. Would you happen to know of a place willing to rent a room to us tonight? I've tried just about everywhere, but being where Nugget came from and all, no one wants us."

Maybe the preacher could put in a good word for them. It was only one night. Then they could go to his pa's cabin and make it a temporary home for Nugget. What his siblings would do when they found out…well, it'd be like losing their parents all over again. Especially for the girls, who'd been sheltered from such things.

"You'll stay with us, of course. It's a shame to have all those bedrooms sit empty when there are heads needing a place to rest. And I told you, it's Frank." The preacher's smile appeared benign, but Joseph saw the underlying power behind it. There'd be no arguing with this man.

And really, it would be foolish. He was running out of money, and with an extra mouth to feed, he had to think beyond his pride. But someday…he'd keep an account of all the preacher had done for him and his family and he'd pay him back.

"Again, my thanks. Your generosity is—"

"None of that." Frank held up his hand. "The Lord has been generous to me, so it's only right that I am generous in return."

Frank reached into his desk and pulled out a coin. "Take this. Go on down to the bathhouse on West Seventh. It's run by a couple of nice widows who will take good care of you."

Joseph didn't need a man of the cloth to tell him he reeked. But every penny he wasted on a bath was a penny less for his family. "Thank you, but—"

"No buts. Maddie, that's my housekeeper, is one of the most particular women you'll ever meet. If you don't go to the bathhouse and take care of it, she's liable to haul you out back and scrub you down herself."

Joseph took the coin and stared at it. Still, it seemed a shame to spend it when he'd just received a letter from Aunt Ina asking for more money.

"Thank you," he finally managed to force himself to say. "What about Nugget?"

"Don't worry about her. Like I told you, Annabelle loves children. Once I tell her what's going on, she'll have Nugget cleaned up, and if I know my daughter, she'll probably have found her a pretty new dress and done her hair all up. You won't find a better person to leave Nugget with than my Annabelle."

Joseph remembered the looks of disgust the other women in town had given them as they'd walked in search of the church. Annabelle was different. She'd taken Nugget's hand and treated his little sister with respect.

All these warm feelings did nothing to dispel his wariness. In fact, it only made them worse. Liking a golden-haired girl such as Annabelle couldn't be on his mind. He'd come to Leadville to solve the problem of how to care for his siblings, and so far, all he'd come up with was another mouth to feed and a few probably worthless pieces of paper.

Thinking thoughts he had no business thinking about a girl was just borrowing trouble. And Joseph already had more than his share.

Annabelle reached to knock on the door to her father's office just as the door opened, causing her to nearly run into the miner's chest.

"Where's Nugget?" Joseph peered around her, invading her personal space.

"She's fine," Annabelle said, stepping out of the man's way. "Maddie's got her taking a bath in the kitchen, so if you could give her a little privacy…"

She entered the office, looking around to see any sign that her father had yet again funded some foolish endeavor. "Maddie also wanted me to tell you that supper's going to be ready at seven. We'll be serving outside so if you could get some men to put out the tables, she sure would appreciate it."

No sign that anything was missing, so at least this man wasn't a thief. One time, a miner stole the gold crucifix from her great-grandfather right off the church's wall. And her father, with his forgiving soul, had let him.

"What'd I tell you," her father said, putting his arm around her. "You don't have to worry a bit about Nugget. Go take your bath so you can be back in time for supper. Maybe some of the miners your father knew will be there."

Joseph cleared his throat. "Are you expecting many?" This time, his voice sounded less raspy, more husky, and less like he'd spent too much time in the mines. She briefly wondered what he'd sound like singing in the church, but then shoved that thought out of her mind.

Her father gave her a squeeze. "Only the Lord knows. But He always provides enough. My dear, sweet Catherine, before she passed, had a heart for making sure those boys had a home-cooked meal. Every Wednesday night, and also after services on Sunday, we invite anyone who wants to eat over for supper. I don't know what I'd do without Annabelle to carry on the tradition."

Annabelle's heart sank at his words. How was she supposed to leave Leadville and move on with her life when her father needed her so desperately?

"Your kindness is much appreciated," the miner said gruffly. So unlike most of the miners who'd grown to expect the handouts. This one was different.

Not that she'd allow herself to see him as different, she told herself as sternly as she could. Seeing miners as individuals and caring for them as people was dangerous stuff. Getting attached had gotten her heart broken more times than she could count. Which was why, after all the tragedies of the winter, Annabelle absolutely was not going to find herself caring about this miner or his child.

She'd do her duty, feed them, give them what they needed, then send them on their way. Just like she did with everyone else. And when the letter from Aunt Celeste came, giving her the means to escape, she was going to do it, and pray that somehow her father would find a way to get on without her.

Because if her heart was forced to take on any more burdens, it would certainly crumble under the weight.

Chapter Three

One would think that by now, Annabelle's back wouldn't ache so much after feeding a hungry crowd. But every muscle in her body hurt. Not to mention her head from the din of all the voices in the backyard. She returned the last plate to the cupboard, looking around the kitchen to make sure her share of the chores were finished.

Despite their best efforts, the floor looked like a herd of cattle had tromped through the kitchen. Maddie wouldn't be pleased. She went to grab the broom when Maddie's voice interrupted her.

"I'll finish in here. The poor lamb is all tuckered out. I've got her on your bed, but I imagine you'd rather her on Susannah's. Why don't you get that fixed up? I've already done Peter's room for the miner."

The miner. Her father had never allowed a miner to stay in the house before. Of course, none had brought a child with him, either. She supposed she should give him a little credit; after all, he'd taken responsibility for a child borne to him by a woman of questionable morals, and certainly in her line of work, he couldn't really be sure that the child was his.

Nugget lay sprawled across Annabelle's bed, her feet tangled in the quilt Annabelle's mother had made. Rosy cheeks had replaced the grubby face, and in the dim candlelight, Nugget looked almost like a porcelain doll. Hard to believe the tiny girl was six years old. Just two years younger than Susannah had been when she died. Such innocence almost made Annabelle want to believe she was making a difference helping with her father's work.

Annabelle pulled out the linens and made up Susannah's bed, trying not to remember the way her sister had traced the pattern of the quilt at night to fall asleep. She forced herself to push aside the memory of Susannah's sweet voice asking Annabelle to tell her one last story. She wasn't ready to confront the loss of her sister.

Every day. Every day her father asked her to do one more hard thing for the sake of his ministry. And every day, she had to shove one more piece of her hurting heart into the abyss.

But as she lifted the sleeping girl off her bed and into the newly made bed, she told herself that maybe somehow it would be worth it. And maybe someday, it wouldn't hurt so much. Though she suspected it wouldn't happen until she could finally leave this place and all its painful memories.

Maybe now that her father had some time to grieve, he wouldn't mind so much letting her go to Aunt Celeste. Maybe there, she could build a life for herself. A life that didn't include putting her heart out to be broken on a daily basis.

"I was going to have her stay in my room." The miner's voice came from her doorway.

Annabelle jumped at the interruption, then took a

breath as she smoothed the covers around Nugget. "I've already gotten her settled. Besides, it's not seemly for her to share your room."

"She's my sister. We can share." He stepped into the room as if he was going to snatch Nugget away.

Annabelle stood. Sister? She hadn't expected that. What sort of man took on the care of a sister when he barely seemed capable of taking care of himself? Yet again, she realized that this man was different. And she didn't like it.

Ignoring the desire to know more about his situation, she looked at him with the same detachment she gave everyone else. "You're a grown man. You deserve your privacy. Besides, just look at her."

As if to prove her point, Nugget snuggled deeper into the covers, giving a small sigh.

"I haven't ever seen her look so…"

Clean? Content? This man didn't seem to know anything about raising a child. But for the first time, she could understand his protectiveness. And she had to give him credit for trying.

Annabelle sighed. There was no escaping the compassion leaking into her heart.

"Nugget's so peaceful, isn't she? It'd be a shame to disturb her." Annabelle gave the miner a smile. "Why don't I show you to your room? It was my brother Peter's."

She swallowed the inevitable lump at the mention of his name. This stranger wouldn't understand how much she'd lost. Hopefully, they wouldn't stay long. She refused to get attached to one more person who was just going to leave anyway.

"I'm not putting him out, am I?" The gruff tone to his voice made Annabelle pause. He seemed uncomfortable with the hospitality. Unlike so many of the people she encountered, this miner wasn't a taker. Her conscience told her she shouldn't judge, but her heart reminded her that it could no longer afford to be open.

"Peter died seven months ago." As many times as she stated that fact, it didn't get any easier to accept.

"I'm sorry for your loss." Words she heard often enough, but the sadness in his voice made Annabelle's heart constrict. He'd lost someone recently, too.

"It gets easier every day." A lie, but since that's what everyone told her, she supposed it must be true for some people. It was the answer she'd learned to give to quiet the well-intentioned words of sympathy that never seemed to do any good.

The miner stepped into her space as she pushed the door open. "Does it?"

His dark eyes searched hers, making her feel exposed, vulnerable. People weren't supposed to ask those questions. They were supposed to move on and leave her to dwell in her private pain.

She turned her head away. "Of course it does."

Doing what she did best, Annabelle pressed on, ignoring the tickle at the back of her throat as she surveyed the room she'd barely dared enter since Peter's death. She'd liked to have said it looked exactly the same, but it didn't. The lamp that had sat on the table beside his bed was gone. Her father had given it to a needy parishioner. The same with the blanket that had always lay across the foot of the bed. Her grandmother had made it, but that hadn't stopped her father from giving it to someone in the mining camp. And if she looked in Peter's closet, it would be empty.

Yes, it was selfish to cling to them; after all, they

were only things. If her father knew these thoughts, he would tell her about storing up her treasures in heaven instead of on earth, and that these things would be far more useful to the people here than they were to Peter's memory.

Those emotions, like everything else, were quickly pushed away. Her father expected her to be a part of his ministry, and that meant making this man feel comfortable in their home.

"Maddie filled the pitcher with some clean water for your use." Annabelle gestured to the dresser. "If there's any other need I can attend to, please let me know."

She turned to leave, but he stopped her. "Wait."

"Is there something else you need?"

His features were cast in shadows, but she could still see the hard catch in his jaw. "I'm sorry if my question offended you. I didn't mean to put you out."

He might as well have taken that pitcher and dumped it on her. Annabelle glanced at the open door. Her father would be up soon, and he would know that she hadn't been very welcoming. She sighed. She was trying, she really was. But her father was so focused on providing for the miners' needs that he never seemed to consider hers.

More selfishness. And none of it helped the man in front of her. The man who looked like he was staring down into the depths of her soul. A place no one, not even God, was allowed to look.

"I'm sorry." Annabelle looked at the floor. Swept clean, of course. If only Maddie had left one stray dust bunny that could swallow her whole.

Annabelle took a deep breath. She'd hurt this man's feelings, and she hadn't meant to. But with all the miners, she had to keep her heart locked up. She'd let one slip past her guard. One to whom she'd given her heart. And he'd deemed his search for riches more valuable than their love.

The miner standing in front of her? Now that he'd had a bath, she could tell that his hair truly was the color of soot, and it curled around the top of this collar ever so slightly. His eyes, too, were dark, and the light caught them just enough that she knew he meant business. This wasn't some miner. Not anymore.

Bad enough that he had to sleep in Peter's room, worse that by closing herself off to him, she now had to admit the truth.

"I lied. I don't know if missing someone gets easier. I wake up every day wishing I could hear my brothers or my sister, and especially my mother, walking through the door. But they don't. And I guess having you here makes it more real that they never will."

Everyone expressed sympathy over her losses. But what she saw shining in Joseph's eyes was deeper, more personal. She couldn't afford to get personal, not again. They were both supposed to say the proper things, like that Annabelle was getting over the loss of her mother and brothers and sister, and that Joseph was sorry to hear about it, and every other pithy comment that everyone said because it was what you were supposed to say.

Because she'd already said all of those deeply personal things to another man, another miner, and despite her offering up everything her heart had, he'd left, chasing after rumors of gold in the Yukon.

Getting personal was no longer an option.

"Annabelle?" Her father's voice boomed through the

room as he pushed open the door. "You've made sure Joseph is comfortable?"

Annabelle let out a long sigh, exhaling all of the thoughts she shouldn't have been thinking. "Of course I have." She turned to the miner. "You have everything you need, don't you?"

He glanced at her, the sympathy still shining in his eyes. "Yes." He turned to her father. "Your daughter is most gracious."

At least he brought it back to what people were supposed to say.

Her father came into the room and kissed the top of her head. "I don't know what I'd do without her."

She smiled up at him, trying not to let the guilt over all of her wrong thoughts drag her down. As much as she hated this position, her father was all she had left of her immediate family.

"I think that's all then." She leaned up on tiptoes and gave her father a kiss on the cheek. "Good night." Then turned and gave the miner as much of a smile as she could muster. "And good night to you, too, Joseph."

Before either man could say anything else, she turned and left the room, retreating to the once-safe haven of her bedroom. There, Nugget slept, her tiny body reminding her that even the slightest bit of sweetness still had a bitter taste. Because as much as she wanted to take this little girl into her arms and give her the love she deserved, Annabelle absolutely was not going to get attached. Not when, like every other child she encountered in her work, Nugget would soon be gone.

Because that was the reality of life in a mining town. People either went broke and left, struck it rich and left,

left in search of a better prospect, or left the earth completely. Regardless of the reason, they all left.

There wasn't enough of Annabelle's heart remaining to let anyone take any more.

Joseph watched Annabelle's retreating figure, her skirts swishing behind her. She moved with the grace of any of the fine ladies he'd encountered, but there was a humility to her that he'd never known.

Back in Ohio, he'd encountered plenty of girls who turned up their noses at the Stones' poverty. Only Margaret had openly accepted him and promised to love him no matter what. She'd been filled with grand dreams of the farm they'd build together and how everything would work out. But when his ma died and he'd made it clear that his siblings were part of the package, Margaret had a change of heart and married another.

He once thought Margaret was made of the cloth he believed he saw in Annabelle, but appearances were deceiving. As much as he'd like to admire Annabelle, he had to remind himself that he had too many other responsibilities to put any energy in that direction.

He forced his attention to Frank. "Thank you again for your hospitality. Your daughter went above and beyond in preparing rooms for us."

Frank gave that wistful look Joseph was beginning to see as the Annabelle look. "It'll be good for her to have another little girl in the house. She used to share her room with her sister Susannah. She likes to pretend that she's fine, but don't let her fool you. Annabelle misses her terribly."

Joseph's gut churned. He'd liked to have credited it to a filling supper after going so long without, but he knew better. Not after her hard-won admission of grief. He'd thought about offering her comfort for her loss, but at Frank's expression, Joseph was glad they'd been interrupted. His thoughts and questions were better left for the man of the house, not a woman he found himself inappropriately attracted to.

"She mentioned this room belonged to her departed brother. I didn't realize that she'd lost another sibling, as well."

Sorrow filled Frank's eyes as he looked around the room. "Yes. This was Peter's room. Sickness hit Leadville hard this past winter. We lost my wife and four of my children. Annabelle is all I have left."

Maddie's biscuits thudded in the pit of Joseph's stomach. Having spent the better part of a month trying to track down his father to save his own siblings, he couldn't imagine what it must have been like to watch them all die.

"I'm so sorry for your loss." Joseph spoke softly, realizing that the other man had retreated into his own grief. "It's good of you to let us use their rooms."

Frank's head snapped up. "What else would we do with them? The good Lord provided, and it seems wrong to not share what He has given us. Just…" He looked around the room, then his gaze settled back on Joseph.

"Go easy on Annabelle. She gets awful mad when I give away any of the family's possessions, and even though she's playing the part of the gracious hostess, I know she's upset."

He gave another wry smile, and Joseph realized that Frank was trying as hard as Annabelle seemed to be in dealing with his heavy losses.

"Then why do this? If it pains her, then perhaps I—"

"I can't allow her to wallow in her grief. Her mother, brothers and sister are with the Lord. There's no reason to be sorrowful."

Except the preacher's face spoke of his own great sorrow. "Having you and Nugget here will be good for her. Already I see a light in her eyes I haven't seen since…"

His shoulders rose and fell. "I know you feel guilty at accepting my charity, but you're doing me the favor. It was good to hear laughter in this house again."

Frank turned to leave, but his final words burned through Joseph's heart.

A house without laughter. Without noise. Even Joseph would admit that this month without the cacophony of his siblings' voices had made for some lonely nights. He'd gotten through by telling himself it was temporary. But for Annabelle and her father, the silence was permanent.

Lord, forgive me for judging.

The biscuits collided angrily against each other, reminding him that he had a lot to beg the Lord's forgiveness for. He'd been angry and resentful over his situation, but as he looked at what the Lassiters were going through, he realized that he had no call to complain.

"Sir?"

Frank turned. "I told you to call me Frank."

Joseph nodded slowly. "Yes. Frank. I… I was wondering if you had a spare Bible in the house."

Silence echoed briefly against the walls. Joseph's heart thudded. It shouldn't have been that difficult a question to ask a preacher.

"Annabelle still hasn't forgiven me for giving away Peter's. Barely nineteen years old, and my boy had his heart set on becoming a preacher. He would have wanted me to share God's word, but Annabelle…she was furious."

The older man's voice cracked. "I'm sorry, I shouldn't have burdened you. I…"

"Forget it." He'd already made Annabelle uncomfortable enough. "I'm sure I can find one in town tomorrow. It's just I— Well, you reminded me of how much I've lost track of my faith."

Some of the tiredness left Frank's face. "I'm glad. As for the Bible, I'll let you read my own tonight. When a man's got a yearning for God's word, it's best to fill it immediately so nothing else sneaks in."

He was about to tell Frank it wasn't necessary, but Frank had already left the room. It humbled Joseph to see how freely the man shared all that he had. A lesson Aunt Ina would benefit to learn. Her last letter had complained of all the money she'd spent on his siblings and that she fully expected to be repaid for her sacrifice.

If he'd tried to pay Frank back, the man would be insulted. Joseph looked around the room that had once been occupied by a beloved son and brother. No wonder Annabelle had seemed so tense earlier. He sat on the bed and ran his hands along the fine quilt covering the bed.

Joseph didn't know much about women's handiwork, and had taken the blankets and quilts in their home for granted. But to Annabelle, who'd been upset over a Bible, this was probably yet another memory of her brother.

"That was the first quilt my wife ever made." Frank's

voice came from the doorway. "Her family was horrified that she was wasting her womanly talents on making quilts instead of embroidering fancy linens. It has some mistakes, but that's why I love it. She wasn't afraid of the mistakes that come with learning."

Frank had crossed over while speaking, then handed him a well-worn Bible. "I hope it gives you the same peace tonight."

The lump that Joseph had been successfully swallowing all evening wouldn't go away this time. Everything had meaning to the Lassiters, yet they were both able to share. Frank more willingly than Annabelle, but even her, he couldn't fault for being stingy.

"Thank you, Frank. Your generosity means the world to me."

Frank gave a small nod. "I hope someday you pass on that generosity to someone else."

The floorboards creaked as Frank once again retreated, leaving Joseph in the cozy room bathed with soft candlelight. He glanced at the Bible, which smelled of the hope and promise of things yet to come. So far, he hadn't found any of the answers he'd been seeking in Leadville. But Frank Lassiter had given him the hope that he'd finally come to a place where he could.

Chapter Four

Annabelle walked into Jessup's Mercantile, Nugget's hand clutched tightly in hers.

"I ain't allowed in here," Nugget whispered.

"You're with me, so it'll be fine. Be a good girl, and I'll let you choose a peppermint when we're done."

She gave the little girl an encouraging squeeze and a smile.

"I don't like peppermints. The men who visited Mama always gave 'em to me, and then I'd have to go away."

After a day with Nugget, none of her experiences should shock Annabelle. But each one put an anger in her heart that wasn't going to be easily erased. How many other children endured what poor Nugget had? Despite her anger, Annabelle felt powerless to do anything.

"I'm not going to make you go away." She gave Nugget another squeeze. "But I will let you pick out whatever treat you'd like."

Nugget's grip loosened in her hand.

"Who is this young lady you have with you today, Annabelle?" Mrs. Jessup greeted her with a smile as Nugget shied into Annabelle's skirts.

"Good morning, Mrs. Jessup." Annabelle returned the greeting. "We have a very special guest staying with us, so I've brought her with me to pick up a few things for Maddie. Nugget, please give Mrs. Jessup your most polite how-do-you-do."

Mrs. Jessup blanched. "Nugget? That isn't the child from…" She glanced over Annabelle's shoulder in the direction of State Street.

Annabelle straightened her shoulders as Nugget let go of her hand and clung to the back of Annabelle's skirt. She reached behind and gave Nugget a pat on the head. "Why, yes, she is. And she's currently our guest, so please treat her with the respect accorded all of our important guests."

"But that child is filthy and full of bugs."

"Am not!" Nugget burst out of Annabelle's skirts. "Mama made sure I didn't get no bugs."

Annabelle put her arms around Nugget and pulled her close. "Maddie scrubbed her clean herself. Didn't find one bug on the sweet little girl." She did her best to keep her voice modulated and calm. Nugget was just a child, after all, and didn't deserve Mrs. Jessup's scorn.

"Is that the dress I ordered from New York City for poor Susannah?"

The horror on Mrs. Jessup's face brought a pang to Annabelle's heart. After all, it wasn't Mrs. Jessup's sister who'd died.

"Why, yes, it is." Annabelle gave a smile in spite of the sick feeling in her stomach. "And I'm sure she'd be pleased that it wasn't getting eaten by moths in some closet. All Nugget needs are a few ribbons for her hair to make her the picture of sweetness."

Wasn't that the very thing Maddie had said this morning? And Annabelle had politely agreed, all the while resenting having to give up Susannah's dress. But now, in the face of such meanness, she'd parade Nugget around with Susannah's beloved china doll to show the world that she didn't give a whit where Nugget came from.

"Your mother would be horrified that you're associating with such people."

Her mother would have been ashamed it had taken Annabelle so long to take up Nugget's cause.

"What people? Nugget has done nothing wrong. She's a good girl who hasn't given me a bit of trouble."

Mrs. Jessup's face turned as red as the bolts of flannel she kept for the miners. "She was raised in that…place!"

"And she's now a guest in my home." Annabelle didn't mean to raise her voice, but when she did, a group of women looking through the buttons stopped and looked up at her.

"I understand that your mother is gone and I'm sure your father has no idea how to explain such delicate matters to a young lady, but let me assure you that no good can come of—"

"What? Taking in a child who needs a home?" Annabelle gathered Nugget closer to her. "My mother and father both instructed me on such matters, and when a sinful woman was brought before Jesus, he asked those without sin to cast the first stone. I am certain that none of us can lay claim to leading such a blameless life."

Mrs. Jessup couldn't have exploded any more brilliantly than the time the old cookstove's pipe had been blocked by a nesting raccoon.

"You…get…out…" she thundered, pointing at the door.

Annabelle smiled sweetly. "With pleasure. I'll be

talking to my father about taking our business to Taylor's. Come along, Nugget."

She grabbed Nugget's hand and ushered her out the door. Once they arrived on the sidewalk, Annabelle tried taking a deep breath, but Maddie had laced her too tight. What a bad day to be fashionable.

Nugget tugged at her hand. "I told you I weren't allowed to go in there."

Annabelle straightened. "That's right. You're not allowed to go in there. You're too good for the likes of Mrs. Jessup."

She scanned the street and looked toward Taylor's Mercantile. Her boast in leaving Mrs. Jessup's had been just that—a boast. Her father was very strict about which stores she shopped in, with all the riffraff that came to Leadville. She wasn't supposed to go anyplace else alone.

But even her father wouldn't be able to fault her disobedience in light of Mrs. Jessup's meanness.

"Come on, Nugget. You might not like peppermints, but I could use a sweet right now."

She grasped Nugget's hand and strode across the street to Taylor's.

Joseph had just stepped through the back storeroom into the main store with Frank and Mr. Jessup when he heard Annabelle's raised voice.

"And now she's a guest in my home!"

Joseph stepped forward to come to Annabelle's aid, but Frank held his arm out. "Let her fight her own battles."

"But that's my sister they're arguing about."

"Annabelle is doing fine. Listen to her."

The pride in Frank's voice was obvious. Joseph had to admit that he hadn't seen this side of Annabelle. She might not think much of him, but she'd protect his sister with everything she had.

Mr. Jessup shifted nervously. "I should probably go out there and…"

"You should," Frank told him quietly. "But first, you need to know that while I respect you as a friend, I'm going to stand by my daughter's decision unless your wife apologizes to her."

"Apologizes?" Mr. Jessup's face turned redder than a hot coal. "After your daughter insulted her and practically accused her of not being a Christian?"

Joseph couldn't help but grin. Annabelle had done just that, and beautifully so.

"No hard feelings, Bill." Frank held out his hand for Mr. Jessup to shake, but he didn't take it.

"Joseph, I know we've spent a lot of time picking out the gear you'll need for your father's cabin, but I believe we'll be taking our purchases elsewhere. Go ahead and set the things down. We need to go make sure the girls are all right."

Joseph did as he was bade and followed Frank toward the door. Mrs. Jessup stopped them.

"Did you hear what that daughter of yours said to me? Without a mother, she's going positively wild."

Frank nodded. "And I couldn't be more proud. Good day, Mrs. Jessup."

As they strode out the door, much to the shocked faces staring after them, Joseph was proud to know her, as well. Annabelle Lassiter was one of the finest women he knew.

He watched as Annabelle crossed the street, firmly clutching his sister's hand in hers.

"Annabelle!" Frank called his daughter's name, and she paused to stop and wave.

The two men rushed over to Annabelle and Nugget.

"Good," Annabelle said with forced cheer. "I'm glad you're here. I've decided that we need to start shopping at Taylor's. My friends assure me that Taylor's is perfectly respectable, but I'm sure you'll want to see for yourself."

Frank laughed. "Annabelle, my dear, Joseph and I were in the back during your argument with Mrs. Jessup. We heard the whole thing."

Annabelle's face fell, and for a moment, without the false cheer or guarded expression Joseph was used to, she looked almost pretty. "Oh," she finally said. She looked down at Nugget, then back up at her father.

"Well, if you think I'm going to apologize, then—"

Her father held a hand up. "I'd be disappointed if you did. I told Bill that unless Mrs. Jessup apologizes to you, we won't be patronizing their store anymore."

Annabelle's cheeks tinged pink, and a smile lit her eyes, the blue even more striking in the sunlight.

All right, Joseph would admit it. Annabelle Lassiter was downright pretty. But that momentary admiration was all it could be.

"But that does leave me in a bind." Frank put his hands in his pockets and rocked back on his heels. "I now need to make arrangements with another store to get supplies for our ministry. As members of our church, the Jessups gave us a good discount."

"Oh." This time, when her face fell, Joseph immediately felt guilty. He hadn't meant to bring grief to them or their ministry.

The false cheer Joseph was used to seeing on Annabelle's face filled Frank's. "It's all right. The Lord will provide. And since I haven't had the pleasure of getting to know Mr. Taylor, perhaps it's about time I did so. He belongs to the new church across town, but God's children are all God's children, right?"

Annabelle nodded slowly.

Frank turned to Joseph. "While I'm conducting business with Mr. Taylor, I hope I can trust you to stay close to Annabelle and Nugget. Though I've also heard good things about Taylor's, I'd feel better knowing they had some protection until we've experienced it for ourselves."

Annabelle gave a small but ladylike grunt, and Frank shot her a look. Joseph couldn't help but grin as he watched the tiny rebellion cross her face. The independent woman didn't like it one bit, but she'd obey.

Joseph held up an arm. "Ladies?"

Though Annabelle took it, he could feel the glower come all the way from her face down through her gloved hand to his arm. Some might call it unladylike, but he appreciated the feisty woman who very clearly knew her own mind.

They walked into the store, and Joseph noticed how Nugget still clung to Annabelle's skirts.

"Are you all right?" He ruffled his sister's hair with his free hand.

She looked up at him, wide-eyed. "Uh-huh. That lady was mean, but Annabelle showed her." Then she looked at Annabelle, like she believed more in Annabelle than she did in him.

"What if they're mean to us here?"

The already proper woman straightened even more. "Then we'll find another store. And we'll keep trying until we find someone who will treat us with respect."

Annabelle's conviction shamed Joseph. With all the places that had turned them away, he'd taken Nugget and slinked away with his tail between his legs. If they had refused Annabelle, she probably would have given them the what-for.

"Thank you." He turned and looked at Annabelle.

She looked confused. "For what?"

Joseph nodded his head toward his sister. "You treat her with dignity."

Her face colored, and she reached for Nugget's hand. "Come on, Nugget. Let's go look at some ribbons."

So far, no one had noticed their presence in the store. Frank appeared to have already engaged in serious conversation with the proprietor.

As they walked toward the ribbons, a woman approached them. "Hello. I'm Mrs. Taylor. Your father said you needed help with your shopping."

Joseph examined her face for any sign of the judgment he'd come to expect with Nugget. But she appeared pleasant and willing to do business with them.

"Thank you, yes." Annabelle gave the woman the kind of smile Joseph wished she'd direct at him. "Our housekeeper, Maddie, provided me with a list of items. But I'd also like to look at some ribbons for Nugget."

Annabelle pulled the little girl off her skirts and in front of her. "Nugget is my friend, and I hope you'll be kind to her."

"Of course." Mrs. Taylor bent in front of Nugget. "Why don't you go select a peppermint for yourself?"

"Thank you all the same, Mrs. Taylor, but my friend doesn't care for peppermint."

How did Annabelle know that Nugget didn't like peppermints? He'd shoved dozens of them at the poor child before she'd finally told him that she didn't like them.

The genuine affection in her face as she looked at Nugget tore at Joseph's heart. And the smile Nugget gave her back was enough to make him melt.

"Well then, come along." Mrs. Taylor's voice was pleasant, accepting.

They wound their way through stacks of goods, neatly displayed. All the while, Mrs. Taylor spoke of the weather and treated them as she would any other customer.

With each step, Joseph felt more of the worry fall off his shoulders. By the time they arrived at the ribbon display, he felt as light as any other man shopping in a mercantile.

"Here are the ribbons. Are you looking for something to match that pretty dress of yours?"

Mrs. Taylor bent to Nugget, giving her a smile that spoke of understanding and kindness.

"Annabelle?" Frank's voice called from the other side of the store. "Can you come here for a moment?"

She immediately looked at Nugget.

"It's all right," both Joseph and Mrs. Taylor said at once. He stopped himself, then looked at Mrs. Taylor.

"She'll be fine, truly," Mrs. Taylor said. "I have a little one myself, and I miss her dreadfully. She's visiting my mother, and I can't wait until she gets back next week."

"I…" Annabelle looked at Joseph.

"We'll be fine."

She nodded slowly, then went to her father's side.

"I promise I'm not like that awful Mrs. Jessup," Mrs. Taylor told him. "Pastor Lassiter told us what happened in her store. I can't say I'm surprised. She's been spreading rumors about us ever since we opened."

Mrs. Taylor put her hand over her mouth. "I'm sorry. I shouldn't have shared gossip about her. I'm sure she means well. It just burns me sometimes…" She shook her head.

"Anyway, on to more pleasant things." She held up a

ribbon. "What do you think of this ribbon, Nugget? It would bring out the pink flowers in your dress nicely."

Nugget looked at the floor.

"It's all right. You can look at the ribbon," Joseph told her.

As he watched the emotions play across his sister's face, he realized how hard it must be to have grown up the way Nugget had. How many rejections had she faced because of who her mother was?

Nugget looked, but didn't touch. She just stared at it, wide-eyed. "Sometimes the men would bring me ribbons."

Mrs. Taylor knelt in front of her. "I'm not like those men. I'm your friend."

Nugget looked up at him, and Joseph nodded. He was quickly learning how precious friendship was in this place, especially with a child like Nugget. She reached for the ribbon.

"May I put it in your hair? Annabelle is going to think you look so pretty."

With deft fingers, Mrs. Taylor put the ribbon in Nugget's hair. The shy little girl preened as Mrs. Taylor held up the mirror.

"See? You look very pretty. Why don't you go show Annabelle?"

Nugget skipped all the way to Annabelle. Joseph watched her with a lightened heart. He'd been worried about his family accepting her, but surely with the acceptance she was finding here, his family would eventually warm to her.

"I knew her mother," Mrs. Taylor said over his shoulder. "Lily was a kind woman. She came to town with a worthless husband. When he died, she didn't have anyplace else to go. So she took up the life she did. She wasn't a bad person."

Her words were meant as a kindness, but they hurt. "Did she know my pa was married?"

"They're always married, sugar. Sometimes, though, we're fortunate, and we find someone who will take us away."

He turned and looked at her. "You?"

Mrs. Taylor shrugged. "Things aren't always what they seem. I didn't know your father, but I'm sure that his relationship with Lily had nothing to do with your mother. Mining is lonely business."

Hard to imagine this genteel lady in the place where he'd gotten Nugget. Also hard not to blame his father, despite Mrs. Taylor's words.

"How do you know all of this?"

She smiled. "Because I've been there. And if you ever need anything for Nugget…"

He watched as Nugget giggled at something Annabelle said to her. "Thank you. It's good to know that she's got so many people who care about her."

Something he hadn't expected. But the longer he spent in Leadville, the more he was learning to expect the unexpected. Just then, Annabelle turned and looked at him, the smile in her eyes blinding.

He couldn't help himself. Joseph smiled back. His growing affection for Annabelle was perhaps the most unexpected of all. And it was something he needed to avoid giving in to at all costs. With all he had to focus on, he couldn't afford to divert his attentions.

Chapter Five

Annabelle headed home with a little girl on one arm and a sedate man on the other. She glanced over at Joseph, who seemed to be focused on the girl who proudly showed off her new ribbons.

"Thank you for your kindness to my sister," he told her softly. "I have never seen her so happy."

Nugget broke free and skipped ahead. Annabelle didn't have the heart to stop her.

"I'm glad to have given her something to be happy about." She smiled. Joseph wasn't too bad. Cleaned up the way he was, it was almost easy to pretend he was just a normal man.

Annabelle stumbled slightly. Joseph wasn't a normal man. And it wouldn't do for her to entertain feelings when she knew she couldn't count on a miner to stick around. Not that she had any intention of entertaining feelings about any man.

At least not here in Leadville. The town was full of shiftless drifters, and the one time she'd let her guard down to trust in someone, he'd betrayed her. Something she'd do well to remember in the presence of this man.

Especially the way Joseph's sparkling smile made her tingle all the way down to her toes. Despite the chilly breeze coming off the mountains, she suddenly felt warm. The lace at the top of her collar itched.

Annabelle quickened her pace. The faster she got home, the faster she could take off her gloves and adjust her collar. Surely the sudden warmth was due more to the clouds moving off the sun than the fact that Joseph had moved closer to her.

"Joseph! Annabelle! Watch!" Nugget spun around and around in a circle, nearly running into a group of ladies.

Joseph dashed forward to catch her before she fell. "Whoa, there, Nugget. This street's too crowded for your antics."

She fell into his arms, giggling. "I was being a dancer like Mama's friends."

Though Annabelle was briefly scandalized by the reference to Nugget's mama's friends, the thought stopped in her brain as she watched Joseph swing Nugget. He tickled her, then placed the still-giggling girl on his shoulders.

There weren't many men in Annabelle's acquaintance—well, there weren't any, actually—who would be so loving toward a little girl. Especially one with Nugget's background. Joseph's gentility reminded her a lot of her father.

Something to keep in mind. Both men were impossible dreamers. Her father because he believed that his work with the miners would somehow make a difference. Joseph because as a miner, he was after the impossible dream of striking it rich. The difference was,

Joseph's dream would take him away as soon as he realized chasing after silver was a worthless dream.

No, entertaining thoughts of Joseph was out of the question. Just because he exhibited fine qualities of character didn't mean he was of good character. Henry had taught her that.

They approached the Tabor Opera House. Its elegance stood out among the dust of Harrison Avenue, reminding Annabelle that profit could come out of the mountains. Maybe some, like the Tabors and a few other fortunate people, made a big strike. But too many ended up on her porch, dead broke, hungry, and willing to risk it all for another chance that never came.

In the end, no matter how many of the dazzling grins he gave Annabelle, Joseph was one of them. A miner whose dreams were bigger than his common sense. Otherwise, he'd never have ended up on her doorstep with a little girl who deserved a better life.

"Annabelle!" Lucy Simms, one of the girls she'd gone to school with, waved her over. "I have news."

"I can spare only a moment," Annabelle told her. "I need to get home."

The other girl's conspiratorial grin did not bode well for a quick conversation. "Papa has given permission for me to take a trip East so I can see the world before I settle down. He's going to ask your father if you can accompany us. I heard him tell Mama that your father has been looking for a proper escort to take you to visit your aunt."

Annabelle's heart leaped at the thought of her father looking for someone to escort her to finally visit Aunt Celeste. Her father hadn't been ignoring her. Why hadn't he said anything?

"Annabelle, watch this!" Nugget's voice stopped her from questioning the situation further as she watched the little girl spin, nearly falling into the street as she did so.

Fortunately, Joseph was there to grab her, then knelt before Nugget, probably to give her a more stern warning about being careful.

"That sounds lovely," Annabelle told Lucy. "I would love to hear more about it, but—"

Nugget had broken free of her brother and was hurtling toward her. "Annabelle!"

"Another one of your father's projects?" Lucy's disdainful look at Nugget was hard to miss.

Annabelle's back stiffened. Coming from Lucy, the thoughts that had consumed Annabelle sounded completely selfish. Was it so wrong to want to leave the ministry for a life of her own?

But as Nugget raced into her arms, tears streaming down her cheeks, Annabelle couldn't bring herself to think of Nugget as a mere project.

"Nothing like that." Annabelle gathered Nugget close. "They're friends. I'm sorry, Lucy, but I really must go."

The look Lucy gave her told her that she didn't believe Annabelle one bit.

What should have been victory at knowing her father had finally relented in letting her visit her aunt now felt like failure.

Which was fine. Annabelle wasn't sure what to believe herself. She took Nugget by the hand and started toward home.

"She's got to learn to be careful near the street." Joseph caught up to them, apparently thinking she'd taken Nugget's side.

"I know," she told him, continuing forward. "We've been gone too long. Maddie will be concerned."

Lucy stepped in with them. "I thought your father was expecting you."

"Yes, yes, he is." Annabelle didn't break stride. "I need to do some work for him, but Maddie is expecting me. I have to be home for them both."

Her words seemed like falsehoods even to her. But she couldn't stay and play mediator, not with her warring heart, or Lucy, or between Joseph and Nugget.

Spots danced in front of Annabelle's eyes. The sun. It was too bright. The air. Too warm.

Somehow, though, the ground didn't seem all that hard when she woke. She hadn't realized she'd fallen—

"Annabelle? Are you all right?" Joseph's voice jarred her.

She nodded slowly and started to sit up.

"Careful." He knelt beside her and offered his arm. "Let me help you."

"I'll fetch Dr. Owens," Lucy said, her voice full of concern.

Joseph helped her to her feet. "I'm all right. I just got a little dizzy. And the boards in the sidewalk were a bit uneven."

She couldn't help releasing Joseph's protective arm as quickly as possible.

Annabelle turned and gave Lucy a smile. "I'll be fine. Thank you for your concern."

Joseph's eyes were on her the entire walk home, making her feel more exposed than when she'd lain on the sidewalk.

What was she supposed to say that wouldn't make her sound like a complete ninny? *I'm trying hard to keep it all together for my father's sake, but everyone keeps pushing in places I'd just as soon keep hidden?*

Even in her own mind, it sounded ridiculous.

Fortunately, they were close to the house, and soon she'd be able to fix herself a cup of tea, then she could rest, and all would be well.

When the house was in sight, Nugget raced ahead. "I'm going to show Maddie my new ribbon!"

Annabelle couldn't help the smile that crept across her face. Nugget was a delightful girl. In spite of everything she had experienced and witnessed, she still maintained the childlike innocence that anyone would be hard-pressed to resist.

"Ah, there it is." Joseph touched her cheek briefly. "I was beginning to think we should send for the doctor after all."

She wasn't sure if the sensation left by his momentary touch was a good thing or a bad one. Certainly the way it made her stomach turn inside and out wasn't a comfortable sensation. Nor was there any comfort in the way his eyes seemed to be searching deep within her.

"I just need a cup of tea."

Annabelle tried to keep her voice steady. The last thing she needed was for everyone to get concerned for her health. Then her father might never let her leave.

"Are you sure?" Though Joseph's touch was gentle, it burned, like getting too close to a fire. She should have taken a step back, but having his hand on her arm was just as—

A team of horses galloped by. She turned her gaze to watch the matched set in the beautiful carriage.

Trimmed out in the finest gold, it had to belong to one of the mining barons.

Annabelle's heart sank as she pulled her arm away. Men like Joseph came to town believing they'd leave in a carriage like that. Few did.

She straightened. "I'm perfectly fine. But the longer we dally, the more likely it is to worry my father."

"He knows you're safe with me."

Except she wasn't. Every kindness from Joseph only punctuated the fact that she couldn't allow herself to enjoy it. Henry had been all politeness and kindness—until she'd truly needed him. And he was gone.

The ache didn't leave until after she was seated in the kitchen, Maddie fussing over her.

"I can't believe you fainted and didn't let anyone call for the doctor. You should have at least had someone get you a carriage." Maddie placed a cup of tea in front of her.

"I got too warm, that's all." As Annabelle sipped her tea, she watched Joseph slip in the back door.

Annabelle looked up at him. "Would you care for some tea?"

"Thank you, no." He turned his gaze to Maddie. "I want to visit my pa's cabin. Frank gave me the information, but I'll admit the directions don't make much sense."

Maddie stirred the pot of soup. "I never venture out of town. Don't want to get mixed up with the riffraff. Annabelle used to go up to the camps with her father. She might know."

Annabelle slumped in her seat. She had purposely avoided going to any of the mining camps since the illness that had taken her family. It hurt too much to see the work they'd done together, and realize that for the ones who'd died, it had been all in vain.

"Of course I'll help." She tried to sound cheerful, but the look on Joseph's face told her that he didn't believe her.

Joseph held up a hand. "Don't put yourself out on account of me."

"I want to," Annabelle said quietly. She wanted to add that she was sorry for not being more welcoming, but that would only serve to get a scolding from Maddie.

Surely he would be able to accept her peace offering after explaining her feelings last night. This was as much as she could give, and he had to be gentlemanly enough to know that.

The door opened, and her father walked in. "The soup smells delicious, Maddie."

Maddie beamed. "I'll get you a bowl, and for everyone else. Joseph is going to look at his father's cabin, and Annabelle fainted dead away on Harrison Avenue. A bit of soup will perk everyone up."

"I did not faint dead away." Annabelle met her father's look. "I got too warm, that's all."

"She did, too!" Nugget piped up. "Fell on the ground and everything."

The worry on her father's face nearly killed her. After having so much illness in the family, the last thing he needed was to be concerned about Annabelle's health. Especially if what Lucy had said was true. He'd never let her leave if he thought she was taking ill.

"I'm fine. It was just warm, and my dress was a bit... tight." She whispered the word, knowing that ladies of her acquaintance often said that they sometimes got a little dizzy if their corsets were too tight. She would have easily said such a thing to her mother, or Maddie, if they were alone. But her father, being a man... still, if it eased his worry, a little diminished modesty would be worth it.

"Well, land's sakes, child!" Maddie set the bowl in front of her with a thud. "Why didn't you just say your corset was too tight? No sense in suffering misery for the sake of fashion. I told you I thought that dress was too much. I don't care what the other girls are wearing. We're getting you upstairs and changing out of that monstrosity and into that nice calico where you don't have to be laced so tight."

Annabelle's face heated. She'd at least been discreet in her words. But for Maddie to be so free in front of... She stole a glance at Joseph, who winked at her.

Annabelle looked down at her bowl. Of all the...

"It's all right, Annabelle. I have sisters. I never did see the point in those contraptions making a woman miserable."

She opened her mouth to say something, anything, to make this man know that such talk was completely inappropriate. But Maddie was tugging her out of her chair.

"Let's get you changed."

If only a change of clothes was enough to fix the woes in Annabelle's life.

Chapter Six

Joseph watched Annabelle leave with a smile. She was like a wet cat when she got all riled up. And even though he assumed he was supposed to take her seriously, it only made him want to laugh. Someday, she'd figure out that she didn't have to pretend with him.

Wait. What was he talking about, someday? As soon as he finalized his pa's estate, he'd be taking what he could and going back to his family in Ohio. There he wouldn't need to worry about getting closer to Annabelle Lassiter.

Frank coughed, and Joseph looked up. He probably shouldn't have said all that about corsets. At home, that's all his sisters ever talked about. But in polite company, it was highly inappropriate.

"I'm sorry. I should have been less frank with your daughter."

Frank smiled. "No need for apologies. When her mother was alive, she had a woman to tell her these things. Poor Maddie isn't equipped for the society Annabelle runs with."

"It must be hard on her, losing her mother."

Joseph took a mouthful of soup, pleased that the flavor was every bit as good as the aroma that had been tantalizing him since this morning.

"I'm sure it's just as hard for you and your sisters," Frank said in a pastorly tone.

Joseph looked around the large table. "We at least have each other."

He continued eating his soup, remembering Annabelle's confession from the previous night. Yes, he'd lost his parents, but he had his siblings left. People to care for, people who counted on him, people who cared about him.

Who did Annabelle have other than Maddie and her pa?

"You must miss them." The knowing smile warmed him even more than the soup. How could Annabelle be devoid of the same warmth?

"I do. But I'll wrap up things with my pa's estate, then return home." Hopefully with enough money to get by until he could support them all. As his ma's sister, Aunt Ina would surely refuse to help their pa's out-of-wedlock child.

"I hope you find what you're looking for," Frank said, then continued eating his soup.

It was too bad there weren't more men like Frank Lassiter in Ohio. He would never forget Frank's kindness. Someday, he'd take Frank's challenge and help someone else in need.

Annabelle returned, wearing a faded dress and an equally faded expression on her face. The wet cat look had been replaced by the look the cat would have after being dried off—slightly more comfortable, but still resentful.

"There you are, Annabelle. And looking just as pretty." Her father's flattery did nothing to erase the scowl on her face.

"You'll feel much better once you get some soup in you. Since Joseph is going to need help finding his father's cabin, you could go with him. It's near Greenhorn Gulch. You know where that is."

"Of course, Father."

She sat down and ate the soup placed in front of her, her face expressionless and her gaze completely on the bowl.

Joseph should learn to accept Annabelle being distant, but she was like a burr under his saddle. He wasn't going to be satisfied until he fixed it and fixed it good. His sister Mary would tell him it was his failing. Having to get to the bottom of things and solve the problem. They'd always thought he'd become a lawman for that very reason. But the pay wasn't enough to support the family and run the farm.

So instead, he was here, chasing down his deadbeat father's estate, and trying not to be attracted to the lovely woman sitting before him. He'd admit it, even in the dress she looked none too happy about wearing, Annabelle Lassiter was still a beautiful woman. And when she forgot herself for a moment, she brought so much light into the room.

But those were thoughts he needed to do his best to temper. Though Margaret's defection had hurt, she'd been right. Joseph could barely provide for the family he had. He needed to focus his attentions on caring for his siblings, not courting a lady.

After lunch, Annabelle took him and Nugget to the livery. They saddled up her family's horses, then rode out of town toward a place her father had called Greenhorn Gulch.

Rocks jutted out around them, and stumps showed where trees once stood. The sure-footed paint Joseph rode had no trouble keeping up with Annabelle's blue roan. The mare was perfectly suited to Annabelle, who seemed completely out of place in this desolate land stripped of what had probably once been a beautiful forest.

"What happened to all the trees?"

"Cut down to make support beams for the mines and places for the miners to live." Her voice had a coldness to it.

"You don't approve?"

She led her horse across a shallow creek. "It's not my place to approve, but I think it's a fool's errand. People are willing to risk everything to get rich, and most of the folk who come out here never do. They abandon their families, leaving behind perfectly good lives in the vain hope that they'll strike silver. When they get here, they're willing to lie, cheat, steal and do anything else to gain an advantage that doesn't exist."

She could have been talking about his pa. He'd come out here with the goal of finding silver to provide what the farm could not. But the little girl sitting in front of him on the saddle was proof of how his pa had discarded his principles.

But he refused to accept Annabelle's evaluation that it happened to everyone.

"Some people get rich."

Annabelle looked over her shoulder at him. "Don't even entertain that line of thinking. Before you know it, you'll be living in the filth, blinded by the tiny flecks you think mean something but turn out to be nothing."

"My papa found a treasure." Nugget, seated in front of him on the ample saddle, piped up. "He was going to build me and my mama a bigger house than anyone else in Leadville."

The glance Annabelle gave him was enough to melt the rocks around them. "So you are one of them."

She turned her gaze to Nugget, and he could tell it immediately softened. "You should just take her back to wherever you came from. Now, before you wind up losing whatever else you have left."

Annabelle probably saw a lot of hardship in her line of work. It was natural that she'd want to be protective, especially of Nugget. But she didn't understand. He had nothing to go back to. Only a family to send for, and he already knew there wasn't a place here for them. His only hope was finding something of enough value in his pa's possessions that he could use it to move the family west.

"All I want is what my pa found. Nothing more. Just enough to get home to my family and make sure they're taken care of."

"That's what they all say." Annabelle clicked her tongue and set her horse to a faster pace. The rocky path had widened until a large mining operation came into view. He'd spent some time working in a similar place when he'd first arrived in Leadville, bringing the ore to the smelter. Tents and ramshackle cabins dotted the area, but Annabelle made no motion to slow her pace.

He glanced behind him, noting that from this elevation above town, the view was so majestic, it was easy to forget the abysmal conditions of the mining camp they'd passed through. On the hardest days, it was this picture of being above the clouds covering the valley below that had kept him sane.

Once they passed through the camp, Annabelle followed the creek back into more rocky terrain. Joseph had to give her credit for her adept handling of the horse. His sisters probably wouldn't have been able to do the same. They came around a rise and into a smaller clearing.

"Hey! This is where my papa lives," Nugget cried out as she tried to scramble down from the saddle.

Joseph held her tight. "Wait. I want to be sure it's safe."

Annabelle slowed her pace, then pointed to an outcropping of rocks. "Based on the map, that's where the cabin is."

"How did you get to know the area?"

She shrugged, and said in a dull voice, "My father's ministry is helping the people in the mining camps. Many of them don't venture into town because they're so afraid that if they leave, they'll miss out on the big strike. So we go to them."

"How often do you come out?"

"I haven't in a while." The familiar look of sadness crossed her face. "Not since everyone got sick."

They dismounted, and she led them to the other side of the rocks, Nugget skipping on ahead into the cabin.

"She's still here!" The little girl ran out of the cabin, carrying a worn rag doll. "I forgot her last time we came to visit Papa, and I've been missing her terribly."

Nugget hugged the doll as Joseph stared at the place his pa had been calling home for the past five years. Sandwiched between outcroppings of rocks, the cabin was little more than a one-room shack built mostly of rocks, twigs and mud.

"I guess we found it," Annabelle said, looking resigned.

"Thank you. I would have never found it otherwise." Even though Nugget had recognized the area, it was clear she wouldn't have found it, either. When she'd tried to get off the horse, she was looking in the opposite direction.

He walked into the dark building, grateful when Annabelle handed him the lantern. She obviously knew what she was doing. Looking at this place, Joseph could see why she sounded so disillusioned.

As he held up the lamp to illuminate the room, Annabelle walked around, lighting the lamps she found.

It was a simple room, with a small stove, a bed, a trunk and a few boxes. His pa had given it a touch of home, the bed covered with a quilt Joseph recognized as the one his ma had tearfully pressed into his arms when he'd left.

One of the crates was turned on its end, like a makeshift chest of drawers, with a picture of his family, as well as a picture of a bawdily dressed woman—Nugget's mother, he assumed.

He walked over to the pictures and picked up the one of his family. If only Annabelle's judgment of the situation hadn't been so true. His pa had abandoned them to give them what he'd claimed was a better life. Only it hadn't panned out, and now Joseph was looking for something, anything, to pick up the pieces.

"That your family?" Annabelle stood behind him, her voice thick.

"Yes."

Nugget entered the room and noticed him holding the picture. "Papa said that someday I'd meet the rest of my brothers and sisters. That's how I knowed you when you comed for me." She pointed at the people in the picture.

"That's Mary, and Bess, and Evelyn, and Helen, and Rose, and Daniel and there's you." She frowned as she pointed at Ma. "And that's the other lady. Mama said she was the reason why I couldn't meet you yet."

Joseph swallowed the unexpected grief and tried to ignore the anger burning his insides. Pa had never planned on coming home. At least not to his ma. Ma had been a good woman. She hadn't deserved this. Once again, he wished his pa was alive just so he could kill him himself.

"She was my ma. She was a good woman."

Nugget's eyes widened. "Papa told Mama she was a shrew."

It was wrong to disrespect your father, but if his pa was here now, Joseph would have no problem punching him. And yet, he could stand here and do nothing—not contradict an innocent child who hardly knew what she was saying, and try to avoid the knowing look in Annabelle's eyes. Not that the girl looking around the cabin knew anything at all.

Annabelle had moved on and was looking at a stack of books beside the bed.

"Your father was a reader?"

"No." Joseph coughed and took the book from her hands. "My sister Mary and I are. Mary thought that if we sent him with our favorite books, he'd have something of us so that he wasn't so lonely."

He glanced over at the little girl now rummaging

through the trunk. His pa had obviously had no problem with loneliness. After having done the math in his head more times than he cared to count, Joseph figured his pa had met Nugget's mother shortly after coming here the first time. Which meant his pa had gone home to Ma after being with Nugget's mother. And then left his ma to return to a woman who— If it weren't for the women present, Joseph would have wanted to smash the pictures representing his pa's lies.

"I'm sure the books gave him some comfort. It looks like he jotted notes in the margins." Annabelle gave him a small smile, as if she was trying to be sympathetic.

Her words made him pause as he looked at the book. Why would anyone jot notes in the margins of *Ivanhoe*? Joseph flipped through the pages and noticed that random words had been circled, and sure enough, when you looked at some of the margins, his pa had made notes.

Only none of them made any sense. One page would have *Mary May* scribbled on the side, then some words would be circled. Why would he write Mary's name on the pages of Joseph's book?

He noticed that Annabelle had begun looking at his pa's other books, sitting on the bed, and Nugget had joined her. He couldn't deny that her treatment of his sister was genuine. One light and one dark head were pressed together, whispering over the books Annabelle was looking at.

"Do you like to read?" He moved back toward them, and Annabelle looked up, a real smile filling her face.

"It's my favorite pastime. I love reading about the far-off places and countries. There are so many wonderful things in this world, and I would love…" She gave a soft sigh, then closed the book she'd been looking at. "Well, my place is here. The only way I get to see the world is through one of these."

A wistful look crossed Annabelle's face, and Joseph realized that there was far more to her dream of travel than she was saying. If conditions were different, he'd want to know more, but how could he give her any indication of his interest and raise false hope in her? Maybe Annabelle's reticence was for the best.

Annabelle ruffled Nugget's hair and stood. "Enough of that talk. Did you find what you were looking for?"

Back to the old Annabelle. Fully on task and avoiding anything personal. Clearly she had more sense than he. Nugget remained on the bed, looking at one of his pa's books.

"I need a pencil," she announced, unaware of the tension in the room.

"Oh, you're much too little for that." Annabelle held out her hand to Nugget. "We'll go pick some wildflowers while your brother finishes what he needs."

Nugget gave her a glare that made Joseph want to laugh.

"Papa lets me draw in his book." Nugget stood, and proudly stomped over to one of the chests, leaving one of the books open on the bed to show a childish drawing scribbled over the pages of one of Mary's beloved books.

Joseph's gut clenched. His sister's favorite book had been reduced to worthless garbage by a pa who had left his first family in need for a new life.

Annabelle caught his eye, and again he saw genuine emotion. Pity this time, and he wanted none of it.

"Such a shame," she said in a quiet voice. "She loves

stories, though, so perhaps I can help her learn to re-spect books. I can remember when Mother was giving us lessons, and Susannah, who was just a baby, got her hands on an inkwell and one of Father's books. I thought poor Mother was going to die of apoplexy. But Susan-nah learned, just like Nugget will."

"I'll teach her," he said gruffly, and went to the trunk where Nugget was still rummaging for something to write with.

"What are you looking for?" He knelt beside her and put his hands over hers.

"I want to make a picture for Papa," she told him, those big green eyes reminding him so much of his sis-ter Mary. Mary, who had the most loving heart in the world, but was going to be so hurt when she finally learned of the horrible sins their pa had committed.

How do you tell your siblings that their beloved pa was an unfaithful liar and cheat?

"You know your papa is gone, right?"

Nugget nodded, big eyes staring at him. "But some-day when I meet Jesus, I'll see him again. And he'll want to see all of my pictures. He loved it when I made him pictures. He'd hand me a book and tell me to make him something pretty."

Joseph's stomach turned over again. How could his pa have been so careless with the things he and his sis-ter held so dearly?

A stack of envelopes caught his eye. He'd recognize that writing anywhere. Ma's. With childish scribbles drawn over it. Even his ma's letters weren't sacred. But why would they be? His pa hadn't kept his marriage vows sacred, either.

Joseph's heart twisted inside him as those letters

beckoned at him. His ma hadn't been perfect, and in most recent years, with their pa gone, she'd been unbearable at times. But he couldn't help himself when he took that stack of letters and put them in his pocket. Tonight he would read them and grieve, both for parents lost, a marriage broken, and the realization that everything promised them had been a lie.

Annabelle watched Joseph talk to the little girl by the trunk. It had been difficult for Annabelle, going through her mother's belongings, and even more difficult for her to watch her father give them all away. But it couldn't possibly compare to the difficulty of going through a parent's belongings with the evidence of that parent's sin right there.

"Nugget? Are you ready to collect wildflowers? I'm sure Joseph would like some time alone, and I know Maddie would be pleased to have a bouquet for the table."

Nugget didn't move from her position. "Papa always has me make a picture for him when I come so that he has something to remember me by."

For the first time, Annabelle realized that as much as she had been focused on her own grief, and tried to understand Joseph's, she hadn't looked too deeply into the grief of a little girl who had lost not only a mother, but a beloved father. Being in this cabin made Annabelle realize that poor little Nugget had been just as close to her father as Annabelle was to hers.

Well, as close as they'd been before the family had gotten sick.

But now…as much as Annabelle tried to embrace her family's mission, she couldn't. And how could she remain close to a man who would eventually see through her attempts to pretend everything was all right when it wasn't?

The backs of Annabelle's eyes prickled with the tears she couldn't allow herself to release. Because if she let herself cry, she'd be too focused on her own pain to be of any use to Nugget or Joseph.

Which was the cruelest trick of all. She'd been fine, just fine, until they'd come into her life, forcing her to acknowledge all she'd lost.

The worst part was that as much as she tried to harden her heart and not let herself love again, she only found it softening toward the sweet little girl and her brother who would soon be gone, just like all the others.

The sunlight nearly blinded her as she exited the cabin. Though she had lit every lamp in the place, she hadn't realized how dark it had been until coming out into the open. Birds trilled in the meadow, singing beautiful but shallow songs of hope. They could afford hope. But for Annabelle, hope was nothing more than a fairy tale. She had to keep herself from believing the myth that caring for Joseph and Nugget would end well.

Joseph would return to wherever he came from, defeated by the dream of his father's riches, taking Nugget with him.

Somehow, she had to find a way to convince her father to let her go East with Lucy and her family. There, she could stay with her aunt and finally have the space to let her heart heal. Until then, she'd endure the best she could, hoping against hope that she'd have some of her heart remaining in the end.

Chapter Seven

Nugget skipped out of the cabin, placing her hand inside Annabelle's with such love and trust, it was hard to remain detached, especially when the skies were so clear and blue. She'd even take away her resentment of the birds, who meant no harm with their innocent songs.

"Are you ready to find some flowers for Maddie?"

Nugget smiled, the grin stretching from ear to ear. "I'm going to press them in one of my books."

They'd passed some young cow parsnip at the entry to the meadow. There, they could not only find some pretty flowers, but maybe even some greens to bring home for dinner. After a long winter with few fresh vegetables, it would be a welcome addition to their supper. Her mother used to say that anytime they had a chance to experience God's bounty, they should. Annabelle's heart gave a pang.

Why did the things that occurred to Annabelle most naturally hurt so much? She should have been able to more easily erase the memories so that she could do a simple task like picking wild plants without that awful prick at the back of her throat.

Nugget seemed to sense where Annabelle was heading, because as they got close to where she'd spotted the wild greens, Nugget took off running.

"Flowers!" The gleeful shout rent a hole in Annabelle's heart. The joy should have made her happy, and she wanted to be happy, but mostly, Annabelle wanted to cry.

Surely her father would let her visit Aunt Celeste if she was traveling with Lucy's family. The sights, and the parties, and being a world away would lessen all the pain.

"Look how beautiful!" Tiny fingers thrust a crisp white flower in Annabelle's face, and even she couldn't deny the sweetness.

"Thank you." She made a show of smelling it. "Beautiful. Perhaps we can find enough to bring back to Maddie."

"What will we put them in?" Wide eyes stared back at Annabelle. Though Susannah had lighter hair and was slightly older than the small girl, Annabelle couldn't help but remember that same face staring at her last summer.

So not fair.

Annabelle turned away before the little girl could see the tears forming in her eyes. It wasn't right to inflict her grief and fear on an innocent child.

"I'll see what I can find in the cabin."

At least she had a viable excuse. And unlike Joseph, Nugget didn't dig deeper into Annabelle's heart or question her motives. Maybe for some, letting go was an easy task. But the harder Annabelle tried, the more it hung on, like the sticky ooze from the creek.

She left Nugget in the meadow, singing a song, and plucking flowers. A small smile cracked Annabelle's face, reminding her of the impossibility of resisting the sweet child.

When she returned to the cabin, Joseph sat on the bed, engrossed in a book.

"Good reading?"

He looked up. "My pa's journal. Not all of it makes sense, but I was hoping it would offer some clues as to where he might have found the silver."

Silver. Always silver. But maybe she could get him to see reason before it caught hold of him.

"They always claim to have found silver, but…" Annabelle shrugged. "There are a lot of charlatans out there who will seed an old mine with a few nuggets to trick people into thinking they've made it big."

She gestured around the cabin. "This is not the home of a man who found silver. You've seen the mansions in town. That's where the ones who strike it big live."

Joseph closed the book and looked up at her. "I know." He sighed, then set the book down. "But he sent money home. More money than our family had ever seen. I've gotten dozens of jobs, but nothing that brought in the kind of money he sent. It had to come from somewhere."

Even in the dim light, she could see the lines drawn across his face. Was he thinking the very thought that had occurred to her? A person didn't get the nickname "Bad Billy" for being an upstanding citizen.

"I don't think it was silver," she told him in the most gentle tone possible.

The look on his face made her wish she hadn't been the bearer of bad news. But he was fortunate to face the truth now. She looked around the room and spied a bucket on one of the crates.

"I'm going to finish picking flowers with Nugget. I found some greens that will be good to take home to Maddie. We've only got a few minutes longer before we need to start heading back. Otherwise, it'll get too dark to find our way home."

Annabelle grabbed the bucket, wishing that the truth wasn't so harsh. But that was the trouble with dreams. Believing in tales, but not having the proof to back it up, meant that disappointment was inevitable.

At least Joseph was able to see the truth sooner rather than later.

Annabelle headed back outside. Once again the light nearly blinded her. But not so much that she didn't recognize another horse. And a man talking to Nugget.

"Hello!" Annabelle waved her hand and started in their direction. The man looked up but didn't return the wave. Instead, he took Nugget by the hand.

Annabelle quickened her pace toward Nugget and the man. "Nugget!"

The closer she got to them, the more her heart thudded. Nugget was tugging against the man's grasp.

"Let go of her!" Annabelle ran in their direction. "Joseph!"

Hopefully if the man heard that there was another man present, he would leave poor Nugget alone.

"Stop!" Annabelle's throat hurt from screaming so loud, but it distracted the man enough that Nugget was able to tear away from his grasp and run in her direction.

Annabelle gathered Nugget in her arms and started toward the cabin. The man took a step in their direction, then stopped. A quick glance over her shoulder revealed Joseph running toward them.

"What's going on?" His shout spurred her to turn and run to him, clutching Nugget tightly.

"The man…he was trying to take Nugget."

Nugget whimpered against her bodice. Joseph's face hardened.

"Get inside the cabin and bar the door. I'll handle this."

Annabelle didn't need to be told twice. This kind of lawlessness ran rampant in the mining camps and surrounding areas. Even being in town could be dangerous, but at least there, no one dared accost an innocent child.

It wasn't until they were safe inside the cabin, the door barred, that Annabelle dared breathe. Just one more reason to want to leave. These ruffians…

Nugget lifted her head, and Annabelle realized that the child's tears had soaked her bodice through.

"Oh, sweet girl…" She smoothed Nugget's hair and began humming a melody she remembered from her mother. Nugget rested her head back against Annabelle, and Annabelle continued humming and rocking the little girl as she tried peering out the cracks in the wall to see if the horrible man had left.

"Don't let him take me," Nugget whimpered. "He's a bad man."

Annabelle lifted the little girl's head and examined her face. "Do you know him?"

Nugget nodded, then peered around at the door as if to see whether the man was coming after them.

"Who is he?" For once, Annabelle wished she would see the miners as individuals, rather than just a whole group. Maybe she would have recognized him.

The child gave a shrug, those wide eyes still focused on the door. "Dunno. But he shouted at Papa a lot."

A man who shouted at the little girl's father a lot who just happened to be at the cabin to try to take her. No, Joseph's father wasn't a legitimate miner. He was something far worse and more scary. How had her own father been fooled into helping this man?

Someone pounded on the door. "Annabelle, it's me. Joseph. It's safe to come out now."

Still clutching Nugget to her, Annabelle opened the door, and Joseph gathered them in his arms. Warmth rushed all around her. She closed her eyes and breathed in deeply of a strong, earthy scent. His hard chest felt so good against her cheek, and his warm body cradled Nugget between the two of them. Safe.

"Are you all right?"

"I'm—" Before Annabelle could finish telling him they were fine, he'd taken Nugget from her grasp and was cradling her like a baby. Of course it was Nugget he was worried about, and the reason he'd gathered them in his arms. She'd been foolish to get wrapped up in a moment of fancy.

Fancy was what got everyone here in trouble.

"I'm sure she's fine," Annabelle told him, clearing her throat, and silently applauding herself for making it sound like she'd known who he was interested in all along. "I didn't see any injuries, so she's just a little scared, that's all."

He ignored her, keeping his gaze focused on Nugget. "What happened out there?"

"I was picking flowers, and Annabelle went to get a bucket. When she was gone, the man came from the trees and asked about Papa's treasure. I told him it was a secret and to go away. Then he grabbed me. But Annabelle saved me."

Dark, sparkling eyes stared up at her. "You won't let the bad man get me again, will you?"

"Of course not." Annabelle reached over and brushed

a hand across the little cheek. "We'll tell my father, and he'll make sure we all stay safe."

A bright smile lit up Nugget's face, and she pulled a hand away from Joseph's embrace. "I saved us some flowers."

Her little fingers were stained from the mush that she'd been keeping in her tiny fist. Annabelle couldn't help smile at the thought that in all of the danger they'd just faced, Nugget was determined to keep her flowers safe.

Joseph set Nugget down. "Why don't you go look at your books while I talk to Annabelle?"

Nugget let out a long groan. "You guys want to talk about the bad man. Mama and Papa never let me hear about the bad man, either."

"You know about the bad man?" The disbelief in Joseph's voice made Annabelle's heart sink. He probably had no idea what sort of skullduggery his father had been involved in. Annabelle didn't, either, but from the whispered conversations she wasn't supposed to hear when her father was talking with the sheriff, she knew enough.

Nugget nodded and looked at Annabelle.

Joseph whipped around. "You knew?"

"Once we were in the cabin, Nugget told me she recognized the bad man as someone she'd once seen arguing with her father. But that's all I was able to find out. Were you able to find anything?"

"No." A dark look crossed his face, and Annabelle could only imagine what poor Joseph must be feeling. "He got away."

Annabelle had gathered that much on her own. "Maybe my father knows something that can be helpful. He's good friends with the sheriff."

His shoulders relaxed, and he glanced in the direction of Nugget, who had turned her attention to the books. "Why would someone want to take a child?"

Because there was a lot of meanness in this world, particularly in a mining town, where the lowest of the low hung around, hoping to find riches.

Unfortunately, most of the people seeking riches weren't kindhearted souls wanting to do good for others. At least that had been Annabelle's experience. What that had to do with taking an innocent child, she didn't know, but she didn't question things like that anymore.

"Because Papa knew where the silver was," the little voice piped up.

Annabelle sighed. Especially when Joseph headed her way and asked, "And did he tell you where it was?"

She couldn't bear to look at him, or to hear the rest of the conversation. Annabelle went outside for a breath of fresh air in hopes that her churning stomach would calm down. The man's sister had nearly been kidnapped, and he wanted to ask about the silver. Maybe she and God weren't on the best of terms right now, but surely the fastest way to ruin was greed. The kind of greed that had men stealing children, and others too worried about the silver to consider their safety.

Please, God. Help me escape this horrible place. Let Joseph and Nugget leave here before anything worse happens.

The futility of her prayers was not lost on Annabelle. She looked around the clearing, realizing for the first time that the horses were gone. What a way for God to answer. She wasn't just stuck in Leadville, but in a ramshackle cabin so far from home that she wouldn't be tasting Maddie's cooking anytime soon.

She turned toward the cabin and saw Joseph standing in the doorway.

"The horses are gone," she said, gesturing toward the empty area where they'd grazed.

"Yeah." Joseph ran his fingers through his hair. "He took them."

Annabelle glanced over the hill toward the low sun. "It'll be dark soon. Too dangerous to leave the cabin now. We'll have to spend the night here, then set off first thing in the morning."

He nodded slowly. "You're taking this better than I thought you would."

"And what is it that you thought I'd do?" Annabelle's face heated. "Have a fit of vapors?"

At his slow nod, the heat in her cheeks moved to the back of her neck.

"I'll have you know that I have spent plenty of time in places worse than this, thanks to my father's ministry. Why, I could even catch us a couple of fish in the stream, clean them, and then cook them up for supper."

The look on his face screamed disbelief. Fine, then. She'd show him. Fortunately, she remembered seeing a fishing rod in the cabin. Without another word, she stomped past him, grabbed the fishing rod, then went back out the door.

"Annabelle! Wait."

She spun around and shot him her best glare. "What? Any other condescension you'd like to send my way?"

"No." He shoved his hands in his pockets. "I was just going to say thanks, that's all. And that I'm impressed. Back home, my sisters would have been horrified at spending the night in a place like this, and even more so at the thought of touching a worm, or cleaning a fish. There's a lot more to you than meets the eye,

Annabelle Lassiter. I see that once again, we've misjudged each other."

She supposed she should have been grateful for his compliment. But his words about misjudging each other grated on her conscience like the squealing wheels of the train pulling in to the station.

Joseph knew nothing of Annabelle's life, or her situation, least of all her capabilities. Yet here he was, admitting that. Trying to do what she supposed was the right thing. Which made her own thoughts on him even worse. She should be trying harder, but something in her fought it and wouldn't let her.

So she let his comment pass and walked toward the creek, where hopefully enough fish would be biting that they could have a decent supper. Walking back to town tomorrow would take considerable energy, and with a little girl to protect, things could get even more difficult.

"Annabelle!" Joseph called out to her again.

She stopped, but didn't turn in his direction. "I need to catch supper before it's too dark to see."

"I don't want you out there alone. That man could come back. We're safer if we stick together. Let me get Nugget, then we'll all go."

His logic made sense. And she shouldn't resent him taking charge. Her mother would tell her she shouldn't resent anything, but there was so much to resent these days.

"All right," Annabelle said, then sighed. At least with Nugget present, Joseph wouldn't be as likely to ask the kind of questions that made her brain whirl and her heart hurt.

Chapter Eight

~

They found another patch of flowers near the stream. This part of the mountains seemed relatively untouched by the mining operations. A few trees remained, and the stream wasn't clogged with the tailings from the mines. If you looked in just the right direction, you couldn't see the town or any of the mining operations. Beautiful.

It was a shame that the cabin wasn't bigger. Joseph could bring his family here to live. Unfortunately, the cabin was too small, too rough, and he couldn't ask his siblings to witness the evidence of their pa's foul deeds. Nugget would be hard enough to accept, but he was confident that once they got to know her, the rest of the family would love her just as much as he did.

Joseph smiled at his sister, who seemed to have completely recovered from nearly being kidnapped. If anything positive could come of such a disastrous day, it would have to be that surely this confirmed the existence of silver. Then, he could save his siblings from the clutches of his aunt Ina. *Please, God, let me find the silver soon.*

He wasn't asking for much, not really. Just for a place

to live and a way to support everyone. He'd thought five sisters and a brother hard enough, but now that he had Nugget to think of, well, he supposed one more mouth wasn't too much more to consider.

Still, it'd sure be nice to buy Mary a pretty dress like the one he'd seen her admiring in the mercantile. He was closer to Mary than to anyone else, and when Ma had gotten sick, she'd taken over the mothering while he'd gone to work. Between the two of them, they'd kept things together, and he hoped to someday treat Mary to something nice for a change.

He glanced over at Annabelle, who'd taken off her shoes and stockings, then tied up her skirts funny so she could fish from the edge of the bank. It would probably offend her sensibilities for him to notice, but with the breeze blowing golden tendrils of her hair about her face, she looked almost peaceful. Back to the pretty girl he'd been admiring.

It was a shame he had nothing to offer her. Nugget was barely six years old, and though Mary was old enough to marry and start her own household, the others still needed his guidance. A woman wanted her own home, and her own family. Not a ragtag bunch of kids who'd lost their parents. Six. Hard enough to ask a woman to take on a child or two, but six, or even seven if you counted Mary, that was a lot. No, he didn't harbor any illusions of marrying and starting a family of his own.

But when Annabelle grinned and sent a splash of water in Nugget's direction, he was tempted.

The cool reception Nugget had been given by the women in town made Annabelle's kindness toward his sister all the more remarkable. She didn't see Nugget as being the child of a sinful woman, but as a child worthy of love.

"Got one!" Annabelle's clear voice interrupted his thoughts. "Joseph, help! It's a big one!"

He hurried over to the bank, where she struggled to reel in the fish. It was a big one, all right, and he wrapped his arms around her to help her pull it in.

Together, they reeled in the fish, water soaking them both as the fish fought for its life. Finally, they were able to get the fish on the bank, where it flipped and slipped, to the clapping of Nugget's little hands.

"Nice catch!" Joseph whirled Annabelle around, grinning.

She smiled, but released his hands. "You think you can do better?"

He glanced at the fish, still wiggling on the bank. "Probably not. But if you give me a chance, I just might."

She blushed when he winked at her, and he was reminded again of how charming she could be.

"I should tend to the fish," she said as she scurried past him.

Joseph grabbed the rod and started preparing it for another fish. Although Annabelle had caught a large fish, it wouldn't hurt to have more. They could take it with them on the walk home tomorrow.

"I'll do it," he said, holding the fishing pole in her direction. "Since you like fishing, I'll handle the messy work and leave you to the fun."

Her eyes flashed. "I can clean a fish."

"I don't doubt it." He smiled, hoping to disarm her once again. "But since you love fishing, I'd hate to spoil your fun."

Annabelle took the pole. "Oh. If you don't mind…"

"Not at all. I hate fishing. Too much standing around and waiting for the fish to bite. I prefer things that are more direct."

"If you're sure. Father and I loved going fishing together, but Mother said…" She turned her head away and started back for the water.

"Why do you do that?" he said to her back.

"What?" She looked at him, her brow furrowed like she was trying to decipher a puzzle.

"Hide." He bent down and grabbed the fish, but kept his eyes on her. "Just when you start to reveal a bit of the real Annabelle, you retreat into a place where no one can see you."

He couldn't read the expression on her face, but then, that was exactly what he was accusing her of doing. Hiding. Pretending. Who was the real Annabelle Lassiter?

"This is the real Annabelle. I like to fish. Some women would say that's not proper. So I only fish when I'm with my father."

A wistful tone filled her voice, and he wondered when she'd last gone fishing with her pa.

"You can fish with me."

Annabelle shook her head. "That really wouldn't be proper now, would it? I'm already going to have to be careful to avoid a scandal for being here, so the more we can avoid the appearance of impropriety, the better."

Annabelle was right. He hadn't thought of the consequences of them spending the night unchaperoned. They shouldn't have come at all. But he hadn't thought twice about it when her father had suggested the idea. Still… Annabelle was a lady, and…

If word got out about them spending the night alone in the cabin together, Annabelle would be unfit for decent company. She'd done nothing other than offer him and his sister her kindness—at the expense of her own grief. And now, because she'd agreed to bring them here, she'd suffer once more.

"I should marry you. To avoid scandal."

He'd never imagined himself saying those words, least of all to someone like Annabelle, but they slipped out. A man of honor, he'd spare Annabelle's reputation.

"But I won't marry you." Annabelle stalked the rest of the way to the water, fishing rod clenched in her hand, stating clearly that the conversation was over.

Nugget tugged at his hand. "That wasn't very romantical."

"Romantical?" He stared down at her. "What do you know of romantical?"

The little girl's face brightened. "When Papa got romantical for Mama, he went to the bathhouse and took a bath. Then he picked some pretty flowers and gave them to her. Mama said it was the most romantical thing ever, and she couldn't wait until he was free to marry her."

She stared at him with a knowing look. "If you're not romantical to Annabelle, she's never going to marry you."

Words from a child shouldn't sting. The comparison to his snake father was the lowest insult he could think of. Especially as they related to marrying a woman he had no business thinking he could marry. The honorable thing was to propose marriage. He had, and she'd said no. End of discussion.

Right?

* * *

Annabelle fought with the line that had somehow been tangled. Imagine! Telling her that he'd marry her, as if it were some kind of chore, like gutting a fish. Was she so unlovable that he wouldn't want to marry her?

Not that she wanted to marry him, of course.

But oh…the nerve of the man. Her finger slid along the line, and the string cut into her skin. Blood oozed out, and she stuck her finger in her mouth.

She glanced over her shoulder. Joseph had squatted by Nugget and together, they were gutting the fish. Her heart wasn't supposed to melt at the sight. She should have been completely unaffected by the way he smiled at the little girl. So tender. Gentle. And Nugget's giggle…

There was so much to like about them. Annabelle recast her line, this time being careful of her injured finger. If only things were different. If she hadn't been abandoned by another miner whose lust for riches outweighed his feelings for her. Mining fever blinded people to what was right. Though Joseph was beginning his quest with what sounded like good intentions, they'd fade once he held that first glimmer of metal in his hand.

But even if Joseph were a blacksmith or a barber, or anything else, Annabelle's heart was too irrevocably damaged that she had nothing left to give anyone. And why should she? She'd lost too much to risk it again.

Another giggle rent the air. Another pang in Annabelle's heart. For all her attempts not to care for the little girl, she couldn't help but wish…

If Susannah had lived, she and Nugget could have been friends.

A tug at her line brought Annabelle's attention back to where it should have been. This fish wasn't as big as the other one, but it still took a good deal of strength to bring it in herself. But she wasn't afraid of the work. Work had never scared her. The strength required to perform such tasks was nothing in comparison to the strength of will it took to handle everything else in her life. If only the rest of her life was so simple as physical labor.

"I'm impressed," Joseph said over her shoulder as she finished bringing it in. "You should have asked for help."

"And spoil the fun?" Annabelle grabbed the fish and pulled it off the hook. "I told you that I love to fish."

The fish wiggled in her hands, and she tossed it in Joseph's direction. "Want to take care of this one?"

"I'd be happy to. It's the least I can do, since you've been so good as to provide dinner."

She watched as he brought the fish to Nugget for them to clean. One more thing she had to appreciate about him. He didn't coddle Nugget or treat her as less than capable because she was a girl.

"I'll head back to the cabin and get the stove ready so we can cook the fish."

Before she could turn back up the trail, Joseph stopped her. "We need to stick together, remember?"

Annabelle sighed. "You're right."

The look he gave her made her feel only marginally better. How, in all of this, had she forgotten that there was a man out there who wanted to harm Nugget? For a moment, she'd gotten lost in the joy of fishing and forgotten that they were all in very real danger.

A bird cried out, and Annabelle watched as it turned

circles in the sky. As high up as they were, sheer cliffs still surrounded them from all directions. Trapped. And with night closing in, the only option they had was to remain united.

She gave another deep inhale before opening her eyes and looking back up at the cliffs.

Along the top of the ridge, something flashed. Like a light, only not so bright. Like a reflection. Was it the man who'd tried to take Nugget?

"Joseph?" She tried to keep her voice modulated, not betraying the worry and fear that would frighten a little girl.

He must've sensed the edge in her voice, because he murmured something to Nugget, then stepped right beside Annabelle before quietly saying, "Is something the matter?"

"Look up at the cliff to the north. Just past my right shoulder. There's a flash of...something." She gazed at him, watching his face as he searched the spot.

"Is it silver?"

If he had been her brother, she'd have slugged him in the arm. Hard. Silver. Because that's all the people around here wanted to see. Joseph's sister was in danger, and all his mind could conjure was silver.

"If it were silver, dozens of miners would have found it by now. I'm worried that it might be someone watching us. Like the man who tried taking Nugget."

At her words, he stilled. Hopefully realizing that chasing after silver was foolishness in comparison to Nugget's life.

"I'm going to take a closer look. We'll return to the cabin. Once you two are safely inside, I'll see what I can find."

Annabelle's heart thudded against her chest. "I thought we were supposed to stay together. I can't protect Nugget by myself."

He stared at her. Long and hard. Like he thought her words were more foolish than the thought of an inexperienced man going after a child-stealing bandit.

"Don't go acting soft and feminine on me now. I know better. You are way more capable than you let on. I have no doubt that if someone came to the cabin, you could absolutely handle it on your own."

Annabelle swallowed. His stare bore into her as if once again he saw deeper into her soul than even God. He was right. No one would harm Nugget. She'd already lost a precious child on her watch. Disease was something she couldn't see coming, and she couldn't stop once it came. But a man… Annabelle straightened her back.

"I could," she finally told him. "But I don't like it."

Then, because she couldn't let his foolishness pass without a remark, she looked him up and down. "You, on the other hand, I have serious doubts about. You don't know this land. And the type of men you're liable to come across…"

"You think I'm weak." The word came out as a slap in the face. No, no one could accuse this man of being weak.

"I think you're green, which is different from being weak. Out here, being green gets a man killed."

A sly smile slid across his face. "Does this mean Miss Annabelle Lassiter is worried about me?"

Oh! He was insufferable! "Fine, then. Take your chances." She spun and strode over to where Nugget was finishing with the fish.

Annabelle smiled at the little girl and pretended to inspect Nugget's handiwork while ignoring Joseph's soft chuckle. Had she said he was insufferable?

"You did a nice job, Nugget. We'll have a wonderful supper tonight." Annabelle picked up the fish. "Let's go back to the cabin and see what kind of feast we can prepare."

The little girl giggled. "My papa used to say that when we finally got our mine in production, we'd have a feast every night. I didn't know he was talking about fish."

More false silver dreams. Annabelle swallowed the bitterness that rose up and smiled. "I'm sure he was talking about a different kind of feast, but I think this'll do just as good."

Nugget rewarded her with a heartbreakingly sweet smile. "You sound like my mama. Mama said we didn't need no feast, just each other."

Scary to be compared to a woman of ill-repute. Only, the more Nugget talked about her, the more Annabelle had to question that judgment, as well. Nugget's mother sounded almost nice, like the sort of person she might be friends with. Except, of course, for the sinful life she led. Which only made Annabelle wonder more. She'd always lumped sinners into a pile, where their badness made them almost intolerable. She'd never taken the time to consider that they might have good qualities, as well.

Her father would have probably given her a sermon on the topic—that all are sinners and fall short of the glory of God. But the ladies at church said that some sinners were worse than others. Only now she had to begin to wonder which sin truly was the worst—the way they treated a sweet girl like Nugget and her mother, who seemed like she was a nice person—or the life Nugget's mother led.

Annabelle tripped over a rock, stumbling, but managed to catch herself and save the fish.

"Are you all right?" Joseph grabbed her to steady her, then looked into her eyes.

How could he have known where her thoughts were going? "I'm fine," she said, then continued on the path.

If she wanted to condemn those who condemned Nugget's mother for being what she was, then she also had to look at her own judgments of people. Like Joseph. Like being upset at miners for vainly pursuing silver at the expense of all else.

Her father had once told her that he wanted to share real treasure with the miners, and that it was his duty to love them where they were at. That there was nothing wrong with pursuing a dream as long as you didn't forget the highest prize.

Annabelle sighed. It wasn't that she didn't like Joseph or even miners. But it was the only defense she had against the pain of what would be the inevitable loss.

Nugget giggled at something Joseph said to her. The little girl, and yes, even her brother, had already wormed their way into her heart. But if she could leave soon, surely the pain would be bearable. It would certainly be more tolerable than prolonging the acquaintance. The longer she was with them, the more the parting would tear at her.

Chapter Nine

Joseph stuffed the paper-wrapped fish in his pocket. True to her word, Annabelle had made their dinner a feast. He hated leaving so late, but Annabelle had refused to let him leave without food in his belly.

Annabelle handed him the shotgun they'd found buried under one of the floorboards. "I think you should take this."

"I've never been much of a shot." He stared at the gun, knowing that if he had to come up against the kidnapper, he wouldn't stand a chance.

Joseph closed his eyes and offered a silent prayer. He had to keep Annabelle and Nugget safe.

"What are you going to do when you meet up with whoever's out there? Invite them to church? Even my father doesn't venture out of town unarmed. When I agreed to the plan of you investigating, I assumed you at least knew how to protect yourself."

Which was the nice way of her saying he was the biggest fool ever. "What do we do about what we saw on the cliff?"

She inclined her head over to Nugget, who was bent

over one of Pa's books. "We can't do much of anything. We have Nugget to keep safe. At least, with the way the cabin is positioned, we'll know they're coming before they get here."

Annabelle held up the gun and said, "I'm pretty good with targets, but it's not as though I've ever shot a person before."

If only Mary could see him now. She'd probably love the fact that he had a whole list of things a girl could do better than he. No, not a girl. Annabelle.

"We do have the strength of the Lord. Why don't you pray for us?"

Except Annabelle didn't rise up to his challenge. Instead, her face fell, and she started to turn away. "Sorry, I can't."

He reached for her shoulder. "Please. Annabelle. Stop turning away from me, and just face it."

Her shoulders fell, and she slowly turned back to face him. A single tear ran down her cheek.

This Annabelle, this Annabelle he knew. It was the sad girl he'd seen try to hide at her father's house.

"Please don't tell anyone," she whispered.

"Tell anyone what?"

Another tear trickled down her cheek. He wanted to reach out to wipe it away, but feared that if he did, it would give her reason to run away again.

"I can't pray, Joseph. God doesn't hear my prayers." She closed her eyes, then her shoulders rose and fell again before she opened them and looked at him. "I'm a preacher's daughter, and God doesn't listen to my prayers. If anyone knew…"

The expression skittering across her face reminded him of one of the rabbits they caught in traps. She truly believed that people learning of her lack of faith would be the end of everything.

"Have you talked to your father about this?"

"No!" Annabelle took a step back. "And you can't tell him, either. It would kill him to know that after all he's done to save others, his own daughter doesn't believe."

His heart broke at the way her face twisted in pain. From his own faith journey, and how his family battled against Christian do-gooders, even if he did tell her father, it wouldn't make a difference in what Annabelle believed. She had to learn to believe on her own.

"Then I'll pray for us," he said quietly. "And I'll pray for you."

"Please don't waste your words on my account," she said, then turned to clean up the remains of dinner.

This time, he gave her the space she required. He'd seen farther into Annabelle's heart than she'd even allowed her father to see. With that, he had to believe that there was hope for Annabelle. Maybe even for him and Annabelle to be friends.

If there was silver, and the threat against them seemed to indicate there must be, then maybe he'd move his family out here. It would be good for Mary to have a woman friend her own age.

He smiled at the thought of Annabelle and Mary becoming friends. They both shared the same deep convictions and inner strength he so admired.

He glanced over at Nugget, engrossed in one of their pa's books. "What are you reading?"

"Papa's words." A sad look crossed Nugget's face. "I miss Papa. He would've made the bad men on the cliff go away."

So much for trying to keep Nugget out of this. "What do you know about the bad men on the cliff?"

Nugget shrugged, then hugged the book closer to her. "They want Papa's silver."

He wished the little girl was old enough to tell him about more than just that their father had silver.

"Can you tell me anything about Papa's silver?" Joseph sat next to her on the bed, but she scooted away.

"No." Nugget hugged the book closer to her. "It's a secret."

Joseph sighed. She was just a child. She probably didn't know much anyway.

"It's all right. You don't have to tell your secret. Come here, and I'll read to you."

This time, Nugget rewarded him with a grin and fell into his arms. He breathed in her soft little-girl scent, cuddling her.

Since he wasn't going to be able to marry and have children himself, he had to enjoy these moments with his sister and cherish them as his own. Mary would call him daft, but she could someday have a family of her own. He would do that much for the sister he'd left behind to care for the others while he hunted for their pa. After the abuse she'd suffered at Aunt Ina's hands while protecting their siblings, well, he owed her. If only he'd known before he'd left just how bad it would be for them. One more reason to be angry at his father.

He caught Annabelle's soft humming as she cleaned up the remainder of their dinner. It was almost enough for him to be able to lose himself in the fantasy of having a real family. It'd be nice to have a woman who loved him to take care of them, and a sweet child of their own to love. But Annabelle wasn't his wife, and Nugget wasn't his daughter.

Margaret had been right about why he'd make a terrible husband. He was too busy with the family he already had to start one of his own. It was a good thing Annabelle had refused his proposal. He could rest with a clear conscience knowing he'd done the honorable thing, but also with the relief that he wasn't forcing a good woman like Annabelle to give up whatever it was she dreamed of.

"Read!" Nugget lifted her head and handed him the book she'd been looking at.

The Bible. Fitting, considering his prayers and Annabelle's confession. Maybe, as he shared the sacred words with his sister, Joseph would find some answers.

But as he opened the first pages, he realized the same thing he'd seen in his pa's other books. His pa had been using it to write his own notes.

Joseph started reading the opening lines to the book, but as the words swirled around in his brain, all he could think about was how they connected. His heart raced. The mines—his pa had secretly written the key to finding his treasure within the pages.

"Joseph!" Nugget tugged on his arm. "More!"

He patted the little girl's head and continued reading about Joseph in Egypt. Later, when Nugget went to sleep, he'd decode his pa's mystery.

Annabelle listened to the soft sound of Joseph reading to Nugget. It was peaceful, being in the cabin with Joseph and Nugget. For the first time since meeting them, her heart didn't hurt. Strange.

She put the last dish back in the crate. Maddie would tsk over her reddened hands when she got home tomorrow, but if that was the worst Maddie could find fault with, it would be worth it. Funny how as much as she'd been longing to go back east to visit Aunt Celeste, she couldn't think of a more contented moment than now.

It had grown dark, and the last remnants of light faded from the one tiny window the cabin had allowed. Their lamps would make them easy targets for intruders, but she couldn't bear to spoil the special time Nugget and Joseph were having. If only she had been given more similar moments with her own baby sister.

But she couldn't. All she could do was give that time to Joseph and Nugget.

Annabelle turned down the rest of the lamps, conserving oil, and making their presence as unobtrusive as possible.

"Everything all right?" Joseph paused in his reading.

"Fine," she said. "Everything's fine."

She stood at the corner of the window, looking at the dark landscape. The bandits could be anywhere, and she wouldn't see them. The door was already bolted, but would it be enough? She spied a large barrel in the corner. Against the door, it would be an additional barrier.

Annabelle started pushing the barrel.

"Let me help."

"I can do it. Nugget—"

"Is asleep." Joseph had come alongside her, and together they pushed the barrel in front of the door. Even in the darkness, she could see his smile. Sometimes she wished she could have his same calm attitude. With all that he lost, how was it that his burden would be so light?

Having Nugget must make it easier.

Annabelle leaned against the door. Wisdom said they should rest. But what if the men came during the night?

"Why don't you take the bed with Nugget, and I'll make a pallet on the floor? We should both get some rest."

She hated the way he could read her mind sometimes. It reminded her too much of how her father and mother had been together. Finishing each other's sentences, often so alike that…well, that didn't describe Annabelle and Joseph at all. Not only did they have no future together due to his mining ambition, but he wasn't the sort of man she could fall in love with. Why, she didn't even like Joseph.

Something tickled her on the back of the neck as a small voice reminded her that telling falsehoods was a sin. Fine, then. She mostly didn't like Joseph. Sometimes, like when he was caring for Nugget, he could almost be all right. Not that her admission made the tickle go away.

Annabelle looked around the cabin. No sense in thinking about Joseph, not now. Not with all the other things they had to worry about.

"I think we should be safe enough for the night. I thought I saw—" When she turned to point out the trunk she'd noticed containing a number of blankets, she saw that Joseph had already beaten her to it. Yet again, he'd known what she had been thinking.

She huffed out a breath. Coincidence, that's all. Joseph wasn't a stupid man. Of course he would remember that the trunk contained blankets. Obviously being in these close quarters was addling Annabelle's mind. She'd be thinking more clearly once she had a good night's sleep and was home safe.

"That's just what I was about to suggest," she finally said, almost forcing a smile, but stopping when she recalled how it usually served only to irritate Joseph rather than placate him as she intended.

Joseph shifted slightly, then looked at her in a way he hadn't looked at her before.

"I know you'd prefer to be anywhere but here, so um…" He shifted again, his shoulders rising and falling. "I appreciate everything you've done here with Nugget and me. I'm not sure what we would have done without you."

She'd been thanked countless times, but none of the thank-yous she'd ever received had made her so queasy. So… Annabelle closed her eyes. She'd done what was needed, nothing more. Which didn't explain why his thanks was so disconcerting.

"Of course I would help." She didn't look at him as she turned toward the bed she'd be sharing with Nugget.

But his silence didn't feel right to her at all.

Obviously she was overtired and overwrought after such a day. Once she'd had a good night's sleep, the jumble in her mind would make sense again. Then she could get them all back home and back to their normal lives.

Chapter Ten

Joseph tried making himself comfortable. He'd slept in far worse conditions, so he couldn't understand why he couldn't fall asleep. He'd need every bit of rest he could get for their trek in the morning.

He could hear Annabelle snoring softly. She'd be mortified if he said anything, but he wished he could tell her that her unladylike noises were actually somewhat cute.

Maybe if he took a look outside one last time to make sure everything was fine, he'd be more comfortable going to sleep. He stood, and in the faint light, could see Annabelle and Nugget curled up together. Absolutely beautiful.

A noise outside the cabin startled him. The men? Maybe his lack of sleep wasn't such a bad thing after all. Joseph tiptoed to the small crack that would allow him a view of the surrounding area. Two riders on horseback were in the distance, heading toward the cabin.

Hating to disturb Annabelle's peace, but knowing their safety depended on it, he crept to the bed, then shook her softly. As her eyes fluttered open, he put a finger to his lips, then pointed to the door.

She nodded, then scooted out of the bed. He couldn't help but notice how she tucked the quilts around Nugget as she left. Someday, Annabelle would make an excellent mother.

Which made Joseph want to smack himself for being so daft when they were clearly in danger.

They went to the crack, and Joseph pointed out where he'd seen the riders.

"Get the gun," Annabelle whispered.

He nodded slowly, wishing he didn't have to let Annabelle do a man's work. When they returned to town, the first thing he'd do was practice his shooting. If the place was so unsafe as for a man to teach a woman like Annabelle how to defend herself, then he'd need it, as well. Especially now that he had Nugget and her silver secret to protect.

As the riders drew closer, she set the gun down. "It's my father."

Though Joseph expected to have to face her father at some point, it somehow seemed more wrong for him to find them in the cabin together.

"Help me move this." She pushed at the barrel they'd only recently put in the way of the door.

There was nothing Miss Annabelle Lassiter couldn't do.

As the riders stopped just short of the cabin, Annabelle ran out, carrying a lantern.

"Father!" Her joyful cry made his gut ache. He supposed he wouldn't have had such a reunion with his own pa. Even more than before, he'd like to punch the man for messing up so many lives. Not only was there the obvious evidence of his pa's infidelity, but now, they had dangerous men after them.

What kind of man had his pa been, really?

Certainly not the kind of man who jumped from his horse and wrapped his arms around his daughter. He'd never seen such affection with his sisters.

Nugget made a small noise in her sleep as if to remind him he had another sister. A little girl who called their pa "Papa," with such fondness he had to wonder if he knew his pa at all. Could a man change? And if he'd changed, why hadn't he cared enough to make sure the rest of his family was provided for?

Annabelle, her father, and another man walked toward the cabin. He steeled himself for what would most likely be a confrontation ending in a marriage proposal. He knew how poorly that had gone over before. But with them being unchaperoned for so long, the preacher was bound to make him do right by his daughter.

Somehow, they'd make it work. And he'd make it up to Annabelle for ruining her life.

Joseph stepped out to meet them, but Annabelle shook her head. "We'll talk inside."

Once inside, neither Annabelle nor her father, nor the strange man made a move to add additional light.

"Annabelle tells me that you may be in danger." The preacher looked at him with a very unpreacherlike expression. "What did you see on the cliff?"

Joseph relayed the details as best as he could remember.

"I know the spot he's talking about," the strange man said. "I'll go check it out."

The preacher gave a nod, but kept his attention on

Joseph. "Thank you for your quick thinking. I'm sure you saved both Annabelle and Nugget."

Annabelle gave a most unladylike snort, and despite the serious nature of the situation, Joseph wanted to smile.

"It was all Annabelle's doing. Her quick thinking and resourcefulness has been a real blessing."

This time, the preacher turned his attention to Annabelle, who appeared to back away from his examination. "Is that so?"

"I just did what I had to do." She looked away, then grabbed the pile of blankets Joseph had left on the floor. "I can make pallets for Nugget and I so you two can trade off with the bed."

"Annabelle—" Her father seemed to want to say something, but she cut him off with a glare.

"Not now. I did what I had to do, and that's that."

Even if he'd wanted to, Joseph couldn't ignore the bitterness that had returned to her voice. Somehow the carefree Annabelle had gotten misplaced with the arrival of her father.

Joseph reached out and took the blankets from her. "It doesn't make sense for you to disturb Nugget. You take the bed with her, and your pa and I will make do on the floor. I haven't been able to sleep anyway."

"That's because you've been on the floor while I've had the bed," she retorted, tugging at the blankets. "You need your rest."

"And so do you." He held them firm, glancing at her father for reinforcement.

"Joseph is right. Go to bed, Annabelle."

Finally. Someone with enough authority to get Annabelle to obey. Not without a fight, though. She practically stomped to the bed, then snuggled down into the covers.

Neither man said a word until Annabelle's soft snore sounded through the room.

"I'm sorry for my daughter's behavior. I realize this situation is difficult." Frank broke the silence first.

"You have nothing to be sorry for. Because of Annabelle, we had a fine dinner and were safe inside the cabin until you arrived."

He glanced over at the mounds on the bed before continuing. "Sir, I realize that my being alone with her is improper. I'd like to assure you that I took no liberties with your daughter's person. But if you feel it necessary for us to marry, I'll be glad to do so."

The words came out all in a rush, lest he lose the courage to utter them.

Frank, though, looked at him, then chuckled softly. "Son, you have a better chance of taking liberties with a mountain lion. Unless she feels it necessary, I won't be forcing you into a wedding."

Which should have left him feeling relieved, only it didn't. Worse, that traitorous part of him almost wished her father had insisted otherwise.

"There's something I don't understand." Joseph moved closer to the preacher so they could talk more. "In town, you acted like Annabelle was near perfect. Here, you seem to have a more realistic view of her."

Frank sighed. "I'm not blind to Annabelle's faults. Still, she's got a good heart. One that's been broken too many times by these mountains. I should never have sent her with you, but I'd hoped it'd bring some healing to her. All it's done is put her in danger."

For the first time, Frank sounded like a broken man

instead of a man of God. "She wasn't always so bitter. But when her mother and brothers and sister died, she let the bitterness take over. If you'd been alone with her then, I'd have made you marry her. Because she'd have been impossible to resist."

It was almost on the tip of Joseph's tongue to tell him that he'd gotten a glimpse of that Annabelle. But he wasn't sure that information would be helpful about now.

Maybe it was time to talk about more relevant information. "Who was that man you brought with you?"

"Slade Holmes. Best tracker I know. When Annabelle wasn't home in time for supper, I figured she might have run into trouble. So I found Slade and came up here."

"I'm sorry I didn't do more to protect them." He glanced over again at their sleeping forms. "I don't know what I'd have done if those men had—"

"Don't fret over what-might-have-beens. The girls are safe. That's all that matters." Frank grabbed a blanket and wrapped it around himself. "I'm going to get some shut-eye, and I suggest you do the same."

"What if the men come back?"

"Slade will give us plenty of warning."

With that, the older man turned and curled up on the floor, the conversation clearly over.

But it wasn't over, not in Joseph's mind. Not with the puzzling woman still snoring softly on the other side of the room. As much as Annabelle held the silver search in disdain, she had to realize that it was the only way he was going to save his family.

A small slant of sunlight roused Annabelle from her slumber. Nugget still lay curled beside her. She sat up slowly, looking around the strange room that had become familiar to her in less than a day. Joseph slept slouched in a chair, and her father was gone.

Slade must've found something.

Annabelle stretched, and careful not to disturb Nugget, slid out of bed.

She walked to the door, wondering if Slade and her father were near. It figured he'd bring Slade along. One more reminder of all she'd lost.

"Morning." Slade's voice greeted her as she stepped out of the cabin.

She didn't look at him. "Morning."

"You can't hate me forever."

Oh, yes, she could. "I don't wish to discuss that particular topic. Where's my father?"

She scanned the area, noting that her father's horse was gone, but Peter's—now Slade's—grazed nearby.

"Maybe if you were a little nicer to me, I'd tell you."

Annabelle sighed. Staying angry did her no good, especially when she knew Slade was just trying to help. But forgiving him in theory was so much easier than in actuality. "What do you want from me?"

"How about a bit of civility? You lost a brother, but I lost my friend. Can't we call a truce?"

A truce. For the man who should have been getting the doctor for her brother but somehow ended up bringing home a pocket full of silver instead.

"What'd you do with the silver?" She hadn't meant to confront him with the question that had been plaguing her for months, but the words bubbled up of their own accord.

Slade's face darkened. "Your father went down to the

camp at Greenhorn Gulch to see if he could get some food and borrow some horses."

"I'll start a fire." Annabelle turned toward the cabin.

She probably should have apologized for her rudeness, but it was hard enough being in his presence without having to also humble herself and admit where she'd been wrong.

Before she could enter the cabin, hoofbeats sounded in the distance. Her father. At least he hadn't witnessed her conversation with Slade. She'd have had to endure another sermon about forgiveness. Then, she'd have had to paste another smile on her face and pretend it was all right when it wasn't.

Nothing was all right. But if she didn't pretend, everything around her threatened to cave in. While she appreciated Joseph's attempts at wanting to do away with the falseness she surrounded herself with, he simply didn't understand it was the only way for her to survive the grief that tried to swallow her whole.

"Hello, Father," she said when he dismounted. "I was about to go inside and build a fire. I believe Joseph has some fish from last night." Hardly a feast, but at least it'd keep her hands occupied so she didn't go crazy.

"No need." He smiled and kissed the top of her head. "I ran into Gertie at the camp, and she's got breakfast for all."

"I wouldn't want to impose. I know how provisions are scarce for them." She gave a half smile in return.

"I told Gertie the same thing." The genuine smile her father gave made Annabelle's insides curl up. "But Collin's had a bit of good fortune lately, so there's plenty."

Yet not enough for them to leave the mining camp and live in a decent house. She'd never understand these miners. They settled for living in squalor and throwing their money back into a pit that might someday pay off.

Or, like Collin MacDonald, throw it all into a bottle that never did anyone, least of all his family, any good.

"That's very kind of her. We'll be sure to send a basket of Maddie's goodies to thank her when we're back home."

Her father sighed. As if he, too, was learning to see right through her. "I know it's going to be hard on you, seeing Gertie. Just remember that she was your mother's best friend, and that she loves you like her own."

"I'll try." It was the best she could do. She hadn't seen any of the MacDonalds since her family died. Her father had dutifully come from his visits to the family to let her know of how they were all doing, but she couldn't bring herself to visit. There were too many reminders of what she'd lost.

"I'll let Joseph and Nugget know." Annabelle went inside before the feelings got to be too much to bear. She knew it was wrong to shut out the remaining people who loved her. But what else was she supposed to do?

She'd tried so hard to build walls around all the things that hurt, and to keep out the people that reminded her of that pain. But now she was being forced to confront it, and that seemed like the worst injustice of all.

The mining camp was like so many of the places Joseph had visited looking for his pa. A sea of tents, rough-hewn cabins, and the stench of unwashed human flesh. However, instead of the wary stares he'd gotten on his trips, the people greeted them as they passed by.

"Howdy, Preacher."

"Morning, Miss Annabelle."

Friendly voices, friendly smiles, and if it wasn't for the tense way Annabelle sat on the horse in front of him, he'd think they were going to meet beloved friends. Children crowded around the horses, and several women looked up from the washing to give a cheerful wave.

The farther they went into the camp, the more Annabelle's back stiffened.

"Are you all right?" he asked in a low voice.

"I'll be fine."

He might as well have asked if she'd take arsenic in her tea. They stopped near the center of the camp, and as everyone dismounted, he followed suit, then rushed over to lift Nugget down, then to assist Annabelle.

"I can do it," she said, her voice laced with sadness.

Her father smiled at him. "Now, Annabelle, you're a lady. Don't fault a gentleman for treating you as such."

When her shoulders fell in that resigned way of hers, Joseph felt half-bad for wanting to help her. Now that he'd gotten to know her, had heard about her pain, he wanted to give her space to deal with it.

"I'm sorry for troubling you," Joseph whispered as he finished helping her off her horse.

He leaned in with one final whisper. "Let me be a friend to you."

Crystal-blue eyes that could have matched the stream they'd been fishing in filled with water as she shook her head slowly. "Please. Let this be."

Frank was oblivious to the situation as he neared the campfire and had already begun chatting with the woman who tended it. Joseph watched as she led him into a cabin that appeared to be even rougher than his pa's.

"Is that where we're going?"

Annabelle shrugged and looked away.

"Annabelle!" A girl slightly older than Nugget came bounding toward them. "It's been ages since you've come to visit."

Joseph didn't have to watch to know Annabelle had stiffened beside him. He could feel it. As much as he wanted to give her some comfort, he had something else to worry about. Nugget had attached herself to his pant leg again. The sweet, cheerful girl had disappeared.

Whatever it was about this camp, he sure didn't like the effect it had on his womenfolk.

His womenfolk. Joseph shook his head. Annabelle wasn't his anything.

"I've been busy," Annabelle finally told the girl, her voice thick.

"We've missed you." The girl's sweet voice didn't waver. "I miss Susannah." The last sentence was spoken with such heartbreaking sadness.

"I miss her, too."

With the way Annabelle's voice cracked at that admission, Joseph wasn't sure she'd have the strength to say anything else.

All of this—everything from the time he'd spent with her in their home until now—it was all about the same thing. Annabelle's crushing grief.

"Annabelle," her father called, coming out of the cabin. "Bring Joseph and Nugget over so we can get washed up and eat."

The smell of frying bacon finally hit Joseph's nostrils. His stomach growled. Though Annabelle's meal had been wonderful, the meager leftovers they nibbled at this morning hadn't done enough to satisfy his hunger.

"Is Nugget the horse?" the girl asked, her voice filled with wonder. "We ain't never had a horse to breakfast."

"Nugget is my sister," Joseph answered for Annabelle. "And she's a little shy, so give her some time to get used to you."

He nudged Nugget to get her to move forward, but her hands dug farther into his pants. "I'm not hungry."

Annabelle was no help in the matter, as she just stood there, staring.

"Let's do as your father says."

With a soft sigh, Annabelle nodded. "Come on, Nugget." She held out a hand, as if that hand would somehow make whatever was wrong with Nugget suddenly all right.

Nugget loosened her hold on his pants, then took Annabelle's hand, still grasping him with the other.

They trudged toward the cabin with painful slowness. Annabelle because she seemed to be doing everything she could to avoid getting there, and Nugget because she wouldn't let go of Joseph or Annabelle.

"I declare, you are as slow as molasses, Annabelle." The older woman stepped toward them and wrapped her arms around Annabelle. And, by default, Nugget.

"I don't know what's kept you from us for so long, but you are a sight. All skin and bones, what is that Maddie feeding you? Or not feeding you, I should say. Well, never mind that, I just fixed a mess of fresh eggs, and we've got bacon and biscuits so flaky you'd think you were eating a cloud. Polly's becoming quite the cook, aren't you, Polly?"

The woman stopped her rambling speech to point out a girl stirring a pot over the fire.

"And you must be Joseph. Frank told me all about

you. Says you've been looking into Bad Billy's estate. Now that's a sad state of affairs if I've ever heard one. Poor fellow got all mixed up with one of them dance hall girls and, well, she foisted someone's git on him. At least he died before he had to deal with the heartbreak of finding out she had the pox. Can you—"

"Don't talk about my mama and papa that way!" Nugget flew from the protection of Joseph and Annabelle, then kicked the woman squarely in the shin before running off.

"Nugget!" Annabelle and Joseph said the name in unison, but Annabelle propelled into action.

"I'll take care of it," she called over her shoulder, running after Nugget.

"And she will, you know," the woman said to Joseph. "Annabelle has a way with children. Such a terrible loss when she stopped coming here to work with the little ones. Come, let's get you a plate."

He looked at the woman, still full of cheer, and completely oblivious to Annabelle's misery.

"Thank you kindly, but I'd better help Annabelle." He looked her up and down. "And while I'm grateful for your hospitality, I would appreciate it in the future if you'd avoid making such comments about her mother or our father."

The woman flushed. "I meant no harm. I was only repeating what I—"

Joseph held up a hand. "I'm sure you didn't. But Nugget is my sister, and I take affronts to her honor seriously."

"Of course. I…" She looked at Joseph, then over at Frank, then back to Joseph. "I apologize."

"Thank you. I'd better see if Annabelle needs any help."

He left the woman standing there and headed in the direction he'd seen Nugget and Annabelle run. It didn't take long to find them, sitting beside a large rock at the edge of camp.

Annabelle held a sobbing Nugget in her arms, rubbing her back, whispering what he assumed to be soothing words into her hair.

"Is she all right?"

"Yes." Annabelle continued rubbing Nugget's back. "She's been so far removed from the gossip for a while that it's hard to have it come back at her. Especially with being reminded of their deaths. Poor little thing misses her mama and papa, and this just brought all the sadness back up."

She smoothed Nugget's hair. "But it's going to be all right. Everyone's entitled to be a bit sad from time to time when they miss someone they love."

The sweet kiss Annabelle pressed to Nugget's head tore at Joseph's heart. She wasn't just offering words of comfort to Nugget, she was telling it to herself.

Who rubbed Annabelle's back and whispered words of comfort to her?

The wind whipped down the hill, cold against their backs, reminding him that a warm fire and breakfast awaited them.

"We should get back."

His stomach concurred, grumbling its opinion.

"You go. We'll just be a little longer." The smile Annabelle gave him was mixed with sadness and unshed tears.

When did Annabelle get to cry over her losses?

Joseph looked around. Though people milled about the camp nearby, they were still out in the wild. "I don't—"

"We'll be fine." Annabelle pressed Nugget closer into her. "She's not all cried out yet. It's best if we let her get it all out."

More advice that he assumed had to have come from Annabelle's own life. Something she probably didn't allow anyone else to see, just like everything in her life. Had things been different for her when her siblings were alive? Back home, he told Mary just about everything. He sure could use her advice now. Of course, he'd never seen Mary cry. But surely she'd know what to do about the situation.

Though Annabelle seemed to have Nugget well in hand, he couldn't help but wish for something to ease Annabelle's pain.

"You're sure you'll be all right?" He hoped the look of concern he gave her would be taken in friendship.

She nodded and gave the kind of Annabelle smile he lived for. Would that their lives were simpler. That he didn't have a family to provide for. Even then, what did he have to offer her, or any other woman?

"Thank you," he said instead.

"Of course." Annabelle snuggled Nugget closer in to her. "She just needs time."

The look she gave him made him wonder if maybe it wasn't just Nugget she was talking about.

But the impossibility of the situation and his rumbling belly pushed him in the direction of the camp. "I guess I'll get back then. Try to hurry. Nugget could also use some breakfast."

At the mention of food, Nugget's head popped up. "They don't want the likes of me at their table."

Then she burrowed back into Annabelle's shoulder.

Annabelle looked up at him. "I'll talk to her."

The memory of Annabelle facing down the woman in the mercantile flashed before him as he realized that his sister would have no greater champion than Annabelle.

"All right." He looked at her. Annabelle needed a champion, too. Unfortunately, it couldn't be him.

Joseph returned to the cabin, where Frank was eating outside with a crowd surrounding them.

"Did you find them?"

"Yes." He took the plate one of the young ladies offered him. "Nugget was hurt by the unkind references to her mother, and Annabelle was making her feel better. She's still grieving over the loss of her parents."

The word *parents* didn't come so hard as it usually had. Not when he'd seen a little girl crying her eyes out over a mama who was gone. Nugget had woven herself into Joseph's heart, and for the sake of his sister, he had to let go of his discomfort with where she'd come from. But it didn't mean he had to forgive his father.

The older woman, Gertie, stood. "I should go to her and apologize. I'm sure Annabelle could use—"

"No." Joseph looked at Frank, hoping he'd give some assistance. "Annabelle is doing fine, and she…"

Was extremely uncomfortable around Gertie and her family. A person would have to be a fool or blind not to see it. But perhaps it would be indelicate of him to expose her in front of her pa.

Frank nodded. "She's still grieving, Gert."

"You know?" Joseph was grateful he hadn't yet taken

a bite of the mouthwatering food in front of him. He'd have choked otherwise.

"Of course I know. I'd be a bad preacher, and an even worse father, if I didn't see how she tries to shut out everyone who loves her. I keep thinking that given enough time, and around the people she used to love, that she'd get over it, but…"

Frank stared down at his feet, and for the first time, Joseph saw him, not as the faith-filled preacher, but as a man who was trying his best for a daughter he couldn't reach.

"How is it that I can't reach my own daughter?"

Annabelle's shameful secret was shared by her father. She feared him knowing, yet he knew. Worse, he blamed himself.

"You can't blame yourself, Frank." Gertie sat beside him and put her arm around him. "She'll heal when the time is right. You just gotta keep praying."

Though Frank didn't seem heartened by Gertie's words, Joseph realized that in all of this, he hadn't kept his promise to pray for Annabelle. True, it had only been a few hours since he'd decided that he needed to pray for healing in her relationship with God and her pa, but clearly, with Frank's pain so plainly displayed, he needed to be more diligent.

"Sir? If I may…" Joseph took a seat across from Frank. "Perhaps you should talk to her about this. When she held Nugget and let her cry, she said that sometimes a person needs to cry until it's all out. I couldn't help but wonder if Annabelle has had that opportunity."

"Annabelle never cries." Hard eyes stared back at him. Now he knew where Annabelle got it.

"Has anyone ever let her? Have you given her an

opening to pour out her heart and share these things rather than let them fester?"

In his own words, he finally saw the truth in Annabelle's actions and words. She was trying so hard to shove down the grief and pain that she couldn't express that it was festering.

Joseph took a deep breath and met Frank's gaze. "Maybe if you talked to her as a father, instead of as a preacher, and just loved her for who she is, instead of her role in your ministry, maybe she could finally heal."

He expected an Annabelle-like outburst to tell him he'd overstepped his bounds. Instead, those eyes softened as Frank said, "Her mother was always so good at that. I'm just as lost as Annabelle without her."

"Then tell her that. I think it would help you both." With that, Joseph turned his attention to his cooling breakfast, knowing that he was dangerously close to interfering more than he ought.

Because as much as he was working toward the reconciliation between Annabelle and her father, he had a feeling that his own homecoming wouldn't be as smooth. Their pa's death would be hard enough to take, but the transition to accepting Nugget as their sister was going to be hard on the rest of his family.

One more thing he needed to be diligent about praying for. As selfish as it sounded, finding his pa's silver would make that acceptance a whole lot easier. But if they had to face poverty with another mouth to feed, he wasn't sure Mary, or anyone else, would be that generous with accepting Nugget.

Chapter Eleven

Annabelle felt stronger as she returned to Gertie's cabin. It wasn't so much that anything had changed, other than the fact that she knew if Nugget was going to be comfortable, she had to be brave. Which meant pretending that it didn't hurt to see Gertie and her children running and laughing like the world was just fine when Annabelle's had ended.

"There they are!" Gertie's cheerful voice rang out, and Annabelle forced herself not to cringe.

"Sorry it took so long." She avoided Joseph's gaze. Joseph, who knew her too well for their short acquaintance, would see right through her.

"You just sit right on down and eat." Gertie handed her a plate while Nugget clung to the back of Annabelle's skirts. But Gertie was wise to that trick. "And you, too, little one. You've got to come out so's I can give you a plate."

Annabelle relaxed slightly as Nugget peeked out. "You're not gonna say mean things to me?"

"No." To Gertie's credit, she squatted down to Nugget's level. "And I shouldn't have said those things about your parents, either. I'm sorry. You must've loved them very much, and I'm sure they must've loved you, too."

Her words brought Nugget out of hiding but didn't remove the suspicious look from her face. "I am mighty hungry."

"Then I have a mighty big helping of breakfast for you."

As Gertie handed Nugget a plate and they all got settled, Annabelle couldn't help but notice Gertie's kindness. Gertie had always been a kind woman. It truly wasn't fair that Annabelle couldn't bear to be around her mother's best friend. She didn't know why it hurt so much, but it did.

Loath to spend any more time here than they had to, Annabelle gobbled up her food as quickly as was polite. At least the first few bites. But she could feel the weight of Joseph's stare on her and she knew.

He knew exactly what she was doing and why. No matter that she hadn't told him the full story. He knew.

Why couldn't he be as oblivious as her father, who sat there, making a whistle out of a twig for the children? He accepted her excuses readily enough, and when she finished eating and suggested that they return home as quickly as possible because Maddie must be worried sick, he would agree.

But Joseph wouldn't.

Tears pricked the backs of her eyes and she tried forcing them away, but they wouldn't listen. She gave them a quick swipe with the back of her hand.

"Is everything all right?"

Of course Gertie would notice.

"The smoke is rather thick, that's all." To prove her point, Annabelle got up and moved to the other side of the fire. But as she passed Joseph, his eyes mocked her.

Stop hiding.

He could add it to the list of her sins.

At least Nugget felt better. She was attacking her breakfast with gusto, enjoying every bite, and completely unaware of everything else around her.

Annabelle didn't want to feel this way. She would've liked to have laughed with Polly at whatever joke Gertie was telling. But the rushing in her ears kept her from being able to even hear it.

Even her father was laughing.

She stabbed some of her eggs, knowing that if Gertie noticed her not eating, there would be questions to answer. If only it didn't taste like slag and there wasn't such a huge lump in her throat to make it difficult to swallow.

"What's your doll's name?" Caitlin had sat on the other side of Nugget and was staring at the tattered rag doll sticking out of the small bag Nugget carried.

"Surprise," Nugget said shyly, but a small smile crinkled her lips. It was good for Nugget to be able to relate to kids her own age. Annabelle knew that. Based on the reception the little girl had gotten in town, she was sure that Nugget probably had few playmates.

"I've got a doll, too. Want to see?"

As Nugget nodded, Caitlin pulled out the one thing sure to shatter the last shards of peace Annabelle had been clinging to.

Bethany. Susannah's favorite china doll.

The plate slipped from Annabelle's hands and crashed into the dirt. Among the remains of her breakfast, she saw spots unlike any she'd ever seen. She'd purposely put that doll in a special place, a place where her father wouldn't find it to give to one of his projects.

Caitlin sat opposite of Nugget, prattling on and on

about how it used to be her very bestest friend's doll, but now it was hers, so she named it Susannah.

A nice gesture that wouldn't bring her sister back.

"Are you all right?" Joseph slipped into the spot next to her and began cleaning up her mess. She could only sit there and stare at it all.

No, she wasn't all right. But she wasn't allowed to say so. She couldn't begrudge a poor child the joy of a precious doll. And yet, she also couldn't find it in her heart to share the child's joy.

What kind of monster was she?

No wonder God didn't listen to her prayers. There was absolutely no good in Annabelle Lassiter.

"Don't worry about it. Your pa and Gertie are over there talking."

His words were meant to reassure, but as she looked over, she noticed her father slipping money into Gertie's hands.

"He's really generous, isn't he?"

Annabelle could only nod. She supposed this generosity of spirit was something to be praised, something clear in the idol worship shining in Joseph's eyes. But what about her? Didn't she have the right to grieve and miss her family? Selfish, yes. But she'd spent so long putting her own needs aside, and just once, she wanted her needs, her prayers, her dreams, to matter.

"What's wrong?" He looked at her with such a caring expression she wasn't sure she could stand it.

"I just want to go home," she whispered.

Joseph nodded. He didn't try to make her stay and face whatever he thought was bothering her.

"I'll talk to your pa." Joseph got up and walked toward her father.

Nugget tugged on her sleeve. "I don't want to go. I

want to stay here with Caitlin. She's going to show me how to fix Susannah's hair."

Annabelle wanted to close her eyes and be transported to anywhere but here. But she was afraid that if she did, she'd see Susannah's smiling face telling her the exact same thing. So she swallowed the lump in her throat.

"I'm sure you'll see her again." Because she would face this irrational emotion. Not for her sake, but for the sake of a little girl who desperately needed a friend.

"When?" Two little girls stared at her, like they were used to promises adults made, but seldom kept. Something she had often been guilty of with Susannah. "Later," she'd tell her sister. Only later never came, and now Susannah was gone, and she'd never be able to do those things with her.

"We'll discuss it with my father."

Who was walking toward them with Joseph and Gertie in tow.

"Joseph says you want to leave. We just got here. Surely you don't want to refuse the MacDonalds' hospitality. You haven't even chatted with Polly yet."

Annabelle closed her eyes. They were supposed to be her family's dearest friends. And once upon a time, before Henry had left with Annabelle's heart, Annabelle and Polly would sit and giggle and admire some of the miners. What had Polly done with the shawl she'd been knitting for Annabelle's wedding trip?

It hardly mattered. There was no wedding, no wedding trip. Henry had gone without Annabelle, all because Annabelle had chosen to nurse her ailing family when the sickness hit. The worst part was, Henry hadn't even said goodbye. Polly had been the one to break the news of Henry's departure.

How could she face her friend now?

She opened her eyes and looked up at Joseph.

"I'm sorry. I didn't sleep well last night, so I'm tired. Of course we can stay."

"What happened to your breakfast?" Gertie pointed at the plate Joseph had cleaned up but hadn't found a way to dispose of yet.

Annabelle stared at the ground. "I'm sorry. I got distracted, and I was clumsy."

She was trying so hard not to offend anyone. To not wrap them up in what was obviously her grief alone. But nothing she did was right. This was why she'd stayed away. Why she couldn't come back. Everything in her hurt, but everyone else had moved on.

"Are you sure you're feeling all right?" Gertie knelt beside her and put a hand on her forehead. "You've looked awfully pale since you got here."

"Nothing a night in my own bed won't cure." She gave another half smile, then closed her eyes and took a deep breath. She would do this. She would make it through the rest of the day in the mining camp, and everything would be just fine.

Her father joined Gertie in front of Annabelle. "She did faint in the middle of Harrison Avenue yesterday. We all thought it was because her corset was too tight, but perhaps she is coming down with something."

The concern in her father's face undid her resolve. She couldn't let him think that his last remaining child was in danger, too. He'd lost so much, and even though she was trying to be brave for his sake, she couldn't have him thinking she was ill.

"Truly, I'm fine." She stood, and at the same time, all the tears she'd been trying to hold back came rushing out. "I just want to go home. I don't want to be here, where everything reminds me of everything I have lost."

The only good thing about crying like this was that she couldn't see anyone's faces to read their expressions. Especially Joseph's. Why his was the most important, she didn't know. But as much as she'd like to save face in front of him, the dam had been breached, and she couldn't stop any of it.

"I miss Susannah. I miss Peter. I miss Mark and John. I miss Mother. And I'm tired of pretending that it's fine. It's not fine."

Nugget wrapped her arms around Annabelle's legs. "It's all right, Miss Annabelle. You can cry just like I did when I was missing my mama. It's all right to miss your mama."

The little girl's kind words sent Annabelle to blubbering like a fool. She had said that very thing to Nugget. *It's all right to miss your mama.* But she had no idea just how powerful those words were until someone said them to her.

Gertie stepped forward and wrapped her arms around her. "Oh, dear heart, I should've thought about that. Of course a young lady would miss—"

Annabelle tried to shrug off the embrace. "Please, Gertie, I can't."

But Gertie only squeezed her tighter, and the tears kept rolling down Annabelle's cheeks faster and faster.

"You have to face this, my girl. You lost your mother, yes, but you have a lot of people who love you. You don't have to lose us, too."

Gertie's words throbbed in Annabelle's ears. Was that what she'd done? In shutting herself off from everything, could she have been making it worse?

Annabelle straightened, and moved out of Gertie's embrace. This time, the older woman let her go. An-

nabelle turned and looked at her father, who held out a handkerchief.

"Thank you. I'm sorry, I didn't mean to go on like that." She blew her nose, an action that would horrify her mother, but she supposed her mother would be horrified by a lot of things she'd said and done lately.

Her father wrapped his arms around her. "No, don't be sorry for your tears. I suppose I haven't been very good at helping you grieve."

He kissed the top of her head, the way he did when she was little, and held her tight. "Your mother would have known how to talk to you, but I… I don't know what to say. I miss her more than you can imagine."

Annabelle looked up. Examined the lines in her father's face, noting for the first time that they'd deepened in recent months.

"You never told me."

"I was trying to be strong for you."

His words mirrored her own. Annabelle blinked away the tears. "And I was trying to be strong for you."

Her father pulled a letter from his pocket, the familiar script staring out at her. Aunt Celeste.

"Your aunt has been begging me to let you visit. The Simms family offered to escort you, but I…"

A long sigh shook his body. "I haven't been able to let you go. You're hurting so much, and I can't let you leave broken."

"I'm always going to be broken if I'm here." She looked around, noting that Joseph had taken the little girls closer to the fire, where they played with their dolls, and Joseph amiably chatted with Gertie and Polly.

She wanted to be able to interact with them. To talk like they did in the old days. But those days were gone, and nothing would ever be the same.

"No," her father said softly. "You're always going to be broken if you leave without fixing this."

But he didn't understand. It wasn't hers to fix. Annabelle hadn't broken anything. She was the one who had been broken.

Annabelle pulled out of his embrace and smoothed her skirts. "So what now? You won't let me leave, and I can't stay."

Her father let out the exasperated sigh she'd grown too used to hearing. "Gertie has been asking us to come up for a while now. I've been making too many excuses. There are a number of parishioners I need to see and I haven't been able to spend nearly the time I'd like up here caring for them."

A familiar tightness closed around Annabelle's lungs. "Please don't ask me to—"

"I'm not asking, I'm telling." Her father stood immovable. "This shouldn't be a chore. You used to beg to spend more time here. No matter how many days you spent up here, you always wanted more. So for you to be so reluctant to stay up here—"

Her father looked her in the eyes, searching in a way that he hadn't done before. "Annabelle, if there is some reason, other than you being upset over the loss in our family, then tell me. Otherwise, we're staying. Long enough for me to finish my work, and, I pray, long enough for you to face the pain that has you so trapped."

And what if she suffocated in the process? Already her lungs felt like they'd been filled with the dreaded slag from the mines. Her eyes burned. And her heart might shrivel up and die completely. That, she supposed, would be a mercy. Maybe then, the pain would stop.

"What will I do while I'm here?" In the past, she'd

visited parishioners, helped with Polly's chores, and then she and Polly would be on the lookout for—

Annabelle closed her eyes. Henry was gone, and who knew what had become of Polly's Tom? Regardless, there would be no giggling over weddings and babies.

"Joseph needs your help. If he's going to find his father's silver, he can't have a child underfoot. Mining is dangerous work as it is, and with the man who tried taking Nugget, he needs someone to take care of her."

Meaning Annabelle. And it didn't diminish the threat of the man who wanted to take Nugget.

"So we're still in danger?"

Her father shook his head. "Slade found some good tracks and he's confident that he'll be able to locate the culprit. You and Nugget will be safe enough with Gertie."

Leaving Joseph alone. "But what if the man comes after Joseph?"

"I'm glad to see you care about them. Now for you to start caring about the rest of the people in your life."

Annabelle drew in a breath. "Of course I care about the people in my life. I just…"

The look on her father's face told a different story. He didn't need to say it. She already knew that wallowing in her grief had been selfish. But remembering the sadness on Gertie's face as she reminded Annabelle of the people she'd been shutting out, Annabelle's excuses seemed rather thin.

"You're right. I should be more sociable toward Gertie and her family. I should talk to Polly."

It wouldn't be enough time to repair the breach, but she could make the effort. Maybe she'd even find the words to mend things with Polly. Of all things she regretted, it was that she'd said such harsh things the last time she'd spoken to the girl who'd once been her best friend.

It wasn't Polly's fault Henry had left. She'd merely been the bearer of bad news, and Annabelle had taken her heartbreak out on the other girl.

So many wrongs Annabelle had to make up for.

Her father followed her gaze to where Polly stood. "It would be a good start."

Annabelle swallowed. Her father didn't know the half of what had gone on. He'd been visiting a sick parishioner while Annabelle sobbed the whole story to her dying mother. None of them had realized how little time her mother had left, and sometime in the midst of Annabelle's pain, her mother had died.

She'd already been grieving the losses of Susannah and Peter. But that day, Annabelle had lost the man she'd thought she was going to marry, her best friend, and her mother.

Maybe Gertie was right. Maybe Annabelle hadn't had to lose everything. But as Nugget's laughter rang out across the camp, Annabelle wasn't sure she could risk opening her heart up again. What if she did everything right, and she still lost everything?

Chapter Twelve

Joseph swung the giggling girl in another wide circle.

"More!" Caitlin cried, the air full of her joy.

Nugget stamped her foot. "No! It's my turn."

He set Caitlin down and looked at the little girls. "You've both had turns, and now my arms are tired. Take a break and play with your dolls."

They ran toward the stumps where they'd set the dolls for a nap, and Joseph took a seat on another old stump. He hadn't remembered youngsters being so tiring. Of course his sisters were older, though Bess only by three years. Still, it had been a long time since he'd heard such laughter. Or maybe it only felt that way.

"Joseph!" Frank walked toward him, but Annabelle was nowhere in sight.

Joseph stood. "Is everything all right with Annabelle?" He wanted to kick himself for his impertinence. It wasn't his place to be concerned for her. "I'm sorry, Frank, I had no right."

"You care about my daughter. You have every right." Frank frowned, then looked over at the girls playing before turning his attention back to Joseph.

But this wasn't attention Joseph wanted. He didn't have the right. Not when he wouldn't be there for someone who clearly needed more stability than Joseph could provide.

"I've tried to be a friend to Annabelle."

Frank nodded slowly. "What are your intentions toward my daughter?"

Joseph sighed. "Friendship is all I have to offer. Back home, I have five sisters and a brother to raise." The giggling girls drew his attention. "And then there's Nugget."

A complication he hadn't dealt with in terms of sharing with his family and figuring out how they were going to incorporate this sweet little girl into their lives. There was no question about his love for Nugget. But telling his siblings, and getting them to accept her...

"Does she know that?" Concern filled Frank's eyes.

He hadn't said so in so many words, but he knew where he stood in terms of Annabelle.

"When we were stuck on the mountain, I proposed in case there were any repercussions to her reputation. She made it clear her answer was no, even if her reputation suffered."

Only Frank stared at him like he was crazy. "Any woman with pride is going to say no under those circumstances." He looked at Joseph hard. "But the way you take up for her, it's got to make her wonder if your feelings aren't deeper."

They were. But feelings didn't make for a decent marriage. He couldn't be the kind of husband she or any other woman deserved.

"I'm sure she understands."

But as the words came out of his mouth, he wondered if this was what Annabelle felt sometimes. Wanting to give the right answer, but not sure if he himself believed it.

Joseph shook his head. "I'll be sure she's clear on my plans."

The preacher looked at him with the same kind of look Joseph often gave Annabelle. He didn't believe him for a second. "It's been my experience that love doesn't always follow people's plans."

Love? That's not what he and Annabelle had.

But Frank didn't give him a chance to refute that statement. Gertie was striding toward them, clearly intent on whatever purpose that brought her.

"Is everything all right?" Frank's attention to Gertie clearly indicated that their conversation was over, as well.

Joseph started in the direction where Gertie had come from.

"Everything's fine." Gertie held a hand out. "I was coming to let you know the living arrangements up here. Annabelle's going to watch Nugget while you search for your pa's silver."

"I'd thought to have Nugget with me." Joseph glanced in the direction of the two girls playing. His sister seemed to be thriving in this environment, but with everything, he didn't want her far from him.

"It would make more sense if Nugget stayed here." Gertie smiled, then glanced in the direction of the girls playing in the distance. "The mountains are no place for a child. With the trouble you faced at the cabin, it's even more dangerous. You'll be able to avoid the bandits easier if you don't have a child to protect. And, well, I could use the company for Caitlin. She's been lost without Susannah, and this is the longest I've seen a smile on her face since."

The longing on the older woman's face would have been enough to get him to say yes, even if he'd been inclined to say no.

As much as it pained him to admit it, Gertie was right. He wouldn't be able to protect his sister and find his pa's treasure.

"Annabelle won't mind?"

Frank and Gertie exchanged an uneasy look. Of course Annabelle minded. She'd made it clear that she'd rather be anywhere but here.

"She understands the importance of keeping Nugget safe," Frank finally said.

Not the same as not minding, but Joseph was hardly in a position to argue Annabelle's cause.

Her father was already concerned about the possibility of Annabelle falling in love with him. Even if Annabelle thought nothing of it, he had to be careful of people's talk. And of taking up for her out of—simple human decency, that's what it was. But her father didn't seem to understand.

"It's settled then." Gertie gave him a wide smile.

What kind of life would it be with people around them who cared about one another? Annabelle had no idea how fortunate she was.

"Come on, girls," Gertie called in a booming voice, and they came running.

He hadn't seen such a big smile on Nugget's face before. It had to have been a hard life, living the way she had. He hadn't asked a lot about what had gone on in that situation. He hadn't really wanted to. It was too painful to hear about the woman who had stolen his pa's affections.

They walked back to the main area, back to the noise and chaos of the mining camp. They stopped at a tent a couple of yards from Gertie's cabin.

"This is where you'll be sleeping," she said with authority. "My boys sleep here in the summer. It's plenty warm when the weather's nice. They're already up working with Collin. The wages are good, and it's enough until Collin makes his own strike."

"And then he'll work that mine?"

"My, no." Gertie smiled in the same indulgent way she looked at the girls. "Pretty much all of the mines here are owned by the big companies. It's too expensive to buy the equipment needed to get the silver. That's the real dream here. To find a big enough strike that someone will buy it and you can go retire somewhere. I've got a sister in Denver, and it sure would be nice to be closer to her."

He hadn't thought of it that way. Of what would happen if he struck silver. "So why would my pa be hiding the fact that he found silver if he was going to sell it to the corporation?"

Gertie shrugged. "Either it wasn't quite enough to interest the corporations, or he was digging deeper to find a higher price." She looked deep in thought for a moment, and then looked at him. "Or the land he was prospecting wasn't his own."

She gave a quick nod and half smile as she looked over at Nugget. "No disrespect to your pa intended. It happens, though."

"Would it explain the people after Nugget?"

Gertie shrugged. "Perhaps. We can talk about that once we get settled."

Gertie pointed to the cabin across the small fire pit

area. "That's where Nugget will be sleeping. She'll be sharing the loft with Annabelle, Polly and Caitlin."

Nugget's face lit up. "You mean it? I get to stay here with Caitlin?"

Both girls squealed with delight, not waiting for a response, but running into the cabin.

"I'd rather have Nugget in my tent. To protect her."

Gertie shook her head. "I'm afraid that wouldn't look proper. I know she's your sister and all, but being that she came from a woman of—" she mouthed the words *ill repute* "—folks wouldn't be comfortable with her in a tent full of men."

Laughter erupted from inside the cabin. "Besides, you won't deny the girls the pleasure of each other's company, will you? It'll be so good for Caitlin."

The happiness emanating from the girls was almost enough to convince him. But Gertie didn't seem to understand how dangerous the situation was.

"But will they be safe?"

Though Gertie looked offended at the question, he had to ask. She hadn't been at the cabin when those men tried taking Nugget.

"Annabelle and Polly will be up there, too. There's no better shot than Annabelle. And Polly, well, this miner tried taking advantage of her at the creek one day, and let me tell you. She done such a number on him that he left town."

Gertie's warm laugh shook her belly. "No, you won't find a safer place for Nugget than with Annabelle and Polly."

He peered inside the tent he'd be sharing with Gertie's sons. "It's awfully cramped. Are you sure I'm not imposing?"

He stood and looked back at Gertie, who'd crossed her arms across her chest.

"You've been giving me all these reasons why you can't, or why this is a bad idea, but let me tell you. You won't find a better offer or a safer place. You'll be well taken care of, but if you can't accept that, then maybe you want to take your chances on your own. I guarantee you will be looking over your shoulder every night. Get much past our encampment, and you'll find plenty willing to slit your throat over a day's wages. Folks find out you've got information on a mine, well…they'll do that and plenty worse if they think it'll get them out of this place."

Her words shamed him. She was only trying to be nice. He'd just been thinking about the wonderful hospitality, and here he was spitting on it.

"I'm truly sorry for any offense. You have to understand, we're not used to this kind of treatment. Back home, our own family and church is barely lifting a hand to help us. Where I come from—"

"This isn't where you come from," Gertie said. "Why do you think we're all here? Every person in this place has come looking to build a better life. I know there are some who think that living in a cabin and taking in wash is no life, but one of these days, we'll be able to afford a house. Maybe it won't be one of those big mansions, but it will be our house."

Wouldn't that be nice? A home where he and all of his siblings could be together without Aunt Ina breathing down their necks, barking orders and threatening them all the time.

If anyone could sell him on the dream of mining, it was Gertie. But then, he didn't need her words to convince him. He already had a mission of his own. Six sisters and a brother, all of whom who needed him. As much as he'd like to find a dream of his own to follow, that wasn't possible right now.

"Thank you, Gertie. I really do appreciate all you've done for us."

"Mama, we're hungry." Caitlin ran to them and tugged at her skirts.

"There's an extra biscuit or two in the cabin." She smiled at her daughter and patted her on the head as she raced off. "We don't do a proper noon meal here, on account of everyone being up at the mine. But I fix them all a good lunch to take with them. Supper's at dusk, and you'll want to be prompt with the way my boys eat."

She looked at him. "I know you won't be going up to the mine, but I'll still pack your lunch all the same. Mind you get home by dusk. As safe as we've made it, it's still not a good idea to go wandering about by yourself."

Her words reminded him of the bandits and the danger they faced. Yes, this was the best option. Frank reappeared. "I've got some visiting to do. Why don't you come with me so I can give you the lay of the land?"

Joseph nodded. They'd wasted so much time already. Though it had done his heart good to see Nugget so happy, it'd do him even better to have her safely settled.

As they walked back to the horses, Joseph asked quietly, "Any word on the men who were after Nugget?"

Frank shrugged. "Slade isn't back yet. I'd put Gertie and Annabelle up against any man if it meant keeping a child safe."

Though he knew firsthand how capable Annabelle was of keeping Nugget safe, it didn't cause him to worry any less. Not with the attempt against Nugget, and the niggling feeling in the back of his mind about his father's death. If someone was going to this length to find his father's silver, his father's death was looking less and less like an accident. Which meant the danger they faced was far greater than they were imagining.

Chapter Thirteen

Annabelle approached the creek where Polly was working on the wash. Lumps of rock lodged in her throat, preventing her from speaking. Not that she had any idea of what to say. What separated them called for a whole lot more than a simple, "I'm sorry."

"Hello, Polly."

Polly didn't look up from the shirt she was scrubbing. "Annabelle."

"I'm gonna be here for a while, I guess, so I thought maybe I could help you with your chores."

Brushing her arm against her forehead, Polly looked up. "Don't make no nevermind to me."

No, there was no easy fix for this. "I'm sorry about what happened, you know, when—" Annabelle swallowed. "I shouldn't have said those things to you. You were just trying to help."

"You accused me of lying about Henry to deliberately hurt you."

The words reverberated in Annabelle's head. The sight of her best friend, her face whiter than the snow she'd been standing in, filled Annabelle's vision.

Annabelle grabbed a shirt and started working. "I said a lot of things I didn't mean. I couldn't imagine that Henry would simply leave without me. Not when he knew I'd just lost Peter and Susannah and Mother was so sick."

Pouring out her heart seemed almost easier when she had her hands occupied. She turned her attention to a spot that wouldn't come out. "I was wrong to accuse you of being anything but a friend. I'm sorry."

"You're going to tear a hole in it." Polly's voice interrupted her thoughts, and she stared down at the shirt.

"I can't get this spot out," she said, holding it up for inspection.

"It'll do." Polly took the shirt out of her hands and stalked over to where she had the other clean shirts drying.

Annabelle sighed and brushed the stray curls off her face. An apology would never be enough to mend the damage she'd done.

Polly turned and stared at her. "You barely knew Henry. Sure, he was handsome and charming and helped you deliver things to your father's parishioners. But we'd known each other our whole lives. And you'd call me a liar before you'd believe that your precious Henry would betray you."

Annabelle deserved every bit of the ire directed at her. Probably even more than that. "I was wrong," she said again, but Polly had returned to her work.

"What next?" she called over her shoulder at Polly.

"Go find my ma and tell her to put you to work elsewhere. You're slowing me down. I'll never get all this done with you around." Polly gestured to the pile of laundry.

"I'm sorry. If there's anything I can do…" She looked

for any sign of understanding in her former friend, but Polly merely frowned at her.

"Just go."

The camp was quiet as Annabelle returned to Gertie's cabin. Everyone was probably up working in the mines. With such good weather, they were probably trying to get as much extra work done as they could.

"Hey, pretty lady." An obviously drunken miner stumbled out of a tent. Disheveled, and smelling more like liquor than the mines, he reached for her with hands knotted with age. An old-timer, most likely. But who could tell with the way this place prematurely aged people.

She turned to go between the tents, but another miner stepped from behind the tent she was trying to go around. Younger, the sandy-haired man also reeked of drink.

"What's your hurry?"

Her father hadn't given her a gun to replace the one that had been in her saddlebag. Which would be a problem living in the camp. She'd gotten proficient at scaring men off with a quick wave of the pistol.

"I need to get back to my friend's cabin. She's expecting me."

The men moved closer, sandwiching her in. "We can't have no delay, now can we?"

Even with considerable distance between them, she could smell the younger man's foul breath. She looked for an escape route.

"Aw, pretty birdie wants to fly the coop," the man in front of her said with the kind of leer that spelled trouble.

This was precisely why young ladies did not venture beyond certain boundaries unescorted.

Her momentary lapse in looking for an escape gave

the man behind her the opportunity to bump into her, pushing her closer to his friend. He might have looked like an old-timer, but he was quick.

"We don't mean no harm," he whispered, his foul odor stinging her nostrils. "Just tell us where the silver is."

Naturally. That's all anyone in this crazy place wanted.

"I don't know anything about any silver," she said stiffly, realizing that a hard object was pressed into her back. A gun.

She tried to take a deep breath to calm herself, but the gun pressed deeper into her back.

"What'd you find at the cabin?" the man rasped into her ear and pushed her forward into his friend.

"Nothing. It was just a cabin." She tried to keep her voice steady, calm. These were no ordinary ruffians, but dangerous men who clearly knew much more about her activities than mere happenstance.

The man in front of her grinned an ugly toothless grin as he rubbed his stubbled chin. "And silver is just a rock."

As his eyes narrowed, she recognized him as one of the men who frequented her father's Wednesday night dinners.

"I know you." She stared at him harder, trying to remember if she knew his name. There were just so many, coming and going, and with trying to stay unattached...

"Our family has done you great kindness. Please repay that kindness and let me go."

Her words only made the man's sneer deepen. Perhaps it had been the wrong thing, to ask for repayment for what they'd done.

"We'll give you kindness, sweet lady." The man behind her rubbed up against her in a vulgar motion that sent her stomach rolling. "You tell us where the silver is, and we won't share you with our friends."

Annabelle gritted her teeth. "I told you, I don't know about any silver. I was merely showing Joseph where his father's cabin was so that he could claim his father's personal effects."

Toothless gave her a murderous look. "We seen him in the mercantile yesterday buying mining supplies with the good preacher. So no more lies. Where's the silver?"

She glared at him and tried to shake free of his friend, but the man pressed the gun harder into her back.

"If he had really found any silver, do you think that cabin would have been as desolate as we found it? Don't you think he would have spent some of it on something nice for his daughter? You know miners. There's no silver."

Her words seemed to catch the miner who held the gun to her back off-guard because the pressure loosened and he hesitated.

"You think she's telling the truth?" The waver in his voice was all she needed.

In a quick motion, Annabelle stomped back, using the heel of her boot to dig into the man's leg, then darted past Toothless. As she rounded the corner past his arms, her heel broke, but she kept running, hoping Toothless would be more concerned about his friend's yowls.

"I'm going to get you, she-cat."

Annabelle ran, dashing between cabins, hoping that somehow the weaving would keep him from catching her. A short distance, and she'd be at Gertie's.

"Gertie!" she yelled as loudly as she could.

"Your friend ain't gonna help you, so save yerself the trouble."

"Help!" Annabelle hoped the word would get someone in the area to come to her aid. She rounded the corner, feeling her ankle in the broken boot give way.

Oh, how she'd wanted these fashionable boots. But what good were they doing her with a bandit after her? At least she'd worn the sensible dress Maddie had forced upon her.

"Please," Annabelle yelled again. "Someone help me!"

A man stepped out of the cabin nearest her.

"What seems to be the problem?" Though his face was grizzled, his voice was kind.

"There's a man…" She gestured behind her at Toothless, who'd slowed up. "He and his friend had a gun. They were trying to hurt me."

Her savior stepped past her. "That you, Bart?"

Bart. Now she had a name for her father and the sheriff.

"Just a misunderstanding." Bart gave a grin that made her stomach turn, then headed in the opposite direction.

The man nodded and looked over at Annabelle. "You're all right now. Bart don't mean no one no harm."

Oh, yes, he did. But she didn't need to belabor that point with this stranger.

"Thank you, sir." She offered a small smile as she nodded and turned toward the direction of Gertie's cabin.

No one was at Gertie's cabin, making her more grateful the unknown man had come to her rescue.

She sat on one of the logs and examined the damage to her boot. The heel had been torn clean off. Her foot… For the first time since the initial pain of twisting it, she realized that it throbbed. And was swelling rapidly.

"Gertie?" She called the woman's name but received silence in return.

Annabelle leaned back and closed her eyes. Maybe if she took a few deep breaths it wouldn't hurt so bad.

The crunch of shoes on gravel jolted her out of her tiny rest. If the men had been following her, they probably realized she was completely alone.

"Please. I've already told you I don't know where the silver is. So just leave me be."

Maybe she truly was a coward, but she couldn't bear to open her eyes and face the victorious sneers of evil men who were going to triumph because Annabelle hadn't truly embodied the Christlike behavior she had been supposed to model.

"What happened?" Slade's soft voice jolted her, and she looked up, but not directly at him.

"Some men accosted me."

He had no reason to take up her cause, so the less she said the better.

"About the silver?" He knelt before her and touched her broken boot. "How bad is it?"

Pain shot through her. "Ow!" She jerked out of his grasp.

"Yes, about the silver. That ridiculous metal that has blinded everyone to decency."

His face contorted as though he'd been wounded more than her ankle hurt.

"I'm sorry, I didn't mean—"

"Yes, you did," he said quietly. "You've been seething in hate for months now. But I'm going to fix your ankle anyway."

Tears rolled down her face.

He took her foot, not at all gently, and attempted to unlace her boot. Even Slade was ignoring what she had to say based on the prejudice she'd expressed.

She should have listened to his side of the story. "What happened that night?"

Something glittered in Slade's eyes when he looked up at her. If she hadn't been so stubborn, they'd have had this talk long ago.

"When I got to Doc Stein's house, he was passed out drunk. So I went to the hospital to see if they could spare someone. But they were busy with the influx of their own patients. I was told to bring everyone there."

Slade shook his head slowly, fumbling with the lace. "I'm going to have to cut this off. I know you prize these boots, but there's no other way."

"It's all right. They're just boots. And they're ruined anyway." Annabelle shrugged, then looked at him.

Really looked at him. Pain filled his face, and she realized that all this time, all the hurt she'd been feeling over her family's deaths, Slade had been feeling, too.

Everyone was hurting. But all Annabelle had been able to see was her own pain.

"I want to hear the rest. About the silver."

He pulled a knife out of his boot as he nodded slowly. "On my way back, I headed to the livery to get a wagon to take everyone to the hospital. I took a short-cut through State Street and got caught in the middle of a gunfight between two men arguing over a poker game. One got away, but the other…"

Pain filled his face, and for a moment, Annabelle forgot that she'd vowed to hate Slade forever. He'd been her brother's best friend, and until she'd decided to blame him for Peter's death, a good man.

"I did the best I could for him, but…"

Slade's hand stilled on her foot. "He pressed a bag of silver in my hand and asked that I send it home to his wife. It was the last thing he said before he died."

He had been doing a kindness for a stranger. She'd hated him for his selfishness when all he'd been doing was a good deed. Annabelle hadn't thought it possible to feel more shame over her actions, but it was so strong she thought she might burst of it.

"I didn't—"

"Don't." He looked up at her with watery eyes. "Somehow I thought it would make a difference if I stayed with him until the sheriff came. I was worried about a dead man, when I should have been getting Peter to the doctor. I never imagined he would go so quickly. Your pa has told me over and over that it probably still wouldn't have saved him, but I can't help but wonder if I'd done it any differently…"

All this time, she'd been casting stones, when poor Slade had been casting them at himself. He hadn't needed her to make him feel bad when he was already doing a fine enough job of it himself.

"You did what you could," she told him quietly. "And I apologize for saying otherwise."

Slade nodded slowly. "What you saw that night was me giving the silver and information about the dead man to your pa so he could track down the family. Frank was going crazy with grief and I thought that giving him something to do would help. I never realized how much I would hurt you."

Her chest ached, and the weight of her actions pressed on her shoulders heavier than any of the boulders in the area. "I should have heard you out."

"Well, now you have." His lips twisted in a sort of grimace, and he finished taking off her boot. As he turned his focus to her injured ankle, she realized the injustice she'd done him. Her family had adopted Slade into their own because he'd had no one. Peter had been a brother to him.

Annabelle should have been comforting him, and they should have worked through all of this together.

"I'm sorry it took so long for us to talk," she said, knowing that being sorry didn't make it any better. "I hope someday you'll be able to forgive me."

The look he gave her was enough to slay her. "Already have."

If his words were intended to make her feel better, he had failed completely. Because now, she felt so much worse for having had the conversation.

Before she could think of anything to say to give him some comfort and heal the rift between them, he changed the subject.

"Your father says those men were after Bad Billy's silver. Was the little girl able to tell you anything about it?"

Annabelle shook her head. As Slade pushed on a particularly painful spot on her foot, tears sprang to her eyes.

Slade stopped his ministrations to her ankle. "I don't think it's broken, but you've definitely injured yourself. I'll see if Gertie has anything we can wrap it with."

He stood, then looked down at her. "When I get back, we'll talk more about the men who were after you. Now that you don't hate me, maybe we can fix this together."

Though she should have been gratified to know that there were rifts in her life she could fix, the nagging pain in her heart hadn't diminished. She wondered if it ever would.

Chapter Fourteen

Exhaustion had set in before the mining camp was in view. Joseph glanced at Frank, who looked even more weary. The older man hadn't been able to stop worrying about Annabelle.

Even Joseph wasn't sure about the best course of action for her. Especially the more he mulled over Frank's words to him about his behavior toward the beautiful girl. Closer to the camp, he realized that it wasn't so much that he was looking forward to being reunited with his sister and finding the silver, but that he'd get to see the smile that continued to haunt his mind.

Before they were within eyesight of Gertie's cabin, a ball of energy hurled herself at him.

"Joseph! You're back!"

Despite the fatigue, he dismounted, then picked Nugget up and whirled her in a big hug. "I think you've grown since this morning."

Nugget giggled. "Papa used to say that, too."

Her words didn't sting the way the comparisons to his pa used to. Time, and Nugget's love, had begun to heal that wound. Not that he was willing to fully forgive him, but at least he could accept his sister's love for the man.

He set Nugget down, then held her hand as he led his horse to the cabin. "Did you have a good day?"

"Yes, but Annabelle got hurt so now Caitlin and I have to stay close." Her lip jutted out in a tiny pout.

Frank stepped forward. "What's this about Annabelle getting hurt?"

"She hurt her foot, and Mr. Slade put a bandage on it." Nugget skipped along without realizing the import of her words.

But both Joseph and Frank picked up their speed. With the way Annabelle had shot daggers at Slade earlier, chances were any interaction between them had resulted in bloodshed.

But Annabelle sat by the fire, Slade next to her, chatting almost amiably.

"Annabelle?" Frank handed the reins to Joseph and dashed toward his daughter. "What happened? Are you all right?"

A wan smile he didn't recognize crossed her face. "I hurt my ankle. Slade says I'll be fine." She glanced at Slade and gave him a look Joseph didn't understand.

Joseph could hardly believe the way their interaction had completely changed in less than twelve hours.

Polly huffed past them. "I'm sure she's fine. She was when she left me at the creek with all the work to finish."

Annabelle stiffened at the words, and any hint of the ease he'd seen in her earlier had disappeared. Slade scooted closer to her. Even though that should have made him feel better, it brought a new sense of unease to him. What was the relationship between Annabelle and Slade?

None of his business.

He had no right to wonder what may or may not be

going on between them. Annabelle wasn't his to claim even if he wanted to.

Her father, though, wasn't going to let it go so easily. "It's nice to see you two together again."

Together again…well, that probably said it all. His chest tightened, and even though he'd like to blame it on the altitude…

How had he developed such feelings for Annabelle so quickly? Especially when he had no right to do so.

"I have a lot of amends to make," Annabelle said quietly. "It was time I listened to Slade instead of judging him."

Even though everyone wanted to see Annabelle in a harsh light, the reality was that she was struggling through a difficult time and doing the best she could to keep it all together. Her admission was a measure of the remarkable strength she had.

If only his circumstances were different.

Slade stood. "Frank, I'd like you and Joseph to take a walk with me. We need to talk about Annabelle's injury."

He looked at Nugget pointedly, and Joseph's stomach sank. They'd left the women and children unprotected. And sure, he knew Annabelle was far better at taking care of herself than he was, but there was something about not being there that made Annabelle's injury feel like a grievous sin.

Once they were out of earshot of the tent, Slade stopped.

"Annabelle was accosted by two thugs. She said she recognized them as men who frequented Frank's mission. One of the men in camp referred to him as Bart."

Frank shook his head. "Not Bart Wallace?"

"Annabelle's description seemed to match. And from what she said about the other guy, I think it's Pokey

Simpkins with him." Slade looked around, then continued.

"I went to talk to them, but they're gone. I imagine they've met up with whoever they're working with. They're not bright enough to be working alone. Plus, Annabelle says they don't look like the guy who tried to take Nugget."

Though Slade's words gave Joseph reason to be concerned, there was also more to give him hope. "So they believe there's silver?"

Slade nodded, but put a finger to his lips. "From what I was able to find out about the claims in the area, including where I found some equipment, it all belonged to your father. I saw signs of a lot of digging and burying."

"So he or someone else was hunting for silver." Joseph had to believe that this meant he could resolve things with his pa's estate sooner rather than later and then he could get home to his family.

Frank also looked around before speaking. "But if all they were doing is prospecting, they wouldn't have bothered covering it up. Usually folks just leave the holes."

"Exactly," Slade said, then motioned for them to keep walking. "Someone found something somewhere, but is trying to keep it a secret. There are dozens of holes, and there's no reason why everything should be covered like that. He's gone to great pains to make sure no one else finds his silver."

Silver. More reason to believe in the security of his family's future.

"What do I do next?" Joseph looked to both men, who clearly had more experience in such matters, for guidance.

Slade looked at him. "I think you'd be wise to not

go it alone. Not without knowing who Bart and Pokey are working with."

Annabelle wasn't safe. She'd gotten away from her attackers today, but what happened when someone else came for her? Or Nugget?

"They're not going to stop until they get the silver, are they?"

Slade shook his head. "I can't see why they would. Greed does things to a man."

No wonder Annabelle was so against mining. Joseph didn't need to be rich. All he asked was to be able to provide a home and a way to make a living to support his brother and sisters.

He looked over at Frank, hoping to hear the man's wisdom on the subject. Frank looked utterly exhausted.

"What do you think, Frank?"

The older man frowned. "I can't understand why whoever is behind this is going to so much trouble. And to endanger my daughter after everything we've done for them…"

Frank ran his hand down his face. "I don't know. Some days I wonder if Annabelle is right and we're wasting our time. But I believe the Lord has called me to be here working in these people's lives."

The life returned to his face, and for a moment, Joseph envied Frank the sureness of his calling from the Lord.

Frank straightened, as though God had again confirmed the calling. "I think you'd be wrong to give up. Your father clearly found something, and I truly believe he intended to provide for his family. I know a few trustworthy men who'd be willing to provide assistance if you'd be willing to share some of what you find."

"Of course," Joseph readily agreed. "I don't ask for

much. I'd never hoped to find a treasure. Just enough to get a place where I can raise my brother and sisters without wondering where their next meal is going to come from or how I'm going to get new shoes for the little ones."

If only Annabelle could understand that. She'd spoken of the greed of the miners, but what about the ones like Gertie's family, who wanted nothing more than to provide for their children?

"I'll talk to Collin and his boys, then." Frank looked over at Slade. "You'd be willing to help Joseph, wouldn't you?"

"Naturally." Slade gave an easy grin. "Now that Annabelle's speaking to me again, I'd like to learn a little more about the man who's stolen her heart."

"I haven't stolen anything," Joseph insisted. "Besides, aren't the two of you—"

Slade and Frank started laughing. "Annabelle?" Slade finally sputtered. "She's like a sister to me. I lost my own kin a long time ago, and when the Lassiters took me in, I was part of a family again."

Now it was Joseph's turn to be embarrassed. And worried. With the way his mind had been playing tricks on him over Annabelle all day, this latest turn made it nearly impossible for him to admit he didn't have feelings for her. The only trouble was that it changed nothing in his life.

When he found the silver, he had a responsibility to uphold.

"Well, that's all Annabelle can be to me, too," he told both men, the words like a foul medicine on his tongue. "She's a wonderful girl, but it's just not meant to be."

Frank's voice was soft. "You could bring your family here."

He looked over at Frank. "What made you think of that?"

"Just thinking. You've told me that's your priority, and that you intended to take them from Ohio anyway. Why not bring them here? There's plenty of things needed in Leadville, good jobs, so if you wanted to pursue my daughter, there's nothing stopping you."

Frank's earnestness almost made him want to believe. But there were so many unknowns. Too many things he had to work out and plan for. He couldn't allow himself the luxury of even thinking about falling in love until after he had his family's future settled.

"That's a fine idea, and perhaps we will decide to stay. But there's much more to consider. Courting Annabelle is not one of them."

"Maybe you should talk to Annabelle about that first," Frank stated.

"And maybe you should let my business be my business. I've already told you that I'll be careful with your daughter's heart, but that's all I'm going to do in Annabelle's direction. It's all I can do."

"But what about your heart?" Frank's quiet question was one he'd already made up his mind on.

"My heart is with my family. My responsibility is to them first."

Joseph cleared the lump forming in his throat. "Let's get back to more important business. Like our next move in finding my father's silver."

With this talk of love and hearts and things best left alone, it was more reason time was of the essence. They were engaged in a dangerous game with everything at stake. No room for any of the impossibilities Frank wanted to discuss.

Slade pulled a map out of his pocket. "Based on what

I could see, Bad Billy seemed to have a lot of claims near the Eastern side of Mosquito Pass and around his cabin. The area near the cabin is where things looked dug up and buried, but as far as I can tell, there's no evidence there's actually any silver there." He pointed to a corner of the crinkled paper. "But there's this one, all alone, in the center of claims owned by Slim Deckert."

Frank rubbed his chin. "Slim probably didn't like the idea that Billy purchased a claim in the center of his claims."

"Billy didn't buy it," Slade stated matter-of-factly. "He won it in a poker game against Slim."

Poker. Joseph shouldn't be surprised that his pa would engage in such activity, given that he'd fathered a child by a soiled dove. But surely there had to be an end to the sinful legacy left by his father.

"I remember that game," Frank said. "Slim was fighting mad over the deal and tried accusing Billy of cheating. But Lon was there, and he'd said it was a fair game."

Slade nodded. "It's the same mine where Billy died."

"Or was killed," Frank said somberly.

Now, more than ever, Joseph was convinced that his pa had been murdered. And with the attempted kidnapping of Nugget and the attack on Annabelle, whoever was after the silver was willing to get it at any cost.

Chapter Fifteen

Polly's dismissal and subsequent lie about what happened at the creek stung. Annabelle had said unkind things to Polly. And yes, she deserved to be punished for her thoughtlessness. But that didn't mean it was right for Polly to be so nasty to her at the creek and then lie to everyone about it.

"How's your foot?" Gertie asked, the familiar kindness in her voice not nearly as painful as her foot.

"It's fine, thanks." Annabelle tried to stand, but Gertie shook her head and clucked at her.

"You sit right back down and put this compress on it. Polly may think you're faking it, but a foot doesn't swell up to twice the size of the other on its own."

Gertie handed her the compress, and Annabelle tried not to wince. Still, it was some comfort to know that Polly's poison hadn't completely taken hold.

"I'm sorry for the inconvenience. I truly appreciate your kindness," Annabelle said, not knowing what else to say.

Gertie brushed her hands on her apron, then frowned.

"I need to get supper started. I'd ask you to mind the girls, but I suppose you can't go chasing after them."

Yes, a lot had changed in her relationship with Gertie. As much as she'd thought it wouldn't matter, given all of the hurt Annabelle felt, she'd come to realize that it actually did, quite a lot.

"I could help with supper," Annabelle offered. "I assist Maddie all the time."

"Can you peel potatoes?"

"Of course." Annabelle smiled. "And as far as minding the little ones, why, they can help."

Just then, the little girls came bounding over, huge smiles on their faces. "Annabelle! Guess what we found?"

Nugget held out a sticky handful of tangled wildflowers.

"Lovely." Annabelle smiled at the little girl. When her foot got better, they'd have to go flower picking again.

"We brought these for you to feel better," Caitlin said shyly.

Annabelle closed her eyes for a moment, giving herself time to collect her thoughts. Yes, her heart hurt, but she had to remember that poor Caitlin had lost someone, too.

"Thank you so much, Caitlin." She made a big show of smelling the flowers, even though they were just a bunch of weeds. Still, as she gave an appreciative, "Mmm…beautiful," the smiles she was rewarded with made it worthwhile.

"Now that I've got my flowers, you two wash up and you can help prepare supper."

"All right," Nugget said with a smile. "Come on,

Caitlin. If we're real good, and there's biscuits, Annabelle might let us help roll them out. Annabelle makes the best biscuits."

The compliment warmed Annabelle's heart, and for a moment, she wished she hadn't been so wrapped up in her own life that she'd failed to do such with her sister. Of course, their mother had, which was where Annabelle had gotten the idea to do it with Nugget.

"You're good with them," Gertie said quietly. "Your mother would be proud."

She looked up at the older woman. "At least I've done something right. I know she wouldn't be proud of how I've been shutting everyone out. I hope you know I'm trying to do better."

Slade's story earlier in the day had made her realize that Gertie, too, probably harbored unspoken grief over her family's losses.

"I know you are," Gertie said quietly. "I just hope you learn to do it for your sake, not for hers."

She turned, then handed Annabelle a sack of potatoes. "Your father was too generous. I invited a few other families for dinner tonight, so you can fix them all. We'll fry them up with the venison the boys brought back yesterday and it'll be a wonderful meal."

Gertie turned her back before Annabelle could respond, and she knew that tonight's dinner with all the other families would be equally uncomfortable. She'd try to put on a brave face, and hope that no one said anything that tore at the tiny pieces of her heart she was trying desperately to hold together.

The sound of gravel crunching beneath someone's boot drew Annabelle's attention. She looked up to see Joseph approaching.

"How's the foot?" Joseph bent down as if he was going to tweak her nose or something, but then straightened, like he'd thought better of it.

"I'll be fine, thanks."

The girls returned, fortunate, since she could tell by the light in Joseph's eyes that he was probably going to say something to dispute her claim.

"Joseph! I'm gonna help Annabelle fix supper!" Nugget's clear voice made it impossible to feel too sorry for herself. Though she'd done a lot of things wrong over the past couple of days, at least this was clearly one area in which she'd done all right.

Concern littered his face. "Are you sure you should be doing anything with your injured foot?"

"I'm just peeling potatoes," she told him with a smile. "I can do that sitting."

"I'll help." Joseph sat next to her in the dirt. Did he have any idea how charming that grin was? Why couldn't he be doing something useful with his life like being a banker or a teacher or a blacksmith or, well, just about anything other than a miner? As soon as he found silver, Joseph would leave, taking Nugget, and where would that leave her?

She turned away before he could see that her cheeks were feeling a bit warm. Surely she was as red as fire.

And really! She shouldn't have been thinking such thoughts about Joseph anyway. About any man. Here, of all places. Where she'd met Henry and carelessly given her heart away knowing so little about him. She'd not make that mistake again.

Stronger in her convictions, Annabelle turned back to Joseph. "Haven't you ever heard that too many cooks spoil the broth?" She dug in the bag of potatoes and began peeling the first one. "Nugget, have you ever peeled a potato?"

The little girl shook her head, and Caitlin stared at her wide-eyed. "Mama says knives aren't for little girls."

Unfortunately, that was just the right amount of inducement Joseph needed. "You girls fetch us some water and I'll help Miss Annabelle."

Miss Annabelle. Her cheeks heated again, which was absolutely silly, given the close quarters in which she'd found herself with him over the past day or so. She was used to much more familiarity from him, and yet, moving to more formal address felt… Something prickled in her heart, stinging and leaving her more alone than ever. Why had she thought that opening her heart to a friend would be a good idea?

The knife slipped in her hand, nearly nicking her skin. Why did she always have to be so clumsy around him?

Her father entered the campsite, and he looked at Joseph, then at her, almost as though he was signaling Joseph in some way. Joseph gave a quick nod.

Joseph cleared his throat. "Miss Annabelle, if I may, I'd like to escort you to the creek for some water."

Did he grow daft all of a sudden? They'd just sent the— Annabelle glanced at her father, who nodded. Of course. Her father had something he wanted to have Joseph talk to her about. Right now, her heart couldn't take any kind of talk. Especially not one encouraged by her father.

Annabelle lifted her swollen foot. "While I do appreciate your kind offer, you might recall that I'm unable to put any weight on my foot."

Polite enough to satisfy even the stodgiest of matrons. She was very tempted to stick her tongue out at both Joseph and her father for being such meddling oafs, but that would only prove just how childish she was. Annabelle sighed.

Fortunately, Joseph looked just as relieved as she felt at the prospect of not having to go to the creek together—code for having a little chat, she was now certain.

"I'd forgotten. Please accept my apologies."

"Certainly." She smiled in the direction of her father. Annabelle dropped a peeled potato in the pot.

"You thoughtless wretch!" Polly grabbed the pot off the ground and glared at Annabelle. "Have you any idea how wasteful you're being? Look how much potato you've taken off with the peel!"

The insides that had finally begun to feel more comfortable in this place knotted up. "I meant no harm," Annabelle stammered. "This is how Maddie told me to do it."

"There are a lot of hungry bellies to fill, and you've just wasted the food that goes into them."

Annabelle looked at the pot of potatoes she'd carefully peeled the way Maddie had shown her. "I've only done a few. I'll be more careful with the others."

Then, because she couldn't bear to look at her father or anyone else witnessing more of her humiliation, she looked at the ground. "As for filling hungry bellies, someone else can have my share of the potatoes. It's the least I can do."

"The least you can do is—"

"Polly!" Gertie banged on one of the pots. "Just because you're cross with Annabelle doesn't give you the right to treat her like that."

She marched over to where Polly stood over her with the pot. "You know how to fix potatoes the way Maddie does?"

Annabelle nodded. "But I can fix them the way you want. Just tell me what to do," she said as quickly as she could.

Please, please, please, please let everyone see how hard I'm trying to be a better person. It was just potatoes, after all. Surely that wasn't something to be declared sinful.

"I haven't had Maddie's potatoes in ages." A smile filled Gertie's face. "So if you know how to fix them, I'll be looking forward to eating them."

Gertie glanced at Polly with a look that dared her to defy her, but that's just what Polly did. "So you're taking her side, are you? Fine. But don't expect me to go without because of her. Bad enough she made more work for me with the laundry. Then she goes off and has to play princess with the hurt foot. Well, you can count me out. I'm through putting up with her."

Polly stomped off, leaving Annabelle feeling like a bug that had been squashed for no other reason than existing. Pure meanness, that's what Polly's words were.

Her stomach churned and turned sour in a different way. This is what she'd done to Polly. She'd said horrible things out of anger and hurt, and it had squashed something in Polly's heart.

"I'm sorry," she mumbled again, knowing that no amount of times she said it would ever change what had caused this mess to begin with.

Joseph placed his hand over hers. "It's all right. She's hurting, too. I'm sure she didn't mean to offend you."

At least the old Joseph was back. Even under the weight of her father's stare, she couldn't ask Joseph to remove his hand. Someone cared for her. Someone understood how awful this whole situation was, and how she'd never meant for any of it to happen.

"Yes, she did," Annabelle said softly. "And I know I deserved it, I just…"

Her throat felt raw and ached like she was coming down with something. But it wasn't that. That she knew, even without a doctor. "I guess I see why they say an eye for an eye makes the whole world blind. I was hurting, so I let the harsh words take over, which led to Polly hurting, and then she needed to be mean to me."

Annabelle removed her hand from Joseph's and picked up another potato and began peeling. "I suppose it'll eventually wear itself out."

Her father stood and motioned to Gertie, who followed him out of sight of the tents. Probably more discussion over how to solve the problem of Annabelle.

Joseph picked up a potato. "Why is Polly so upset with you?"

"Because." Annabelle sighed. There was so much to the story that Joseph didn't understand. That no one understood. Because the one person to whom she'd bared her soul was gone.

"I was in love once. With a miner. I thought Henry a good man, and he helped with my family's ministry. But then the sickness hit over the winter, and Henry wanted to leave. He wanted to avoid getting sick, and besides, there was gold in Alaska."

She set another potato in the pot, trying to focus on

the task at hand so her heart didn't ache the way it always did when she remembered how selfish Henry had been. "I was needed at home to care for my family. He promised to wait. But then Polly came to see me. Told me he'd left without saying goodbye. I called her a liar."

Her knife got caught in the potato, and Joseph took it from her. "Let me do that. You just focus on the story."

"There is no more." She sucked in a deep breath as she turned to look over the fire. It should have been warm, only all she felt was cold inside. "I asked why she would deliberately hurt me with such lies when she knew how I was hurting already. I'd already watched as they'd taken Susannah's and Peter's bodies out to the icehouse to be kept until the ground was thawed enough to bury them. I couldn't imagine why Henry would abandon me at such a time, so Polly must've been lying."

The fire popped, and Annabelle jumped, bringing her attention back to Joseph. "Turns out, Polly was telling the truth. I believed in a scoundrel over my dearest friend."

"Your dearest friend should have understood."

Annabelle reached for another potato and began peeling again. "Maybe. But I hurt her, and I shouldn't have."

"Even if Polly was hurt by your words," Joseph said quietly, "she had no right to speak to you like that. Or even to tell lies about you."

She looked up at him. Why did he have to be so wrong for her? "Thank you." She finished the last potato and brushed off her skirt. "I wish…"

No, she couldn't say what she wished. She wished too many things that would never come true.

"Well, I suppose it doesn't matter." She turned her head, wishing she could stand and get away from the closeness of this man who confused her so.

"It does matter. And I..." Joseph looked in the direction her father had gone, then back at her. "Annabelle, your father has asked me to get something straight with you. As a gentleman, I need to be sure that I don't dishonor you in any way."

Not another proposal. Annabelle's heart fluttered in the pit of her stomach. If he asked, she'd almost say yes. Except the retelling of her story reminded her just how little she knew of Joseph. She'd known Henry far longer, had known him to be honorable, and been betrayed.

"Your father is concerned that you might have...feelings...for me." His shoulders rose and fell as he glanced again in the direction her father had taken Gertie. "I assured him that we were merely friends, but he felt it necessary to clarify my intentions."

If a person could die of mortification, she'd do so right at this very moment. How could her father be so... so... Annabelle sighed. She did have feelings for Joseph. But they weren't the sort a person ever acted upon.

Joseph cleared his throat. "You know my situation. I have a brother and sisters to care for back home. I intend to move them west somewhere, but I can't promise anything to anyone. All I know is that my duty lies with them. I can't be a proper husband to any woman knowing that I have seven others to provide for."

He looked at her with such tenderness, it made her heart want to break. "If I were to take a wife, I would want her to be every bit as bold and strong as you. But I can't. It's impossible for me to marry. Not when I have the children to raise. It's an impossible burden to put on anyone."

He had said as much before. Yet this time, it made her heart ache in an unfamiliar way. "Of course your family must come first," she said, hoping it sounded sympathetic to his cause. It wasn't as though she wanted him for herself.

Joseph's slow nod only made her feel worse. "Good. So then we have an understanding. Your father will be much relieved to know that your heart isn't entangled."

She forced a smile to her face, not caring if he saw through it or not. Over Joseph's shoulder, she could see her father and Gertie returning. For all they saw, it was a perfectly amiable conversation that wasn't creating strange feelings in her stomach. She was fine. Just fine. Or at least she would be once these feelings left. Because they all knew that based on both his words and hers, anything between them was an impossibility.

The old Annabelle had returned. Joseph watched as she greeted her father with a smile and a too-friendly tone. On the surface, the conversation had gone well, but he knew better than to trust her glib answers. But what else could he do? Carrying on the conversation meant digging in to the places of each other's hearts that neither was willing to risk. He simply couldn't afford to, and whatever Annabelle's motivations, it didn't matter.

Frank stared at him with a keen eye, questioning. Joseph gave a small nod to indicate that they'd had the conversation.

"All is well?" Frank addressed the question to Annabelle, but looked at Joseph.

"Yes, Father," she told him in a perfectly proper tone.

"Joseph and I are clear that neither of us have intentions toward the other."

Frank looked almost shocked, taking a step back. Gertie's soft gasp all but accused Annabelle of being impertinent. Then again, the whole situation bordered on impertinence. Things had been fine between him and Annabelle until her father had decided to protect his daughter's honor.

Joseph rubbed his temples. He couldn't fault Frank. If he'd thought anyone trifling with any of his sisters' affections, he'd have insisted upon the same conversation.

Annabelle indicated the pot beside her. "I have the potatoes ready. If someone could put them on the fire, I would be much obliged."

The rest of the evening passed with the same sullen silence he'd had from Annabelle when they first met. No one could accuse her of being rude, and some would probably even say that she was pleasant. But she wasn't Annabelle.

Why should he care? He wasn't supposed to have these feelings. Joseph rose from his spot by the fire. "I'm going to retire for the evening."

None of the other men had come in, so Joseph lit a lamp and began looking through the books he'd brought from his pa's cabin. The first book appeared to have strange markings and notes in the margins. Almost as though he'd used it as a sort of diary, only it wasn't straight prose. Certain words were circled, but even put together, they made no sense.

Annabelle might claim there was no treasure, but his pa wouldn't have gone to all of this trouble to throw people off track if there hadn't been. He'd covered it up too carefully. And that wasn't the sort of man his pa was.

Plus with the attacks on Annabelle and Nugget… someone was after something.

Perhaps the silver wasn't worth pursuing. Not at the risk of… Joseph sighed and closed the book. What alternative did he have? How else would he provide for his family?

He picked up his pa's Bible and began searching through it. Entire passages had been underlined, not just the random words of his other book. It should have brought comfort to Joseph to know that his pa had read God's Word. How could he then justify his relationship with another woman when he had a wife waiting for him at home? His pa's first priority should have been his family, yet he'd created this whole new life without them. He could have accepted that his pa had fallen in love. But what was love when you had a family to provide for? Certainly the Bible didn't condone such a life.

Joseph wasn't going to be like his pa, forsaking family for love.

He tried reading the pages, but they seemed tainted, coming from his pa's Bible. *Lord, I know these feelings about my pa are wrong. Please help me forgive.*

Those words seemed easier to think than to live out. The words in the Bible jumbled in such a way that he could barely read them.

Maybe the Psalms would give him some peace. King David had struggled with his enemies, so perhaps his words would comfort. As he flipped to the right section of his Bible, Joseph noticed that his pa had again circled random words. None of it made sense.

Until…

As he looked back and forth between the pages of circled words, he began to see a pattern. *The. Key. To. The. Silver.*

Dear Lord, he had found it. His pa had been circling words in his books to indicate where his silver had been hidden. Joseph pulled out his journal and began copying words. Not all of them made sense, and not all of them were as easily connected as the words he'd found. His pa had left a map to his treasure, only he'd done it in a sneaky way so that others couldn't figure it out. *Please Lord, let me be able to decipher the code.*

He looked around the tent. With so many people after his pa's silver, it wasn't safe to leave the books lying around. He'd already put Annabelle and Nugget in danger, and he couldn't risk Gertie's family, as well. Tomorrow he'd find a safe place.

The tent flapped open, and Slade entered.

"I didn't know this was your tent."

Slade eyed him, then shrugged. "I stay here when I'm at camp. Collin's boys stayed up the mountain tonight, so it's just the two of us."

Even though he had no problem with the other man and would be working with him to find his pa's silver, something about the way Slade looked at him didn't sit right.

"I'm just finishing my Bible reading, so if you'll give me a minute to put the books away, I can turn the lamp out."

Slade gave another shrug. "Doesn't make any difference to me. I've learned to sleep where I can."

He laid out his bedroll and made motions of getting ready for bed, but Joseph could feel the other man watching him.

Joseph turned down the lamp and settled in to sleep.

"What's your plan for tomorrow?" Slade's voice broke into the darkness.

"I'm at your mercy. I think going to the site we were talking about earlier today makes a lot of sense."

Slade grunted. "Be ready to ride at first light."

The man's snores soon filled the tent, and Joseph wished he could have the same ease. But every time he closed his eyes, he remembered the look in Annabelle's eyes as she talked about the heartbreak she'd endured. He understood that pain. If it weren't for their already awkward situation, they could have comforted each other. But they'd crossed too many lines, and Joseph couldn't afford to get any more emotionally involved with Annabelle.

He tucked the blanket tighter around him. He wasn't supposed to care. Didn't care. Fine, did. Now he was getting to be as bad as Annabelle. Only in this instance, the worst of his lies were the ones he told himself. No, they weren't lies. Just the uncomfortable results of the reality he found himself in. Here, in the dark of night, in the presence of the Lord, he could admit that he might be falling for Annabelle.

Please, Lord, if it's not too much to ask, could You also help me get over my feelings for Annabelle? They're entirely inappropriate, and I want to behave honorably toward her.

Chapter Sixteen

When Annabelle woke, her foot wasn't throbbing as badly. The swelling had gone down. At least she'd be able to do some work today and not be a burden. She shifted the two little girls sleeping almost on top of her, curled together like kittens, noting that Polly was nowhere to be seen. She sighed and struggled to put on her boots. Thankfully Gertie had lent her a more practical pair of shoes. If Polly was already up and working, Annabelle would be scolded for remaining abed.

Her ankle was tender as she stepped on it, but she'd manage. The fire hadn't yet been stirred up. Annabelle grabbed a poker and began stirring the ashes, exposing the red-hot coals. She then added a few pieces of the wood. The fire sprang to life almost immediately.

Remembering where Gertie kept the coffeepot, she pulled it out and began taking the steps to prepare the coffee.

The calm, quiet air felt more peaceful than what Annabelle had ever felt inside the mining camp. Mixed in with the smoky fire, she caught a hint of the pine from the remaining trees. They would soon be taken for the mining operations, she was sure. For now, though, she could watch the soft pink stripes of dawn crest the mountain, highlighting the majestic pines around them. Absolutely amazing.

In such a moment, it was almost easy to believe in God. No, that was not right. She had never stopped believing. God was still there. Still painting the sky as He directed the sun over the mountain like He did every morning. Her mother used to quote the Bible at these times—"This is the day the Lord has made, let us rejoice in it."

Annabelle's heart gave a flutter. In this moment, in the perfectly wonderful sunrise, her heart could rejoice at the magnificence of the Lord's creation.

It didn't mean that anything changed in their relationship, and certainly offered no proof of any affection the Lord might hold for her. But still she could enjoy the work of His hands.

She brushed off her skirts and looked for a bucket to get some water from the creek. As she stood, she realized that in that memory of her mother, the pang in her heart wasn't the crippling grief it had been all these months.

"Good morning!" Gertie's greeting made her jump. "I see you've already begun making the breakfast preparations."

"Just the fire. I was going to start the coffee, but I realized that there's no water, so I need to go to the creek."

Gertie held up a bucket. "No need. But we are low on wood. If your ankle is feeling up to it, you could gather some."

"Of course." Annabelle gave a small smile. "It doesn't appear to be troubling me overmuch."

She started for the woodpile, grateful that Gertie had

given her something to do other than remain idle. As she got closer, her ankle began to throb. She'd tough it out.

"Annabelle!"

She spied Joseph coming from the other direction and sighed. Everyone else would accept her "I'm fine," but Joseph would probably see through it.

"Good morning." She didn't bother trying to smile, since with him it was a wasted effort.

"What are you doing? Your foot—"

"Is feeling much better, thanks. Gertie needed more wood."

He let out a long sigh, the kind that meant she had yet again managed to exasperate him. Well, that was fine by her, since he'd made his feelings for her clear last night. It didn't matter to her one bit what he thought of her.

"Why don't I help?"

"If you like." She shrugged. "Aren't you supposed to be heading out to look at your father's other properties?"

"Slade was gone when I woke."

"I'm sure he'll be back soon. Someone probably needed his help, and being Slade, he went to do it."

He looked at her solemnly. Studying her. "You know a lot about the goings-on here."

They had reached the woodpile, and Annabelle began picking up the wood they'd need for the fire. "This used to be like a second home to me. But anymore—"

"You don't want to get involved," he said quietly.

She straightened, then stared hard at him. "Why would I? Leadville might be a fast-growing city sure to rival Denver, but it is still a dangerous place. People get sick, people die, outlaws come, or they tire of trying to strike it rich and head home. Or worse, they do strike it rich. But you know what they do then? They leave.

Even the Tabors, with their magnificent opera house, do you think they spend their days in this place? No. They have their mansion in Denver, just like everyone else."

The back of her throat had a slight tickle, like everything she'd been going through wasn't enough.

"You want my honesty, Joseph? Here's honest. You've offered me friendship. But where will that leave me? If you find your father's silver, you will head home to your family. One more person I care about gone. Trust me, remaining unattached is the only way I can survive. I've lost too much."

She turned to head back to the camp, her ankle giving slightly as she stepped on it. Well, she'd endure it. Just as she'd endure Joseph's silence every painful step of the way home.

Because in the end, he knew she was right. Her father was worried she might form a romantic attachment to the man, but given that she could barely afford for her heart to like him as a friend, falling in love was simply not an option.

Clearly, Joseph knew it, too.

Annabelle paused near a darkened tent and even darker fire to rest for a moment.

"Excuse me." A woman poked her head out of the tent. "Could you spare some wood?"

Her throbbing ankle screamed no, but the wail of a baby from inside the tent made her heart insist.

"Of course." She made one trip, she could do another.

Annabelle set the wood in the woman's fire pit and tried to stir up some of the coals, but she could already tell there was no heat left in them.

"Why don't I bring you a coal from our fire?"

The woman rewarded her with a soft smile. "Thank

you. I'm afraid I haven't gotten the hang of mining camp life."

"It's no trouble at all. I'll return shortly." At least without the weight of the wood in her arms, the pressure on her foot wasn't so bad.

When they were out of earshot, Joseph said, "You're a better person than you think, Annabelle Lassiter."

"Not really. I'm just doing my duty. The woman needs help. You can't turn a blind eye to a woman needing help."

"Many would," Joseph said quietly.

Not a Lassiter. But this wasn't an argument she needed to have with him. Not in the interest of keeping their distance. Joseph did things to her heart that she didn't like. Made her feel things that she didn't want to feel, least of all for a man like him.

They returned to the cabin, where Gertie had already started breakfast.

"I'm sorry it took so long," Annabelle said by way of partial apology and as an introduction to the situation with the woman she'd just met.

Polly glared at her. "You can't even get wood."

Annabelle tried counting to ten, and she tried to hold her temper. But honestly…how much was she supposed to take? Her father would tell her to turn the other cheek, but what did that look like when someone else was constantly belittling you?

"Actually," she said with as much calm as she could muster, "I met a woman on the way back who asked if she could have some wood. She's new here, and she had a baby crying in the tent. I gave my load to her, and I'm bringing her some hot coals to get her fire going again."

Polly's indrawn breath wasn't nearly as satisfying as it should be. She didn't want to get in the jabs against her former friend, the way Polly was keen on doing to her. All she wanted was peace to reign again.

Annabelle's words sprang Gertie into action. "Oh, that poor dear. I wonder if that's Isaac Johanson's wife. I meant to call on her yesterday, but with everything…" She cast an apologetic look at Annabelle.

"It's all right. I'm sure you can visit with her later. But right now, I'd like to get some coals to her. It's chilly out still."

Gertie rewarded her with a smile. "Yes, I think that's good." She handed Annabelle a bucket with some coals in it.

"If you'll give me just a moment, I'll send you with some leftover biscuits. It isn't much, but with a jug of coffee, it'll take the edge off. You'll invite her to have breakfast with us, won't you?"

Annabelle tried to nod, but Gertie kept talking and piling things into a basket. "Give her one of these blankets. I like to keep them on hand for the new little ones."

Gertie bustled past her and for a moment, Annabelle forgot that her world had changed so completely. It was like the old days, when Gertie and her mother had conspired together to make sure everyone had what they needed. Just last Christmas, they had come together to make sure every child in the camp had received a gift.

Annabelle's heart constricted. It had been their last major project before her mother had gotten ill. She took a deep breath and swallowed her unshed tears. Her mother would have loved this.

A sleepy-eyed Nugget came down the stairs. "Where did you go? I was lonesome without you."

For all of Annabelle's promises to keep her heart to herself, loving this sweet child was irresistible. Her heart did another flip. Joseph's reminder of his impermanence in her life was something that she'd do well to continue remembering. When Joseph left, so would Nugget.

But when the little girl jumped into her arms, Annabelle couldn't stop herself from hugging her back. "Nonsense, silly girl. You had Caitlin to keep you company."

"But she's not you." Nugget sighed into her hair.

Annabelle swallowed. Someday this would be easier.

"Well," Annabelle said as she released Nugget, "you'd best get washed up because Gertie is getting breakfast ready. I have an errand to run, but then I'll be back."

Gertie handed her the wrapped biscuits. "Don't take no for an answer, because I won't hear of it."

"Yes, Gertie." Annabelle pretended not to notice Polly's scowl as she headed back to the woman's tent.

Joseph grabbed the basket out of her hands. "I'll take that. Your limp is getting worse, and you don't need to aggravate it by carrying such a load."

"Annabelle?" Gertie stopped and looked at her. "I thought you said your foot was better."

The snort from Polly was enough to make her ignore the throbbing in her foot. "It is. Just a twinge now and again. Nothing to keep me from giving a warm welcome to a woman who needs it."

She didn't care if her smile was fake or not. For the first time since her mother had died, she had a purpose, and the hurt wasn't as great. Even the pain in her foot was tolerable.

"I'll look after her," Joseph said. Which seemed to seal the deal as Gertie nodded, and Polly's scowl deepened.

Once they were out of earshot of the cabin, Joseph spoke. "You need to go easy on Polly."

Annabelle stopped and stared at him. "Me? I don't understand."

The way he pressed his lips together told her that she obviously had missed something. Probably that whole forgiving seventy times seven thing.

"I overheard her at the river fighting with some guy named Tom. Apparently, she heard him mentioning to some of the other guys that you looked quite the picture the other day in town. She thinks you encouraged his attentions and are trying to steal him from her."

"Why, that's the most ridiculous thing I've ever heard." Surely Polly knew her well enough to know that she would never do such a thing. "Polly knows that I would never be interested in one of her beaus."

Then again, Polly had once thought that Annabelle would never think her a liar. So much had changed with a few careless words.

"I know," Joseph said quietly. "But Polly believes otherwise, and that's probably the source of her attitude."

The sincere look in his eyes made it hard to remember all the things she needed to focus on. Like the fact that he was the last person on earth who could be a friend to her.

"I'll talk to her." One more hard thing to do, but it seemed like everything in her life was a hard thing. Because she couldn't bring herself to continue the conversation with Joseph into the next logical step, which would be to let him know that they had to do something about Nugget's continuing attachment.

Yet it seemed like the more she tried pulling away from Joseph and his family, the closer they all seemed to get.

Chapter Seventeen

Annabelle had never looked so beautiful as when she held the tiny baby while its mother ate. Again, he couldn't help but think she would make an excellent mother. Her care for Nugget had shown that, but now, with such a tiny infant in her arms, it was a beautiful sight.

Why did it have to be so hard?

He tore his eyes off the captivating woman and watched the other woman gobble the biscuits. It had clearly been a long time since she'd had a substantial meal.

"Where are you from, Meg?" he asked the young mother after she'd eaten the last of her food.

"Kansas." She gave a wry grin. "Isaac wasn't meant to be a farmer, poor man. He tried, he really did."

Joseph had heard many similar stories since being here. So many people wanting a better life. Of course, he had been a good farmer, that wasn't the problem. But when the bank owned it and demanded higher payments than any reasonable man could afford and still keep food on the table…

He glanced back at Annabelle, who'd handed the baby back to its mother. She wouldn't understand what it was like to do without. Nor would she understand the willingness to do just about anything to make sure loved ones had food to eat.

"What made you come here?" He turned his attention back on Meg.

A dark look crossed Meg's face. "His brother had written, talking about all the money there was to be made. Isaac sold everything we had and sent some of the money ahead for his brother to get us a place. Only…" Meg sighed and cradled her baby tighter.

"When we got here, we found out his brother had gambled it all and then some. There were no houses to be let, and even if there were, we didn't have enough money. One night, some men attacked Isaac, and said that if he didn't come up with the rest of the money his brother owed, they'd harm me and the baby. So he gave them the last of our money. Now we're here, and Isaac is working at the mine in hopes he'll make enough to support us."

How he hated the look on Annabelle's face. It was as if all this served to prove her theories on the evils of mining true.

He shot a glare at Annabelle, then returned his attention to Meg. "Did you talk to the sheriff?"

"For as much good as it'll do us." Meg shook her head. "He said he'd look into it, but he said not to hold out much hope."

Annabelle took the woman's hand. "At least you're all safe. As far as catching those horrible men, you should talk to my father. He's a minister in town, and he knows just about everyone. Sometimes he can find out things the law can't."

Even though Meg shook her head, a tiny light shone in her eyes. Joseph couldn't help but notice that she squeezed Annabelle's hand back, clinging to it like a lifeline.

"All I want is enough money to get us back home. I know Isaac wasn't cut out for farming, but mining isn't for him, either. Perhaps if we went back to my parents, they'd let us stay with them for a while until Isaac can find other work."

"We'll do what we can to help," said Annabelle, a little too cheerful to have fully grasped the situation.

Annabelle stood, then looked around the campsite. "Would it be too forward of me to ask what supplies you have? We keep a number of things for people in your situation, and—"

"We won't be taking charity."

"I wouldn't dream of offering you charity," Annabelle said in a gentle voice that spoke of having done this dozens of times. As much as she fought it, she was a natural at caring for others. If only she'd open her heart to see that. "These are the leftover supplies from people who've done just as you're saying you'd like to do. When they leave, they have no use for these things, so they give them to us and ask us to give them to the next family."

Not only was Meg not appearing convinced, but she'd stiffened even further.

"Truly, Meg. It's what we do here. When someone's done using an item, they leave it for the next person who comes along. No sense in it going to waste."

Meg softened slightly, and Joseph had to give Annabelle credit for trying. When she wasn't thinking about the pain of her losses, she had such an incredible heart for others.

"I…" Meg's face indicated a debate between practicality and wanting to protect her pride. Joseph knew all about that. Had faced the same debate upon encountering the Lassiter family.

"I know." Joseph stepped in and gave a smile as he peeked down at the baby. "It was hard for me to accept their help at first, as well, but I've found that they aren't just about giving handouts, but are true friends."

Some of the wariness left Meg's face. "They helped you?"

"Are helping. I came looking for my pa, and found that I had a sister." He relayed his tale and as he shared his family's need, Meg continued to soften. True, he did not share the most private details, such as how bad things were for his family back home, but at least she would understand that Annabelle meant to be her friend.

Which clearly Annabelle did, because as he relayed his tale, she'd once again taken the baby into her arms and was playing with it quietly.

"Emma is the sweetest thing," Annabelle said, wrapping the baby snugly in her own shawl. "I can't believe how chilly it's gotten."

Annabelle's smile at the young mother melted his heart. If he was to keep his promises to both her and his pa, he needed to find a way to maintain his distance.

Joseph looked up and noticed clouds rolling in over the mountains. The sky was already darkening, which meant a storm would hit before afternoon.

He tried not to groan at what would be an inevitable delay in his mission.

"I'm not used to this weather," Meg said. "Back home, summers were so hot. I thought Isaac's brother was funning us when he told us to bring our winter things. But one of the women in town said that they've had snow in June here. June! Can you imagine!"

Annabelle nodded. "I remember it well myself. It wasn't much snow, of course, and it melted right away, but it was still quite the surprise."

Why did her smile have to be so engaging? Even though she was talking to Meg, and not him, he felt just as drawn in by the woman as Meg clearly was. Her face was animated, and her smile crinkled her eyes.

Joseph turned away, unable to continue watching Annabelle. He couldn't afford to be given one more reason to like her.

As he turned, he noticed Slade riding in. Though they would be unable to visit the sites until after the storm passed, this would give them a chance to discuss their plan.

Annabelle must have noticed his change in attention, and she followed his gaze, then stood. "Slade." She looked at Meg. "We must talk to him about what happened to your husband. Perhaps he can be of service where the sheriff was not."

She didn't wait for Meg's answer, but held the baby tighter to her as she moved in Slade's direction and waved.

"Slade!"

He dismounted and came toward them, handing his reins to a boy before arriving at the camp. "Good morning, Annabelle. Joseph." He nodded in his direction before approaching the ladies.

"Slade, this is my new friend, Meg. Her husband was

attacked by some ruffians, and I'm hoping you can help find these horrible men."

Annabelle relayed the story with such passion that any doubt he'd ever had about her character and willingness to engage with others was wiped away. She had been listening, with all her heart, and was acting upon it.

Stop it, Joseph. She wasn't his to be thinking this way about. He knew better. Had warned himself multiple times to avoid doing so.

He turned his attention to Meg, who was engaging in the conversation with Annabelle and Slade.

No, that wasn't good. Because her engagement only reminded him of how Annabelle's warmth had drawn her out. Even as the baby gave a slight cry and Annabelle handed her back to her ma, he couldn't help but think of how wonderful Annabelle was with a baby.

He gave a small cough. "Since you have it all in hand here, I think I should go check on Nugget."

Without waiting for an answer, he retreated to their own camp, where he could find at least a moment's peace from his thoughts of Annabelle.

Annabelle watched Joseph retreat, feeling the chill in the air more acutely in his absence. She'd given up her shawl for the baby, and now her arms were starting to prickle against the coming storm.

"I'll make some inquiries," Slade said, as he, too, watched Joseph leave. "Now if you'll excuse me, I need to catch up to Joseph to tell him our plans."

"Of course." She gave him a smile, the kind she hoped Joseph would be proud of. "I appreciate you taking the time."

He nodded, then left, leaving her alone with Meg and the baby.

"Thank you," Meg said when they were alone. "I am so glad the Lord brought you to us. He's clearly watching over our family."

Annabelle held out her arms for the baby. "Do let me hold Emma again. She's such a dear. I'll take you to breakfast with Gertie, who will want to hold her, then I'll never get to hold her again. She does love babies so."

That warm memory, and the sweet baby placed in her arms, put a tiny crack in Annabelle's heart. Gertie did love the little ones. How could Annabelle have shut her out for so long?

They walked to Gertie's, Meg chattering about life in Kansas. Annabelle had no idea how hard farm work was. It certainly sounded just as difficult and desolate a life as these miners faced. Getting up with the sun to work in the fields all day, laboring for a crop that could be wiped out by drought, fire, animals, disease and a host of other problems.

How was mining any different?

Annabelle shook her head. Farmers weren't risking their lives and putting families in danger. They didn't spend their earnings on whiskey, women and gambling.

Joseph didn't, either, a small voice told her.

Nonsense, she told herself right back. There were plenty of reasons to dismiss Joseph.

He was leaving.

Which was why she would put him completely out of her mind.

Fortunately, it was easy enough to do when they arrived at Gertie's because Joseph wasn't there. Nugget was, and she immediately launched herself at Annabelle.

"Annabelle! You were gone ever so long!"

She smiled and wrapped her free arm around the little girl. "I was visiting my new friend, Meg. And this is her baby, Emma. Isn't she a dear little thing?"

Gertie swooped upon them. "I love babies. Let me have a look."

Just like that, the baby was taken from her arms, and Annabelle gave Meg an "I told you so" look.

Meg smiled shyly, but was immediately engaged in Gertie's enthusiastic banter as she placed a dish of food in front of the woman. Though Annabelle was pleased to see her so well taken care of, it was almost a shame to give up her job. For a few moments, it had felt like she belonged again. Back before everything in her life had become so hard.

For Nugget, though, it was a welcome change. The little girl hadn't let go of her hand. Again, Annabelle's conscience panged at the thought of this little girl leaving her. Nugget had lost so much already. Was it fair to make her lose someone else?

"What have you been doing while I was gone?"

Nugget scowled. "We had to go wash dishes with Polly. Only she got mad at us and chased us away."

That didn't sound like the Polly she'd once been friends with. Had Annabelle's attitude soured her old friend so much? Then Joseph's words came back to her. Polly was jealous. Over nothing.

"How about I go talk to her?" Annabelle ruffled the top of the little girl's head, then withdrew her hand. "And when I get back, we're going to do something with that hair of yours."

A comment that earned her another scowl, but that was fine. She didn't want to push Nugget away exactly, but if a few hair brushings was all it took to diminish Annabelle's popularity, she'd take it.

"I'm going to the creek to talk to Polly," Annabelle said over her shoulder at Gertie and Meg. "I'll be back shortly."

She avoided the path that she'd taken yesterday where she'd run into those men. Her ankle was now throbbing again. But she couldn't put off this errand. Polly's attitude was affecting everyone else.

Her trip to the creek was quieter than it had been the last time, and she easily found Polly, clean dishes in one pile, and already beginning the wash for the day.

"Hi, Polly."

The other girl didn't turn and look at her. "Go away. I don't need you slowing me down again. You tell Ma—"

"What? Something that you'll contradict later?"

Polly spun, her face red. "So what? You're going to tell on me now?"

Annabelle took a deep breath. "No. I'm sorry. I shouldn't have snapped at you." This making up was harder business than the idea had originally sounded.

"Look." She took another step in Polly's direction. "I know I said some awful things. I deeply regret them. But what I regret even more is that I've lost a good friend. So if we can talk about whatever else is bothering you, I'd like to clear the air. Even if you don't want to be friends again, at least we could be—"

"Nothing." Polly's stare was full of pure hate. "You are nothing to me, and never will be. You think you're better than everyone else, and you don't give a whit for anyone other than you."

The backs of Annabelle's eyes and throat stung. She could own a certain amount of selfishness, but surely Polly knew that there was more to her than that.

And if Joseph hadn't spoken to her about Polly earlier, she might have walked away. But this wasn't about Annabelle's behavior, not really.

"Joseph said he heard you and Tom fighting this morning. Something about you thinking he and I were engaged in a flirtation?"

Annabelle stared at Polly, ready for her to spew more venom in her direction. But Polly didn't say anything, not even as Annabelle could see the steam practically rising out of Polly's head. When she blew, it wasn't going to be pretty. But better here than with the little girls again.

"I have never encouraged Tom. I've always seen him as your beau, and I've always believed that the two of you were going to be married someday. I would never interfere with that. Regardless of what you think of me, I want you to be happy. And if he's—"

Polly shook her head furiously. "Just this past fall, you were telling me about how I could do better. I never imagined you were giving me such friendly advice because you wanted him for yourself."

Annabelle's heart hurt at the memory. She had told Polly that she could do better. Because frankly, Tom was on the lazy side. If Polly married him, she'd end up just like her mother, working hard to take care of a family while her husband squandered it all on whiskey and cards.

But that wasn't something she could say to her now. Not with their friendship so damaged.

"I was wrong to judge," Annabelle said instead. "I

didn't know his heart, and I should have listened to you. I'm sorry. I've truly never had designs on him."

Her stomach ached at the way Polly looked at her. She could list dozens of reasons why she didn't like Tom, but they would only be taken the wrong way.

If she were to chase after a man, it would be someone like Joseph. She closed her eyes. Why couldn't she stop thinking of the impossible?

"I am so sorry that you don't think better of me," Annabelle said, opening her eyes to look at Polly. "I know I deserve it after how judgmental I've been. But if you could find a way to at least call a truce, for the sake of the others around us, I promise I'll do what I can to make amends."

It had taken a long time for Annabelle to find friends like Gertie and Polly, but with a few thoughtless words, she'd ruined it. Worse, though, it seemed like Polly now thought her capable of even more foul deeds than she would ever contemplate.

"You can never fix this." Polly spat out the words like Annabelle was a bug she'd swallowed. "Just leave. We don't want you here."

If only it were that simple. Because if she could go, she would gladly go visit her aunt, build a new life for herself in the city, and forget about the mess she'd made.

Polly returned to her work with the wash. This was not how Annabelle had envisioned the conversation going. Perhaps she'd been too ambitious thinking they would be able to forgive, and maybe even hug. But surely she could have done better than to have broken things between them even worse.

Chapter Eighteen

"I'll only be gone a few hours." Joseph tried prying Nugget from his legs, but she was having none of that. She'd seemed perfectly content remaining behind the day before with Annabelle and Caitlin, but today seemed to be a completely different story.

"You're just like Papa! Always leaving." The little girl's lip jutted out in such a perfect pout that Joseph was almost convinced to remain behind. After all, the sky looked like a storm was moving in.

Fortunately, Annabelle, as always, seemed to know the perfect solution. "None of that," she told Nugget firmly. "Joseph will be back in time for supper. You're going to be so busy playing with Caitlin that you'll hardly notice him missing. Now go get the brush from Gertie so I can fix your hair. Then we can play by the creek for a while."

Though Annabelle ruffled the little girl's ratted hair with a gentle wave and a smile, the set to her eyes brooked no argument, and Nugget released his pant leg.

"You promise you'll be home for supper?" The big eyes blinking at him would have extracted his promise even if he'd had other plans. He'd be home for supper, no matter what.

"I already did. Now listen to Annabelle, because I'm sure she has a wonderful day planned for you."

He hugged his sister, and then she scampered off like she'd gotten exactly what she wanted. Joseph shook his head. He'd never understand females.

"As always you know how to handle her." He smiled at Annabelle, who shrugged.

"Children aren't so difficult. I've always enjoyed them."

The genuine smile that filled her face reminded him of his previous thoughts about her and motherhood. "You're going to make an excellent mother someday."

He might as well have slapped her for the shock that registered on her face. Or at least that's the expression he thought he'd caught before she replaced it with a more serene but blank look.

"Perhaps someday. But I have no intention of marrying anytime soon. There's a lot of world to see and a lot of things I'd still like to do."

She'd spoken wistfully of her ambitions in the cabin. He still knew so little of her, despite feeling like he'd known her all his life.

"Like what?"

"Go back East, for one. I haven't seen my mother's family since I was small. My aunt Celeste has asked me to come visit, and my father says that once he's convinced my heart is healed, I can go."

An expression he didn't recognize skittered across her face. "I know it sounds silly, but I'd like to go to the balls like Mother described. Certainly, we have the theatre and other pleasant diversions here, but Mother says that the social scene where she grew up was delightful. After all, that's how she met my father."

And in that instant, Joseph understood. Annabelle's future wasn't here. Not the way her eyes had lit up at the thought of her mother's descriptions of the balls. He'd never been to any such thing himself—could not imagine what would draw anyone to them. But he'd seen his sisters giggle over pictures of ladies in their finery, and knowing how similar in character Annabelle was to his sister Mary, understood the draw.

A trip back East and a fancy ball—those were things Joseph could not reasonably expect to provide for Annabelle. Not with so many mouths to feed and feet to shoe.

If anything was capable of convincing Joseph that he needed to put Annabelle out of his mind, it was hearing of her dreams for her future. He cared too much for her to ask her to give up her dreams when she'd already lost so much.

Annabelle seemed to sense the change in his mood. She reached out and touched him lightly on the arm. "I'm not going to abandon you, Joseph. My father has asked me to be of assistance until Nugget is properly settled."

A sly smile stole across her face. "In truth, I've come to love that little scamp, and I don't think I could leave until your family's affairs are in order. And I do hope you'd allow me to write."

Joseph nodded, willing himself to find a way to speak. In her grief, he'd caught the unspoken story of the sacrifices she'd made. The things she'd given up for her father's ministry. Here she was, sacrificing one more thing. While he could tell by the light in her eyes that she didn't view her time with Nugget as a sacrifice, he couldn't ask her to do it any longer than she had to.

Annabelle Lassiter was an amazing woman, and she deserved to have a life of her own. *Lord*, he prayed, *help me set Annabelle free*.

Joseph already knew that he had to find the silver as quickly as possible, but knowing that one more life hung in the balance made it all the more urgent.

He bade Annabelle goodbye, then climbed onto the horse Slade had waiting. Hopefully they'd find silver today.

Slade had taken a look at the clouds moving over the mountains and declared that the storm would go around the area. He had been partially right.

They came to a narrow ridge, and looking across the valley, he could see the rain fall on Leadville. Glorious. The valley was packed with houses and other buildings. He could see why some of the townspeople still grumbled about wanting to make Leadville the state capitol. The city boasted growth that he hadn't seen the likes of anywhere near home.

"Your pa's mining claim should be just over the next ridge," Slade shouted back at him.

Once they crossed the ridge, Slade pulled out a map, then pointed at an outcropping of rocks. "That's it. This claim used to belong to Slim Deckert, but then he lost it in a card game to your pa. Slim thought it was a great joke he'd pulled over on Bad Billy, since none of his crews had found anything other than pyrite."

Joseph picked up a shiny rock. "I take it this is pyrite."

"Yep. No offense, but your pa was known for being a fool. There's sayings about suckers here in Leadville, and your pa could be described by just about every one of them."

He knew Slade was being honest, and with the anger he had against his pa, he hadn't expected the words to sting so much. It was bad enough having the foul deed that had come to light, but it seemed like there was a never-ending string of missteps that had him wondering how such a miscreant could have fathered him.

What a tragic end. Though fitting, for all the fool-ishness his pa had done. Living a fool, dying a fool.

"Doesn't look like there's anything here." Slade rubbed his jaw and looked at Joseph. "Frank says you still have family back home. Why don't you sell the claim, take the money and go home? I'm sure there's some wide-eyed sucker that'll buy it. We've enough land brokers in town who'll gladly do the job for you. In fact, I can rec-ommend a guy."

Suckers. If Slade hadn't used that word, he might have thought about the idea. But how could he live with himself, knowing that to provide for his family, he'd just done to another what had been done to them? Sold them down the river on a raft made of false dreams. No, he had to see this through.

"There's evidence that my pa found silver. He sent money regularly."

Slade snorted. "Gambling, probably. He's been kicked out of every saloon in town dozens of times. Everyone knew he didn't mean no harm, which is why they let him back in, but…" He gave Joseph a look of pity. "Everyone wins at the tables now and again. That's how they keep you coming back. Which is why it'd be best if you just went on your way."

Maybe Joseph was being a paranoid, but it seemed like Slade was in an awful big hurry to get rid of him.

The man's demeanor was pleasant enough, but there was something about his words...

"What's it to you if I stay or go?"

Slade shook his head. "None of my business. Just figuring with your family and all, you'd want to be with them."

The easy answer did little to ease the prickle on the back of Joseph's neck. Still, what could he say to contradict a man who had been nothing but helpful?

"What do you make of the attacks on Annabelle and Nugget?"

Slade eyed him intently. "I'm not convinced Bad Billy found silver. But I do think he was into something. Whatever you've been digging into is making people nervous. If there's something going on, I want to stop it before anyone else gets hurt."

It wasn't the first time he'd heard hints of his pa's less than honest dealings. Which made him consider Slade's idea of going to one of the local land agents and selling his pa's claims. But how could he, in good conscience, have potential buyers be swindled? And, if something illegal was going on with his pa's claims, would it put those people in danger? As much as Annabelle thought he and everyone else ignored her warnings about chasing after silver, he wasn't going to sell someone else on a false dream.

Mary would tell him that he was overthinking the situation. Too bad she wasn't here to talk to him and give him advice. What would be best for everyone?

He looked around the site, wishing it were as simple as a sign saying Silver Here.

If his pa had been killed, why here? Was the chasm

a convenient place to dump a body, or did it signify something more?

Joseph went over to where Slade was poking around some rocks. "What kind of illegal activities was my pa involved in?"

Slade picked up another rock, then looked at him. "I guess we've all made it sound like he was a pretty bad guy. Truth is, when he wasn't drinking, he was a decent fellow. Pleasant enough when you came across him in the street. But he got into scuffles in the saloons, and there were accusations of cheating."

A drunk and a cheat. But it didn't add up. "None of this makes any sense to me. If my pa wasn't a horrible person, then what could he have done that would have people trying to harm Annabelle and Nugget?"

The rocks clattered where Slade dropped them to the ground. "My theory is that some of the people he cheated at cards are trying to get their land back."

Which would mean— "So there is silver?"

"Naw." Slade shook his head. "They're dirtier than Bad Billy. They probably want to seed the mines to make it look like there's silver, sell it to some sucker to make a tidy profit. Then, the sucker runs out of money and is so desperate for a way home, they sell it back for a pittance. And then the cycle begins again. Happens all the time."

And Slade was suggesting that he do the same thing. After all, no one would buy this land except for the hope of finding gold or silver.

Maybe Joseph was a sucker, too, but he had to believe that his pa hadn't completely died in vain. There had to be silver out there somewhere. His family was counting on him. And he wasn't sure he could live with himself given the alternative.

"Let me think on it. I'm not ready to completely give up on my pa's dream."

Slade nodded slowly. "You do that. Lots of folks waste everything they have on hopes of finding gold or silver. Most of them lose everything. I'd hate to see that happen to you."

Another reminder of Annabelle and her words on the subject. She had more wisdom than anyone gave her credit for. She just didn't understand the difficulty in separating the wise decision from the only chance he had at getting enough money to save his family.

The ride home wasn't nearly as pleasant. In fact, the storm he had thought they'd so cleverly missed had come upon them with a vengeance—punishment for the stupidity of thinking they could avoid nature.

Joseph pushed his horse hard, trying to keep up with Slade, but Slade was a more skilled rider on a faster horse, and he didn't seem at all concerned about leaving Joseph behind.

Nothing about the site where Joseph's pa had died looked even remotely possible for having silver. At least according to Slade. Which meant that all the maps and even his pa's strange code had done nothing to help.

It was tempting to stop in town at one of the land offices to see if he could sell the claims. But all he could think of was the sadness on Annabelle's face about miners and their false dreams. Could he sell that to someone else? Could he live with putting another family through what his had been through?

No, he couldn't.

His horse slipped on the wet rocks. Continuing was

becoming a suicide mission, but as he glanced around, he saw no safe place to take cover.

Lightning struck nearby, sending tiny ripples of electricity through him and making the horse's hair stand on end. Not deadly, but a warning of the power of nature. The horse reared, and Joseph did his best to control it as rocks slid under them, the edge of the ground giving way.

Though Joseph managed to get the horse settled, it had caused him to lose sight of Slade against the wind and rain. Another loud boom reminded Joseph that they were too high, and on a horse, he was almost the tallest thing around.

"Slade!" The shout went unanswered, and Slade was nowhere to be seen.

More ground gave way, and Joseph fumbled, trying to get out of the saddle, but his foot remained stuck in the stirrups. Both man and horse slid down the embankment. Behind them, rocks crashed, following like an avalanche, only with rain and mud and boulders.

"Come on." He signaled the horse and spurred him sideways, out of the path of the rocks, but with his stuck foot, was largely ineffective in controlling the spooked horse.

The horse reared and sidestepped as rocks whizzed past his head. Joseph ducked and pressed his body close to the horse, not sure which was the more dangerous move—remaining on the animal, or taking his chances among the rocks.

As he looked up, he heard a boom, then another shower of boulders headed his way.

The next lightning bolt lit up the sky, for all the good it did. All it showed was the direness of the situation.

A wall of water rushed down the side of the hill. Frank had warned him about flash floods, but never did he imagine that the water would rush past like a raging river at spring thaw. Joseph looked for an escape. At the rate they were going, they'd be caught in the water in no time. If a boulder didn't catch them first. He spotted a break just to the right. Now if he could convince the horse to take it...

Tugging as hard as he could, he turned the horse toward the open space. It, too, spotted the chance at safety, and bolted in that direction.

Faster than he'd ever imagined a horse being able to go, the animal charged into the opening, then raced down the mountain. It was all Joseph could do to cling to the horse and pray that they would both somehow arrive at the bottom safely.

When they got to the bottom of the hill, a tree slid past them. Rocks were still coming down to the left of them, and a huge pile of boulders, rocks, trees and miscellaneous debris had gathered where he and the horse would have ended up had he not spotted the break. Another few steps, and they'd have been caught up in the flood.

Thank You, Lord.

He'd heard that storms in the mountains could be bad, but he'd never expected this. Between the rain loosening the ground at the edge of the hillside, and the lightning knocking down trees and shaking boulders loose, combined with the flash flood, it was amazing he'd survived.

He found a safe place to stop, then got off the horse. With the storm this bad, and so much lightning around, it was best to take his chances on foot. After a few paces, he could see Leadville, which from his vantage point would be a lot closer to wait out the storm in town than trying to get back to camp.

The rain worsened, pouring like a waterfall without breaks to indicate droplets. Hopefully Annabelle would keep Nugget… Joseph shook his head. Of course Annabelle was taking good care of Nugget. She loved his sister, and he couldn't have asked for a better caretaker.

His mind started to wander in the direction of thinking of Annabelle as a mother again, but he stopped. No. Joseph glanced up at the sky. Better to be struck down than to continue tormenting himself. He'd find the silver, then send Annabelle on her way to the life she'd always dreamed of.

When he finally arrived in town, he was sure not a dry spot existed on his person. The streets were rivers of mud, and Joseph couldn't remember ever seeing them so empty. Everyone had taken refuge from the storm.

He brought the horse to the livery Frank patronized, glad that Wes, the proprietor, came out to greet him.

"Got caught in the storm, did you?" Wes took the reins and led the horse into the stables.

Joseph nodded and took off his hat, shaking the water from it, knowing that it did no good.

"Want to come in and dry off?"

"Thanks." Joseph followed him into the stables, thankful that something around him was actually dry, even though the smell of wet horse and manure burned his nostrils.

"I think Betsy has some coffee on. We're about the same size, so I'll lend you some dry clothes."

"I'm obliged to you."

"None doing. Frank's a good friend, and I know he'd do the same for me."

More of the same hospitality he'd grown used to. Such a dichotomy between the people like Frank and the rest of the world. Clearly Frank's people loved as Christ loved, and gave freely. They'd been taught well. How could they be otherwise with Frank's example?

Wes led him into the neat living quarters off the stable. "It's not much, but with land prices here in town, it's the best we can do."

"It's fine." He looked around the room that Wes and his wife used for their home. Everything, including a cookstove and bed, was contained in that tiny room.

"Betsy, can you get our guest a cup of coffee while I find him some dry clothes?"

"Gracious!" Betsy hurried toward them. "Let's get you by the fire to dry off. You'll catch your death. What were you thinking, going out in that storm?"

"It caught me unawares. We were out looking at some of my pa's claims, hoping to find clues as to the location of his silver. On the way back, I got caught in a flash flood."

He didn't bother explaining about Slade, or how it was really the expert's fault they were in this mess. Especially since Betsy was shaking her head and clucking about risking one's life for silver.

"You sound just like Annabelle," he said as a way of trying to be friendly and breaking the ice.

Betsy stepped back. "Annabelle? I'm nothing like her. She's a preacher's daughter."

"Betsy…" Wes's warning came from the corner.

"It's all right." Joseph accepted the blanket Betsy handed him. "Sounds like you just need to get to know

Annabelle better. She's one of the kindest people I know. She's been helping take care of my sister, and I can honestly say I don't know what I'd do without her."

Betsy stared at him for a moment, then looked over at Wes. "That's what he's been telling me, but I don't know. I can't imagine her wanting to be friends with the likes of me."

Joseph wanted to continue defending her, but the more he rose to her defense, the more it looked like his feelings were more... Well, they... He shook his head. The woman was going to drive him crazy by the time he was done.

"Maybe you should invite her over. I'm sure she'd be honored to have you as a friend." Joseph's stomach ached. That was the worst part of the situation and him trying to be her friend. He'd be leaving soon, and things would be all the worse for Annabelle.

Betsy turned away, like she didn't want to continue arguing the point. Joseph had to start learning to mind his own business, especially where Annabelle was concerned.

Wes returned, carrying a pile of clothes. "Betsy'll turn her back while you get these on."

Joseph changed as quickly as he could. "I'm finished," he said as he buttoned the last button on the shirt.

"Based on you riding Frank's best horse, and what you've said, I presume you're Billy's boy." Wes looked at him, studying.

"Yes."

It couldn't be that bad if Wes already figured him out, but still supplied him with clean clothes anyway, right?

"Did you know my pa?"

Wes nodded slowly. "I took care of his horse. Had to sell it, though, to pay his past due on the stabling."

If his pa had silver, why couldn't he pay the stable?

"Mighty fine horse." Wes stroked his chin. "I always wondered where he got the money for it."

"Maybe he won it in a card game."

Wes shook his head. "Not Billy. He was terrible at cards. Used to say that losing was God's punishment for adding that to his multitude of sins."

It sounded almost as if Wes knew his pa. "Were you friends?"

"As much as a body could be, I suppose." Wes handed him a cup of coffee. "Billy mostly kept his own counsel. Visited that girl he had over on State Street, but didn't spend too much time getting friendly with others."

The description didn't fit with what he'd been told about his pa. "Everyone I've talked to has spoken poorly of him."

The fire crackled in response, because Wes just stood there, as though he was carefully considering his words.

Then finally, "Well, I suppose he didn't do much to endear himself to anyone. Especially Slim Deckert. When Billy heard he'd roughed up one of the girls over at Miss Betty's, he went and beat the daylights out of him. No one understood why he'd take up for a woman like that, but Billy just muttered that he had a daughter her age, and that she had to be somebody's daughter."

Another story that didn't mesh with either his view of his pa, or the stories he'd heard. Though the name intrigued him. Slim was the guy his pa supposedly cheated to get the mine he'd just looked at.

"How did that make him unpopular?"

Wes shrugged. "There's two types of people in this town. One that wants to get rid of the women. They'd just as soon have them sent away and everything cleaned up nicely. The other type wants them so's they can use them, if you know what I mean."

The collar of the unfamiliar shirt felt tight around Joseph's neck. Yes, he knew what Wes meant. Because clearly his pa had taken advantage of the latter.

"Billy, he wasn't neither. He saw a man for who and what he was, and he didn't make no pretense otherwise. Didn't matter if a man wore fancy clothes or drove a nice rig. If the man was a snake, he called him a snake. The snakes around here didn't like that none."

Wes's eyes narrowed as he motioned to Joseph to lean in more. "There's plenty of folks who wanted your pa dead, and not for any of the reasons you'd think."

Not a very helpful answer. "But was there silver?"

"I don't know. No one knows for sure. Only Billy, and he's dead now."

So close to answers, yet none that he sought. "Is there anything you can tell me that would be helpful? I just looked at a mine he supposedly won in a card game from Slim."

"I've heard that tale." Wes shrugged. "And even though Lon, the dealer, supports Slim's side of the story, I never bought it. Like I said, Billy was terrible at cards."

Which only made everything all the more murky. And made his pa's death all the more likely to have been murder. But it didn't give him any answers.

"If anyone knows anything, it would be the kid," Wes continued. "Billy doted on her. When her ma took ill, he cared for that little girl himself. Paid Miss Betty well to keep Lily and the child."

Money he could have sent home. While part of Joseph admired that his pa did the honorable thing with his mistress and their child, the other part stung at the thought of his mother and siblings struggling. How was he supposed to forgive a man for letting one family starve while supporting the other?

"Why'd he keep them at that place? Surely he'd put them in a house or something like that."

"For a while, they lived at his cabin. But when Lily got sick, she needed to be close to the doctor. None of the decent boardinghouses would have her, given her old profession. Besides, her friends were all at Miss Betty's."

It was strange to think that a person would be more comfortable in a house of ill repute than anywhere else. Especially with a child.

"Plus, if you ask me—" Wes lowered his voice again "—I heard talk of some men out to get Billy. I imagine he wanted to keep his family safe."

"How do you know all this? And why doesn't Frank know?"

"Billy was afraid of putting the preacher in danger. He figured he'd risked enough by giving him his papers to hold, but the preacher's safe is the safest in town, other than at the bank. And Billy had his reasons for not wanting to go to the bank."

"But that doesn't answer my question. How do you know all this?"

"Because…" He lowered his voice even further.

"Oh, for land's sakes, Wes. Just tell him already. I'm not some delicate flower you have to protect."

Betsy came and stood in their midst. "I used to work at Miss Betty's with Lily. Wes and I fell in love, but given my profession, we were afraid that if people knew, they wouldn't do business with Wes anymore. So we pretended like I was new to town, and everyone believed it. Except Billy, who recognized me from his visits to Lily."

She gave Wes a sharp glare. "Billy would sometimes bring Lily over to see me. None of the womenfolk here in town were all that friendly to me. I always imagined that they figured out who I really was, even though no one has ever said anything. It's like no matter how hard I try, I can't get the stain of my former job off me."

The longing on her face wrenched Joseph's heart in two. "You told me I should seek out Miss Annabelle. But I ask you, what do I have to offer a fine young lady like her? I'm not fit company, and if her pa knew what I used to do, he'd never allow it."

Obviously Betsy didn't know Frank all that well. "If that's so, then why does he let her take care of Nugget?"

"She's a child. She hasn't done anything wrong. Not like me."

The pain in the woman's eyes made him realize that she had far more in common with Annabelle than she thought. He looked over at Wes, then back at Betsy. "Clearly you haven't been to church enough. Because there you'd learn that all have sinned and fall short of the glory of God. Anyone who would judge you is just as guilty of sin as you are."

"I knew I liked you," Wes said with a grin. "I can see why Frank is so keen on you. You're a good man. I hope you find your pa's silver. If anyone deserves it, you do."

Unfortunately, he was learning that finding silver

had nothing to do with deserving it. Just like the misfortunes that befell people. Frank and Annabelle didn't deserve the tragedy they'd experienced, but it had come anyway. So, too, had the hardships come to Joseph and his.

But somehow, some way, Joseph was going to make it right.

Betsy handed him a bowl of soup. "Eat this. After being in that storm, it'll do you good. Keep you from catching cold."

Between sips of soup, Joseph further relayed the events on the mountain. Even as the soup warmed him, his bones ached with the chill of being so close to death. Again, he couldn't help but thank God for keeping him safe. Surely, by the worried expressions on his new friends' faces, God's hand had been on him the entire time.

"Wait a second." Wes stared at him. "You're telling me that right before the big rockslide, you heard a boom?"

Joseph nodded. "Yes. Lightning must've struck and loosened the rocks."

"I don't think so. It would do that to a tree, maybe, but boulders? A slide that big had to have come from something like dynamite. Your story sounds a lot like what miners have described as being caught in when they've set the dynamite wrong."

The concern on Wes's face brought the chill back to Joseph. "It did sound different from the lightning strikes, now that you mention it."

Wouldn't Slade have known the difference? "So why didn't Slade come back to see if I was all right?"

He'd told himself it was because the situation was so

dangerous, but wouldn't a man of God, the right-hand man of the preacher who'd assigned him to take care of Joseph, have checked?

Betsy's eyes narrowed. "I'll tell you why. Because Slade's dirty. The preacher doesn't see it, because he always sees the best in everyone. I'm telling you, Slade is the worst of them all."

Wes nodded, his lips drawn in a thin line. "You can tell a lot about a man by how he takes care of his horse. Slade's ruined many a good animal. I don't like to speak ill of anyone, but I have to agree. If I were a betting man, I'd go all in on the notion that Slade caused that landslide."

It just didn't seem right. Not with how highly Frank regarded the other man. "Has he been in any trouble? Done anything that would make you think…?"

Wes shook his head. "Nothing that could be proven." He frowned. "Not even enough that I could go to the preacher with. It just seemed like I'd be speaking ill of someone without cause."

Unfortunately that didn't do any of them any good with Annabelle and Nugget at stake. Surely he wouldn't hurt Annabelle. Not since they'd made up.

"He wouldn't hurt Annabelle, though, would he? I mean, everyone says—"

"Don't trust him with her," Betsy said too quickly. "We learned real quick at Miss Betty's to be busy when Slade came around. He liked doing things, bad things, and the more the girl cried, the better he liked it. I'm telling you, he might put on a pleasing attitude in public, but that man likes hurting people."

Betsy didn't need to go into detail for Joseph to feel sick.

"Why would he finally show his true colors now?" Joseph looked at the two, hoping that there was some way they could be wrong. That all of this wasn't true. Because if it was, Slade was on his way back to the camp with no one there to protect Nugget and Annabelle.

Wes looked at him intently. "Because you must've been close to finding the silver. I always thought that your pa's death was suspicious. He was having an assayer come all the way up from Denver, so why would he get drunk and accidentally fall into a ravine the day before?"

Because his pa had always had a weakness for the drink. "Maybe he was celebrating prematurely."

Or maybe, based on Slade's evasive answers, he was pushed.

"Slade was trying to talk me into selling the claims to a land agent."

"Who'd he recommend?"

"He didn't say."

But with the strong hints that Slade gave, Joseph was sure he'd probably had someone in mind. He'd almost been convinced to go ahead and do it. And maybe, had Slade been patient enough to not try to kill him, Joseph would have.

Now, knowing what he knew, Joseph had no choice but to see it through.

First, though, he had to find a way to keep Annabelle and Nugget safe.

Chapter Nineteen

❧

Gertie had decided that Annabelle's foot wasn't healed enough to help with the laundry or much of anything else. Probably not a bad thing, considering that if she stepped on it just right, tears still sprang to her eyes. So she'd brought the children to collect wildflowers. Still within sight of the camp, but far enough that Annabelle could have a moment's peace while two little girls scampered in the meadow and picked flowers.

Annabelle had found a nice rock to sun herself on, and the girls' laughter was enough to almost lull her into a nap. Not that she'd do such a thing, of course. Especially since every time she closed her eyes, Joseph's smile haunted her.

Fortunately any other flight of fantasy in regards to the man too handsome for his own good was interrupted by Gertie's dinner bell. She held out her hands to the little girls. "I believe we have enough flowers to decorate the table. Let's take these back to Gertie to see what we can come up with."

The little girls gathered their baskets and took Annabelle's hands. Except Nugget's grasp seemed a little less firm than usual.

Gertie's cabin was within eyesight. "Caitlin, could you bring the baskets to your mother? Nugget and I will be right there."

Caitlin nodded solemnly, then scampered off. Annabelle knelt in front of Nugget.

"What's wrong, sweet pea?"

She wrapped her arms around Nugget, who remained stiff and didn't return the embrace. Annabelle kissed the top of the little girl's head.

"You're going away." Nugget finally looked up at her, tears streaming down her face.

"Where did you hear that?"

Nugget sniffed. "Your pa was telling Caitlin's ma. Then I heard you telling Joseph."

Annabelle rubbed Nugget's back. She should have been happy at the victory of finally being able to leave, but all it did was make her feel as miserable as the tears running down the little girl's cheeks. "So are you, remember? Joseph is going to take you to meet your other brother and sisters. You're going to finally be a family."

Light shone in Nugget's eyes. "You're coming with us?"

"No." Annabelle shook her head. "It wouldn't be proper. But I know they're going to love you."

"What if they're mean?" Nugget asked in a tiny voice. "Who will protect me?"

Annabelle closed her eyes. *Please, Lord. You don't answer prayers for me, but could You please honor this little girl? She doesn't deserve this.*

She opened her eyes and looked at Nugget. "You'll have Joseph."

"He's not you."

How did a person respond to such a thing?

"We'll write letters. And perhaps we can find a way to visit."

From the child's expression, she could tell that Nugget wasn't too keen on either of those ideas.

"I want you with me always."

Nugget flung her arms around Annabelle and clung as though she expected someone to separate them right away. But Annabelle wouldn't be so fortunate. She already knew that. She'd have more time to fall deeper in love with the girl so that when she was finally wrenched away, her heart would be broken into tinier pieces than it already was.

The pain of losing shouldn't be as bad, having already lost so much. But it seemed like this time, it was even crueler, given her vows not to be attached and the way Nugget had crawled in anyway.

As Annabelle and Nugget headed for the cabin, the first drops of rain began to fall.

"Come on, sweet pea, we've got to hurry if we're going to stay dry."

"Look what we have here." One of the men from the previous day stepped in their path.

Annabelle grimaced as he gave her a toothless sneer. From her discussion with Slade yesterday, she surmised him to be Pokey Simpkins, which meant the other guy must be Bart Wallace. Not that knowing their names changed anything.

"Looks like our sparrow that got away," Bart said.

Annabelle turned to run in the other direction, but Tom, the very man she had been fighting with Polly over, had come behind her. "I don't think so. You and the brat are coming with us."

"Run, Nugget," Annabelle shouted, but it was too late.

Bart had her securely in his arms, and even though the little girl was kicking and screaming, it did no good.

At that moment, the sky decided to open up into an all-out downpour. Everyone within shouting distance was scurrying for cover and shouting their own instructions to their people to keep safe.

No one heard their cries for help.

Tom bound her wrists with a rope. She tried kicking at him, but he laughed when she missed, and her injured ankle gave way, landing her squarely in the mud.

"Aw, the lady got herself all dirty."

The men cackled with glee, as if it was the funniest thing they'd ever seen. Too bad Polly wasn't around to see Tom with her now. Of course, she'd probably help with whatever nasty scheme these men had in mind.

"Mebbe," Tom said. "But just like a juicy piece of fruit, a bit of dirt ain't gonna stop me from plucking it."

She might be a lady, but there was no mistaking his reference. Too much time working in her father's ministry had taught her more than she'd ever wanted to know. There had always been a meanness to his eyes that she'd never trusted. And now she knew why. She'd been right all along in her instincts about this man, but being right didn't help her now.

Pokey brought around a horse. The men hoisted her up then tied her to the saddle. Tom got up behind her and spurred the horse on.

"Nugget!" She twisted to try to see the child.

"Don't you worry your pretty little head none. She's coming. Just by different route so's we can fool any rescue party."

Lightning lit up the sky around them. "'Course with this storm, no one's going to be able to track us anyways."

He stuffed a cloth in her mouth. Old and tasting of

stale…well, something old. Worse, it made her feel a little woozy.…

When she woke, she was inside a cave, tied up. Nugget slept next to her, also tied. Her heart wrenched at the thought of everything this child had been through in her short life.

"About time you woke up, princess." Tom kicked her in the side. "You got me into a heap of trouble, let me tell you."

She stared at him, the gag too tight around her mouth to say anything.

"Yes, sirree…" He pulled a knife out of his boot and began playing with it. "Polly overheard me talking with the boys about our plans, and I had to do some fast thinking."

Tom leaned in close, his foul breath stinging her nose. He flicked the knife along her cheek. "You're scared, ain't ya? I loves me some scared girls. Something I have in common with the boss man."

She struggled and tried using her body to strike at him, but he moved away, laughing.

Pokey and Bart entered the cave.

"Anyone follow you?"

"Nope." Bart grinned. "They haven't sent out a search party yet. No one realizes they're missing."

"Good." A familiar voice sounded in the background. "All the more time to find out where the silver is before I have to get back."

She looked up to see Slade standing before her.

"Surprised?" His eyes gleamed in the firelight. "You were right about that night Peter died. I had to see a man about some silver. Only there was no wife I sent it to."

Slade stared at her with more hatred than she'd ever felt in her own heart. "You have no idea what that night cost me. I'd worked so hard to gain Frank's trust, to be able to hear about all the claims and mines. Playing his errand boy so that I could get the inside track. And you know what?"

He stepped in closer, shoving Tom aside. "You had to go ruin it all with your silly tantrum about how it was all my fault your stupid brother died. Your pa asked me to stay away until you cooled down, making it harder for me to find the big one. I knew then, I'd make you pay."

His laugh shook her insides. "But look how convenient. Not only are you going to pay, but you're going to get me my silver."

Pure evil. That's what Slade's face looked like. Being right was no consolation for what stood before her. He pulled the gag down off her mouth.

"What do you want from me?"

"The kid knows where the silver is. One of the girls at Miss Betty's said she overheard the kid talking about seeing her daddy's silver."

He gave her another cold stare. "The kid trusts you. Make it tell us where to find the silver."

Nugget stirred beside her, but didn't wake.

"She's just a child. She doesn't know where the silver is. She couldn't even get us to her father's cabin. When we got to the clearing, she led us in the wrong direction."

Madness. That's what this all was. Nugget could no sooner help them than she could. And the crazy look in Slade's eyes told her that he wasn't going to take no for an answer.

"Besides, you know how children are. They have wonderful imaginations. They—"

Slade's hand came across her cheek in a stinging blow. "I've wanted to do that to your smart mouth for a long time. You never did know your place. Get the kid to talk."

"There is no silver." Annabelle stared at him. Or at least in his direction. She could still see spots.

"Don't lie." He struck her again, on the other side, and as his hand made contact, she tasted blood.

"I've seen the silver. Billy used it to pay Slim for his worthless claim. Was spitting mad when he found out that Slim seeded it. Now get the kid to tell me where the real mine is."

Tears prickled her eyes. How could he endanger a child like this? "You'll need to free my hands so I can wake her up."

Slade's head jerked up and down. "Fine." He gestured to Tom.

"Cut her loose." Then he looked over at his other men. "If she tries to escape, shoot her. We don't need her. Just the kid."

If Slade had no problem with hitting her and kidnapping a child, he could do much worse to Nugget. Annabelle took a deep breath as Tom cut the ropes at her wrists.

"Nugget," she whispered when she was free. Annabelle shook the little girl softly. "Wake up, sweet pea."

"My head hurts," Nugget said as she struggled awake. "I had a bad dream."

The little girl blinked, then looked around, her eyes widening as she realized it hadn't been a dream.

"Annabelle," she cried, burrowing into Annabelle's arms.

Annabelle stroked Nugget's hair. "They want your father's silver."

Nugget whimpered and looked up at her. "I thought he was our friend."

She had, too. He'd fooled them all. The worst part was how her father was going to feel when he realized that he'd been betrayed by someone he'd loved like a son.

"I'm sorry, Nugget."

"Enough." Slade held up a hand like he was going to hit her again. "Get her to tell me where the silver is."

Annabelle squeezed her precious charge. "It's going to be all right. But you have to help us get out of here by telling Slade what he wants to know."

Nugget's eyes darted over to Slade, then she looked around at all the other men, her gaze resting on Tom.

"Papa always said you were a snake."

"Shh." Annabelle pulled Nugget closer to her. "We can talk about this later. But right now, we've got to do the right thing."

Nugget pulled away. "Papa said it was a secret."

Slade's chuckle made Annabelle's heart sink. The problem with the child's reasoning of keeping her father's secret was that she didn't understand that men like Slade didn't care about promises or secrets. He'd do whatever it took to get what he wanted.

"Please," Annabelle said, looking at the little girl. "Tell him what he needs so we can get safely back to Joseph."

Another laugh from Slade. How had she missed the pure evil in this man? How had her father?

"Joseph won't be joining us this afternoon. Or ever." His features twisted into a sneer that skittered down Annabelle's back into the darkest pit of her stomach.

"What'd you do to him?"

"Joseph?" Nugget's whimper as she slid back into the protection of Annabelle's arms made her heart hurt.

Slade smiled. "I didn't do anything to him. Wasn't

my fault he couldn't keep up in the storm. Just too bad about all the lightning."

His yellow teeth stuck out from his tobacco-stained lips. "There might have been some dynamite involved. But in a storm like that, you never can tell. It'll be weeks, maybe even months before they find the body. With all the rocks on top of him, and then the flash flood washing everything away, who knows where his body ended up."

Familiar grief welled in Annabelle's heart. Why, God? Why, when she'd finally agreed to opening up her heart, did He have to take away Joseph, too?

Sure, he was going to leave anyway, but it was so much easier to think of him as being away, where she could write him and stay in touch, than it was to think of yet one more loved one gone forever.

Nugget hadn't spoken, but the wetness against Annabelle's bodice said all that needed to be said. The little girl had lost both mother and father, and now a beloved brother had been taken, as well.

So unfair.

"Now…" Slade leaned in, so foul that she had no idea why she never saw how completely indecent he was. "Since we have that cleared up, why don't you tell me what I need to know."

He reached for one of the tendrils by Annabelle's face, winding his finger in it. "It would be a shame for you and the kid to come to the same end."

The sinking feeling in Annabelle's gut told her they probably would anyway. If Slade was going to kill them no matter what, why convince Nugget to tell them what he wanted? It didn't seem right for so much to be lost for Slade to win.

Annabelle pulled Nugget tighter to her chest. "She just found out her brother is dead. So back off for a minute or else we'll both gladly take a bullet just to spite you out of getting the silver."

"Don't toy with me, you witch." Slade used his grip on her hair to pull her head in toward his, their faces barely an inch from touching. "I will get my silver, with or without your help. I'm sure your father will do just about anything to get his precious daughter back."

So much for her grand plan. Because he was right about her father. He loved her far too much to let her go easily. Tears filled her eyes as she realized how selfish she'd been in wanting to leave. She couldn't let her father be hurt by all of this.

"All right," Annabelle said softly. "I'll do what I can to get Nugget to cooperate, but you've got to give us room. You've waited this long for the silver, surely a few more hours won't make that much of a difference."

If there was ever anything to convince Annabelle of the sheer evil in Slade, it was the way the light shone in his eyes at her offer. He'd thought he'd won. And if there was anything that ever prodded Annabelle into action, it was this.

She was sick and tired of everything evil and rotten in this world winning. This time, if it cost her everything, including her life, Slade would not win. She just had to figure out how to make that happen.

Despite the rain not letting up, Joseph returned to the stable and began saddling one of Frank's other horses.

"You're crazy to go out back out there," Wes told him, handing him a bridle.

"What else am I supposed to do? Based on what you just told me, there's no way that avalanche was an accident."

He bent to check the cinch on the saddle. Wes

grabbed his arm, forcing him to look at him. "Why do you think I'm asking you to wait?"

Joseph straightened and looked at the other man. "Someone tried to kidnap Nugget. Annabelle was accosted in the camp. And the man that her pa is trusting to keep us all safe just tried to kill me. You'll forgive me if I'm not going to hesitate in making sure they're out of harm's way."

Lord, I don't even know how I'm going to do that.

"There's no way you'll beat him to the camp."

Hopefully, Slade would be counting on the fact that Joseph was dead, and was waiting in camp for the storm to let up before doing anything. But why would he act now? They'd come no closer to finding the silver than they were when he first started looking.

Except…

The Bible.

Joseph shook his head. He hadn't told anyone what he'd found in the Bible. Hadn't had a chance. He'd have liked to have shown it to Frank or Annabelle, but for whatever reason, he hadn't felt comfortable trusting Slade.

Maybe God had been protecting him more than he knew.

Joseph looked around for the saddlebag he'd had on the other horse. He hadn't even thought about whether or not the contents had remained dry.

"Where's my saddlebag?"

Wes pointed to a rack. "I hung it to dry. But what do you need with some old clothes and a couple of rocks?"

Rocks? "What about the Bible that was in there?"

"You really are a praying man," Wes said with a grin. "Well, rest your mind about that. It wasn't in there, so you must've left it at the camp."

Joseph's stomach turned. He'd put it in the saddle-bag. Hadn't wanted to trust leaving it in camp. Slade must've switched it out on the mountain. Joseph had his back turned, looking at his pa's land. Plenty of time for him to have made a switch.

He should have been more careful. And he shouldn't have assumed that Slade wasn't paying attention to his Bible reading last night. Slade obviously knew what Joseph was looking at.

"No, that means Slade took it. Last night, I figured out that my pa had used it as a key for the location of his silver. I had it in my saddlebag until I could talk to Frank and see what he thought of the code my pa left. I couldn't figure out what all the references to the places meant."

The loss of color on Wes's face was all Joseph needed to know. He turned and grabbed another saddle. "Then I'd best come with you. If Slade thinks he has the key to where the silver is, then there's no telling what he'll do to finally get it."

Chapter Twenty

The men were poring over a Bible. How could a gang of kidnapping thieves get any more ridiculous?

Nugget had ceased crying, but she remained listless in Annabelle's arms. Her brother's murder must have sucked the last bit of life out of her.

Annabelle looked around for something to use as a weapon. If she got out of this alive, she would absolutely insist on having one of those tiny pistols to hide under her skirts. Fortunately, the men seemed to be focused more on the Bible than on them. Fine time for a Bible study. She supposed she should find comfort that something her father had taught Slade had sunk in.

If only she knew which cave they were in. The landscape would give them a clue, if she could convince them to let her outside for a moment.

"Slade," she called, trying not to disturb Nugget. "I have to use the necessary."

"So?" He slammed the book shut, and the men scattered.

"Could you please escort me out so I can take care of my needs?"

Her face was warm at the thought of discussing such a personal though fabricated matter with him.

"Nope." His grin taunted her.

"Boss," Tom whispered, "maybe you could get her to…"

She didn't catch the rest of it as the two men put their heads together and began whispering furiously back and forth.

Nugget stirred. "Don't leave me alone with them. They're bad men."

Annabelle shifted the little girl so she could whisper in her ear unobserved. "I want to look around outside so I can see if there's a way to escape."

"Don't leave me." Nugget's wail nearly pierced her eardrum.

Slade looked in their direction. "Don't worry, she's not going anywhere."

He sauntered over to them, Bible in hand. "But we might let her stop and do her business on our way to the silver."

Or maybe they could find a way to escape at that time. "If Nugget tells you where it is."

"Don't need the brat." He sneered in Nugget's direction. "There's enough clues here that we'll find the silver."

He held up the Bible, and at closer look, she realized that it was the one Joseph had taken from his father's cabin. Slade had probably killed Joseph to get it.

"Then let us go." She said the words with as much bravado as she could muster, but in reality, she knew that Slade no longer had any reason to keep either of them alive. Especially since he had to know that she'd turn him in to her father and the sheriff when they got free.

"There's a few pieces we don't understand. But between you and the little one, we'll get it faster. And I owe a guy, so I'd rather get the money quick-like, if you know what I mean."

She looked down at Nugget, whose eyes had widened. Slade, too, drew his attention to the little girl.

"Where's Nugget's secret house?"

At Nugget's indrawn breath, Annabelle knew once that location was revealed, Slade would have the silver.

So close. But she wasn't going to give up. Not until the last breath had been ripped from her. She was done with letting evil take everything from her. Done.

"By the monkey rock," Nugget said in a quiet, shaky voice.

The monkey rock. Completely not helpful in the description, since many of the rocks looked like shapes of other things. They were like clouds. People saw different shapes in all of them.

"Which is where?" He pulled Nugget out of her arms and shook her.

"Leave her alone!" Annabelle jumped up and reached for Nugget, but Slade was just as quick to keep her away.

He looked at the other men. "Get them ready to travel."

Slade kept hold of Nugget, tying her to his saddle. Tom grabbed Annabelle.

"Be a good girl and don't fight."

Not likely, considering Slade was ready to leave with Nugget. She couldn't let him take her. Hopefully on the way, she'd figure out how to get them both free. Right now, though, it wasn't worth fighting, or even wasting her breath on screams no one would hear. Best to save her energy for when she could get Nugget.

As Tom dragged her outside, he whispered, "You even think about trying to escape, and we'll kill the brat."

The rain had stopped, leaving puddles everywhere, and the kind of mud a person could sink in. Maybe she could use it to her advantage.

Annabelle pulled a pin out of her hair and let it drop to the ground. Though tiny, the small rhinestone on the end would hopefully be a clue to anyone looking for them.

Once Tom had hoisted her onto his saddle, she managed to get another pin loose and dropped it into the grass nearby. Maddie had called those pins an unnecessary vanity, but at least they were distinctive to anyone who knew her. Slade hadn't been around enough lately to know they were hers.

They headed east, and Annabelle memorized every bit of terrain. When she got out of this, she would be sure that the sheriff searched every inch for anyone else linked to Slade's gang.

If someone spotted one of her hairpins.

As they turned out of the canyon, Annabelle recognized the landscape. Not too far from the cabin, and an easy journey to the camp.

"Can we stop for a moment?" She looked over her shoulder at Tom and gave him her most pleasant smile. "You never did let me use the necessary."

Her skin crawled as she batted her eyelashes at him, trying to appeal to him in a feminine way. If Polly was mad at her because she thought he'd been flirting, then maybe she could use it to her advantage.

Tom gave a half smile back. Shy, like her being nice

to him was an unexpected treat. Annabelle tried not to gag.

"Boss!" he yelled. "We need to stop."

Gloating would only ruin her chances at this point. Though it would be easy for her to get away here, it still left the problem of getting Nugget free. She had no doubt that Slade would harm her in retaliation. Even in the fun games her family had played together, Slade was known to be a ruthless competitor.

Slade rode toward them. "What's the problem?"

"The necessary." Annabelle twisted her face into an expression that she hoped looked like she had to go really bad. Her mother would be horrified at how unladylike she was being, but if it saved her life, and that of a young child, surely it would be worth it.

He glared at her, then at Tom. "Now?"

"I'm afraid if I wait any longer, and all the jostling on the horse…"

Tom got off his horse. "Boss, if she ruins my saddle…"

"Fine." Slade pulled out his pistol. "But if you try anything, remember I've got the kid."

She swallowed, then scooted off the horse. "I understand."

No, running away was not an option. Especially given that Slade had one hand on Nugget, and the other held a gun.

"I'll just go behind those bushes." She stared at him, daring him to argue.

"What happened to your hair?"

Annabelle reached up, realizing that with all the pins she'd taken out, it was starting to look a mess. She couldn't afford for Slade to look too closely or start wondering about the missing pins.

"I told you, all the jostling is rather uncomfortable. I keep trying to push my hair back up out of my face, but it's not as though any of you are taking care to make this an easy ride."

The gleam in Slade's eyes made her realize that he was enjoying every moment of tormenting her. The more miserable she said she was, the more he enjoyed it.

"We don't cater to prissy spoiled brats here. Guess you'll have to make do."

She gave him the kind of haughty look she knew he expected from her. Though she was learning to be more than the child everyone thought her, now was not the time to prove she'd changed. The old Annabelle was exactly what Slade needed to see.

"When my father finds out—"

"We'll be halfway to Mexico with the silver." He leaned forward and ran a finger down her cheek. "And I haven't decided if I'll kill you first, or keep you around for entertainment for a while, and then sell you. Pretty golden hair like yours will fetch a mighty fine price."

Slade rolled one of her curls around his finger, then gave it a sharp yank. Had he pulled any harder, she was sure she'd have a bald spot. It took every amount of energy not to kick him in the shins.

She brushed past him and headed into the bushes. She relieved herself as quickly as she could, then took three of her hairpins and fashioned them into an *A*. Maybe that would help anyone looking for her.

Now to find a place to leave it unobserved by the bandits, but in such a way that anyone looking for her would spot the clue.

As she walked back to the horses, every bandit's eye was on her. At least they weren't underestimating her abilities to try to escape. Because she would. With Nugget.

She spied a rock, that if she could just get the hairpins on it, would hopefully put them in view of anyone coming from the direction of the camp.

"Ouch!" Annabelle pretended to stumble on her way to the horse. She scooted toward the rock, pretending to try to right herself. Then, because it was so close, Annabelle went and sat on the rock, making a show of examining the foot she'd injured the day before.

"I do hope it's not worse." She glared at Slade. "It's the same ankle I hurt yesterday. I should have listened to Gertie about keeping off it longer. Then maybe you wouldn't have been able to kidnap us. We'd be safe in the cabin right now."

Annabelle started to cry, thinking she'd have to fake the tears, but as they flowed readily, she realized what a mess everything was. Her words were supposed to have been a ploy, to distract the men from noticing her setting the pins for someone to discover them. But they were true.

Slade strode toward her, his face filled with disgust.

"Even if you'd stayed at the cabin, we'd still have gotten you. Probably easier and without a fuss. You think your pa or Gertie would have objected to me taking you two for a ride?"

His confidence made her realize just how he'd fooled them all. If Slade had come to the cabin and offered to take her for a ride, she and everyone else would have agreed.

"Then why kidnap us?" She stared at him defiantly as he hauled her to her feet.

He grinned. "Because it's more fun this way."

With great ease, Slade picked her up and threw her over his shoulder. "Wouldn't want you to hurt your foot any more, would we?"

How had she not seen what a bully Slade was?

Slade handed her to Tom, who helped hoist her back onto the saddle.

"No more delays," Slade said as he tugged again on one of her loose tendrils.

Another hairpin clattered to the ground, and she couldn't help but hope that was the first one her rescuers found. It would serve Slade right for his meanness to be the instrument of his downfall.

When Joseph and Wes arrived at Gertie's, the rain had stopped, but the place was in an uproar.

"What's going on?" he asked Gertie.

"Annabelle and Nugget are missing," she said, looking over at Frank. "They were picking flowers, then the storm hit. I just don't know where they could be."

Polly slammed a pot to the ground. "I'll tell you where they are. She's run off with Tom, despite all of her protests about not being the sort to dig her claws into someone else's man."

He couldn't believe that Polly's petty jealousy was keeping everyone from looking for Annabelle. "That isn't what happened." Joseph glared at her, then turned to Frank.

"There's a lot Wes and I need to catch you up on. But we'll have to do that as we look for Annabelle and Nugget. Slade has them, and—"

"No, he doesn't." Polly stood and squared off with him. "I saw her ride off with Tom. Nugget wasn't with them. He had his arms around her, and I can assure you, she was not upset about it."

He stepped aside and addressed Frank. "Tom must be working with Slade. When we were on the ridge, Slade tried to kill me. He stole my pa's Bible out of my saddlebag. I believe it holds the clue to the location of the silver."

The doubt on Frank's face, along with Polly's screeching in the background made it almost impossible to believe they'd get Annabelle back safely.

"It's true," Wes said, breaking in to the conversation. "I've seen Slade and Tom hanging around town together. I'm sure he's got other men who've got Nugget. We need to find them—fast."

Frank's Adam's apple bobbed as he looked from Wes to Joseph. "You're certain Slade tried to kill you?"

"Yes. As I said, I'll give the rest of the details on the way. We've got to find Annabelle and Nugget."

Which seemed almost hopeless given that Frank was still doubtful about the circumstances of his daughter's disappearance, and that without his pa's Bible, they had no idea where…

Joseph glanced around the people gathered. "My pa referenced something about Nugget's secret rock house in his Bible. Does that sound at all familiar?"

Gertie nodded. "The girls were talking about one. Caitlin!"

She ran toward the tent, where a teary-eyed little girl emerged. "Did you find Nugget?"

"No."

Joseph watched as Gertie bent down in front of her daughter. He prayed Caitlin would know where it was.

"I heard you girls talking about a secret house. Do you know where it is?"

Caitlin nodded. "Nugget said it was by her papa's cabin, at monkey rock, and that someday she'd take me there to play in her treasure room."

All this time, Nugget had probably known where the silver was.

"Thank you, Caitlin." Joseph bent and gave the little girl a hug. "I promise, we'll do everything we can to find Nugget."

Please, Lord, don't let this be a broken promise. Nugget had to be safe, she just had to be.

"I know where we're going," he told Wes, who was already headed for the horses.

Joseph looked over at Frank. "Are you coming?"

The older man nodded slowly. It was clear he still couldn't wrap his mind around Slade being behind everything, but hopefully, during the ride, with Wes to help explain what he knew of the man, it would become clearer.

Now he just needed to pray that they'd reach Annabelle and Nugget in time.

Chapter Twenty-One

❧

When they reached the turnoff for Nugget's father's cabin, they didn't turn, but rode on.

"The cabin's that way," Annabelle said, twisting to get Tom's attention.

"We're not going to the cabin, Miss Know It All." He yanked on Annabelle's hair in imitation of Slade.

What was it with these men and her hair? At least it gave her an excuse to pull out yet another hairpin to leave as a marker. She dropped an extra one, and another closer than what she ordinarily would have in hopes that they'd pick up on her clue and keep going.

What must her father be thinking right now? Had they gotten word of Joseph's death? Did he know Slade was the culprit, or would her father be wondering who could have taken her?

Did they even know they were gone?

Annabelle pushed those thoughts out of her head. She wasn't going to give up. She simply couldn't. Too many bad things had happened already, and she wasn't going to let this have the same end.

They reached an outcropping of rocks, which must've

been the other side of where Joseph's father had built his cabin.

"There!" One of Slade's men pointed in the direction of a rock formation.

Tom dismounted, then yanked her off the horse. "Walk."

She did as she was bade, eager to catch up with Slade and to check on Nugget.

When they got to the base of the formation, Slade turned toward Annabelle. "Get the kid to tell me where the silver is."

Annabelle started toward Nugget, who raced into her arms. "That man is mean."

"I know." Annabelle hugged her tight. "Is the silver here?" she whispered.

Nugget nodded. "Papa said I shouldn't tell anyone."

How could she convince a child to betray her father's confidence? Worse, how could she get the information about the silver to Slade in such a way that he'd let them live, at least long enough for them to escape?

"You know that the mean man is going to hurt us if you don't tell him?"

Tears ran down Nugget's face. A child so young should not be responsible for all the things she'd had to face.

With a look braver than her age, Nugget wiped an arm across her face, took Annabelle's hand, then tugged her in the direction of Slade.

"In that cave," Nugget said, pointing at a small fissure in the rock.

Slade went to the spot Nugget indicated, staring into it. He tried squeezing into the space, but his body was too big.

"How'd he get the silver out? Is there another entrance?" He returned his attention to Nugget.

She shook her head, then said quietly, "I got the silver for him."

If there was anyone Annabelle wanted to hurt more than Slade and his men, it was Nugget's father for putting a child in this position. How could he?

Slade, though, had no such thoughts, as a wicked grin crossed his face. "Then get it for me."

Nugget glanced in Annabelle's direction. "Annabelle has to come with me. There's enough room. Mama used to come so's the bats wouldn't get me."

Bats. Annabelle swallowed. Well, if she had to choose between bats and bullets, she supposed bats were the best option.

"You wouldn't be trying to pull anything, would you?" Slade got right in Nugget's face, but the little girl remained unmoved.

"She's a child," Annabelle said. "What exactly do you think she's going to pull?"

Slade turned to his men. "Where's the dynamite? Let's just blast it out."

The men whispered amongst themselves, then Bart came forward. "Slim used it all on Joseph. There isn't any more."

For a moment, Annabelle was sure Slade was going to shoot him on the spot. Then Slade looked over at the one she presumed to be Slim.

"Then Slim had best get in to town and get us some more."

Slade returned his attention to Nugget and Annabelle. "I guess it's time for you to prove there's really silver in there. Go in and get me some silver."

Nugget scrambled into the cave, and Annabelle followed, barely able to squeeze into the tight space.

"Nugget?"

Annabelle could hear a soft scrape, then a light shone in the distance.

"Crawl on your belly to my light."

She did as the tiny girl ordered, finding herself in a large cavern.

"Papa told me to come here if anyone ever tried to get me to tell them where the silver is."

Nugget shone the lantern around to indicate an empty cavern that had shiny flecks of some sort of mineral adorning the wall. Unfortunately, it wasn't gold or silver. That much Annabelle knew. "Mama called it my secret house."

Annabelle closed her eyes. They were safe for now, but once Slade realized they were not coming out, he'd just get dynamite and blast them out.

"But how do we get out?"

Nugget shrugged. "Papa always came."

"But your papa is dead. Is there any other way out?"

Annabelle took the lantern and looked around for some sign that the cavern had another exit. Every fissure in the cavern appeared tighter than the one they'd just entered. Nugget went to one of the spaces and pulled out a blanket.

"I want my mama," she said, plopping down on the hard ground and wrapping the blanket around her.

Annabelle joined her and pulled the little girl into her lap. "I know. I want my mama, too."

Because her mother would know exactly what to do. She always did. At some point, Slade was going to get impatient for the silver. And if he found dynamite, and the rocks exploded around them, they surely wouldn't survive.

Lord, please. Help me find a way to get us out safely. We can't have come this far for nothing. My faith is so lacking, but the Bible says that if you have faith as small as a mustard seed... Surely I have that much in me. Otherwise, I wouldn't be calling on You now.

Annabelle wasn't sure what else to say, so she cuddled Nugget closer to her and tried peering around in the limited light. If Nugget had faith that her papa would come get her, there had to be another way in if the way they'd entered was too small for a man.

"Nugget? Will you tell me where the silver is?"

The little girl sighed. "You won't tell the bad men, will you?"

"I won't tell them." *Please God, let me not break this promise.*

But Nugget seemed to know Annabelle was weak. "Yes, you will."

So Annabelle continued her search, shining the light and running her hand along the surface of the cave walls. She stumbled over a pile of rocks.

Could this be it?

She started digging among the rocks, moving them aside in hopes that they would lead to a passageway. Each rock seemed heavier than the last, but it didn't make a dent in the pile.

"It's not there," Nugget said, moving to stand beside her.

Great. Annabelle let out a long breath. She'd been working to get them out of the cave, and Nugget was still trying to protect her father's silver.

"Then where?" She tried keeping the exasperation out of her voice, but she was running out of options.

Nugget looked at her with big, watery green eyes. "I promised my papa."

"Then at least tell me how he got in."

Shadows crossed Nugget's face, and she'd liked to have thought that it was because Nugget was carefully considering the idea. That meant there had to be another way.

"Papa came in from the big rock." Nugget pointed, and when Annabelle swung the lantern, her heart sank. The big rock was bigger than the two of them put together.

"Some other bad men came for Papa once, and he told me to stay in here until it was safe." She walked to the spot where she'd found the blanket, then pulled out a canteen. "The food's gone, but Papa left us water and this lantern." Nugget held up the lantern that illuminated the cave.

This was not what she was looking for. But maybe, if she got Nugget to tell more of the story, she'd find out something that could help them. "How long were you in here?"

"Ages." Nugget let out a long, dramatic sigh. "But then Papa pushed the big rock out of the way and he saved me."

"Annabelle!" The echo through the cave reminded her that they didn't have ages. They had only as much time as the men had to bring dynamite in from town. Which, if they rode hard, only gave them a couple hours.

She turned toward the opening from which they'd come. "We're still looking. It's all a bunch of rocks."

"You best find me some silver."

If only Annabelle and God had been on good enough terms that He would listen to her prayers. But maybe…

Lord, please help us. Help me find a way to save us. To save Nugget. You saw fit to save me when all of these good people died in spite of all my prayers. Why did You have to take Joseph, too? And now to leave me in this situation where only You can save us? This time, if You have to take someone, let it be me instead of a little girl who hasn't done anything wrong.

Because that, of all things, was her greatest fear. That somehow, God would once again take someone she loved and leave her behind to regret.

Annabelle took Nugget in her arms. "They're not going to be patient much longer. Please, if there is silver, tell me where to find it."

The little girl looked up at her with tears in her eyes. "You don't believe me?"

But this…breaking a child's heart, was probably the worst of all her sins. Faith was supposed to be about believing in things unseen. These men had never seen the silver. Joseph had never seen the silver. But they were all willing to fight for it. How much so should her faith be?

She couldn't even believe in silver when she was supposed to believe in God.

"I just…" Annabelle hated the way her heart churned. "I've seen no evidence…no…"

A voice inside the back of her head asked her if she hadn't seen evidence, or if she hadn't seen the evidence she'd wanted to see.

Annabelle took a deep breath. "I'm sorry, Nugget. If you say there's silver, then I believe." She had to choose to believe.

Annabelle looked Nugget in the eye. "I know your father said to wait here for him, but what did he say to do if he didn't come?"

The uncertainty in the child's eyes didn't give her any comfort. But Annabelle had to do something. Otherwise, sitting here, thinking about the men after her... Men who'd killed Nugget's father. And Joseph... No, she couldn't think about him. Not now. Otherwise, the pain might completely immobilize her.

Nugget's voice piped up. "Papa said for me to sing some songs so I wouldn't miss him so much while I waited for him to come. I could sing one my mama taught me."

The earnestness in the small child's voice gave Annabelle the strength she needed to keep fighting. "That sounds like a great idea."

As Nugget began singing "Rock of Ages," Annabelle looked around for something to use as a lever. If the rock moved one way to get Nugget out before, surely she could find a way to make it work again.

Joseph slowed his horse just before the turnoff for the cabin. Maybe his pa had left more clues there. Something to tell him where to find the secret rock house or Monkey Rock.

Lord, please. Help me find Annabelle and Nugget.

Something glinted off a rock in the sunlight and caught his eye. He stopped and looked closer. The letter *A*, made out of Annabelle's hairpins.

"Frank!" He twisted in his saddle and waved at the other man. "I've found something."

Without waiting for Frank's answer, Joseph jumped off the horse and picked up the pins. He searched the area around where she'd left the clue. She'd been here, but which direction did they go?

Frank joined him where he stood and examined the pins. "I've always appreciated that she didn't worry herself into a tizzy the way so many ladies do. I just wish…" He shook his head.

Joseph put his arm on the other man's shoulder. "Don't wish. We're going to find her and Nugget, and we'll bring them home safely. Then you can tell her all the things you wish you could have told her."

Like that fact that he was kidding himself to think he could only be her friend. No other woman would have the kind of gumption Annabelle did. And in the face of being kidnapped, she still found a way to fight. She'd given his sister her heart and loved her in spite of all the reasons a respectable woman wouldn't be so kind to Nugget. Even though she had to face her own grief to do so.

If anyone could hold her own against Slade and his gang, Annabelle could.

Joseph held up the pins. "Annabelle left us some clues. Do any of you see anything that looks like a monkey rock?"

The men scanned the area, and Joseph's stomach sank at the realization that none of the rocks in the area looked like a monkey.

"I found another pin!"

Frank's shout gave Joseph more hope. Annabelle had left them a trail. Surely as they followed her clues, they'd find a monkey rock.

They were headed east, by the looks of things. He turned toward the other men. "What's east of here? Anything that would be like a monkey?"

Wes's face turned white. "I know where they are. It's not monkey rock, it's long key rock, and it looks like a long key."

He watched as the other man shook his head slowly. "I can't believe the silver was there the whole time. He even tried to get me to buy the claim off him, said he needed to send money home. Said he didn't want just anyone to have it."

Hearing of his pa's honor, or what looked to be it, caused Joseph's gut to churn in an unfamiliar way. No matter how much he thought he knew about his pa, it seemed like there was always something more to be learned. Just as he'd been unable to fit Annabelle into a box, so too, had he failed to do so with his pa.

Joseph went to his horse, prepared to travel to Long Key Rock, but as he headed in the direction of the pins, Wes stopped him. "That's the way they went, but I know a back way. They won't be expecting us from that direction, so maybe we can get a jump on them."

Wes turned toward the men who'd ridden from camp with them. "Someone get the sheriff."

They followed Wes through a tight canyon, so tight that they could barely fit their horses through. If Joseph had been in charge of navigating the passage, he would have been tempted to turn back. It seemed to be nearly impassable as his horse slipped on some rocks.

"Careful!" Wes called behind them. "We're almost there."

A large boulder blocked their path. Wes jumped off his horse. "We'll lead the horses through here. Funny, I don't remember this boulder being here before."

They managed to squeeze past the boulder, and from there, Wes's description of being almost there didn't seem to be so far off. The canyon opened up, and to their right stood a large rock formation. Ahead, nothing but sheer cliffs and the edge of the mountains. From his vantage point, facing the villains directly seemed almost the smarter choice.

"We can tie up the horses here." Wes gestured at a tree with well-worn ground. "Looks like this is probably where someone else did."

That someone being his pa? Or someone else? Joseph examined the rock formation that Wes said was the rear of the rock where they'd likely taken Annabelle and Nugget. He clambered up the pile of debris. Piles of rock had been dumped here and there, almost as if someone was searching for silver but hadn't found it yet. Someone had been prospecting here.

The other two men joined him, scrambling up the rock, looking for a way to sneak around the front. A fissure in the rock appeared to be almost large enough for a man to squeeze through. If his pa had hidden silver in here, he'd made it nearly impossible for anyone to get to it. But maybe that was the challenge. The way he'd kept it safe all this time.

And why two people were in grave danger.

Joseph peered into the rock opening. Could there be a way through here to where Annabelle and Nugget were being held?

A sound, almost like someone calling Annabelle's name, reached his ears. Joseph squeezed in deeper. Could they have escaped?

"Annabelle...." The word echoed to his ears.

They were there. Had to be.

He squeezed back out of the cave and motioned to

Wes and Frank. "I can hear someone calling to Anna-belle through here."

Without waiting for their answer, Joseph returned to where he'd positioned himself.

"I've got a lantern." Wes's voice sounded behind him, and light filled the tight space.

Joseph pressed against the wall, realizing there wasn't enough room for two men to walk comfortably in the space, which dead-ended only a few feet ahead of him.

"Annnnnnnaaaaabellllllleeee...." The voice came again. "Bring out my silver, or we're going to use dy-namite."

Dynamite. The hair on the back of his neck stood up as the air grew distinctly colder.

In a cavern like this, who knew how stable the rocks around them were. Dynamite could get them all killed.

A child's voice singing "Rock of Ages" echoed through the cavern. Nugget.

"Give me the lantern." He reached back to Wes, who handed him the light.

Joseph held it up, shining it against each side of the rock around them. Surely there was some passageway to lead them to the girls.

Light seeped through the crack of the boulder that Nugget had said her father pushed aside to get her out. Was it one of Slade's men? Or someone come to save them?

"Rock of Ages, cleft for me. Let me hide myself in thee."

Though Nugget's childish voice spoke of Christ, An-nabelle looked around for a hiding place in the rock they were already hiding in. Was there a deeper place for them to find themselves in?

A small voice inside her told her to have a little faith. And she was reminded that she needed to simply believe.

"Annnnnaaabellleee…." Slade's voice came from the other end, though sounding closer than his previous threats had been. "Bring out my silver, or I'm going to use dynamite."

Surely he wouldn't be threatening dynamite if he was sending someone else in through the other side.

"Nugget." Annabelle got the little girl's attention, and indicated to the rock. "I see light coming from there."

The little girl jumped up. "Papa!"

She ran to the boulder and clawed at the crack. "Papa, we're here. The bad men are trying to steal our silver."

"Nugget!"

Joseph. Tears clogged her throat at the sweet sound of a voice she'd never imagined she'd hear again. Annabelle closed her eyes and breathed a simultaneous prayer of relief and prayer for his safety. Against these evil men, Joseph would be no match.

Still, he was alive. All the regret over his death could be erased. She could love him, and let him love her in return.

If they got out alive.

She spoke low and urgently, not wishing for their voices to echo back to Slade. "We're both here, and we're safe. But I don't know for how much longer. Slade is threatening to use dynamite if we don't bring out silver for him."

"Papa moved the rock out of the way to get me out of here," Nugget added.

"Who else is there?" Slade's voice called out. He yelled something to his men, probably to either look for the other entrance or ready the dynamite. Neither would end well for them.

Annabelle knelt in front of Nugget. "Can we send some silver their way? If we tempt them with something, it will give Joseph more time to get us out of here."

Nugget looked in the direction they'd come from, then back at the boulder. "But Papa said..."

"If there's a lot of silver, it won't matter if we give them some. Besides, it'll give the sheriff a way to find them."

The little girl examined her like an older, wiser, person would. Weighing the risks and benefits of her plan. But mostly, she looked like she wanted to cry.

Nugget nodded slowly, then walked over to another rock. "Behind there."

It looked like any other rock in the place. Part of the many piles of rocks that seemed to lead nowhere. But she trusted Nugget. Annabelle pushed against the rock, but it didn't budge.

"Help me."

Nugget joined her, pushing with all the might the little girl had. Her face reddened with the exertion, but nothing seemed to move.

From the direction of the other boulder, Annabelle could hear sounds of scraping at rock, but no movement.

"Annnnaaabellle...." Slade's voice threatened.

"I'm trying," she called back. "Truly. I just need to move this rock."

She pushed harder, using all of her strength. Nugget

grunted as she helped Annabelle push against the rock, which began to move slightly.

Finding silver would give them more time for Joseph to get through the other entrance.

"Dynamite can move the rock."

His voice sounded closer, like he'd managed to find a way through the tiny passageway.

Nugget seemed to realize that, too, as she cast a worried look in Annabelle's direction.

"Come on." She motioned to Nugget, and pointed at the other boulder.

They moved to the other boulder. "Slade is coming," Annabelle said in a harsh whisper.

"Push!" Annabelle said loud enough for Slade, or whoever he might be sending after the silver, to hear.

They gave a couple of shoves at the rock, just as Slade entered the larger cavern.

Annabelle's heart stuck in her throat, and she willed it to go back to normal. To cling to the hope that Joseph would find a way to get them out.

Slade's clothes were torn and covered in dust from using a pick to get to them. Dirty, messy work, and he clearly wasn't happy about having to do the work himself. And, she noted, he'd had to leave his gun behind. Maybe they stood a chance after all.

He tossed the pick at them as he held up the lantern. "What kind of trick is this? There's no silver here."

Annabelle shook her head. "Nugget says it is. She said her father came for her from behind this rock, so it must be here."

Slade looked even more imposing than ever. "That so?" He shone his lantern around the rock. "Yes, we'll need some dynamite."

Hopefully Joseph had heard.

Nugget tugged on Annabelle's skirt. Annabelle looked down at the little girl, who looked terrified at the prospect. "Papa said—"

"I don't care what that no-account papa of yours said," Slade roared as he spun in their direction. "All's he had to do was give me some silver and we'd have been square. But that lyin', cheatin'—"

"Enough!" Annabelle gave him a stern look. "There's no call to use such language."

Then, she looked down at Nugget. "Or dynamite. Clearly, with these tunnels, this is an established mine. We need to dig out the access to the silver, and when we have a better sense of the layout, then you can dynamite where appropriate. If you randomly blast things, you're going to make an awful mess, and I'm sure it'll be that much harder for you to get your silver."

Slade leaned in at her, his eyes gleaming with enough avarice to make her wonder how anyone could have seen anything other than what a cold, hard man he was. His laughter rang through the cavern, surely carrying through to the other tunnels where the others could hear. They were in grave danger.

Slade kicked the pick. "Start digging."

Annabelle took the pick and started swinging it, aiming for the gap in the rock where she knew Joseph would be, but far enough away that she wouldn't strike him with debris. She hoped.

"Help. Please," she said the words as quietly as she could, but Slade immediately jumped up.

"Who you talking to? Who's there?"

Annabelle spun. "I suppose your praying was just

for show, so you have no idea what it looks like to truly pray."

Her own words shamed her. How long had she merely given lip service to her faith? Making people think she believed when she had none? Even now, her faith was weak, so weak she could hardly defend it. But here, in the cleft of the rock, she had to believe that she was in the protection of a greater rock.

"Your God's not going to help you. He didn't help your family. Didn't help mine. You think you've uncovered some elixir to make Him listen?"

She closed her eyes, trying to drown out the shame of his words. But just as the familiar darkness threatened to overtake her, another truth sprang to the back of her mind. And her mother's voice came to her, clearer than anything else she'd heard in a long time.

It said in Isaiah, "For My thoughts are not your thoughts, neither are your ways My ways," declares the Lord. "As the heavens are higher than the earth, so are My ways higher than your ways and My thoughts than your thoughts."

It didn't matter what her thoughts were, or how she perceived the situation. The Lord's purpose was far greater than she could see. She just had to believe.

"You hated me," Slade's voice taunted. "Because I didn't get the doctor in time to save your brother. You thought I was too busy going after silver."

Annabelle's eyes flew open, and she looked at him. "I put my faith in the wrong man."

"That you did." He gave the kind of laugh Annabelle imagined only came from a truly wicked being.

And, with the most callous of looks she'd ever seen, he grinned. "Sorry."

Rage boiled inside Annabelle at the unfairness of it all. How long she'd suffered for her supposedly rash judgment of this man, which, as it turned out, had been right all along. But then she remembered a passage from Genesis, when Joseph's brothers feared that he would take retribution for what they had done to him. "You intended to harm me, but God intended it for good, to accomplish what is now being done, the saving of many lives."

Whether Annabelle had been right or wrong, the Lord knew, and not only would He take full accounting of all that had gone on, everything, including all of this, would be used for the Lord's purpose.

Oh, how she'd resented her father trying to comfort her with placating words of how the Lord's will would be done. But now she understood. The Lord saw, and He knew.

Annabelle had a choice. To act in accordance with what the Lord had commanded her, or to act on her pain.

A flash on the other side of the rock caught Annabelle's attention, and she noticed that Joseph had almost worked his way through.

"May the Lord have mercy on your soul," she whispered, setting the pick down with a loud clank, and going to where Nugget sat, whimpering.

"What's that?" Slade looked past her, toward the spot where Annabelle had been digging.

Moments later, his face mottled with rage, he spun. "You've been stalling so's they can—"

"Annabelle, get Nugget out of the blast area so we can blow this rock." Joseph's voice rang through the cave.

She didn't need another invitation. Annabelle grabbed

Nugget by the hand and yanked her in the direction of the other tunnel. Though Slade's men waited at the other end, at least it would offer them some protection from the blast until Joseph could get to them.

Slade shoved at her back. "Make way, you stupid—"

An explosion rocked the cavern. Rocks and debris flew everywhere, filling the area with so much dust Annabelle could hardly breathe. She covered her mouth with a sleeve as she pulled her handkerchief out of her pocket to cover Nugget's. At least it would afford the child some protection.

The heavy weight of Slade's body pressed her to the ground, and she shifted to keep most of the weight of the two adults off a squirming Nugget.

"Are you all right?" Annabelle choked the words out, thankful that at least she knew Nugget was alive. Slade, on the other hand, remained a dead weight on top of her.

Nugget coughed, and Annabelle thought she might have heard the little girl say yes.

"Don't try to talk. The dust's too thick."

"Hey, boss!" A man's voice called from the other end of the tunnel. "You ready for us to get the silver?"

Though the heavy man on top of her was most uncomfortable, at least he wasn't able to answer and warn them that rescuers were on the way.

"There's a lot of dust," Annabelle called back. "Best wait a while."

She could hear murmuring, probably the men discussing why she'd answered instead of Slade. And no quick retort came to her to explain. Instead, she felt the weight being moved off her, giving her room to shift toward a dim light.

Two familiar eyes glowed back at her.

Joseph!

Without thinking, she wrapped her arms around him, feeling the warmth of a body she'd believed dead.

"Shh…it's all right. Where's Nugget?"

Of course. Annabelle should have realized that his sister would be a priority in his mind. She shouldn't have… Her face heated. Had she truly put her arms around this man? No matter what she might have vowed otherwise, she'd had no business doing so.

As Annabelle moved out of the way, she heard yells and gunshots coming from the end of the tunnel where Slade's men had been waiting. "The sheriff?" She looked for confirmation from Joseph, who nodded.

"Your pa is waiting on the other side."

He picked up Nugget, then led Annabelle through the cavern, where dust still settled.

"Keep your mouth covered. You don't want to breathe in all the dust." He pressed a handkerchief into her hand, which she gratefully took. It was a sight better than her sleeve.

She followed him out into the sunlight. A setting sun, but sun nonetheless.

"Father!" She ran into his arms, and he hugged her tight to him, tighter than she could ever remember being held.

When he finally pulled away, he picked at her hair. "Why, Annabelle, I do believe you've got silver dust in your hair."

He ran his fingers along the strands, then held his hands up to look. "Joseph! Wes! Look here! There really is silver in that mountain!"

The men gathered round, exclaiming over the silver in Annabelle's hair, and as they examined her further, even among the folds of her dress. Nugget merely lifted her head from her brother's shoulder and gave a shrug as if to say, "I told you so."

On the way back to the camp, she shared what she'd discovered with her father, whose face grew more ashen as he realized the depths of the perfidy of a man he'd loved like his own son.

But they passed camp, taking the trail instead toward town.

"Aren't we stopping at the mining camp?"

Her father shook his head. "There's men to be put in jail. Plus, you could use a bath and to sleep in your own bed."

Annabelle closed her eyes for a brief moment. A bath and her own bed sounded just about perfect. Only… "What about Gertie? I'm sure she must be worried sick."

Even when Annabelle chose to shut the other woman out, Gertie had loved her. It was time Annabelle let her.

He pulled his horse to a stop in front of her. "We sent a rider to let them know what happened. Getting you safely home is the priority now."

"Do you think we could go up and see her soon? I know she won't be satisfied until she hugs me herself."

The look on her father's face was the final piece of healing she needed. "I'm sure she'd like that."

But then the wrinkles on her father's forehead deepened more than she'd ever seen. "I'm sorry, Annabelle. I was blind to a lot of things, like your pain. You were hurting, and instead of talking to you, I assumed I knew what was best. I forced you to help in a ministry that you didn't believe in."

Annabelle swallowed, wishing she could say something to ease the pain in her father's voice. "It's a good ministry, Father."

"But it's not your ministry. Can you forgive me for being so blind? I feel it's my fault for placing you in danger by forcing you—"

"No." Annabelle wished they weren't both on horseback so she could reach for him and offer him some comfort. "If I hadn't been here, Slade would have taken Nugget, and there would have been no one to protect her. But I was here. And it all worked out, all of our mistakes, for the saving of lives."

Her father brushed his hand across his eyes. "You are something else, Annabelle. Your mother would be so proud. Just as I am."

She'd never imagined her father would ever say such a thing of her. In that moment, all of the pain she'd endured through this ordeal was completely worth it.

Joseph slowed his horse alongside them. "Is anything wrong?"

"No," her father said. "I was just telling Annabelle how proud I was of her. And, if she still wishes, I'll be putting her on the next train East to visit her aunt Celeste."

Annabelle's heart leaped. Finally! After all this time. But Nugget's tiny gasp made her stop. How could she leave Nugget?

Her father had been right. Having been forced to confront the pain and push past it, her heart didn't hurt so much anymore. The people she loved were safe, and she wanted to cling to them rather than push them away.

"Father, I…"

Her throat seemed to swell, and it wasn't from all the dust she'd breathed in. Everything she'd ever dreamed of was being offered to her with no price, and yet, it felt wrong somehow.

"I shouldn't have been so selfish in keeping you here."

Her father's voice was gruff, but she wasn't looking at him. Rather, she couldn't keep her eyes off the lone tear trickling down Nugget's cheek.

Her place was with Nugget. But how could she insist? Joseph had said nary a word to her since her rescue, and he'd already made it clear that his future was about taking care of his family, and...

There was no room for Annabelle in Joseph's life. Though she was ready to accept his love, he had none to give.

"Thank you, Father," she said quietly, no longer feeling joy in her newfound victory.

Then she looked over at Nugget. "Remember what I said. We'll write. And if Joseph is agreeable, then I can visit, or you can visit me. It'll be all right. You'll see."

But her stomach churned. None of it felt right. Joseph would have what he wanted. His silver, his family, and Nugget. And though Annabelle was also finally getting what she wanted, she didn't want to leave anymore. But she had no right. Not to Joseph, and not to Nugget, as much as she'd grown to love them both.

It should be enough for her that Joseph finally had the means to provide for his family. Annabelle's prayers had been answered.

Chapter Twenty-Two

They rode to the Lassiters' house, where everyone was promptly dispatched to take baths and get into clean clothes.

After Joseph had a bath and his soiled clothing was taken to see if any silver dust could be found in its folds, he wandered to the back porch, where he sat while everyone else made merry in the house, with an emptiness he couldn't quite describe.

Everything should be perfect. Slade's men were in jail, and now that Slade had finally come to, he would soon be joining them.

Nugget was safe. Joseph had the silver he needed to provide for his family. In fact, he'd spent a good deal of the time on the ride home talking with Collin MacDonald, who'd given him solid information on the next steps to opening his mine and making it profitable. From what Collin said, if the vein opened by the explosion was as deep as it appeared, they could be looking at one of the largest fortunes to be gained in Leadville history.

They'd been back at the house for less than an hour when all the local mining barons or their representatives began coming to call. Everyone was willing to buy him out at a handsome price. Haunted by Slade's words about all the people wanting to take advantage of others, and seeing firsthand what greed would do to people, Joseph decided that he couldn't risk anyone else being taken advantage of. He'd see his father's mining dream through.

With recommendations from Frank and Collin, Joseph had already begun to put a team in place to open his father's mines. Collin's sons had remained behind to guard the newly opened silver vein until he could put together a security team.

In his wildest imaginations, he'd never thought his father's dream could so richly come true.

Joseph wanted to throw back his head and laugh at the irony of how everything had worked out. His only regret was that his father hadn't lived long enough to see it. Yes, regret. While he didn't approve of all his father's choices, he'd come to realize that his father lived a complicated life. Even his father's bad choice of taking a mistress had a bright side. Joseph couldn't imagine life without his precious sister.

It was, as Annabelle said, all for the benefit of saving many lives.

Joseph was going to miss her and their partnership. He knew if he asked, she'd stay.

But even now, with the promise of real wealth in their future, he couldn't ask her to give up her dreams.

As if to confirm his belief, he heard Maddie in the kitchen. "We'll have to go shopping to buy you new dresses for the trip. I'm sure Celeste will want to have new ones made when you get there, but we don't want you going in rags."

"That sounds lovely."

Without being able to see Annabelle's face, he couldn't

read her attitude, but the clatter of something falling to the floor was unmistakable. Annabelle didn't want to go.

"Oh, you! You go on and sit on the porch or something. You're too excited to be of any use to me."

Annabelle murmured a reply, then the door opened and closed behind her as she joined him on the porch.

"Exciting times, eh?" Joseph smiled at her as she sat beside him.

"Your family will be so happy."

Annabelle gave him the kind of fake smile that made him want to dig deeper. But he'd given up that right. Maybe someday, when she'd had her taste of the world, she'd come back to Leadville, and maybe they'd both be free to pursue the what-if questions they'd been unable to face.

"They will. I've already begun the arrangements to bring them here. My sister Mary will be able to take care of Nugget."

Joseph wasn't leaving. "You're staying?"

"I've just said that."

The dark hid whatever expression might have flashed across Annabelle's face. But he knew it wouldn't make her happy to be so easily dismissed. What else was he supposed to do? If she thought she was needed, Annabelle would stay.

And he couldn't have her sacrifice her dreams again.

"What about until then?" Annabelle's voice drifted to him, almost too soft to hear.

"Collin said Polly was undone at the knowledge of Tom's involvement in everything. It will do her good to get out of the camp for a while. She'll be down in the morning to help with Nugget."

Annabelle tried to push away the pang in her heart at the mention of Polly's situation. Her friend had been through so much, and then to find out that the man she thought was going to marry her was so… Annabelle sighed. People were never what they seemed.

She stole a glance at Joseph. He'd barely spoken to her since her rescue, and even now, things were so different from how they used to be.

Everything had worked out perfectly. Joseph was staying in Leadville. Annabelle was leaving on her dream trip.

So why did she want to cry?

The stair beside her creaked. "Nugget wanted to say good-night to Annabelle before Frank takes you to the hotel."

"The hotel?" Annabelle looked up at Maddie and spied a miserable-looking Nugget on her shoulder, then brought her gaze back to Joseph. "Why would you and Nugget stay at a hotel, when there's plenty of room here?"

"I don't need to impose any longer." His voice was quiet. Firm.

"But I thought—"

"It's for the best. We've got arrangements to make, and I don't want to be in the way." His tone was nothing like that of the Joseph she'd come to care for over the past few days. In just the space of a few hours, he'd turned into a man she hardly recognized.

One of the things she hated about silver was how it changed people. It turned decent men like Slade into greedy monsters. Hardworking men like Gertie's husband into gamblers and drunkards. And friends into people too good to share your roof anymore.

"Come give me a hug, then, Nugget." Annabelle tried to keep her voice steady, so that the little girl at least wouldn't know how desperately her heart was breaking right now.

Nugget slipped out of Maddie's arms and into Annabelle's embrace. "I want to stay with you."

She did, too. But when she glanced up at Joseph, he gave her a stern look and a shake of his head that told her she dared not agree with the child she dearly loved.

"Joseph will take good care of you." Annabelle held the little girl tight against her, breathing in the sweet scent she'd forgotten how much she loved. The air was so still, she could hear Nugget's heartbeat, mixed with the choked breaths of a little girl trying not to cry.

"It's going to be okay," Annabelle said, trying to be as cheerful as she could with her heart breaking.

Joseph wasn't just hurting her with his decision to pull away, but the little girl he'd so fiercely claimed to be protecting.

Maddie cleared her throat. "I need to see if a few of these other things fit Nugget before you go. The child's got to have at least a change of clothes, though I'm sure you'll be wanting to buy her new ones."

Joseph gave a small jerk of his head, and Nugget followed Maddie in, leaving Annabelle alone with him again.

"You're sure you can't stay here? Nugget and I—"

"She's already too attached. And with you leaving, I don't want to make it worse."

His jaw was hard, unflinching. And if it wasn't for the tiny spot of tenderness in his dark eyes, she'd think she wasn't even looking at Joseph.

"I promised her we'd stay in touch."

He shook his head. "You'll forget all about her once you get settled with your aunt. I hear she's already planning a fancy party in your honor."

"I would never forget. She's worried that when she meets the rest of your family, she'll face the same rejection she's met from others because of her birth. I could help ease some of that."

Joseph looked like she'd stuck a knife into his gut. "They're good people. They'll accept her. She needs to learn to rely on her family." The "not you," wasn't spoken, but Annabelle heard it loud and clear. This wasn't the Joseph challenging Annabelle tone she'd gotten used to. This was something darker, like that of a changed man.

She'd never expected that finding silver would change Joseph. But surely there was hope.

"I could stay," Annabelle offered. "I needn't leave right away. I can help get Nugget settled with your family, and—"

"No."

His easy dismissal and refusal to even hear her out stung worse than anything Slade had ever done to her.

"But if she's eased into the situation, and has people she knows around her, it won't be so bad when I—"

"You've done enough."

Who was this man, and where was Joseph? "Can we just talk about this? I mean, we—"

"There is no we, Annabelle. I've always made it clear that my family has to come first. Go visit your aunt. Live your life."

Before she could try to argue further, the door opened again, and Maddie ushered Nugget out with a bundle of clothes. "You come back and visit me anytime, you hear?"

Nugget nodded solemnly but made no move toward Joseph.

"Come on, Nugget, it's time to go." He held out his hand, and in the time it took for the sob welling inside Annabelle to finally find its way out, they were gone.

Chapter Twenty-Three

Annabelle hadn't seen Joseph in the days leading up to her departure. She'd even dallied over her shopping in hopes that she'd spot him or Nugget in one of the stores. But she hadn't been so fortunate. When she boarded the train to Denver, she did so with every ounce of her body wanting to throw herself to the ground, kicking, screaming and protesting that she didn't want to go.

But of course, she wouldn't. Not when she'd fought so long and hard to make this trip. Not when she'd finally earned her father's respect and belief in her dreams.

Not when Joseph was so cold.

Her father had somehow managed to procure her a seat in front of a family traveling with a little girl who might have been about Nugget's age. Though she was sure it wasn't intentional, there was something almost cruel about it. Especially when her chosen traveling companions were Lucy Simms and her mother. Mrs. Simms, apparently, had a fondness for children.

The little girl kept twisting in her seat and looking at Mrs. Simms wistfully. Which, of course, Mrs. Simms encouraged with her questions for the child.

Eight hours of this just might kill her.

It wasn't just the loss of Nugget she'd felt so keenly, but that of Joseph. Every time she thought of Nugget, she couldn't help but think of Joseph. And while she'd strengthened her relationship with her father, and their conversations were no longer as stilted, he didn't talk to her the way Joseph did. He didn't see her the way Joseph did.

How had finding his father's silver blinded him so?

Since rescuing her and Nugget from the mine, Joseph had barely talked to her.

So why did the thought of leaving him break her heart?

"I don't know what I'm going to do with the lot of you." His sister Mary smacked Joseph on the back of the head with a newspaper as she joined him at breakfast.

The table was full and set for everyone to join them, but so far, at half past the time they were due, Mary was the first to arrive.

"What's that supposed to mean?" He stared into his coffee already knowing her answer. He'd made a mess of things, thinking that this transition for his family would be easy.

Mary reached past him for one of the hotel's fine biscuits. "The girls are still pretending that the little one doesn't exist, and Daniel eggs them on. Then there's the two of you. The little girl, who won't say a word, and you, who's got the personality of a wet rag in a rainstorm."

He looked up at her. "A wet rag in a rainstorm? That's the best you can do?"

"You know what I mean." Mary took a sip of her

tea and stared at him. "It's like the life has been completely sucked out of you. Sometimes I think we were better off—"

"Don't say it." Joseph glared at her. "After everything we've all been through, everything I've done to get us all together."

He'd failed, that's what. The air in the dining room had suddenly grown a lot warmer. Possibly from Mary breathing down his neck. As he adjusted his collar, a bundle of energy and tears ran into his arms.

"I hate them. Papa said they'd love me, but they're horrible and mean, and I want Annabelle."

The only person Nugget would speak to was him. And mostly it was to ask if she could see Annabelle, or if Annabelle had written. Her train wasn't scheduled to leave for another hour yet, and already his baby sister wanted her to write.

He looked up at Mary, a silent plea for help.

"Nanette, you need to sit in your own seat."

Nugget looked up and glared at her older sister. "It's Nugget."

"Nanette is a good name, and it's listed in the family Bible as your given name, so you'll learn to answer to it."

Joseph rubbed the bridge of his nose. Ever since Mary found that entry in their pa's Bible, she'd insisted on calling Nugget Nanette, which had only made things worse. Annabelle would have found a way to smooth things over.

But he couldn't impose on her, not when it meant delaying her own dreams. No, he'd find a way to do it without her. After all he'd put her through, nearly getting her killed in the process, he owed her the freedom of her own life.

"Annabelle thought Nugget was a fine name," Nugget said, sticking her finger in the jam.

Mary turned her attention back to Joseph. "I would have at least liked to have met Annabelle. I can't imagine why she couldn't have had the decency to respond to my invitation to supper. She could have given me some idea as to how to manage Nanette. Instead, I've got to deal with her and five mutinous siblings who are all furious that you'd do this to them."

Joseph finally looked at his sister. "I didn't deliver the invitation."

"I beg your pardon?" The glare he got was no worse than he deserved. But he couldn't have borne it any other way.

"I didn't deliver it. She was busy with preparations for her trip."

"And she couldn't have delayed it by a few weeks, or even a few days?"

Mary's tone was enough to set the fire back in him. "It wasn't her choice. It was mine. I made her go."

Every morning, he questioned that decision. Wondered if he'd just taken her up on her offer of helping ease the transition with Nugget, if maybe his entire family wouldn't be ready to kill him right about now. If maybe they could write, and she'd…she'd what? Be willing to give up everything she'd dreamed of to raise his siblings? No. He couldn't do that to Annabelle.

Joseph reached for the pot to pour himself another cup of coffee, but Mary took it from him. "Now why would you do a stupid thing like that? It's as plain as anyone can see that you're in love with her. Mooning about, but dodging anytime you catch a glimpse of her so she doesn't notice you."

"I'm not the man for her," he said quietly. "She's wanted this trip for a long time, and I'm not going to stand in her way."

Mary shook her head, her face filled with disgust. "You didn't even tell her how you felt, did you?"

"There's no point." He refused to meet her eyes. "I know how she feels about mining. Annabelle doesn't want this life, and even if I were to convince her to stay for a while, she'd resent not getting to live her dreams."

"Is this because you asked her, or because you assumed and made the decision for her?"

He hadn't asked Annabelle. In fact, he'd pretty much pushed her out and forced her to go on that trip even when she'd tried to offer to delay it for him.

"You don't understand." He addressed Mary while hugging Nugget to him and smoothing her hair. "My responsibility lies with all of you. And Annabelle—"

"Could help you with that responsibility if you'd give her the chance. Why are all men so pigheaded as to think that they need to make the decisions for us?"

Joseph had never known Mary to be a bitter woman. But the anger spewed at him wasn't just about his treatment of Annabelle, but of something else.

"What's really going on? How is this situation with Annabelle suddenly about all men?"

Mary dabbed her lips with her napkin, then tossed it on the table. "Because it is. And because from everything I've seen and heard, you've found yourself a good woman to love and rather than going after it, you're hiding behind the excuse of providing for a family that's got everything it needs. You are just like Pa."

Her barb hit him firmly in the part of his heart that was still struggling to forgive a man who didn't deserve it. The table shook as Mary pushed back in her seat and stood. Even Nugget raised her head from his shoulder and looked up at her.

"Worst of all, you're hurting an innocent little girl because of your pride. Maybe Aunt Ina did take the switch to the younger ones more often than I'd like. But at least she never broke anyone's heart with her cruelty."

Mary stormed out of the restaurant, leaving Joseph alone with a teary-eyed little girl and a table full of food with no one to eat it.

No one had ever accused Joseph of being cruel before. Nor had anyone compared him to their pa. He'd only thought to spare Annabelle the trouble of being forced to decide between the duty of caring for a child who needed her and the dream she'd been putting aside for too long. But had he asked his pa about his reasons for his actions, would he have said something different than what Joseph had assumed?

Had his pa tried to get their ma to move the family west? Had he fought his feelings for Nugget's ma? Wes painted his pa as an honorable man who rubbed people the wrong way for not taking the side they wanted him to.

Joseph had done a lot of judging, and misjudging, as he'd been quick to accuse Annabelle of. But this last judgment was one he needed to let go of. Joseph needed to forgive his pa, and in forgiving, needed to let go of his own expectations of people and let them make their own decisions.

He looked down at Nugget, a child too young to understand the pain of his thoughts. "You never even got to say goodbye, did you?"

Nugget shook her head, messy half-curled hair that spoke of the others' neglect bouncing in every direction. Mary was trying, he'd give her that, but he could see the strain in her eyes when she looked at Nugget or had to do anything for their sister's care.

"Are they terribly mean to you?"

In front of Joseph, they put on a good front, but he'd seen past it. He'd just been helpless to do anything about it. With getting everything ready for their arrival, and trying to procure a house for the family, and putting things in order with the mine...

Nugget's slow nod tore at him.

Those things should have been secondary. And in his pride, he'd ignored the fact that Annabelle would have been able to help him. He hadn't even given her the consideration to discuss it.

"I'm sorry, Nugget." He pressed the little girl to his chest. "How about we try to catch that train to say goodbye?"

Nugget jumped off his lap and ran for the door.

Harrison Avenue was overly congested, already filled with wagons and people and more activity than he'd imagined normal for a day like today.

The train whistle blew when they were two blocks from the station.

Surely Annabelle was onboard by now.

Nugget's pace slowed. "It's too late."

"Sometimes they get delayed. We'll still try."

His spirits sagged when they arrived at the platform just as the train was pulling out.

He calculated how much money he had on him.

Based on getting his own family here, Annabelle would most likely have to spend a day or two in Denver to catch whichever train would take her east. So if he bought a ticket for the next train, they could get to Denver and then…

Surely they'd have a few hours to talk.

Nugget let go of his hand.

"Sweetheart, I'm sorry." He turned so he could bend down and talk to her, but she was gone.

"Nugget?" Joseph spun, looking around the station for the little girl. Though the train had departed, people still milled about, catching up on their business, and carting luggage to and fro.

"Nugget!"

He walked in the direction of the departing train. Had she run after it? Joseph picked up his pace, scouring the area for any sign of her. A porter laden with baggage bumped into him, blocking his path.

"Watch it!" the guy yelled as Joseph darted around him.

And then he stopped short.

There was Annabelle, kneeling in front of Nugget, her back to him. He took a deep breath, trying to compose himself as he approached.

"I cannot imagine what has gotten into your hair. You must've been tossing and turning all night to undo your curls and have only half your head fixed."

Annabelle put her hand in Nugget's hair, mussing it slightly before declaring, "Well, there's nothing that can be done, I suppose. We'll braid it, and you'll still be cute as a button. What do you think of that?"

Nugget didn't say anything, but looked up at him,

causing Annabelle to turn her head slightly until she noticed him. "Oh!"

Annabelle stood, then took Nugget's hand before facing him. "It seems like you've let her run absolutely wild since I've seen you last."

Her words rushed past him. "What are you... You're supposed to be..."

She looked at him long and hard. "I never could tolerate a bully. And frankly, your behavior toward me in regards to my leaving is nothing short of being bullied. Nugget needs me, and I'm not going to shirk my responsibility toward her just because you act like a bear about it."

Joseph closed his eyes. So that was it. More of Annabelle doing her duty. The worst of it was, he almost wanted to let her. But he couldn't. Didn't she understand that as much as everyone wanted to make him the bad guy, this was killing him?

"She's not your responsibility." He opened his eyes and looked at her. "You need to live your life, Annabelle. Follow your dreams."

"Of course she's my responsibility. I love Nugget, and I..." Annabelle looked away for a moment, then back at him. "Well, you don't leave the ones you love. Not when they need you and you need them."

The lump in his throat made it hard for Joseph to swallow, let alone speak. Annabelle had already done this for her father. And now for Nugget? It was too much.

But what was he supposed to do, to say? The selfish side of him wanted to keep her here, to be close to him, to help Nugget, to help Mary figure out how to keep peace, to...to do dozens of things, all of which had everything to do with him and his needs and none to do with hers.

"Please, Annabelle," he finally said. "I'll buy you a ticket for the next train. This is what you've always wanted, and I—"

"You have no idea what I've always wanted." She stamped her foot in such an insolent way that he wanted to kiss her. But that was beside the point.

"Yes, I admit that when we first met, I wanted nothing more than to leave this place and stay with my aunt, and discover the world outside. But I've grown since then. I've changed. And I can't believe that you'd think that the woman standing before you is still that silly girl who thought of nothing more than wearing the latest fashions."

Her words shamed him. Mostly because he'd tried so hard not to fall in love with that silly girl, but as he watched her grow into the woman standing before him, he'd realized that there was nothing about her, including her silliness, that he didn't love. He hadn't given her the courtesy of an explanation, and now it was time to make good on changing his earlier regrets.

"All right, Annabelle." Joseph took a deep breath. "What do you want?"

The triumphant grin she gave him nearly slayed him. Did she have any idea what that grin did to a man? Of course she did.

Joseph shook his head, trying to rid himself of all inappropriate thoughts, especially the urge to kiss her senseless.

"I want to stay here and see to it that Nugget is properly settled in with the rest of her family. I want to go back to the camp and spend more time with Gertie, and maybe get Polly to start talking to me again. I want you to talk to me like you used to, and for us to be friends again."

Friends. Joseph wanted to kiss Annabelle senseless, and she wanted to talk about their friendship.

"I'm sorry, Annabelle. That's not possible. I can't be friends with you."

"Oh." Her face fell, and those pretty little dimples that punctuated every point she made disappeared. "I don't know what I did to offend you, but maybe I could—"

"You misunderstand."

He hated the thought of baring his heart like this, of putting himself out for Miss Annabelle Lassiter to reject, but he also couldn't bear the thought of her feeling guilty over ruining yet another relationship.

"I can't settle for friendship with you. Not anymore. I see you differently. Not as a friend, not as a sister, but in such a way that is entirely inappropriate for…"

Were her cheeks turning pink? And, in the difficulty of him explaining a rather embarrassing and untenable position, a saucy grin twitched at the edges of her lips.

Annabelle was actually enjoying this.

Worse, when he looked over at Nugget, the little imp had started giggling.

But perhaps worst of all, others had stopped what they were doing and were completely, without any shame, eavesdropping on the conversation.

Joseph straightened. "Well… I think that about covers it." He held out his hand. "Nugget, come on. We need to…"

Escape was the first thought that came to mind. But Nugget stood there, shaking her head.

"You are never going to get her to marry you like that. You have to get romantical and tell Annabelle that you love her, then take her in your arms, and—"

"Nugget!" Both he and Annabelle said it in unison.

And when Annabelle knelt to the little girl, her face still red, Joseph understood.

"I told you why I sent you away," he said quietly. "You thought it was because my regard had changed. The truth of the matter is that I wanted you to stay, desperately. Not for Nugget's sake, though that's a bonus, but for mine."

Annabelle finally looked up at him, murmured softly to Nugget, then stood.

"I thought that the noble thing to do when you love someone is to give up what you want for what they want," Joseph continued. "But I didn't find out what you wanted, only made assumptions based on what you'd told me. I love you, Annabelle. And I wanted your dreams for you more than I wanted mine. I'm sorry that it caused you pain."

"Of course it caused me pain. Because I love you, too, and I didn't know that you loved me back. So it's all forgiven. I'm here now, and here is where I will stay."

They stood there in silence for a brief moment, interrupted by a tiny voice that asked, "Are you going to kiss her now?"

So he did.

Epilogue

One year later

Annabelle stood on the porch, watching for the children to arrive home. At half past three, they should have been there nearly a quarter of an hour ago. She smoothed the apron over her rounded belly and debated about taking it off. There was still so much baking to be done for tonight's church supper. Maddie was having a tougher time keeping up with the miners' needs, so Annabelle had agreed to do some of the cooking at her home.

The men were due at any time to help carry everything to the church. Now that Annabelle's condition was more advanced, both Joseph and her father said she shouldn't be lifting heavy things. Which meant relying on others helping her for a change. But as she glanced back down the street, worries about whether or not the children had met with foul play took over.

There were, Annabelle told herself, five of them. Surely together, they were safe enough walking home from school. At least that's what Joseph always argued. Evelyn, Helen, Daniel, Bess and Nugget could take care of themselves. A handful, but most of the time, Mary and Rose were such a big help that Annabelle hardly noticed.

However, on days like today, when Annabelle scurried down the street toward the school, she wondered how she thought she could manage all these children, help with her father's ministry and care for a baby besides. But if something happened to the children—

Annabelle's heart constricted, and she turned the corner. Nugget came running toward her, screeching, "Mama!"

She embraced the little girl, and continued in the direction from which Nugget had come.

Daniel was engaged in a fistfight with another boy, and the girls were egging him on as other children circled the fighting boys, cheering.

"Daniel Edward Stone!" Annabelle pushed through the crowd. "I insist you stop this minute!"

"Not until he apologizes for what he said about my sister!"

Before he could get another punch in, her father and Joseph arrived and pulled the two boys apart.

Nugget huddled at Annabelle's side. "Mama, please don't be mad at Daniel."

The little girl had taken to calling her Mama shortly before her wedding to Joseph. Even though certain people, like the unfortunate boy whom her father was sternly lecturing, didn't seem to want to forget where Nugget came from, most of the time, no one remembered Nugget wasn't her daughter. And, as Annabelle tightened her arm around the little girl, she wasn't sure she could remember a time when Nugget wasn't hers.

"You know fighting is wrong," Joseph told Daniel sternly.

"So's what he said about my sister."

Though Annabelle knew she needed to remain quiet and let Joseph do the parenting, part of her wanted to cheer for the fact that the boy who once refused to even look at Nugget, let alone call her sister, was now fighting for the little girl's honor.

"The other boy started it," chorused Evelyn, Helen and Bess.

Annabelle looked down at Nugget. "That so?"

Nugget shrugged. Apparently, she wasn't going to risk her newfound solidarity with her siblings.

Joseph escorted Daniel to where they were waiting, and Annabelle noticed her father walking the other boy down the street. Probably to talk to his parents.

The other three girls trudged behind, their heads low, as though they thought the other boy had Daniel's beating coming. Annabelle sighed. Raising Joseph's siblings was not for the faint of heart. But watching them heal from the pain of their rough past and come to love one another was worth it.

Joseph came along Annabelle's other side and slipped his hand in hers. "Never a dull moment, is it?"

"Of course not." Until she'd found herself with a houseful again, she hadn't realized just how much she'd missed having the warm bodies, the laughter and even the fights to add color to her life. Some days, she still missed her siblings, especially Susannah, and most days, she desperately missed her mother. For only a mother could advise her on how to handle this rambunctious crew.

A carriage was parked in front of their house.

"Caitlin!" Nugget pulled away from Annabelle's hand and dashed in the direction of the carriage, her siblings following suit.

Annabelle looked over at Joseph. "I didn't know

Gertie was coming down today. I thought they were waiting until Saturday."

"I thought you'd like having her sooner." A knowing look filled his face. "You've been overly tired lately, and she told me to send for her if you needed help."

No, Annabelle didn't have a mother to advise her on such things. But she had Gertie, who loved her like one. Even though Gertie would never replace her mother, and there were times when having Gertie around increased the ache of her mother's absence, mostly, Annabelle didn't know what she'd do without the other woman.

"Daniel, what have you done to your eye?" Gertie's exclamation told Annabelle that Gertie probably had plenty of experience dealing with her own sons' fights. Later, the other woman could help her figure out how to handle this latest development.

Annabelle turned to Joseph and kissed him softly. "Thank you. You always seem to know just what I need."

He kissed her back, then grinned. "Or maybe I want to get a little time alone with you myself. Won't be much longer until we've also got a baby to manage, so I figured I'd best take advantage while I still can."

This time, Annabelle didn't stop herself from throwing her arms around him. Well, as best as she could fit, anyway. She was, after all, expecting a baby. And even though some ladies in town said it simply wasn't done when one was in such a delicate condition, she kissed her husband until they were both breathless. Let everyone say what they will. Annabelle Lassiter Stone had opened her heart to love, and now that she'd found it, she wasn't about to let anyone tell her not to show it.

* * * * *

Jessica Nelson believes romance happens every day and thinks the greatest, most intense romance comes from a God who woos people to Himself with passionate tenderness. When Jessica is not chasing her three beautiful, wild little boys around the living room, she can be found staring into space as she plots her next story, daydreams about raspberry mochas or plans chocolate for dinner.

Books by Jessica Nelson

Love Inspired Historical

Love on the Range
Family on the Range
The Matchmaker's Match
A Hasty Betrothal
The Unconventional Governess

Visit the Author Profile page
at Harlequin.com for more titles.

FAMILY ON THE RANGE

Jessica Nelson

He shall call upon me, and I will answer him:
I will be with him in trouble; I will deliver him,
and honour him.
—*Psalms* 91:15

Dedicated to my sister Josephine, who has Mary's heart. And to my niece Jayla, who is Josie.

Chapter One

June 1920
Oregon

"Bag the body and don't forget to ink his prints." Special Agent Lou Riley moved away from the man who had met his demise in the bowels of an illegal liquor operation. He slipped Wrigley's peppermint gum into his mouth and gnawed on it as he thought through his circumstances.

This dead witness meant more time on assignment trying to track down the one who'd hired the foreign bootlegger to do his dirty work.

Prohibition in Oregon wasn't a thing to be trifled with. After a decade of chasing murderers, traitors and thieves in his job as special agent for the Bureau of Investigation, Lou guessed helping the local police track speakeasies and distilleries served him well enough.

Better than the more dangerous spying he'd done until this past year.

He rubbed the back of his neck, feeling the stress of a hard day's work combined with personal pressures.

Day before last he'd left his secluded ranch to tackle this assignment. His housekeeper, Mary, had everything under control at home, but he couldn't shake his unease. Over a year ago his niece and his best friend, Trevor, had married, and ever since he'd been thinking about the past. About people long gone. And lately, when he saw Mary, a strange tension filled him, which was odd because they'd always had an easygoing rapport in the twelve years she'd been his employee.

Not that his job ever kept him home with her for long.

Grimacing at the kink in his left shoulder, he wheeled around and left the dim building. An overcast afternoon greeted him, heavy with mist and promising rain. He nodded to one of his field agents as he picked his way to the bureau's automobile.

Summers in Oregon weren't exactly sunny. Not warm, either. He missed the aridness of his home in east Oregon, the openness of the desert range. Small cities like this one tended to weigh him down with memories. Buildings pressed in on him....

He shrugged the morbidity away.

Every time he went home, saw Mary, he left feeling this way. Maybe it was her trusting smile or the way her eyes lit with welcome when he walked in the door. Like someone else's long ago. Mary's look stirred up memories, blew the dust of time off them—he stopped himself, stuttering to a halt near a gutter. He couldn't go there. Not ever again.

"Hey, mister!"

Lou turned slowly at the intrusion, his hand moving to the weapon at his hip beneath his coat. "You talking to me?"

"That's right." A shadow slid out from an alley to

Lou's left, heavy Irish accent lilting the man's syllables. "You the agent in charge down the road?"

"What's it to you?"

"I got information on who was supplying the gig down there." The man moved closer, and Lou caught a whiff of sour fish as well as a glimpse of green eyes and blond mustache.

"Let's take this downtown. Put it on paper." That pesky muscle cramped in Lou's back again and he fought not to wince. He was thirty-six years old, but he felt sixty today.

"I'll just slip you the information here, quiet-like."

Lou's brows lowered. He looked down the street. His agents were busy coordinating the bust, but something felt off. Every instinct warned him to draw his weapon.

He never discounted his instincts.

Drawing his revolver, he beckoned the man. "Come into the light."

"And get pinned for bootleggin'? Not on your life, mister."

"Then stay right there. I'll get a pen and—"

"This won't take long." The man pulled back suddenly.

Lou's skin prickled.

Shadows closed over where the man had been as he slipped from view. Alert, Lou spun away from the blond and faced the road. A sharp ping split the night before his chest caught fire in a familiar, unwelcome sensation.

Pivoting, he backed into the shadows. Shouts from down the road reached his hearing, but whoever had shot him took off. The sound of the shooter's footsteps was distinctive, a smart uneven clip of metal against cobblestone. Almost like spurs…. The sound faded, merging with other, faster steps.

His shoulder burned. He groaned as the strength left his legs.

This was real bad. Worse than a shot in the leg or shoulder. Body numbing, he crumpled to the ground. He couldn't keep his eyes open. The sounds around him muffled and the last image he saw was Mary's dark eyes, the curve of her lips when she opened the door to welcome him home.

Would he see her again?

Loneliness never killed a person.

Or so Mary O'Roarke tried to tell herself as she mentally prepared for a visit with her mother. Surely once she stated her wishes, her mother would then see reason and quit insisting on living by herself.

Oregon's summer sun rolled above Mary, hot though not quite to its zenith. She slowed her mare outside the Paiute encampment where her mother lived. *Alone.* With no one to rely on. It was not the way an elderly woman should live, and she'd told her mother so many times.

Only now did she have the means with which to help her, and no one could stop her, not even her stubborn employer who owned the ranch where she worked and, until recently, lived. She'd bought an old friend's house next to the ranch, the first home she'd ever owned in all her thirty years, and maybe that might convince her mother to come back with her.

Feeling hopeful, Mary turned the horse in the direction of her mother's dwelling.

The encampment consisted of tents and campfires. The odor of rabbit flesh hung in the air. The government did not appear to care that native Paiutes preferred homes made from various woods and sagebrush, and instead provided them with only the means to make tepees. Mary nodded to those she passed. Some wore the rabbit robes for which her mother's people were known. Others, mostly men, dressed in the white man's garb. Trousers, hats.

She came to her mother's tepee and dismounted. No hitching post for her mare, so she tied the reins to a straggly shrub nearby. Children whispered and giggled, circling but not coming close. A stray dog loped over and the children chased it, their ill-fitting clothes doing nothing to hinder their laughter.

A wistful smile pulled at Mary's lips. She'd longed to have children many years ago. Before the trauma of her past had wrenched her from any chance of a normal life. Perhaps she'd grown too old now, too set in her ways…. She certainly knew nothing about the ways of motherhood. Sighing, she bent near the entrance of her mother's tent.

"It's Mary. I've come to visit."

A rustle ensued. Then the grunt that was Rose's answer. Mary twisted the flap to the side and entered the tent. The interior never failed to elicit a strange sense of distance. This was her mother's life now, a return to her roots, but it had never been Mary's life. The setting filled her with disquiet and a peculiar sense of displacement.

As a child she'd lived in the white man's world. Her father was Irish and while he worked the docks, her mother had used her beauty to bring in money at various brothels. It had been an odd childhood, full of travel and sporadic learning. When she was twelve, her father had abandoned them, followed shortly by her mother.

Tasting bitterness, Mary swallowed and prayed for peace.

"You brought me something?" Her mother sat to the side, high cheekbones cloaked with lined, leathery skin. The map of her broken life.

"Yes, willow and sagebrush bark." She placed the offerings next to the stack of intricate baskets Rose weaved to sell.

They lapsed into awkward conversation. Mostly talk of weather.

"I have my own home," she told her mother at last, warming to her subject. This was why she'd come. To coax Rose into living with her. At her mother's look of surprise, Mary continued, "I've bought Trevor's house. Now that he's married, he plans to find a place in town for when he and Gracie don't stay at the ranch. I would like you to come live with me."

An old argument, but she tried again, hoping this to be the day her mother might surrender.

"Interesting," Rose murmured, stroking the thick rabbit robe on her lap. "Now you will be alone with your employer?"

"Lou?"

"You have great *besa soobedda* for him."

"A what?" Though Mary spoke some Paiute, she wasn't fluent and disliked when her mother used language she hadn't taught her only daughter.

A crooked smile lifted the corner of Rose's lips. "*Besa soobedda* is love, the sweet emotional bond between a man and his wife."

Mary stiffened as a peculiar heat seeped through

her. She'd lived at the ranch for twelve years and never had she entertained such a thought about her employer. Granted, he was charming and funny. He had hired her as his housekeeper when she was eighteen, offering his home as a refuge after she'd been rescued from the notorious slave trader Mendez. Lou's kindness would never be forgotten. But love?

"We have no such love," she denied. "I feel a sister's affection for him." Even as she spoke, she wondered if that was true. When she'd told him goodbye yesterday, there had been the oddest regret creeping through her. Unnerved, she continued, "I should leave if you do not wish to come with me at this time."

"Wait!" Her mother struggled to a standing position, and Mary tried not to cringe at how age and worries had stolen her mother's strength. Perhaps loneliness would not kill her mother but rather another more obvious ailment. She swallowed hard at the thought.

Rose shuffled toward a trunk at the other side of the tepee. Bending, she opened it. "I have something for you."

"I want you to come home with me. I need nothing else."

"This is important."

A small blond head popped up out of the trunk. "Hiya!"

Mary started. "What is that?"

"I'm a little girl." The child clambered out of the trunk and gave Mary a decidedly mischievous smirk. "Are you going to be my mother?"

Startled, Mary groped for words. Finally, she said, "I'm not a mother to anyone."

"Oh, but I need one. Just for a bit, you see, until I go

home to my real mama." The girl shot a cheeky, gap-toothed grin up at Rose, who reached down to stroke the girl's head.

The movement snapped Mary from her shocked paralysis. "You have someone's child? Do you know the penalty for such a thing?"

Rose met her accusation with a steady look. "She is in danger. You have a home apart from Lou now. You can hide her."

"No." She shook her head, feeling her braid swing against her back. "No, I can't do it."

"My daughter, I need you." Her mother shuffled forward. "I cannot keep her much longer."

Mary glanced at the child, who'd shifted her attention to the baskets and studiously went about picking one apart. "Who is she?"

"I don't know."

"My name's Josie Silver," the girl put in. "I live in Portland but my mama's not home right now."

"Where is she?" Mary asked. "How about your father?"

The girl lifted her shoulders. "I don't know, and I don't have a papa. I want to stay here."

Mary glared at her mother. "Where did you find her?"

"Half-dead near Harney Lake, one week ago."

She shuddered. "That's horrible. You should've taken her to the authorities."

Her mother grimaced. "I wasn't supposed to be out there."

"Mother."

"Don't berate me. You say you follow Jesus. A woman in town says He helps the poor and motherless. This child is that, and I—" Her mother peeked at the girl and lowered her voice. "I'm begging you to hide her until I send word it's safe."

"This makes no sense. How do you know she's not safe?"

"Her guardian has posted a reward for her."

"You said you didn't know who she is? Return her." Mary frowned. Where was the problem if someone had offered a reward? They already knew the child's mother's name. Confused and feeling lost in the maze of her mother's reasoning, she backed toward the door flap.

"I know the guardian," her mother said quietly. "He is not a man to be trifled with."

Uncharacteristic impatience rushed through Mary. "Take care of the matter, then." She had no room, no time, for a child.

I'm afraid.

The thought slammed into her. Tension hovered at the base of her skull, knotting and twining the muscles of her neck.

Her mother moved closer, bringing her once-beautiful features near. "I knew him when you were a child. In my past."

Mary's hand flew to her lips, but the movement didn't stifle her gasp.

"Yes." Her mother nodded. "Now you understand. He is a bad man, and I do not know why this child lay in the desert like a starved and wounded animal, but I will not return her. He will come looking, and it will be impossible for me to hide her from others."

"I'll take her," Mary said through numb lips.

It was true she could take the child to her new home,

but for how long? The girl couldn't live with her indefinitely. The authorities must be contacted.

What would Lou say about a child near his secluded ranch, a haven he'd created for secret agents of the Bureau of Investigation and not for child rearing?

The little girl stared at her with big eyes, and she winced.

Why should she care what Lou thought? Yes, he employed her to keep his house, but she'd just bought her own home, her first step toward a more independent life. Determination straightened her backbone. If she was going to stop being afraid, to start living again, then she must put Lou and everything he represented behind her.

Could she do that, though?

Thank goodness he wouldn't be home for several weeks. That gave her time to return Josie to her mother and persuade her own mother to come live with her. Because if Lou were home, he'd protest, and she didn't know if she had the backbone to stand up for what she thought was right.

Chapter Two

An uncomfortable dryness at the roof of Lou's mouth woke him. His tongue felt oversize, and his throat worked to swallow. He opened his eyes to find himself in the dark tones of his bedroom. A sense of claustrophobia wrapped galvanizing tentacles around him.

He tried to shove upward, but fierce pain in his chest snatched the breath from his lungs. Forced to lie still, he took shallow breaths while the pulsating daggers near his upper rib cage ebbed. Only thirty-six. It wasn't fair to feel this way.

"Water," he croaked.

Movement to his left, and then a firm hand slipped under his neck. Relieved, Lou allowed his head to tip forward so he could drink from the proffered cup.

The hand took the water away too quickly. After resting his head back on the pillow, Mary crossed his line of vision, disappeared, and then reappeared on his right side.

Hair pulled back in a bun, she might've passed for any Irish lass but for the duskiness of her skin and the high cheekbones that pronounced her native heritage. As usual, the sight of her stunned Lou for a moment.

His lids lowered and he watched as she bustled with his covers, stretching and straightening. Finally, she patted them, a satisfied look relaxing the line of her full lips. She turned her gaze to him.

Immediately he noted the strange look in her eyes. Normally she appeared serene, gentle, timid even. Today, however, wariness shadowed her gaze, something he'd only seen in her eyes when she dealt with others. Never with him.

He didn't like that something was wrong with her. He would fix it, whatever it was. Frowning, he ignored the burn in his throat to speak. "Something's wrong."

Her eyelids flickered before she turned away. "You're still thirsty."

The water she brought him slid down easy, coating the soreness with cool relief. Cleared his head, too, so he could more closely examine the situation. Something was off. Mary's evasion, that look on her face...

"Help me up," he said.

She set the cup on his dresser and then returned, sitting at the edge of his bed, just out of reach. Her scent, a strange mix of sage and flowers, filled his senses and taunted him.

"I won't help you sit up. You might tear your stitches," she replied. Her pronunciation was technically correct, but an exotic flavor rounded each of her words, courtesy of her trilingual skills.

"How long have I been out?"

"You left the ranch a little less than a week ago. I believe two days into your assignment you were shot and then taken to the hospital. They removed the bullet and telegrammed James."

Her mention of his ranch hand and long-time friend failed to comfort.

"Did they catch the shooter?"

"No one has told me much. James picked you up from the hospital and brought you here. He drove to town this morning to find supplies to keep your wound clean, but he should be back this afternoon." Her brow lined. "You have been going in and out of consciousness for days now. How do you feel?"

Confused. He felt confused and bothered.

"Sore," he answered shortly. "Where's my M&P?" His Smith & Wesson military and police revolver had kept him company for almost twenty years. He didn't plan on losing it now.

The lines in her forehead deepened. "I put it somewhere safe."

He pushed up, purpose fueling his movement. His vision blackened for a moment as his upper body throbbed with pain, but he ignored the sensation.

"Bring it to me," he managed to say.

"You can't move like that." Mary leaned over him, her features drawn with worry. "You almost died. Someone tried to kill you, and that's why the bureau decided it was best to get you here, to the safe house. You are on temporary leave until you recover."

Lou closed his eyes and waited for the nausea and torturous aches in his body to pass. This couldn't be happening. He needed his job. The last place he wanted to be stuck at was the ranch.

"Let me give you some pain medication." Mary's voice drifted over him.

"No," he said, voice rough. "Not yet. This place isn't safe."

"Mendez is dead."

Lou forced his eyes to open when what he wanted more than anything was to sleep. "He might've passed our location on to one of his buddies."

Twelve years ago, Mary had been kidnapped by a man called Mendez. She'd been his first kidnapping and, thankfully, had been rescued by government agent Striker, aka Lou's friend Trevor, before Mendez could sell her.

Unfortunately, her rescue hadn't stopped Mendez from becoming a notorious slave trader, known for trafficking women down to Mexico.

Trevor spent the next ten years as a shadow, tracking Mendez and rescuing what women he could while hiding behind his nickname, Striker. And Mendez had developed an obsession to pay Striker back for foiling his moneymaking kidnapping schemes. Out of fear, and knowing Mendez wanted to use Mary to draw Striker out from his anonymity, she'd been hiding on this ranch until two Christmases ago, when Mendez had found her again. He'd attempted to kidnap Mary but had accidentally taken Lou's niece, Gracie, instead.

Thanks to Gracie's ingenuity, she'd escaped and had been found by Trevor. Mendez and his men had died of poisoning unrelated to their kidnapping plans, but Lou couldn't shake the feeling this place wasn't safe anymore. He didn't want Mary to see the depth of his worry, though. She had enough burdens to carry.

Feeling exhausted yet unwilling to surrender consciousness, he met her gaze. "Trevor and I buried Mendez. You don't have to worry about him. But our cover is gone…." He paused for breath. He'd been shot before, stabbed, even, but never had he felt this tired.

"Take the medicine." A note of stubborn finality crept into her voice. "I will speak with you about this later."

Lou blinked hard against the tide of sleep pulling his lids closed. Mary wavered in front of him, holding out some foul-smelling concoction. She pressed the spoon against his lips, and he grabbed her wrist. Keeping his gaze pinned on hers, he swallowed but didn't let go of the delicate bones beneath his fingers.

Her eyes widened, and a blush spread across her face at his touch. She tried to pull away, but he tightened his grip.

"Thank…you." He struggled to speak without slurring, to give her a reassuring smile.

"You shouldn't talk right now." She lifted her other hand to his brow, smoothing his hair with warm, firm fingers. "I hear the wagon. James will be in at any minute."

It seemed only a second to Lou until he heard his ranch hand and old friend James in the room. "Got him laudanum. Some Oregon grape root, too."

Mary rose and disappeared from Lou's view. He stifled the urge to shout and demand someone help him up from this bothersome bed. They came back, James smirking down at him.

"Had to go and get yourself shot, boss?" He swiped the hat off his head and rubbed the gnarled mass of hair above his ears. "Leave us with all the ranch work while you catch them bootleggers, and now look at ya."

"Can you watch him for me?"

"I don't need watching," Lou told Mary crossly, annoyance temporarily strengthening him. "Get a message to Hayworth that I need to be moved. Maybe to headquarters." Surely his superior would approve a move under the circumstances.

James bent over him and squinted. "You sayin' the ranch ain't safe?"

"Not with me here. These people mean business. If Mendez found us, chances are someone else…will… too." Lou struggled for breath, hating the weakness of his body. If he'd just gone with his gut instead of standing in the road like a yellow-bellied pansy, he might be flushing out criminals at this very moment.

Now he was trapped here. Forced to see Mary every day, when every second just looking at her made him remember more and more of his past. It didn't used to be this way. He didn't like how things had changed.

He aimed to get out of here before things spiraled out of control.

"Let us take care of you." Mary swished over, bringing medicine with her. "Here, gently now."

Lou took the medicine, unable to fight the droop of his lids any longer. Mary's and James' voices became distant murmurs, then faded away.

He wanted sleep, but instead images from the past flashed through him. His mother and father. His brother with his wife. His niece, Gracie.

And Abby.

Sarah had named Abigail after her mother. He moaned, thrashing his head, willing the images to leave. To stop assaulting him.

His chest burned, but he couldn't tell if it was the wound or his heart.

More laudanum. That was what he needed.

"Mary," he whispered.

Nothing.

"Mary." He tried again, forcing his windpipe to push out more air. A creak followed his plea, but he didn't smell her.

An odd sound cut through the air. Like a…giggle?

He cocked an eye open. With the medicine swimming through his blood, the room tilted to the side. The doorway wavered, and for a second he thought he saw a thatch of blond hair beneath the doorknob.

"Abby," he breathed. A hard rush of pain splintered through his chest, cutting off his air and making his eyes burn. Just one more look. After all these years, he wanted to see her one more time.

He waited. A second later the door creaked again, and Abby poked her head through. She shot him a wide smile that showed off teeth with a gap between them the size of Texas. Had he missed her losing teeth, then? It seemed she'd just started cutting them.

Sarah said she ate everything in sight. A smile curled up inside Lou like a soft blanket over his heart. "Abby, come here. Give Daddy a hug."

Her giggle sprinkled through the air, light and fuzzy, followed by a sweet rush of darkness that took him to a warm and gentle place.

Lou Riley was seeing dead people.

Unable to shake the morbid thought, he opened his eyes. Bright morning sun poured through the window, highlighting the suspiciously clean lines of his room. Mary had been in again, dusting and cleaning. He groaned, wincing as a nasty throb of pain jolted through his temples.

His chest felt better, though. He tried shifting in the bed. His bandages crinkled with the movement, and a definite soreness invaded his muscles. No fever, no infection, which was a good thing. He'd be glad to discontinue this medicine, glad to get his head turned straight, glad to put an end to the dreams plaguing his sleep.

"There you are, sleepyhead." Mary floated into the room, her hair a shiny ebony in the morning light. Her features appeared smooth and even, a hint of worry not evident. He must be doing great.

Despite his aches, he grinned at her. "Right where I've been the past week."

"Oh, not that long." Blushing in response to his flirtatious smile, she set a tray on the bed.

Lou sniffed the air. "Pancakes?" he asked hopefully.

"Yep."

He took a closer look. "Is that a…rattler?" He glanced at Mary. The burnished rose color of her cheeks deepened.

"I was experimenting with shapes. A little artistic license. I'm not sure how that was placed on the tray." She frowned and didn't meet his eyes.

Interesting. He took the plate she held out to him and loaded up. Days of no food had made him famished. His stomach hurt just looking at it all. But that snake… A frown took possession of his mouth.

He settled against his pillow, carefully moving the plate to his lap. "You know, my mom used to make me and my brother animal-shaped pancakes."

"Really?" Mary fiddled with the sheets on the bed.

"Oh, yeah." He nodded, never taking his gaze from her face. An uneasy suspicion was taking root. "Moms do it for kids all the time."

"Not all mothers," she interjected.

"Creative moms." He amended the sentence with a flourish of his fork. "Speaking of kids, you might want to lighten my laudanum dosage. I've been seeing things."

Mary moved toward the dresser, her back to him. For a moment, Lou was distracted by the waves of hair that fell like a silk waterfall against her shoulders. He'd forgotten how dark her hair was, thick, and blacker than a sky bereft of stars.

In all their years of knowing each other, he didn't think he'd ever touched her hair before. In fact, he made certain not to unnecessarily touch her. To give her space and to help her feel safe. His general policy regarding women involved distance. Women were lovely creatures, interesting, a tad difficult, but getting mixed up with a woman took more stamina than Lou was inclined to expend.

Relationships meant pain. He'd learned that early on.

Clenching and unclenching his fingers, he willed the itch to touch Mary to leave.

"What have you been seeing?" she finally asked.

He studied her, noting the stiffness in her shoulders. "Things that shouldn't be here."

"Oh?" She pivoted toward him.

The look of obstinacy on her face might've made him laugh if he didn't realize it meant something he wouldn't like.

"A kid," he said flatly.

She didn't respond at first. Then a serene mask settled over her face. Her armor. Seeing it confirmed his suspicion that she was hiding something. A lead weight settled in his belly, feeling almost like disappointment.

"What's going on?"

Her eyelids flickered. "You haven't been seeing things. There is a child here, found abandoned by the lake. But she's not staying long," she rushed on. "I've made efforts to find her mother and hope to hear something soon."

He groaned. Impatience and a different kind of pain burned through him. He wanted to leap off the bed and make her see reason. His limitations, this inconvenient injury, might prove to be his undoing. "The girl can't stay. This place is too dangerous for a child. Take her to the sheriff."

He waited for Mary's reaction to his words. As usual, she withdrew. He could sense the retreat, see it in the way she backed up, eyes shuttered, face expressionless.

How many times had he seen this look of hers? From the moment she'd been brought to the ranch, bruised in spirit, a desperate eighteen-year-old in need of rescuing, he'd known she was different. Vulnerable. He'd taken her under his protection, watched out for her even though he'd only been twenty-four and dealing with his own sorrows.

Lou ground his teeth, trying not to scowl and failing. She met the look with a guarded demeanor.

"I know you're angry." Her voice came out tiny, quiet.

"I'm not angry, but it's important for that little girl to be home. I can find her family within a day."

"No." She moved forward. "You have to stay in bed. Rest and recuperate."

Suddenly the door to the room whipped open. James stood in the doorway, hair askew and whiskers bunching.

"Josie's gone."

Mary whirled, her hand to her chest. "You were supposed to watch her!"

"The little whippersnapper slipped out of my sight," James grumbled. "She wanted cocoa."

Mary picked up her skirts before casting Lou a worried look. "I have my own home now. You can't tell me who's allowed to stay there."

He narrowed his gaze. It sounded as if she was referencing her mother, the only person she argued with him about. Otherwise she never spoke up, never acted feisty. His niece, Gracie, must've influenced her more than he realized.

It was a nice change from her natural timidity.

Almost smiling, he made to speak but was interrupted by a harsh knocking from below. The sound reverberated up the stairs. Every muscle in his body tensed. No one should be knocking on a secluded ranch's door.

"Get me my derringer." He pointed to his dresser, where he hid a backup.

"Where?" Mary moved toward the dresser.

"Behind, on the floor."

She reached down and picked it up, then brought it to him.

Their fingers brushed when she set the heavy weapon in his hand. She was warm, gentle, and she shouldn't be exposed to danger. His grip tightened as he drew the weapon from her and slipped it beneath the sheets.

Her eyes widened, never leaving his, irises dark with strain. "I have to find Josie."

Lou nodded. "James," he said without looking at his employee, "answer the door. Mary, find the girl and keep her safe."

They rushed out, and Lou leaned back with a grunt.

His head hurt. At least the butt of his gun lay solidly in his palm, cool to the touch, reassuring with its heavy weight and the promise of security.

He looked to the thick door, which remained cracked, and listened for sound from downstairs. If Mary and James needed him, he'd be useless. Did he even have the strength to stand? Shifting in his bed, he gingerly sat forward.

A rush of dizziness pressed in on his head, and the edges of his vision grayed. Groaning, he lay back. How could he have let this happen? He should've stayed away from the prohibition problems Oregon had. But he loved challenges, and aiding the local police gave him something to focus on.

Frowning, he cradled his gun and watched the door.

A rustle sounded. Voices drifted up, low tones, calm sounding. Maybe it was just a homesteader passing through. A lot of his neighbors were leaving their small ranches, abandoning them to the wild desert of Harney County.

The rustle caught his attention again. Ears perked, he held his breath.

A ball of pink rolled out from under the bed and into his line of sight.

Chapter Three

Lou jerked back, causing shards of pain to splinter across his chest. Gut tight, he eyed the little girl as she stood and brushed off her fluffy dress. Her hair was a mass of blond curls that framed a round face, complete with a dimple and a decidedly crooked smile.

"Hi, mister. My name's Josie." She skipped to him and shoved her hand in his face. "Nice to meet ya."

He ignored her hand, giving her the darkest glare he could muster.

Her eyes were a deep blue, almost violet. He'd mistaken her for Abby, but now that she stood before him, in the light of morning, he could see the differences. Abby's eyes had been a bright blue, like his.

A lump clogged his windpipe. Her hair had been dark, like her mother's, and straight as a horse's mane. This girl before him wore a smile that showed off rows of teeth, complete with gaps. Abby hadn't lived long enough to get all hers, let alone lose any.

Because his mouth felt drier than Oregon's Alvord Desert on a summer noon, he couldn't speak, could only wordlessly watch this little person, the kind he'd stayed away from for more than a decade.

"Are you okay?" The girl poked his arm, her touch a hot brand that seared through his skin, straight to his heart. "You look scared. I promise I won't hurt you. I just need a family for a little while." She flashed that dimple at him again and winked.

Caught off guard, a rusty chuckle broke loose, sounding like an old gate he used to hear creaking in the breeze outside his childhood home.

"Who's your father?" he asked.

"I don't have one," she said simply. She rounded the bed, grabbed the water off the bedside table and carefully brought it to him. The look of concentration on her cherubic face did something funny to Lou's middle, almost made him want to smile again. When she reached the bed, she brought the water close to his mouth.

"You sound thirsty. Sometimes my dog is thirsty, too. I always bring her water."

"Thank you." He took the cup and sipped, mind working overtime. Surely a family was looking for this girl. She looked clean and bright, rosy cheeks, healthy hair, unbothered by whatever had happened to bring her here. "You know you'll have to go home."

Josie tilted her head, her never-ending dimple bugging the tar out of him. The girl was too cute for her own good. She'd cause trouble, no doubt about that.

She appeared to be mulling over his words. "I don't think I have a home anymore," she finally said.

No father and no home? He found that hard to believe.

Footsteps in the hall turned Josie's head. There was something familiar in the cadence of the steps.... He couldn't place what. Then the low rumble of men's voices reached him. James sounded ornery and gruff. He didn't recognize the man's voice, though it held a definite Southern lilt.

Someone from the bureau, then? They could help find Josie's parents, or at least put her in an orphanage. The thought of an orphanage unexpectedly filled him with regret, a physical punch that stole the breath from his lungs.

He shot Josie a glance.

Her fingers bunched into her dress, and she stared at the door like a deer caught in the sights of a rifle. The flush that had reddened her cheeks earlier had fled, replaced by an unnatural pallor that pulsed dread through Lou's veins.

"What's wrong?" he asked.

Josie turned eyes too terrified to belong on a child his way. "He's a very bad man," she whispered.

The voices outside the door rose in argument. At any moment the door could open. Lou positioned his gun under the sheets and jerked his chin toward the edge of the bed. "Get under, and don't say a word."

Mary peeked around the door frame of the downstairs study. After racing through the house, searching for Josie, she'd hidden in the study while James spoke with the man at the door. The visitor sounded urbane and sophisticated. She'd caught sight of a pressed suit and slicked-back hair as the men went up the stairs.

Was it someone from the bureau? Why else would James bring this stranger into the house? Heart pounding, she moved around the corner and into the empty hall. The rising sun splashed light against the dark floor she'd waxed yesterday morning.

She loved this home, had lived here for all of her adult

life, but it was time to grow up. With time, Trevor's house would feel like hers. She picked her way to the stairs, listening to the low sound of masculine voices.

As she moved upward, the voices escalated. A sense of urgency propelled her to the noise. She reached the top and spotted an unhappy-looking James with the stranger, standing outside Lou's door.

"I was just fixing to show this man out of the house," James said, his tone a warning.

Oh, no. The man must have forced his way upstairs and she was sure James didn't carry his weapon in the house. But he did have one stashed in the guest room....

Wetting her lips, she smoothed her dress and started their way. "Gentlemen." She forced her lips into a smile, shivering inside when the man swiveled toward her. His eyes were the same purple color as Josie's, but where the child's were alive and bright, his looked dark and forbidding.

Evil.

An inner warning she'd developed as a young girl encased her body, chilling her to the core. This man intended wickedness, of that she was sure. Smile pasted to her face, she drew near Lou's door, sliding her body in front of the knob. She needed to distract him.

James gave her an imperceptible nod of approval before turning to the stranger. "This is Mary, our housekeeper. She the one you've been looking for?"

The man's gaze traveled the length of her, a leer in his eyes if not on his lips. Dread pooled in her belly, and she had to force herself to meet his stare, to be calm in the face of his unrelenting perusal. This man fed on control. It made him feel powerful.

She'd met enough like him in her mother's former life to read the sins on his face.

Finally, the man looked at James. "No, the woman I'm looking for is much older. I was told you housed a Paiute, but evidently this lady isn't the one." The man gave her a slow, ugly wink. "I could offer you a better job. Higher pay." His gaze flicked over her work dress. "Nicer clothes."

"Perhaps you know the woman's name for whom you search?" she managed to say, though her tongue cleaved to the roof of her mouth.

"I only know she took something of mine, and I want it back."

Mary gulped, despising the fear that froze her veins and rooted her to the floor like an ice statue.

James broke the tension by clapping a hand on the stranger's shoulder. "Well, now you've met Mary and she's not the one, so why don't I get you some vittles and drink before you get on your way."

"Will you reconsider my offer?" The stranger directed his question to her.

She couldn't speak, could only shake her head.

"Very well. A pleasure meeting you, ma'am." He inclined his head, but she had no intention of reciprocating. None at all.

A hard look passed over his face when he realized her snub. James strode down the short hall to the stairs, beckoning the man to follow, but he paused in front of her, lips a thin line against his pale skin. "You're a scared little lady." The corner of his mouth tilted. "I like that."

Her heart stilled in its beating, paralyzed, until he pivoted and sauntered after James. Then it resumed a frantic pounding that flushed blood through her body so fast her knees grew wobbly and she thought she might vomit.

Get control. She had to be stronger somehow. Take

charge of the situation. There was no way on earth she'd let Josie return to that monster. If she had to keep the girl in hiding her entire life, then that was what she'd do.

Inhaling several deep breaths, she sagged against the door, letting her body calm and forcing her face to relax. If she went into Lou's bedroom right now, he'd know with one look that something was wrong.

The last thing he needed was action, and knowing him, it would be his first instinct. If he discovered this man was looking for Josie, what would he do? The question filled her with uneasiness.

Somehow she had to work harder to locate Josie's mother. See if she was a more fit parent than the malevolent stranger she'd just met.

Squaring her shoulders, she straightened and let herself into Lou's room. His window faced south, exposing a bright sky scattered with fluffy clouds that spoke nothing of evil. Only of good. Of a loving God who'd rescued her from men like the stranger who'd just visited.

A cleansing calm spread through her. She walked to Lou, who lay on the bed watching her, an alert expression on his handsome face.

"Who was the visitor?" His eyes, those shining orbs that had caught her attention from the moment they'd met, glinted at her.

"A stranger." She gingerly sat on the side of his bed, careful not to bump his body. "How is your wound?"

"Burning, but not as much as my gut. Something's wrong, and I want to know what."

"The man was looking for a Paiute woman. He said she took something of his."

"Josie," Lou stated, giving her a hard look, not his usual smile.

"The man didn't specify but I'm assuming so." Stomach quivering, she clasped her hands. "My mother—"

"The woman who abandoned you?" he interrupted, his face darkening.

"She found Josie near Harney Lake, half-dead. Since I have my own home, she asked me to hide her until things were safe."

"Safe from what?" Lou tried to push up from the bed but stopped, a grimace crossing his even features. "Never mind. You have no business keeping her and you know it. That's called kidnapping."

"No," she protested shakily. "I've telegraphed the Portland police, and they're trying to locate her mother. My mother claimed to be familiar with the father and said he's put up a reward for Josie, but when I rode into town the other day, I saw no such thing."

Lou settled back, the whiskers on his chin drawing Mary's attention. He needed a shave badly. Her gaze traversed the face of a man who'd protected her for so long. Now that time had passed. Now was the moment for her to stand proud and strong. To rise as a woman in charge of her own life.

She could not allow him to take Josie away. This matter belonged to her.

But as she studied him, she realized that despite his good looks and charming smile, he was still exhausted and in need of her care. The epiphany brought a tender warmth to her chest. "I will make you a special meal tonight."

"You will, huh?" Familiar crinkles appeared at the corners of his eyes. "Josie might have something to say about it."

Mary's warm feeling dissipated. "She will not be an issue. You will not have to see her."

"Too late." He gestured to the floor. "Come on out, Josie."

Scrambling ensued before the towheaded girl popped out near Mary's feet. Stifling a surprised squeal, she frowned at the girl. "I've been looking everywhere for you."

Josie squirmed, eyes cast down. "I just wanted to meet Mister Lou."

"We met, all right."

"She's staying with me," Mary put in, worry welling up at Lou's tone. He sounded distant, more removed than she thought possible. "You have no part of this decision I've made."

Her statement seemed to incense him. He grew agitated, rustling the sheets as he attempted to sit. The stubborn man was sure to hurt himself, but she made no move to help him. "The sooner you lie still, the sooner you'll heal."

"Do I really have to leave?" Josie asked in a plaintive, little-girl voice.

"Yes."

"No." Mary glared at Lou. She opened her arms, and Josie ran to her, snuggling in, her hair smelling like the lavender Mary had rinsed it with this morning. Smiling, she tightened the hug.

"We're going to find her a safe place, but first, you need to realize that she knows more than she's telling." Lou's tone caught Mary's attention. She looked up into his serious face. "Ask her, Mary. Ask her who the man at the door was."

Chapter Four

Children complicated matters.

And that was why Lou didn't want them around.

He hated lying in this bed, waiting while Mary sat beside him with that stoic look stuck on her face. Deliberating. The little girl buried her head in Mary's embrace, ignoring Lou and his demand.

Josie was in a heap of trouble. He could tell that much. None of her own doing, of course, but her safety was a priority now. He wanted things to return to normal, and he didn't want to worry about this little girl. Somehow it was up to him to get this mess straightened out.

"I will ask who this man is when the time is right," Mary said at length. Her arms tightened around the girl.

She already felt protective. He admired that, but she'd get her heart broken. He frowned, knowing he felt the same way, too.

"Josie."

The girl made a muffled noise and didn't look at him.

"Josie," he said again, lowering his voice and injecting some sternness into it.

She shuffled around, hair mussed about her face, eyes bright. Her little lips puckered into a pout. "What?"

"Will you tell us who that man is?"

Mary stroked the girl's forehead, her skin a rich color against Josie's blond curls. Josie blinked at him. "I don't wanna."

Chagrined, Lou told himself to be patient. This wasn't a case. Just a little girl who needed to go home, who needed to be safe. Especially before his concern for her turned him crazy. Or worse, drowned him in the sorrow of his losses.

"We want to help you find your mommy," he said with his most winning smile. It worked regularly on women of all ages and didn't fail with the girl. Obviously charmed, her dimples flashed.

"My mommy doesn't feel good. I'm not s'posed to bother her."

"Sweetie, she probably misses you," Mary said.

"She sleeps too much." Josie's dimples disappeared.

"Do you know your address in Portland? A phone number?"

"You sound grumpy, Mister Lou. I think you need a nap."

"I agree." Mary gave him a look that was the equivalent of sticking her tongue out at him. It made him almost want to smile.

She'd changed from the frightened young woman brought to his door years ago. She'd pulled her hair to the side, exposing the lovely bone structure of her face, the deep mystery in her eyes.

He mentally shook himself. What was he thinking? She was practically a sister.

He glared at the subject of his errant thoughts. "Are you making me something to eat?"

"You just ate pancakes."

"I'm still hungry."

"I will, Mister Lou," piped up Josie. "Be good and I'll bring you some soup. Right, Miss Mary?"

"How about meat?" he asked hopefully. The gurgle in his stomach wasn't getting any quieter. A man needed something to stick to his ribs.

"You'll get what's best for you." Mary shot him a quiet smile as she ushered Josie out the door.

"Wait," he called out.

She paused at the door, but Josie ran off. He heard the pitter-patter of her feet, and then she yelled for James in a voice that could wake a corpse in its grave. Even though seeing her pained him in ways he didn't want to explore, he couldn't help the reluctant tilt that grabbed his lips and wouldn't let go.

"She's something."

"Yes, she is." Mary cleared her throat. "Was there anything else?"

"Just keep talking to her. Soon as I can get up I'll take her into town. Find her a safe house."

"She's my responsibility, Lou. I'm praying about what to do."

He arched a brow at her and she had the grace to flush.

"I'm sure God wants me to find her family," she said. "In the meantime, I want to take care of her."

"God doesn't need to be brought into this. Do the right thing."

"I will." Eyes flashing, she shut the door harder than necessary.

He sighed and relaxed against the pillow, just now realizing how tense his muscles had become. How long did he have to stay in this sickbed? Why, the last time he'd been wounded he'd been down only a few days and then a new case cropped up and he'd headed out.

But a week had passed this time, and he still couldn't sit up without feeling dizzier than a bootlegger spending too much time in a speakeasy. If he stayed here much longer… He didn't think he could take much more of Mary's God talk. Let alone seeing Josie every day.

This wasn't a good place for the little girl. That man was looking for her, and he'd be back. They needed to find her mother and a different place so no harm would come to her.

And then there was Mary. After being kidnapped, sold by Trevor's mother, Julia, surely she should see that God didn't care anything for her or her life. It was a lesson he himself had learned the hard way. He just hoped the whole situation with Josie didn't deal Mary too harsh a blow. Maybe he'd warn her somehow. Soften the news.

Smothering an oath, he shifted position. Why should he warn her? The idea suddenly struck him as pompous. Who was he anyway?

Just a federal agent who wanted nothing to do with God, women or kids. And now he was stuck with all three.

Never had Mary met a more grumpy man than a bedridden Lou Riley. Gritting her teeth, she carried his breakfast tray up to his room, Josie tagging behind her. "After this can we go see the horses? And the cows, too? I've never touched a cow. Can I touch a cow, Mary? Just one time?"

"We'll see," said Mary. *We'll see* had become her answer to Josie's constant questions. Was it safe to let a little girl near the cows? She'd learned to ride horses at a young age, but probably not as young as Josie. The girl had proudly told her and James last night at dinner that she was five years old, almost six. A smile tugged at Mary's mouth. She looked down at Josie, who was marching past her on the steps, stretching her little legs to skip a step at a time.

"Be careful you don't trip on your new dress," she reminded her. The past few nights had been spent creating a wardrobe for Josie. She'd loved every stitch.

"I'm not gonna trip." Josie stood at the top, arms folded proudly across her chest. "Can I take Mister Lou his breakfast?"

"You'll stay in the hall."

"But I miss him."

Mary balanced the tray on her hip while fumbling for the doorknob. What should she say to such a sweet comment when it was obvious Lou felt uncomfortable with Josie? "I'd really like to get the kitchen cleaned up so we can go outside. Maybe you could sweep the floor?"

"By myself?" Josie's face brightened. Her arms swung back and forth, and then she started hopping on one foot.

"Absolutely." Mary grinned. Could children see past a distraction? Josie didn't seem to. "You did a wonderful job practicing with me the past few nights. It's time to put your skills to use."

"Yay!" She spun, twirling the skirt of her spring-green skirt. She leaped down the stairs so quickly a little hiccup of fear filled Mary's throat.

When Josie disappeared from view, safe from the treacherous descent, Mary tried the doorknob again. The door swung open, and she sidled in. "Breakfast."

"Lots of bacon, I hope." Lou stared at her from where he sat propped against the headboard. The sickening pallor that had tinged his skin the first week was now gone. He looked much healthier.

And too handsome for his own good. Or hers.

A rush of longing pulsed through Mary. She missed Lou's ready smile, the twinkle he usually handed out so generously. The longer he was cooped up, though, the more it felt as if he disliked her.

Even now he wouldn't meet her eyes. Perhaps it was better this way. Better to break off her dependency on him before he left again on a new assignment. Gaze downcast, she focused on getting the food settled on his side table. Clinking filled the room, and the sound of their breaths, quiet and steady.

So be it, she thought grimly.

Ignoring him, she went to the curtains and pulled them open. Sunlight poured in, a giant wave of light that bathed the room. The sound of rustling followed by Lou sipping his coffee pounded against her ears. Normally she loved silence. Reveled in its clean reliability.

Not now. Lou didn't know how *not* to talk. The silence in this room clouded her peace, its unnaturalness filling her with disquiet. She risked a glance his way, her heart thudding in her chest.

He was watching her.

Hair disheveled, eyes like sapphires in the morning light, his gaze trained so deeply on her that a pleasant shiver cut to her very core. She swallowed hard and broke the connection.

"You stare at me," she said, gaze trained on the wall behind him.

"Do you mind?"

"It is…odd." *But not unwelcome.* The realization startled her. She turned her back to him, whisking to the closet and pretending to look through his clothes. "Are you in need of anything laundered?"

"Mary—" Lou's voice broke off on a ragged note.

"Yes?" As if against her own will, she found herself facing him across the room. She was too aware of the pulse slamming through her veins, too aware of terror, and something different, something unnamed, working in her throat.

At that moment, James poked his head past the open door and gave a gruff throat clear before looking at Lou.

"Telegram," he said. He shuffled in and flipped a small white envelope onto Lou's lap. He glanced at Mary. "You got a young'un dusting up a bunch of dirt in the kitchen. You know that?"

Oh, no. Darting the men an apologetic smile, she raced out the door. By the time she reached the kitchen, she felt calm enough to dismiss Lou's strange perusal from her mind and focused her attention on the sprite standing in the middle of the kitchen, a cheeky grin on her face.

Mary stopped at the entrance, her gaze scanning the room. Everything looked fine. Shining floor, broom propped against the wall. She relaxed.

"Well, it looks as though you've done a marvelous job. How about we visit those cows?"

She followed a rambunctious Josie out the door. Together they trekked toward the stables and barn, stopping to pick flowers on the way. Josie's blond curls glimmered as she hopped through the sparse grasses and shrubs. Desert flowers, in various stages of bloom, drew the little girl's attention and her high-pitched giggle sparkled like glitter on the breeze.

The sun warmed Mary's face, while the sage-scented air seemed to lift the worries from her heart.

Be anxious for nothing, but in everything, by prayer and supplication, let your requests be made known to God.

In this moment, she chose not to fret over Josie and her lack of family. Nor could she allow Lou to take the joy from what she wanted to build in this place. A peace she'd prayed hard for filled her soul.

Who knew what God intended? Josie's laugh rang clear and charming. Perhaps He didn't plan for her to be alone the rest of her life after all.

Chapter Five

"Take me into Burns."

James ignored Lou's demand, bending over the bed to check his pulse and blood pressure. Before coming to the ranch, James had been a physician who'd succumbed to the lure of alcohol and lost all he held dear. He'd recovered from his addiction but never practiced medicine again, except for times like this when his skills came in handy.

All night Lou had studied the telegram he'd received, ready to take action as soon as he could rise without being beset by dizziness. Or guilt.

Had he made the right choices? He wasn't sure, but changing the things he'd set in motion didn't seem possible now.

James set his stethoscope on the bed, frowning at Lou.

"What?" he asked shortly, temper rising at the look.

"Going into Burns is a foolhardy task."

"I've got things to do. Get the truck ready to go."

"Trevor say you could use it?"

"Grab the car, then."

"I ain't drivin' your fancy Ford." James's whiskers bunched in a scowl, but his eyes were keen.

James seemed to know what was going on but wanted to stop Lou anyhow. Odd. "I need to telegraph the Portland office and arrange for travel."

"Can you stand yet?"

"I can." He'd tried last night and succeeded, if only for a few seconds. Not James's business, though. "In a few days' time I'll be ready for the trip. My vitals are fine, and I'm going stir-crazy in this house."

James nodded at the telegram, which he'd propped on the side table. "That the reason?"

"They have a lead on my shooter."

"What about Mary? The girl?"

"Mary stays here. I'll take the girl—" A crash interrupted him, shaking the house with its force.

James jumped up. "Hoo boy, that girl is in some trouble."

"Where's Mary?" His pulse notched up. Crazy child causing all sorts of trouble.

"She went to town. Stay in bed." On that command, James shuffled out of the bedroom as fast as an old man could hobble.

Determination filled Lou. Mary was in town, leaving the child here? With little protection? No, sir. Not on his watch. He might be have difficulty being around kids, but that didn't mean he'd ever let something bad happen to one. He swung his legs across the mattress. They felt heavy and unnatural; his vision swam, but he pushed through until his legs hung over the side of the bed and his hands were planted against the edge of the mattress. Head hanging, he closed his eyes and fought dizziness.

He could do this. Although his stomach bucked against the movement, he waited the feeling out, allowing his body to readjust to his change in position. The wound in his chest throbbed dully, but the pain wasn't incapacitating.

Hadn't he made it through the war? Memories crashed through him: the noise and the smoke, the gut-searing terror of knowing tomorrow might never come for him. And yet he'd completed various espionage activities, shadowed criminals, hunted killers. Only to come home and get gunned down at a low-level speakeasy. The irony was ridiculous.

Very slowly he opened his eyes. The first item he focused on happened to be Mary's Bible, resting on a folded blanket near the door. Groaning, he looked away.

God and Lou hadn't been on speaking terms in a long, long time. Not since God had failed him, taking his child and his wife. Leaving him alone. Unaccountably, his gaze flitted back to that silent black book. Its pages had once been a lifeline for Lou.

No longer. Now they dredged up a past he resisted, a past he thought he'd buried.

Years-old grief clogged his throat.

As his eyes stung, little feet pattered into view, stopping right next to the Bible.

"Mister Lou, I brought you something."

He lifted his head. Josie looked a mess this morning, her hair a frightful nest of twigs, snarls and… Was that paint clinging to her forehead?

"Leave me," he said, but when the little girl's face crumpled, he immediately felt regret churning his stomach. Or maybe it was the swaying floor. "What do you want?" he managed to say.

"I brought you cookies. Sweets make me feel better, and you're looking awful peaked. Sometimes I hear you yelling, but you don't sound mean, just sad."

Lou eyed her, noting the brightness of her eyes beneath the clumps of goo and mess straggling around her face.

"Here." She stepped forward, thrusting a cookie beneath his nose.

The scent rose to greet him, a thick mix of chocolate and some kind of nut. Praline, maybe? He took the cookie, watching Josie as he did so. "Mary's a good cook, isn't she?"

"Yeppers. Much better than Doris."

"Who's she?"

"My old cook."

Maybe sensing Lou's change in mood, the little girl hopped around his room, her dress flouncing. It was a mass of pink ruffles and ribbons, a frothy creation that under normal circumstances should give anyone a toothache.

Munching on the cookie, he slowly straightened and was relieved when the room didn't shift around him. Maybe a little sugar did the trick. Could be a trip into town would happen after all.

"Where'd you leave James?" he asked, watching as Josie twirled in front of his bed.

"He ran outside yelling. His face was purple, like a flower. He needs cookies, too." She cocked her head, fingers trailing over the silk of her dress. "Do you think I look like a princess?"

Lou choked on his cookie.

Hacking and coughing, he brushed the crumbs off his knees while he tried to regain his senses. He'd never heard something so preposterous. A princess? Yet, as he studied her, with the morning light streaming in ribbons across her features, highlighting her hair, making her eyes twinkle with hope, a strange emotion clutched at him.

He cleared his throat. "You're the prettiest princess I've ever seen."

A grin wider than the desert outside his window spread across Josie's face. Before he knew what to expect, she launched herself at him. Pain radiated through his upper body, and he felt useless as she entrapped him. His hands rested on his knees while she hugged him, her little-girl arms feeling impossibly frail as they wrapped around his neck.

Before he could stop himself, he realized his hands were patting her back. Hugging her back. He dropped them to his legs.

"Josie," he said, spitting a wayward hair from his mouth and pulling away, "you stink."

She stepped back and, folding her arms, pouted at him. "Princesses don't smell."

"They do when they mess with things. What'd you do downstairs?"

"She knocked over a can of paint from that big case I'm trying to move." James stood in the door, glowering at Josie. "You'd best come clean up before—"

"Do I have to?" She wheedled a pretty smile toward Lou.

The stinker. Unbidden affection surged through him. "A princess always takes responsibility for her mistakes."

"Oh, fine." She stomped out the door, her little shoulders ramrod straight.

James chuckled. "You need anything before I follow that whippersnapper?"

"When is Mary returning?"

"Soon."

"Send her up. We've things to discuss."

James nodded and left. Lou stared at the door, hating how the empty feeling in his stomach got worse when everyone was gone. He rubbed at his neck, almost feeling the imprint of Josie's arms around him. Would his little Abby have been so affectionate? Yes, because hugs had been common in their home.

Love and warmth and family. All gone.

The hollow in his chest deepened into a gaping void that wrenched through him, a chasm in his soul he could never escape. This pain worried him more than any shoulder wound. Why did Mary have to be so stubborn? Even more, how could he have let himself get shot?

He wanted to blame Mary.

He definitely blamed the shooter.

Because of them, he was starting to remember what he'd fought so hard to forget.

And the memories burned worse than any bullet ever did.

After Mary left the Burns general store, she paused on the walkway to let the morning sun warm her. Around her, people nodded at her as they ran their errands. No one stared. This was a good town.

She let her head drop back a bit so the summer rays could touch her cheeks and chase the chill from her soul. After the few errands she'd finished, she'd yet to find a flyer with Josie's name or face on it, let alone someone who could share information on the homeless child. No response from the Portland police, either.

It seemed the girl had appeared out of nowhere, with no kin to claim her. Except that man with the violet eyes…. She hadn't the courage to ask if anyone spoke with him. Shaking the shudder away at the thought of him, she resumed walking toward where she'd tethered her mare.

"Mary. Mary, wait!"

A woman's voice broke Mary's walk. She whirled and grinned as Alma Waite bustled over.

"Oh, you dear girl. How have you been?" Miss Alma's bright hazel eyes winked up at her before the elderly woman gathered her in a honey-scented hug.

"I'm well, thank you."

"You should visit more. I'm in need of pies and cookies for the Independence Day celebration."

"I shall make you some. I've been a mite busy lately." Mary released Miss Alma and moved beneath the shade of a storefront. Might Miss Alma know of Josie's parentage? While the woman who'd brought Mary to faith years ago knew everything about everyone, she wasn't a gossip.

"Well, we've missed you." Miss Alma tittered as she dug through a bag at her side. "I bought yarn and threads for you. That Grant woman has finally left the sewing circle and we've a hole now…one we'd like you to fill. Ah, here they are." Triumphantly she shoved the bag at Mary.

She took it, feeling a blush warm her cheeks. "Thank you. I shall think on your kind offer. How much are these?"

Miss Alma waved a hand. "Pishposh. They're a gift. I worry about you. Alone on that ranch."

"I have James and Lou—"

"No female companionship at all. It's not healthy. At least we used to meet for church…." Miss Alma trailed off as Mary shifted uncomfortably.

Since Lou had gotten shot, she hadn't been to church. Was it two Sundays she'd missed?

"My sweet girl, is there anything I can do for you?" The elderly woman, who had more fire in her than a rowdy pony, sported a soft look upon her face.

Mary hugged her again. "We're fine. I'm actually looking for some information, though." She thought of the man who'd come calling and decided to hedge a bit. "My mother found a child, and I'm having trouble locating the girl's parents."

"Oh, my." Miss Alma's hand went to her ruffled breast. "Why, I haven't heard a thing. Where did your mother find the child? Does she need a place to stay?"

"No, no, she's safe," Mary replied, flustered by the questions. "Perhaps you might keep your ear to the ground, as it were, and if you find out anything, let me know?"

"Of course I will."

They said their goodbyes, and Mary watched the lady who'd saved her life bustle away. Not her physical life, but her emotional one. Childhood chaos aside, she'd been a mess when Trevor first brought her to Lou's. Miss Alma had nursed her back to health and introduced her to God, to a Jesus who saw past skin and circumstance to the very heart of a person. Who loved despite a person's flaws or parentage.

Feeling cozy from memories, she wheeled to the

right and headed toward her horse. One more stop and then she could go home.

Home.

Humming her favorite hymn, Mary set out for the Paiute encampment. Sunlight warmed her shoulders and bathed the path before her in brightness. If only her own path could be so clear. With Lou injured and Josie running wild, she wasn't sure what to do.

And there was that way Lou had looked at her the other day—intent, dark. Her belly flip-flopped at the memory. She shook herself.

No matter what occurred in the next few weeks, she must disentangle herself from Lou, from the ranch, from everything that made her dependent on him.

The encampment loomed before her, scents reaching her as she came closer. Her mother's tent had no smoke, but that didn't mean she wasn't home. It was a warm day after all.

As she stopped before the tepee, an older man appeared from behind the tent's flap. He peered up at her, eyes black in the light.

"I am looking for my mother. Rose." That had been her name in the past, but Mary didn't know if she'd kept it or reverted to a traditional name.

"Rose not here." The flap fluttered closed as the man disappeared.

Around her, kids laughed and a dog barked. Sweat trickled down her neck as she roasted beneath the sun, trying to process the man's words. Not there? Had she left on her own? Or had the man with the violet eyes found her?

Whatever faults her mother might have, Mary didn't

want harm to come to her. Maybe he meant she'd gone to a general store, perhaps to sell goods?

She debated pestering the man again or riding back to town. Her sense of decorum made the decision for her. Sliding the reins over her mare's neck, she turned the horse back to town.

Once there, she discovered no one knew of her mother's whereabouts. How strange. She glanced at the general store, where she'd caught up with Miss Alma, who'd reinvited her to the sewing circle. When she asked about her mother, the women in the store shrugged and said she'd been to town early in the morning to sell her baskets. They hadn't seen her since.

Feeling a heavy sigh forming, Mary led her mare down the road going out of town and in the direction of the ranch. Ahead, a lone horse hitched to a pole stomped his hoof. The mare whickered and edged to the left, bumping Mary.

"Come on, girl." She soothed her with a pat on the neck as they moved farther left, away from the nervous stallion at the post.

Raised voices ahead slowed Mary's gait. Male voices, sharp and angry. She remembered that sound altogether too well. Cringing, she hugged closer to the horse, hoping to sneak past. It was her hope the men were too involved to notice her.

Here, at the outskirts of town, there was no telling what riffraff lingered. She wet her lips. She could always jump on the horse and gallop away, but that would certainly draw attention. Drawing a deep breath of horse, dust and sunlight, she trudged forward, wincing when one man's voice rose particularly loudly.

From beneath lowered lids she scanned the area and

saw nothing amiss. Tilting her head, she looked to the left. The space between two buildings resembled an alley. It was dark and deep, the perfect place for an argument. She shuddered and kept going. She'd just passed the opening there when the sound of a grunt followed by a thick thud startled her mare.

The horse jerked and the reins slipped through her hands, burning her palms. With a clatter of hooves and a flurry of dust, the mare left her standing slack-jawed in the road.

Instinctually her arms rounded her rib cage. Miss Alma's gift bumped against her hip. She hurried to the opposite side of the road, hiding behind a stack of onion barrels. She glared at the speck of her horse on the horizon, no doubt heading home. She must find a new one, and soon, before the mare worried Lou and James needlessly. But who could she ask?

Miss Alma might still be in town. Surely she'd give Mary a ride for part of the way, or possibly send a message to the ranch somehow....

Mind made up, she stepped away from the barrels and promptly stopped. A man appeared at the edge of the alley across the street. He stood tall and narrow, and something about his posture sent a shiver of foreboding through her.

Pivoting, she headed toward town. Footsteps sounded behind her. She picked up her pace, knowing only a few yards farther the streets teemed with shoppers.

The footsteps increased, faster than hers, until she felt a presence beside her and smelled the overpowering odor of cologne. Pulse clanging in her ears, she looked up and met the gaze of the violet-eyed stranger.

Chapter Six

Lou was sitting by the window when he saw a mare race into the yard. The horse pranced nervously near the porch before galloping toward the stables. An empty saddle went with her.

Biting back an oath, he rose from his spot, palming the wall until his vision became normal and the dizziness passed. His legs felt rubbery, but somehow he made it to the post of his bed. James had helped him earlier to the window. Now Lou wished he'd left some crutches in the room. He could barely breathe.

Taking a deep, steadying breath, he shuffled to the opposite bedpost, the one closest to the door. *Don't fail me,* he urged his body. Finally, his neck clammy and a sheen of sweat pebbling his forearms, he made it to the door.

"James," he shouted. His voice sounded like a croak. Scowling, he tried again. The sound of footsteps padded up the stairs. Little feet.

He'd never been so glad to see Josie. He rested his head against the door frame and waited for the girl to appear. Sure enough, she plopped herself right under his gaze, a big smile on her face.

"Hey, Mister Lou. Whatcha want?"

"Get me James," he said.

"Okeydokey."

She pattered off, but the image of her guileless face remained, taunting him with memories. Swallowing past his dry throat, he allowed himself to slide to the ground.

In moments, James was clumping up the stairs, his breaths heavy and labored. Lou saw his feet stop at the head of the stairs. "That whippersnapper said you was dying."

Squinting, Lou looked up at the man who'd been with him for so long, a former doctor whom Mary had taken from a life of homelessness on the streets of Burns and brought to the ranch for healing from too much drink.

He tried to keep his voice steady and careful. "Mary come back yet?"

James heaved, bending at the waist and meeting Lou at eye level. "You sayin' you sent that stinker runnin' like a herd of wild mustangs was after her, and you ain't dying? You jest want Mary?"

"Did she take a horse?" Lou continued calmly, training his gaze on James.

James growled and straightened. "She did."

"Check the stables, see if her horse returned."

"Now, how'm I supposed to know which horse she took?"

"Find out." The snarl took more energy than Lou thought it would.

"What's going on?"

"Is Miss Mary missing?" A little voice trembled

from the stairs, snagging Lou's attention and putting an ache in the vicinity of his heart. He couldn't meet her gaze. Something had happened to Mary and he hadn't been there to protect her.

Just like Sarah.

Sourness coated the roof of his mouth.

"Don't you worry, Josie. Everything is going to be okay." He jerked his chin at James. "Pull out my car. We're going to town."

For once, the old man didn't argue about driving a fancy Ford.

Soon, they were on their way to Burns. Lou stared out the window, his whole body aching, his worry amplifying every pain. Getting down the stairs had proved to be a terrible chore, one that had required lots of stops and support. He grimaced at his reflection, knowing he looked haggard and not caring one iota.

His strength might be on the low side, but James said the wound looked to be healing nicely. Only a few more days and he ought to be able to hunt that shooter down, if the bureau or local police hadn't found him already. He'd check on that in town.

He felt his lips tugging farther downward. Where was Mary? If anything happened to her…. He clenched his legs, letting his fingers dig into his thigh, needing a different kind of pain to take his thoughts from what his life might be like without her in it.

Even though, according to the telegram sitting in his room, in a few months' time he might never see her again. Guilt joined the worry, creating a ruckus in his head.

"You're quiet," James remarked from the driver's seat.

"Not much to talk on."

"She's probably fine. We'll find her. Give her grief over this whole thing."

"Watch out the window," Lou said. "She could be laying somewhere, hurt."

A rattler could've spooked her horse, and though Mary had been riding a long time, she didn't have a close bond with any of the horses. They wouldn't think twice about leaving her.

"I hope Josie behaves for Horn," said James.

They'd left the girl with their neighbor, though she'd been unwilling. Only the presence of a fresh batch of puppies had seemed to mollify her.

"I'm sure she'll be fine. Seemed happy enough with those pups."

"You heard anything on your shooter?" James dodged a shrub growing in the middle of the road.

The movement jolted Lou, sending an arcing pain through his shoulder. He winced, waiting for it to subside. "Nah. They think he's related somehow to that speakeasy we busted." Enforcing prohibition laws didn't necessarily fall into the bureau's jurisdiction, but they'd found some creative loopholes to catch criminals. Whatever it took to capture the bad guys, Lou was for it.

They didn't make any more small talk the rest of the way. A sick feeling persisted in Lou's stomach. As they drove into Burns, he felt a new resolve take hold. They hadn't found Mary on the way, which meant she should still be in town.

He was going to chew her out good.

Feeling grim, he shuffled behind James, a crutch under his good side's arm and James on the bad side, supporting him. They entered the police station. James's gait was stiff, and Lou was ready to punch something.

The feeling worsened when he saw Mary sitting on the bench. With her hair pulled back, neat and clean, and her profile strong, she looked neither worried nor scared, but serene.

A burst of adrenaline exploded inside Lou, rushing through his body with the power of a locomotive. He growled.

She startled, turning to face them, surprise plastered all over her face. Her mouth made an oval shape, and then she broke into a smile.

Heat shot through him, anger and fear melding into an emotion so powerful he could barely hold himself to where he stood. Yet he resisted, forcing a calm he didn't feel, holding back when he wanted to yell and stomp the way Josie had when he'd taken away the cookies she'd filched yesterday morning.

Mary must've sensed his mood because she stood slowly, casting a look to James before meeting Lou's eyes.

"You're angry," she stated, and the sound of her smooth voice flavored by exotic syllables only heightened his turmoil. "I can explain."

"Get in the car."

Her features changed, becoming impassive. "Thank you for coming to get me."

He jerked his head to the door and watched as she glided past, head high, shoulders straight. She hadn't learned that posture from her mother, or from Julia, Trevor's mom. No, that walk was all Mary. Proud, graceful, aloof… Another growl erupted.

"Let's go," he said.

She made it to the car before they did. They found her in the back, staring blankly out the side window and not meeting their eyes. Once they'd cranked his tin lizzie and hit the road, Lou still found it hard to speak. He knew from past experience that yelling at Mary solved nothing.

Not that he liked to yell, but when she stared up at him with those deep brown eyes, passive and quiet, it stirred him up, made him itch to get her to respond to him, not to ignore him the way she did others.

"What happened, Mary?" James interrupted the horrible silence that had filled the car since they'd picked her up. She could feel tension radiating off Lou and it scared her stiff.

She swallowed hard, afraid to speak, afraid Lou might explode.

He'd never, ever lifted a hand toward her, not even during their most volatile argument years ago when she'd asked to let her mother come live with them. Intellectually, she knew he wouldn't hurt her.

But emotionally… Sometimes she dreamed of the men who'd visited her mother. Sometimes she woke from nightmares, drenched in sweat, trying to rid her mind of the paralyzing fear that overtook her.

"Speak yer mind. I'll boot this shot-up agent out of the car if he yells, okay?" James cast a crooked smile back at her. She attempted to lift her lips, though the pit of her stomach ached.

She glanced at the back of Lou's head, marveling at the blondness of his hair, how it had grown too long and remained straight and fine. Not like her own thick locks. She'd inherited the Paiute ebony color but Irish curl. At least that was what her mother had always said.

She frowned. No one had seen Rose. It was as though

she'd just disappeared. Kind of how the man with the violet eyes did when the police chief interrupted them on their walk toward town. Her eyes fluttered closed for a moment as another wave of relief swept through her.

"Mary girl, are you okay?"

She opened them and looked at James. "There was an assault in Burns."

The car jerked. "What did you say?"

Confident she could keep her voice steady despite the unrest raging inside, she nodded. "I was leading my mare out of town when I heard scuffling. A tethered stallion nearby was restless, so I brought the mare to the other side of the street. Two men in an alley were arguing—"

"You should have rode out of there," Lou interrupted. His voice was gravelly and raw, completely unlike the talkative man she'd come to know through the years. Somehow this gunshot wound had changed him, and she wasn't sure why.

"I didn't want to alert them to my presence," she responded defensively.

"You did the right thing," said James.

His backup emboldened her. "As I tried to hurry past, there was a sharp sound, not a gunshot, but something striking a hard object. The horse startled and ran off on me. You should train them better," she couldn't help saying pointedly to Lou.

"So, that's it?" James asked. "Why didn't you borrow a horse and get on yer way? We've worried over you, Mary girl."

She felt a flash of remorse, followed by unexpected warmth. Though she'd been housekeeper for these two men for twelve years, they'd all kept to themselves, minding their own business while maintaining an un-spoken loyalty to each other. Since Josie had come, things had changed. The girl, or perhaps the familial situation, had tempered loyalty into a new bond, some-thing stronger.

"You shouldn't have worried," she answered. "Once the sheriff stepped out to speak with me, all was well."

"What happened with the scuffle you heard?"

The grate of Lou's tone surprised her, but he was an agent, trained to pick up on minute details. She had been foolish to think she might hide anything from him.

Still, she hesitated to tell him for fear of what he might do.

"Girl, you'd best spit it out." James waggled his eye-brows at her, perhaps trying to induce a smile.

But violence did not inspire smiles. Heart heavy, she looked at her clasped hands, debating whether to snag the lumpy-looking blanket on the floor to cover their cold-ness. "There was a man in the alley," she finally said. The memory of that thud shuddered through her and she pressed her fingers more tightly together. "Beaten."

"Is he dead?" asked Lou.

"The physician is not sure he'll make it."

"Who found the man?"

"Not me. But I pointed the way."

"You just walked into the sheriff's office and told him a man was in an alley beaten to a pulp."

Irritated by Lou's casual, almost sardonic tone, Mary frowned. This was the part she did not wish to share. She glanced out the window, at the rising mountains in the distance and the land she called home. "After the mare bolted, I walked toward the interior of Burns, hoping to catch Miss Alma to ask for a ride to Horn's spread." Their neighbor lived only miles away. "But as I walked, footsteps sounded behind me. Then caught up to me. A man desired to make conversation, and I obliged until we reached the heart of town."

"What man?" Suspicion dripped off Lou's words, thick and heavy.

"He does not matter. The sheriff will find him and I pray charge him. A man like that should not be allowed to roam."

Lou shifted in his seat but did not turn to look at her.

"Are you in pain?" she asked gently. "I picked up a few things in town."

"No," he said, voice tight. "I want to know more about this man following you. Do you think he knows what you told the sheriff? If this man thinks you're a threat—"

"I'm safe at my new house." At least she hoped that to be true. Lately, Lou seemed anxious, and she did not know if his rattled emotions came from being confined to bed or if there was another reason, something secret…. She swallowed at the thought. "The man… I've met him before. He knows where we are and can come at any time to your ranch, but he does not know of my new home."

"What do you mean you know him?" Lou swiveled and pinned her with a piercing blue glare.

"Remember the stranger who visited last week? He is one and the same."

"What's his name?"

"He never said, but he has violet eyes, like Josie."

"He might be her guardian." A thicket of hair fell over Lou's brow as James bounced across the uneven terrain.

"He didn't ask for a little girl," Mary retorted. She did not care for the accusing look on Lou's face, as though she had done something wrong or immoral. "This man is dangerous, and I don't believe he has any right to Josie."

Lou sighed and ran his palms down his face. "James, you heading to Horn's to pick up Josie?"

"Fixin' to veer off now."

"Good. If we haven't heard from the authorities about Josie's family in a week's time, we'll take her to Portland ourselves. I have unfinished business there. The ranch isn't safe for Josie. That man was there once and now he's been sighted in Burns—"

"It's too soon." The protest rolled off her tongue before she could stop it. "You'll reopen your wound."

Lou grunted. "I'll be fine. Someone must be looking for her. James wired the bureau for me days ago, and they think they've found Josie's mom. If not, we'll track down another relative."

They knew? Even the police hadn't been in touch with her. She slumped down. It was for the best. It had to be.

Movement on the floor startled a gasp out of her.

The blankets reshuffled and out of their haphazard mound popped a blond head. Josie scowled up at Lou. "I'm not going back and you can't make me."

Chapter Seven

Why did the man have to be so stubborn?

Mary's legs itched to pace, but she squelched the urge and forced herself to sit quietly as Lou moved across his living room floor. Only days after Lou had picked her up from the sheriff's and announced that Josie was going home, he insisted he was well enough to travel into Portland.

Truthfully, he'd made it down the stairs on his own, but that did not mean he was fit for travel. She eyed the way he shuffled across the floor, noting the pallid tone of his handsome face because he insisted on venting his frustration by moving about. No, he needed more time to recover.

More important, Josie did not wish to live with her family. Specifically her uncle, who she'd confessed to being the stranger who'd visited. The little girl's alarm fueled Mary's own dismay. Surely a man wanted for the kind of assault he'd dished out on the man in the alley should not have the care of a child. Not to mention the way he'd ogled Mary....

"Did you hear me?" Lou stopped in front of her, a frown on his full lips.

She lifted her gaze to his. "I did not hear."

His hands sliced through the air in an impatient gesture. "Pack a bag. We're leaving tomorrow morning. If you don't pack, you're not coming. I've received information that reports Josie's mom has returned to Portland."

"It is a large city," she said slowly. "Do you suggest we knock on each door?"

Lou grinned, the movement lighting his face and tugging at her heart. Here was the smile she'd missed, the crinkle around his eyes and curve in his cheek. "That, my dear, is taken care of. We've an address, and I already sent a telegram requesting a meeting with the mother."

She picked at her skirt, unable to bear looking at the triumph splayed across his features. This would be the end, then.

"Mary, aren't you happy?" He dropped down in front of her. She saw the wince that flashed across his face before he masked it. Eyes alight, he peered at her. "She needs her home. Her mother. This place is no good for a child. I'm going to make sure she and her mother are protected."

He was right, of course. Allowing Josie to stay only fulfilled her desires. A lonely desert with scattered neighbors could not possibly meet a child's need for companionship. She stared down at her hands, which she'd clasped in her lap.

Lou sighed. "I wish you'd talk to me. Communicate."

"I have nothing to say."

"Say we're doing the right thing here. That you want to give a mother back her daughter."

Her head shot up as a bolt of anger darted through

her. Her nerve endings tingled with the prickly feeling. "If this mother wants her daughter, why has she not been scouring the countryside for her? Posting pictures and letters? I have seen little evidence that Josie is wanted."

A gasp came from the front door, followed by pattering feet as the little girl raced away. Mary cringed.

"She needs to stop eavesdropping," Lou said in a grim voice. He rose very slowly, and Mary could tell he'd fatigued himself.

She wanted to run after Josie but didn't know what she'd say. The truth was, no one but that dreadful man had looked for the little girl. And Mary wanted her to stay. To be family.

Lou was still looking at her, seriousness shadowing his expression. Why did he want Josie gone so bad? Why did he shy away from the little girl and even seem afraid of her at times?

"And if I do not wish to travel with you?" she asked, watching him carefully. "You will be forced to care for Josie yourself. To see to her needs. To be her sole caretaker."

"If you don't pack, then you won't go. That's all there is to it." He stood, turning away so she could no longer see his face.

Empathy battled with frustration. She could go with him now, but that would leave Josie in a bad place. The thought of leaving the little girl hurt too much to dwell on. If she refused to go, what could he do to her? Not much, she surmised.

Mind made up, she stood, straightening her skirt with the movement. He shuffled around, shoulders straight despite the obvious pain striking his features.

She leveled her gaze on him, refusing to let him see how horrible she felt that he was in such distress. "I will not go until you can move without pain."

"That so?" he said quietly. Challenge filled the blueness of his eyes and an unwelcome ping of excitement zipped through her. These weeks together were revealing a side to her nature she hadn't suspected existed. A side that seemed to enjoy his challenges, to revel in tension.

The thought was discomfiting, at best. She returned his stare, even though her stomach roiled and her palms slicked.

After a tense minute of silence, she spoke, her voice clear and even, much to her relief. "I must find Josie. She should not have heard our conversation." It hurt to think her words had caused Josie pain. She, who tried so hard to be quiet and speak wisely, had been undone by her unreasonable, blasé employer.

"I'm coming with."

She swished forward. "You can hardly walk. Lie down and recover if you wish to return Josie."

"That girl's leaving tomorrow." As Mary passed, Lou reached out and gripped her arm. His touch imprinted her skin with heat.

"Why do you care so much? She's just a little girl." Slowly, she removed her arm, amazed she felt no fear at his handling but rather wary at what she did feel: a nervous tension that had nothing to do with fear.

"This place isn't safe for her." He gave her his profile.

"So you've said, but why? It is unlikely that man would think she's here." She studied the stubborn line of his nose, the shape of his square, unyielding jaw. Somewhere a little girl cried for a home she'd lost, and here she stood, interrogating a man who didn't seem to care.

Annoyed at herself, she let out a huff. "Never mind. It's obvious I'm not the only one who has trouble communicating."

Aiming that last comment at the doorway, she stalked out of the sitting room and then hurried down the hallway. James was rocking on the front porch when she burst out the door. An uppity wind brushed past, tangling her skirt and hair in its wake.

"Have you seen Josie?"

"Went thataway." He pointed in the direction of Trevor's house. Her home.

"Thank you." She darted off the porch and ran to the house. Halfway there, she had to stop and gasp for air. This was her fault. Maybe Lou was right. Maybe Josie needed to be with her mother. Perhaps there was a reason the woman hadn't searched for her daughter. Josie had mentioned illness.

Then again, some mothers, for one reason or another, couldn't expend the energy to find their children.

She frowned and kept walking, trying to ignore the whispery accusation toward her own mother who'd dropped her off with Trevor's mom at the age of twelve and never looked back. Not until it was too late and the emotional damage had been done.

Her breath hitched. Taking a moment to inhale and exhale, to remember God and how He'd protected her, was not only good for the lungs but good for the soul.

As she inhaled the cleansing scents of pine, sage and desert brush, her pulse slowed and her vision sharpened on the little house that grew larger as she drew near. A curtain flickered in the window.

Feeling deep chagrin, she kept her legs moving until she'd reached the door. Opening it, she stepped into the house. The living room smelled like cookies. Sugar cookies. Tinged with the underlying aroma of wood floor polish. A comforting welcome.

"Josie?" She shut the door behind her. "Sweetie, please come talk to me."

"I don't want to talk." Her mulish voice drifted from the sofa. A blanket covered a misshapen lump but didn't quite reach the stockinged foot peeking from beneath its edge. "I'm going to run away."

Unsure, Mary stayed rooted near the door. Should she take the girl to task for talking in such a way? Or should she go hug her…? Indecision was a heavy coat she couldn't seem to shrug off, so she just stood there, kneading her fingers against her skirt.

If only she owned an instruction manual for parenting.

Finally, Josie flipped the blanket off. Her blond curls stood at attention, static fuzzing them up into a rat's nest. An unruly giggle snickered past Mary's lips.

Josie's eyes narrowed. "Go away."

"This is my home."

"Then I'll go." Huffing, she threw the blanket to the floor and gave Mary such an ugly glare that another laugh sprinkled out from somewhere.

"You're laughing." If possible, the glare turned uglier.

"Oh, honey, I was worried." Instinctually, she dropped to her knees and held out her arms. "I'm so glad you're okay."

"But no one wants me, so what do you care?"

"When I was a young girl, no one wanted me, either."

The confession came unbidden. "It is a lonely, horrible feeling to be unwanted."

Josie eyed her arms and Mary held her breath.

Slowly the girl walked over. "Why didn't anyone want you?"

"I was inconvenient."

"What's that mean?" She settled on Mary's lap, the child's warm weight shooting giddiness to a place in her heart that had been neglected far too long.

"It means I wasn't easy," she said against the aroma of Josie's hair. "I want you, sweet girl. Raising a child is hard work. But it's also wonderful joy. I was very blessed that God sent me a friend when I was a wee bit older than you, and He showed me I was loved." Trevor had been family for a long time. Despite her loneliness, she prayed he and Gracie were enjoying their trip to California.

Josie snuggled beneath Mary's chin, her arms rounding Mary's back as she pressed closer.

"No one is inconvenient to God," Mary murmured. "He loves you so much and no matter what happens, you must know that He wants you. I will pray God sends you a friend, sweetie."

The girl wiggled, pulled back and met her gaze. "Will you pray he sends me a family?"

"Made it down the stairs, I see." James hovered in the sitting room doorway, chewing a stem of unfortunate grass. "You still ain't fit for travel."

Lou sighed, his recent talk with Mary bothering him too much to let him care what James said. The hand knew his medicine, and no doubt the man was right. "Looks like we'll be waiting one more week."

"Sounds good." James came into the room and plopped down on a couch, the grass twisting between his teeth. "Miss Alma cornered me in town this morning."

The huff James emitted coaxed a grin to Lou's mouth. "Don't tell me you don't like her attentions, old man."

"The woman smells good, it's true, but she's plain nosy. Always trying to ask me over for lunch, or worse, to visit that little church she and Horn got going."

"She give you any food this morning?" He was feeling a bit hungry and it might be a good distraction from the memory of how Mary had felt when he'd grabbed her arm. Warm. Fragile.

"It's in the icebox." James interrupted his meanderings.

"You mean the refrigerator?"

"Whatever you youngsters call that newfangled contraption." James's completely white whiskers twitched on the word *contraption*.

With a start, Lou realized the ranch hand was getting older. He had at least twenty years on Lou, which meant he must be pushing sixty.

He eyed his employee. "If you need help with ranch duties, let me know. I'll hire on a few extra men."

"I'm fine. 'Sides, thought you were selling it?"

Startled, Lou glanced at the door before realizing his nonverbal slip.

James cocked a brow. "You didn't tell Mary yet?"

His gape annoyed Lou. "It's not set in stone. She's got her house now, and it shouldn't matter what I do."

"You're her source of income. And mine, come to think of it."

"I know." Lou growled. It was a problem, one he was determined to find a solution to. "The ranch is having a hard time making money. The cooler weather is doing in ranchers all around us. I talked to Doc about you joining on as assistant in Burns since the town is growing so much. He seemed amenable to the idea."

"It'll be hard to get Mary a job, seeing her skin's dark."

"The people in Burns are familiar with her. I don't think she'll have trouble, but no matter what, I'll make sure she's taken care of." Even if he went broke doing so. She deserved the best, and he'd make sure she had it.

"And how about her feelings on the matter? She's uncomfortable around people. Given her history—"

"She'll be fine," he interrupted. He couldn't escape the subject of his housekeeper no matter where he went, it seemed. "She takes stuff to town all the time. Miss Alma will watch out for her, and I'll take care of the financial end."

"Speaking of that woman, she's invited Mary to some kind of lady event on Saturday. So's you best stay here till then." James flashed him a pointed stare before pushing himself out of the seat and heading for the door.

"What time?"

"Noon."

Great. Another week trapped at the ranch when he could be tracking down his shooter. After returning Josie first, of course. Though he was trying to draw that out until he heard a little more about her family. No matter how uncomfortable she made him, no way would he put her in a dangerous situation.

He shook his head, got to his feet. He didn't want to think about Josie or Mary. He just wanted to return to the way life was before.

Simple.

He headed to the door, feeling weak but not dizzy. The fact that his legs carried him to the hallway without buckling was reason to say thanks to the Creator… if they were on speaking terms.

And they weren't. Mary could keep her God for all he cared.

The God he used to serve…

He slowed near the stairs, breathing heavier than he'd like. Maybe he'd rest a bit on the porch. Get some sunlight and fresh air. Take his mind off matters too weighty for a beautiful summer day.

He shuffled to the door, let himself outside and found a spot on the steps in a patch of sunlight that immediately seeped into his bones and spread through him in a liquid spill of relaxation.

Decisions, decisions. He closed his eyes and leaned against the railing. What was he going to do? The ranch's secrecy had been compromised, but even worse, the weather proved that trying to ranch in this desert was a futile effort. Scents caressed his face. Would he miss this place? It had served its purpose, but he didn't need it anymore. Yet he hesitated. Mary seemed more than ready to move on. Now that she had her own place, she'd probably have her mom move in.

That foolish mother who'd abandoned her daughter to run off and search for a man. Granted, she'd been looking for Mary's father, but that didn't excuse things, to his way of thinking. And then there was Mary's kidnapping and the huge part her mother, unbeknownst to Mary, had played in it. He frowned. Mary was asking for trouble by inviting that woman to live with her.

Could she handle any more betrayals? His gut hurt just thinking about it.

The memory of Mary's arm beneath his palm, warm and small, heated his cheeks. She hadn't seemed afraid of his touch, didn't cower the way she had the first few years she'd been hired on as housekeeper. Not that he'd touched her often.

Nah. She was like a little sister. That was it. Someone he cared about and wanted to protect.

Even if she seemed determined to escape protection by moving into Trevor's old house.

As he rested, a sound tinkled in the distance, reaching his ears on the breeze. The laughter grew louder, uncontrolled giggles that swept over him in a swirling dance and left him listening for more.

He opened his eyes, shading his vision with a hand against his forehead. Nothing to the front of the house. Cautiously he stood, scanning the periphery of the house, but he still couldn't distinguish the source of the sound.

A strange and painful yearning had started in his chest, right below the vicinity of his wound. As shrieks floated on the afternoon's breeze, lingering in the scents of summer, the warmth of sun, Lou found himself drawn forward, away from the safety of the porch and toward the laughter that seemed just beyond his reach.

He poked past shrubs and sparse grasses, toward a lush little valley that lay behind the house. The tiny indentation of land was always filled with wildflowers and grass in summer. A verdant patch, one of the many that had fooled neighbors into thinking the Harney desert area might make good land.

As he walked to the sound, a wedge of guilt niggled at him. Mary should know he figured on joining the ranks of sellers. He just needed to find the right moment to tell her. Had planned to before getting shot. Though he didn't farm, cattle sales had been declining for a good number of years now. There was no reason to keep this place anymore.

He ignored the guilt and kept up toward the valley, the growing laughter hooking him as thoroughly as the bass he used to catch with his brother when they were kids.

As he neared, his steps slowed, the sounds he heard filling him with a mixed kind of joy and pain. It was moments like this, in the sun-drenched air, that he wished desperately to hear Sarah's laugh one more time, to see the crooked toothless grin Abby had given him the day he'd left on assignment.

Before he'd come home to find— Nope, he wasn't going there. Forcing the memories to the side, he reached the edge of the valley.

Only feet away, Mary and Josie twirled in rhythmic abandonment. His breath stuttered to a stop, then rushed in as adrenaline began knocking through his system.

Josie's blond curls bounced and glistened, moving with the sound of her giggles as she spun through the flowers, around and around, a purple bloom clutched to her chest. Mary was spinning, too, and when his gaze landed on her, he couldn't look away.

Her hair was down, flowing, a midnight veil taking flight as she spun. The dress she wore clung to her body, molding against lithe legs and rounded hips. Her face tilted to the sky, eyes closed, lips parted, her arms rotating with her body.

And then the little scene was over. Both girls collapsed on the ground, laughing on their backs as their world no doubt tilted perilously from one side to the other.

Lou swallowed hard, backing up. He felt like an interloper. An intruder on their carefree fun. The image of Mary burned in his mind. The woman he'd considered a sister...

The lump in his throat seemed to magnify and with a sudden decision he pivoted and marched back to the house. But the speed of his walk did nothing to erase what he'd seen. What he felt.

One thing was for sure: whatever he felt toward Mary was far from brotherly.

What was he going to do about that?

Chapter Eight

Mary found out about the invitation to the quilting bee approximately two hours before she was to arrive. Lou showed up on her doorstep as she and Josie slid the final batch of cookies into the oven. Damp tendrils stuck to her neck from the hair she'd pinned this morning but that had escaped in strands during baking.

She wiped her hands on a towel as Josie ran to the front door.

"Mister Lou," she shouted, her voice's pitch making Mary wince.

To his credit, Lou didn't back away but managed to give the girl an awkward pat on the head. Then he turned his startling blue gaze on her. Since the other day when they'd argued over when to take Josie to Portland, he hadn't brought up the subject with her again. In fact, she'd barely seen him.

It was almost as if he was avoiding her. Frowning, she finished rubbing a towel over her fingers before setting it on the little table she'd inherited from Trevor.

"Do you need something?" she asked Lou.

"Nope, not on your day off." He gave her a crooked

grin, lounging against the wall near the still-open door. Sunlight from the rising sun surrounded him and a strange catch crowded her throat.

Josie scampered past Lou, stopping in a square of light. "Can I go outside, Miss Mary?"

She nodded her assent and the little girl was gone.

"Miss Alma wants you to join a ladies' group today. I'm sorry that I forgot all about it until James reminded me. If you get ready now, we can be there early," said Lou in a penitent voice.

"We?"

His arms crossed. "I'm going to drive you."

"A horse would serve me fine."

"Not for me. There are things we should…discuss." He pinned her with an electric smile, his gaze sliding from her eyes to her mouth.

She wet her lips. "What things? I have said that which needed to be said."

He left where he stood, his smile widening as he advanced. She backed up, though what she felt in her belly was not terror but a rather more alarming emotion.

Edged against the wall of the kitchen, she could go no farther. Lou trapped her, moving so close she smelled the mint of Wrigley's on his breath.

"I saw you yesterday." His fingers crept to her neck, and his touch was feather soft against her skin.

She suppressed a shiver.

"With Josie, in the flowers. And I realized that—" A pained expression crossed his face. His words cut off, and his hand left her neck, leaving her skin cold and lonely.

"Realized what?" she asked, her voice as tremulous as the state of her knees.

His gaze shuttered, growing distant as he backed up. "If you want to go, be ready within the hour." He spun and left her against the wall, more shaken than she'd been in a long time.

Nerves aflame, she set about gathering her quilting supplies. She put them in a basket and then made a smaller basket for Josie. As she calmed, her mind turned to the event ahead.

Miss Alma had always been generous and kind, a woman of great wisdom. But she couldn't help wondering how wise this outing might be. How would the other women react to her presence? She had no desire to be subjected to the ill-mannered treatment her mother's people often experienced. Even though the people of Burns had been good to her in a distant way, she'd never actually interacted with the townsfolk in a companionable, talkative setting like a quilting bee.

But the trip into town *would* give her another chance to inquire about her mother's whereabouts.

Lou arrived promptly at eleven. James scooted out of the passenger side of Lou's automobile, but her employer remained inside, a scowl visible on his face.

"I'm here to watch Josie. Where's that wild thing at?" James chomped his tobacco.

"She's here somewhere." She tore her gaze from Lou and turned to the house. "Josie, it's time to go." She stepped toward the corner of the house. Maybe Josie had scampered out back. "I'm taking her with me. You don't have to watch her, James."

"Figured I'd take her shooting."

Mary whirled. "I think not."

"But he promised." Josie popped out from the corner of the house. "I don't wanna go sew. That's boring."

Mary sighed and closed the front door. She stepped onto the grass, moving toward the little girl, whose face was set in a stubborn yet adorable pout. "Every girl should know how to use a needle, Josie. It will come in handy."

The skill had kept her out of the brothels.

Josie's head tilted. "Do I have to?"

Mary looked at James, who shrugged. There appeared to be a slight curl to his lip, as if he was amused. Well, that was that, then. She would not force Josie to quilt. Times were changing and women had more options these days. Even she'd taken shooting lessons from James and had bought her very own pistol.

"Very well. Please be safe."

"Really? I can go?" Josie squealed and vaulted into Mary, her arms chained around her waist. "Thank you!"

Touched, she looked down into Josie's eyes. "You're welcome."

A high-pitched blast cut through their hug. Lou on the horn.

"Okay, girlie. Let's get on." James patted Josie before capturing Mary's gaze with a serious look. "Remember, these ladies invited you. They want ya there."

"Thank you, James." She vowed to remember that. She watched as Josie followed James across the expanse of ground between her new home and Lou's ranch house. Their chatter hung behind them, fading from hearing as they grew more distant.

She turned to the car. The baskets she clutched suddenly felt heavy and cumbersome. Though the sky burned a bright, sizzling blue, promising a warm day, tension knotted her stomach.

Lou reached across the front seat and opened the passenger door. "Let's go or you'll be late."

Once they were on their way, bouncing across uneven terrain to the road that led to Burns, Mary finally felt as if she could take a breath. Lou had said nothing to her. Perhaps he would skip this "talk" he'd spoken of.

She had no wish to discuss her private life with him. Or with anyone, for that matter.

"You're going to have fun, you know," he said, breaking into her thoughts.

She pulled her basket closer. Josie's sat on the floorboard, unneeded now. "I go only for Miss Alma." And to find her mother.

He cast her a look loaded with curiosity. "You've lived on the ranch how many years? Ten?"

"Twelve," she said stiffly.

He let out a low whistle. "Twelve years. That's a long time. You ever gone to a quilting bee? Never mind. Your knuckles are white on that basket."

Surprised, she looked down. Deliberately she released the basket.

"Now, you bring neighbors things all the time. There's nothing to be nervous about. Just be yourself and they'll love you." Lou gave her one of his half grins. "Charm these ladies and then we'll head up to Portland at the beginning of the week."

"You're not well enough yet."

"I'm fine. We'll take the train. My wound's closed up, there's no infection, minimal pain."

"Josie doesn't want to go."

"She's a little girl. She doesn't have a choice."

"Everyone should get a choice," she choked out. Her

hands were back on the basket, and she didn't care. The basket's handle dug into her ribs.

Lou sighed heavily. She glanced over. The rugged lawman had slowly been returning to his carefree, light ways, yet the subject of Josie always seemed to sober him.

"I know you didn't get choices when you were young. And when you were older, Trevor brought you to the ranch and we asked you to stay awhile. To be safe. But time passed and you never left. Why not?"

Mary stiffened. "This is not about me. Josie is afraid of that man. We do not know that he is her guardian. She shouldn't be left in his care."

"Even though we're leaving her with the mother, I'm still going to make sure she's safe."

"*My* mother found her and risked much to shelter and care for her. Where was this *mother* when Josie was left for dead in the desert? I do not trust this type of mother." Too late she realized that her outburst condemned more than Josie's mom. Her face burned.

There was an awkward silence in the car. She looked out the window, fastening her attention to her beloved rocky horizon. How she adored this place. Dry and vast, teeming with wildlife and plants carrying all sorts of value.

They were almost to Burns when Lou spoke. "I'll pick you up in the afternoon. Save me some of those cookies I know you have hiding in that basket."

She managed a small smile. "I left many on my counter. You may help yourself when we get home."

"Thanks, sweet Mary. You're the best cook I know." His smile broadened.

The action sent her pulse scurrying. To cover, she let out a gentle snort. "I'm the only cook you have."

"I know." Sporting an annoying grin, he pulled up next to Miss Alma's home.

She lived in a cozy, small house surrounded by blooming flowers. Behind the home, land sloped up in jagged crests to the horizon. Mary paused with opening her door.

"Do you see that grassland plateau?" she asked Lou.

"Over there, behind the house?"

She nodded. "My mother took me there to forage when I was young. Her mother took her, and her mother before took my grandmother. During this season it is ripe with food. Bitterroot. Biscuit root. The food of my mother's people."

"I see women out there in the mornings sometimes. Didn't know they were finding food."

"It is only in these warm months that it can be found, but enough can be gathered to last a winter."

"You're making a point."

"Yes." She held his gaze, wanting him to understand. "My mother taught me of the past. She cared for me—"

"If this is another plea for your mom to live with you, stop now." His expression hardened. "That woman dropped you off with Trevor's mom and didn't look back. At a brothel. I won't ever understand what you see in her."

"I am not asking your permission, nor pleading for anything," she told him sternly, though her stomach twisted like well-wrung laundry. "What she did was ill-advised."

"No. It was wrong."

Oh, he made her angry. Setting her jaw, she jerked

the car door open. She bolted out and shoved the door
shut, its well-aimed slam puncturing the air and giving
her a deep satisfaction. Mule-headed man. Why couldn't
he see that forgiveness meant more than harboring ills?
What had happened to make him so unforgiving? It
wasn't as though Rose had wronged him. She'd left her
child with a friend, little knowing the "friend" would
end up selling Mary, years down the road.

And yet even that horrific experience had brought
her to this place. Harney County, Oregon. To a ranch
inhabited by three independent men. To a town that
was home to a woman named Miss Alma, who taught
Mary the way of the cross.

She stepped to Miss Alma's door. Shoulders straight,
basket up. She could face this on her own.

Mary couldn't face another cookie.

She shook her head at the kind lady who'd just offered her another sugar cookie. Miss Alma's house was
filled to the brim with women, patterns and treats. The
ladies chattered as Mary huddled in the corner chair
she'd chosen. Though no one had outright snubbed her,
she'd felt the surprised looks when she'd opened the
door.

Though she knew one or two ladies, most were
strangers. Women who lived in town and rarely traveled outside its limits. No wonder they were startled to
see a new face.

Of course, Miss Alma bustled around as friendly as
a pup and sweeter than the desserts currently loading
her counters.

Mary looked down at the stitching on her lap. She'd
traded a few of her own gingham squares for a lovely

ivy pattern another lady claimed to have picked up in New York City.

"Ooh, I like that." One of the younger ladies present, perhaps near Gracie's age, scooted close. "Are you making the entire quilt in that color scheme?" The girl's russet hair fell against freckled cheeks and she had an upturned nose that reminded Mary of a curious cat.

"I am considering ivy and greens," she answered.

"Lovely." The girl held out her hand. "I'm Amy Donovan. Gracie is a riding friend of mine."

"Oh…" Mary stared at the hand. Did this Amy really expect her to shake hands like men? Not that she disapproved, the movement simply surprised her.

"Go on, grasp my hand. It's quite fun and perfectly acceptable."

She took Amy's hand and was rewarded with a vigorous pump.

"I'm so glad you came. It gets awfully stuffy in here sometimes. Quilting has its merits, but my aunt, whom I accompany, spends all her time tittering about who said what and who's cut their hair into a bob. I've been missing Gracie dreadfully." Amy's eyes, a pretty brown, widened. "Say, do you ride? This weather is perfect for a good gallop."

"I miss Gracie, too" was all Mary could think to say. No wonder Amy and Gracie had found each other. Chatterboxes, the both of them. Yet she quite liked their loquaciousness.

"When will she be home?" Amy pulled out a long stretch of squares and started working.

"Perhaps in a few weeks." With Josie and Lou both suddenly appearing at the ranch, she hadn't even thought about Gracie and Trevor's return.

"Well, the sooner the better. Sometimes I'm afraid all the ranchers scooting out will leave us with a ghost town."

Mary pricked her finger, despite the thimble she wore. "What do you mean, scooting out?" She sucked the pain from her finger and then returned to her sewing.

"Well, this weather and all. With the Indian summers gone, lots of ranches are up for sale. I heard some homesteaders are just leaving their places without even trying to sell."

"You don't say," Mary murmured. How sad. The high desert of Oregon was a difficult soil for agriculture, though the land grew rich with herbs and roots. One had to know where to search.

"And did you hear of Mr. Baxley?"

"No, I'm afraid not."

"Oh, the poor thing was beaten horribly and died from his injuries. There was this good-looking man skulking about and I've heard gossip that he's the murderer."

Mary's gaze snapped up. "Is he still in Burns?"

"Oh, no." Amy's head shook vigorously. "Our lawmen wouldn't allow that. Though there's no proof. Only conjecture."

"Everything going well over here?" Miss Alma appeared in front of them. She wore an absurd hat laden with all sorts of funny little things that made Mary smile. They hovered above her happy face and bobbed with her movements. "Mary, dear, those snickerdoodles were wonderful. You must give me the recipe and bring something to the picnic tomorrow. Now, may I get you ladies anything?"

"We're doing just dandy, Miss Alma. Thank you, though." Amy flashed a broad grin, but the elderly lady was already swishing off to the next group of women in her crowded living room.

The rest of the afternoon passed uneventfully, though Mary couldn't shake the troublesome feeling nagging at her. Could she have done more to help Mr. Baxley? And how had the violet-eyed man escaped conviction so easily? Perhaps Lou would know.

At precisely three o'clock Miss Alma's door swung open, and a broad-shouldered Lou Riley filled the door frame. Gasps and titters resounded through the room. A few of the younger girls gaped as Mary gathered her belongings and said goodbye to Miss Alma.

She turned to the door and then paused, her heart stuttering in her chest. No wonder the girls were catching flies. Lou lounged in the doorway, one shoulder propped against the frame, his legs crossed at the ankles, hands pocketed in his blue jeans. His leather hat hugged his head at an angle that mimicked the smirk on his lips.

He swirled a toothpick lazily with his teeth as he surveyed the room. The sun slanted in from windows behind Mary, highlighting the mischievous sparkle that winked in his blue eyes.

The man knew the effect he was having, and she didn't know whether to be amused or outraged.

Finally, he took out the toothpick and straightened. Not a woman stirred. He slid the hat off his head, gave Mary a slow wink that filled her with hot mortification and proceeded to dazzle the women with the kind of smile that turned a woman's heart.

"Hello, ladies," he drawled.

Chapter Nine

"**I** am not impressed." Mary hoity-toitied her way to the Ford, posture so stiff Lou figured she could carry a basket on her head the way he'd seen women on the continent of Africa do. Or maybe just plain old books like the stuffy girls back East used to practice with.

"With what?" he called after her. He wasn't going to bother trying to keep up while she threw the most abnormal fit he'd ever seen. Maybe this quilting thing had gone worse than he suspected. Though when he'd walked in, everyone had seemed peaceful enough. Miss Alma had even piled him down with cookies to take home, with clear instructions to send James out for a look at her pipes within the week.

"You know what," Mary retorted.

He barely caught the words before they were followed by the solid *thunk* of the passenger door. No matter. He ambled down the driveway, marveling at how much better he felt. The slightest twinge in his shoulder was his only reminder of that bullet.

Soon enough he'd track his shooter down and get some answers.

But first things first.

He kept an eye on the passenger side as he rounded the front of the Ford. A bright sunny day like this called for good spirits and happiness. Instead, he found himself dealing with a grumpy woman who was going to get even grumpier when he talked to her on the way home.

After cranking up his tin lizzie, he yanked the driver's door open and slid gingerly into his seat. Mary wouldn't look at him, her lovely profile a stark reminder of the reality he'd been trying to avoid since the other day.

She was beautiful.

Beautiful.

The word could barely get past his brain. Just thinking it made him feel guilty, as if he might ruin her somehow. Because she'd been almost like a sister to him, or so he'd thought, but now as he gazed at her proud chin and clenched hands, he realized he knew nothing about this woman who'd been his housekeeper for so long.

Nothing except that she'd been thrown aside in the worst of ways before being mistreated at the hands of greedy, criminal men. He felt his mouth tighten as he pulled onto the road. Why would she want anything to do with men ever again? His good humor dissipated.

They drove in silence while he waited for her to speak. When it became obvious she was too stubborn to talk about what was bothering her, he cleared his throat.

"Do you…" He paused. Asking personal questions went against the grain. He'd never done it before. Had always given her the space he thought she needed. But now it seemed he should get involved somehow. Find out who this woman was. He tapped the steering wheel with the base of his thumbs. "Do you want to talk about your annoyance with me?"

"No."

"You seemed upset back there."

"I'm fine."

Irritation crowded his throat. "Sometimes talking helps you feel better. Sharing your feelings."

"I don't have feelings to share," she snapped. Out of the corner of his eye, he saw her swivel toward him. "Why do you care, anyhow? A man who involves himself in nothing that requires emotional commitment? Those ladies are kind and giving. You shouldn't toy with them."

"I made their day exciting."

She looked away.

"And you disapprove?" Yes, he'd complimented them. He'd looked at their needlework and asked questions. At no time had he been insincere, and yet there was censure in Mary's tone. He stared sightlessly at the road, reminded again why he didn't ask questions. Why he didn't get involved.

"I don't... I'm sorry, Lou." Now her voice had softened. He glanced over and found her staring at him, eyes wide, the deep darkness of them stitching a surprising thread of awareness through him. "I had no call to speak to you in such a way. You've been nothing but kind to me from the moment I stepped foot into your home."

He cleared his throat. "The things I said in there, I meant them. Those ladies are making incredible quilts any person would be honored to own. A woman needs to know she's special, that she has something to offer...." He trailed off, thinking of his Sarah and the canvases she'd painted. She would never paint again.

"I'm happy you meant those things, Lou. I apologize again. Perhaps I'm on edge because of our situation."

He focused on the road, wishing the forlorn quality of her voice didn't bother him so badly. "No problem at all. I think this is the first time I've seen you frazzled in public before."

"I've never been frazzled, as you say."

"Last year."

"Excuse me?" Her voice rose, but he recognized humor creeping through.

"I recall a particular batch of dough that wouldn't rise for you."

She made a noise that sounded suspiciously like a laugh. He fought back a smile.

"Mary, you've got nothing to apologize for. Besides, we have bigger things to discuss, and I don't want my behavior today impacting any decisions we make."

Her heavy sigh rested between them. "Do you mean Josie?"

"Yep. There was a telegram waiting for me today. From her mother."

Mary said nothing, but the tension in the Ford felt thicker than churned-up cream.

"She wants Josie home as soon as possible," he added. "Claimed she's been ill and thought her daughter was visiting relatives. There's no getting around this telegram…. If we're not on a train within the week, she'll press charges."

"Her story is plausible," Mary said quietly, and he heard the resignation in her voice.

He ached for her, a steady, unnerving pain beneath his sternum. He knew what it was like to lose loved ones. "This never could have lasted," he said gently.

"It just felt so blissful, so perfect." He felt her stare. "I've been…lonely, I suppose."

"Since Gracie and Trevor left?"

"No."

He glanced at her then pulled the wheel to the side

to avoid a shrub growing in the middle of the rough desert road.

"For years now, I think," she continued. "It took meeting Gracie to realize I was nothing but a shadow of a person. And now, seeing Trevor so happy and fulfilled, it's as though a light has been cast on this deep, hollow well that's my life."

Lou frowned. She talked as if he and James meant nothing to her. "You might want to explain, because I've always liked having you at the ranch. James and I depend on you."

"You've both been blessings. A sanctuary for my soul. But what you've liked hasn't been me, it's been good food and clean clothes."

"That's a bunch of hogwash."

"Is it?"

He swerved to the side of the road and slammed on the brakes. "You better believe it."

Her eyes widened and her lips parted. The Ford chugged, mindless of the emotional state of its passengers. Over the various odors associated with automobiles, he caught the clean whiff of Mary's scent. That tantalizing, exotic flavor that had so tormented him when he'd been stuck in bed.

Scowling, he leaned toward her. "You haven't been just a housekeeper in years, little lady, so get used to the fact that you mean more to us than some woman doing the laundry. You're special. And you know you could've left at any time, but you didn't. Why not?"

"I—I don't know." Her eyes never left his face, studying him as though she wanted to read the depths of him.

Deliberately he held her gaze. "You've been afraid."

She broke the visual standoff. "Perhaps. Can we go home now?"

He slammed the clutch down, and the Ford jumped forward. "Holding things inside isn't healthy." It struck him how alone she'd been for the past twelve years, how unnatural that aloneness must be. "Don't you want to move on with your life? Maybe not get married, but form relationships? Time slips away too fast and you'll be old before you know it."

"I find your comments ironic. While you've been traipsing all over the world, I've built the friendships I want. It is you who has been alone. As for secrets…" Her voice trailed off.

"What?" he said, more harshly than he'd intended.

"I see the way you look at Josie. There is something you hide from, perhaps run from." She shifted, and he felt that probing gaze again, digging, searching.

He gripped the wheel. "So we both have issues. I'm just worried you'll never have a normal life. You're young, smart and talented. You should use your skills to create a better life." This was the moment he needed to tell her the truth. Why did he feel so badly over it?

"I'm selling the ranch," he said quickly.

There was a sharp intake of breath as she absorbed that information.

"I'm going to make sure you're well cared for," he rushed on. His face felt so hot he could light a wildfire with his cheeks. "You could work for the new owners of the ranch. I noticed a small store for rent in town. Maybe you'd like to open a shop or something." He chanced a look at her and his stomach flopped at the look on her face.

Expressionless and pale.

Why did she hold everything in? This was all his fault.

Jaw tight, he stared forward. "You hear me?"

"I hear you. I'll pray and see what God wants me to do."

"God? Really? And you think He'll answer you?"

"You think He won't?" she countered, and a new strength had entered her voice, challenging him, battling the belief that had helped him survive the loss of his wife and child.

"Experience has proved that when a man needs God, He doesn't show up."

"Perhaps you've measured God by the wrong experiences."

His teeth ground. Sharp pain shot through his chest. Suddenly he was overwhelmingly angry, so enraged he wanted to spill everything that had happened, show her just how faithful this God of hers was. But a man didn't talk about things like his wife and daughter dying in his arms. It didn't feel right to share, even though the words pulsated on his tongue, straining to rip free of the cage he'd put them in.

"Lou," she said quietly, "I don't know what happened in your past, but you're not the only one to have suffered pain." A small catch in her voice caught on the word *pain,* leaving it hanging between them, a shattered sound in the noisy automobile.

In that moment, the anger drained out of him, leaving him tired and empty. He opened his mouth, rotating his jaw, trying to loosen what felt tighter than his trigger finger on a loaded gun.

He wanted to explain to Mary, even though she was the type who never nagged for explanations. She was the kind of woman who waited patiently, who didn't press for what she wanted. It was both her strength and her flaw.

The road stretched before them, long and windy, the jagged horizon only hinting at what lay beyond.

"Sometimes it's easier to blame God," he finally said. Because she didn't seem to blame Him for the things that had happened to her, which made him wonder why he did.

"True."

He made to look at her, but a figure ahead on the left grabbed his attention.

"Lou, there's a woman walking on the road."

"I see her." He steered to the right, passing her safely and at a distance. The woman's silver-laced black hair streamed behind her and she wore the traditional garb of a Paiute.

Mary twisted in the seat, peering behind them.

"Stop," she said.

He looked at her. "Now?"

"Yes, stop the car!"

He slowed, but before he'd fully stopped, she opened her door and scrambled out.

Mary darted across the rough road, the sun in her eyes as she raced toward her mother. "Mother," she shouted.

Rose shuffled along, ignoring Mary, even when she skidded to a stop in front of her. She placed her hands on her mother's shoulders, mindful of the fragile frame beneath her fingers. "Where are you going?"

"You should not be here," her mother whispered. Her gaze landed somewhere behind Mary. Wind raked up the dusty road.

Mary squinted against the debris. "Come with me, to my home. It isn't safe for you to walk these roads alone."

"No."

"Please, I can take care of you."

"There is danger in these hills…." Rose's voice trailed ominously.

A cold tremor shivered its way down Mary's spine. Sometimes it seemed danger lurked everywhere. Running from it solved nothing.

And yet the vacancy of her mother's gaze was alarming, to say the least. Frowning, Mary slid her hands away and tried to meet her mother's eyes.

"Where are you going? I will take you."

"He will find us." Her mother's shoulders began to shake, small ripples of movement almost lost in the dirt-laden breeze. Long strands of hair whipped over her features, lashing at her skin as if punishing her.

Mary didn't want her mother to be punished. Not then and not now. She stepped forward and gathered Rose in a hug, inhaling her earthy scent.

"The ranch is secluded. No one shall find us there." She smoothed hair from her mother's brow. "The little girl, we must take her to her mother soon, but I need help in the meantime. Will you come?"

A sound cut through her words. Lou sidled up next to them, arms crossed, something near a scowl playing about the corners of his lips. "What's going on?"

"Mother needs a place to stay." She tilted her chin at Lou, daring him to defy her.

"She has a place."

"Not now. Something's happened." She glanced at her mother, who still looked as though a wisp of wind might tilt her over.

He moved closer. He stepped in front of her mother, and his closeness urged Mary to move back. The aroma of his cologne penetrated her senses, dredging up good memories. Her first Christmas at the ranch, exotic gifts he'd brought her from his travels.

"Rose, why aren't you at home?"

His deep voice brought Mary out of her musings. She focused on her mother, who stared blankly ahead. Refusing to answer. Stubborn. As she'd always been.

"Mother, answer him. We will help you, but we must know what we face."

Lou made a sound in his throat. "Just leave her. She's probably packing up and leaving without a word. She's got a habit of doing that." He cast a concerned look at Rose before turning his piercing gaze on Mary. "Come on. We've got things to do."

"I can't leave her."

"You can and you should." His hand waved dismissively. "She doesn't want our help. Let her deal with her own problems. We've got enough of our own, plus what she added."

"But—"

"Let's go." His curt tone brooked no argument.

Still, she hesitated. "Mother, look at me. Please."

Slowly Rose's gaze slid to meet Mary's. Dark and unblinking. She'd seen too much pain. Mary's heart hurt with the thought. She held out her hand, hoping her mother would take it. "You are welcome in my home."

"Not if she doesn't say what's going on."

Rose's gaze shifted to Lou. "I will say, but you won't like it."

Mary dropped her hand, letting it curl into a slight ball at her side. A gust swept dirt up from the road, but her mother didn't even blink. She held Lou's look long and tight.

"There is a very bad man," she pronounced. "And he wants the girl."

Chapter Ten

"Tell us something we don't know, lady." Lou lowered the brim of his hat and glared.

"It doesn't matter if he wants her," Mary said, ignoring her bothersome employer. "She's going home to her mother." It was hard, but she forced those words out.

"This is true?" Her mother's brow arched.

"Yes." She nodded to the sack in her mother's hands. "Is that everything you own?"

"Everything that's important."

"What about your baskets? Should we go back and get them?"

"They are all sold. I will go with you, on one condition."

Lou let out a loud, annoying snort. Mary formed a glare and flung it his way. He reached for her arm and none too gently propelled her a few feet from her mother. "What do you think you're doing?"

She pulled from his grasp. "I'm inviting my mother to stay with me. That is none of your concern."

"She's not riding in my tin lizzie."

Though she felt weak inside for fear, something compelled her to retort, "Is that so?"

Lou looked a bit taken aback at her spunk. But not angry. Relief unfurled inside.

"She's got a condition, Mary. That isn't right. This whole situation is wrong and I'm not going to stand by and watch her hurt you again."

"She never hurt me." At his look, she grimaced. "Not much," she amended.

"Regardless, I don't trust any friend of Julia's. She says she's running from this guy who's looking for Josie, but what if she's working for him?"

It was true her mother and Julia had been friends, which was why her mother had left her to live with Julia and her son, Trevor, at the brothel. But Mary had no reason to believe that her mother had anything to do with her being sold to Mendez at eighteen and she certainly wouldn't hold another's actions against her.

"You're too suspicious."

"Nope. I'm not. It happens all the time. Like I said, she doesn't need to be close to you. I'm putting my foot down about her."

He had a very satisfied look on his face that would've made her smile if she wasn't so angry. Her hands fisted, palms slick. She swallowed hard.

"I do appreciate your concern, but you know nothing of why my mother left me with Julia. You have judged with no knowledge." He made to interrupt and she held up a hand. "If you will not give us a ride, then we shall walk."

"You're taking her side?" He had the temerity to look aghast.

"This is not about sides. It is about right and wrong. To leave my mother alone is wrong."

"I see."

"I hope that you do." The words rolled off her tongue, succinct, surprising her.

Lou barked a quick laugh without mirth. "Fine, then. Try to fit her in."

"Are we going to the picnic?" Josie watched as Mary drew a pan of snickerdoodles from her Glenwood gas-and-coal stove. She inspected them, feeling very thankful for the modern range she cooked with. The cookies were perfect.

"Do we have to go to church first?"

"Don't worry, you'll like it." She patted Josie's hair, which hung in the two neat braids her mother had formed while Mary baked. "Miss Alma and I sing wonderful songs, and you're going to meet some of my friends."

Mary didn't attend a traditional church but rather met with other Christians at a neighbor's property. Mr. Horn preached the sermons and sometimes people brought instruments. Mostly those with homes on the outskirts of the desert attended, though Miss Alma often came from town.

"Thank you for my dress, Miss Mary." Josie's eyes sparkled, and Mary couldn't help grinning back. The girl had picked a lovely green to border her white dress. Mary had sewn it together and added matching bows.

"You're welcome, my sweet girl. Ask my mother if she can put your bows on."

"Okay." She skipped out of the room, her new Mary Janes tapping a happy tune.

These snickerdoodles were the last batch. She popped one that had cooled in her mouth, then set about searching for a basket to put them in. She sneaked a few into a hankie for the ride to Horn's and arranged the rest neatly.

Once done, she found Josie jabbering away to Rose, who sat with a smile on her face. The creases in her skin seemed less deep somehow, as though weight had gone from her soul.

Mary smiled and crossed the room. "It's time to go. Are you sure you won't come, Mother?"

"I am certain. Perhaps I'll take a rest."

Her mother woke early now, perhaps because she'd spent more than the first half of her life sleeping through sunrises and well into the afternoon. Mary nodded and guided Josie toward the door.

"We'll be home in the afternoon."

Rose nodded, and her eyes slipped closed.

As Mary shut the door to the house, she heard Josie shriek, "Mister Lou!"

She barely caught the girl by a pigtail as Lou's fancy Ford pulled up to the porch.

"Hop in, ladies." He winked at them. "I'll be your chauffeur today."

Josie squealed with delight. Mary frowned but helped the little girl into the car. She settled where Rose had sat yesterday.

Even now, a day later, it was a strange sensation to know she'd done something out of the ordinary, that she'd risked Lou's disapproval to do what she felt was right. But it had also been empowering and thrilling. For some reason, he'd allowed her to load her mother into his Ford and bring her back to the ranch.

Perhaps he'd felt bad for her at the time. After all, she'd brought up her past, and she knew the things she'd gone through caused him grief. She didn't wish to use her past to get her way, however.

"You coming?" He beeped his horn, making her start. Her basket tilted.

"If these snickerdoodles spill..." she warned.

"Yes, ma'am." He shot her that grin of his.

Mouth tight to cover the ratcheting speed of her pulse, she scurried to the passenger side and loaded up. The trip to Horn's homestead took almost an hour, thanks to the bumpy, rutted road. A horse could handle the trek much faster. Josie and Lou kept up a stream of chatter while Mary attempted to darn an old sock. A useless endeavor considering the uneven terrain. Finally, they arrived. Josie bounced in the back as she waited for Mary to exit the car. As soon as she stepped foot outside, Josie escaped, slipping past her and running toward Horn's place.

Families milled around, unpacking lunches beneath the shaded trees.

"Josie, come back."

"Aww." She sped back, though. A good listener.

Mary handed her the blanket she'd brought. "Could you please find a place for us to sit? And if you see Mr. Horn, let him know I'll be there shortly."

"Okeydokey!" Josie popped a smile and snatched the blanket. She ran toward the other kids, who played near a sturdy elm. She was easy to see from this distance.

"She's going to get dirty quick," Lou remarked.

"I know." Mary smiled. "You may pick us up in four hours or so."

His head cocked to the side. Morning light danced in his eyes. "Thought I'd stay and keep an eye on things."

"Surely you do not believe Josie's uncle will find his way here?"

He shrugged. "Better safe than sorry. If he did, we'd

spot him right away. Either way, it's my job to keep an eye on the girl until we get her home safe to her ma."

"Of course," she said, refusing to dwell on the disappointment that filled her at his words. "Come along. You know many of these people, I believe. At least by face."

"But I plan on sticking close to you." He winked again, and a flush warmed her skin. "May I carry your basket?"

She allowed him to take it. Not knowing what to say, she picked her way toward the picnic area. Neighbors had spread their blankets in a grassy area beneath a sprawling elm. Children frolicked in the grass, shrieking and laughing. Josie ran amidst them, her giggles lost within the group.

"They having a service today?" Lou asked beside her.

"Probably a little something." Did he sound worried? She glanced at him and saw that he did indeed look unnaturally tense. "Mr. Horn is easy on the ears."

"Not worried about that."

"What, then?"

"There you are!" Miss Alma's bright voice cut off anything he planned to say next. "I shall take your wonderful desserts. I saw that darling girl of yours. Is she an orphan?"

"No." Was it horrible to wish she was? Battling a sense of guilt, Mary gestured to the basket. "I hope they'll do."

"Of course they will. Now, did you bring James?"

"No…"

"Tsk, tsk. I needed to speak with the man." Miss Alma whisked the basket from Lou, barely offering him a glance before tottling off toward the tables set up near the trees.

"She's a bundle of energy, huh?"

"You really don't have to stay." As soon as the words left her mouth, she regretted them. For how long had she been praying Lou would attend service? Maybe there'd even been a secret hope inside that he'd change his views on God, soften a bit. She'd never had the nerve to pray out loud for meals until his niece, Gracie, had come. That had been how ornery both James and Lou became, though James tended to approach the mention of God in a more intellectual manner.

But Lou closed up completely. All emotion, much like Trevor. As though he'd been hurt. She sidled a look toward him. The breeze ruffled through his hair. He caught her staring and gave her a tight smile.

"I'm staying," he said. "There's no way I'm missing your desserts."

She sniggered. "You'll be going back to work and needing new clothes if you keep this eating up."

"A well-fed man is a happy man."

"I wish that was true."

"Me, too." He sighed and looked toward the horizon. The mountains rose sharply against the sky, steep and dangerous. Much like the feelings spreading through her.

Yet she didn't know how to stop this warmth…no, this fire. She'd always felt tender toward Lou. How could she not? He'd taken her in at the darkest moment of her life. Kept her safe.

But lately…things were changing, and she wasn't quite sure what to make of it.

Stuck in God talk.

Last thing he wanted, but here he was, settling down on the blanket, with Mary only spaces away from him, her scent mingling with the aromas of fried chicken and flowers. Mr. Horn had instructed everyone to take seats so they could have a short preaching before the picnic.

It had been years since he'd attended any kind of Christian event. What had coerced him now was beyond his ken, but he'd just have to starch his backbone and ignore the rumbling of his stomach.

Truth be told, a picnic had sounded bunches better than sitting home by himself. James planned to stay home reading, but Lou preferred action of some sort. He wasn't a reader, never had been.

Josie came scrambling over, hair flying in her face. She stopped in front of him and brushed knotty strands from her eyes. "We gotta sit still now, don't we?"

Lou made a face and she giggled. Plopping down beside him, she leaned her head onto his arm. A lump formed in his throat but he didn't move away.

Horn moved into sight. People had arranged their blankets in rows, just like a church. The man went to the front.

"Morning, everyone."

The group replied with murmurs, mornings, et cetera. An interesting mix of folks here. Mary wasn't the only Paiute. There was also a Chinese man on a far blanket. Miss Alma with her fancy hat and pleated dress sat next to a family who wore homespun clothes and no shoes.

Feeling more comfortable in this mix of people, he leaned back on his elbows and stretched his legs out. He felt Mary's glance but got caught in Horn's words and didn't meet it.

"Troubles come our way. Hardships." Horn cleared his throat. "But God brings us through. He delivers us from the snare of the enemy and fills our souls with peace. I thought today it would be nice to read the nineteenth chapter of Psalms and sing a few songs before we dig into these scrumptious vittles the ladies worked up."

"Pa fried up his special chicken recipe," a young girl called out.

Horn chuckled. "He sure did. Who'd like to read?"

Miss Alma stood. Lou heard the bustle of her voluminous skirts from where he sat.

"I shall," she said. She adjusted the petite glasses on her face and held up a heavy-looking book. Her voice surrounded them and suddenly everything faded but the clarity of her words.

"'Because he hath set his love upon me, therefore will I deliver him. I will set him on high, because he hath known my name. He shall call upon me, and I will answer him. I will be with him in trouble, I will deliver him, and honor him. With long life will I satisfy him, and shew him my salvation.'"

Lou squirmed on the blanket, glad when she was finished. A heavy sense of regret crept through him. For what, he wasn't sure. Miss Alma sat and then, suddenly, Mary stood up beside him. She opened her mouth and sang "Amazing Grace." The others followed until the entire area filled with the sound of voices.

Mary's voice was a husky soprano. He'd heard her humming throughout the years as she worked but never had she sang so lovely, so invitingly, of God and His grace.

The song he used to sing. Years ago. As a child and young man. The God he'd trusted. Mary thought Him worthy of trust. Still… Josie wiggled beside him. He glanced at her blond curls and thought of Sarah and Abby. Their passing had been so long ago. Why did the memories still hurt so much?

He blinked as the singing faded and an odd silence

descended on the group. Then Mary began "How Great Thou Art." A chill rippled through his body at her words.

Her face was relaxed, her lips rounding and changing as she sang. Her hands lifted and swelled with her words. She was happy here. At peace.

Because of God.

Deep down, in a place he didn't care to explore, he felt the truth of it. That he'd turned his back on Jesus and everything he'd been raised with and now he felt pain and bitterness. But Mary had embraced what he'd spurned and it had changed her.

He blinked as Josie slid her hand into his. He looked down at her broad smile and vowed to protect this little girl. Whatever it took. He returned Josie's squeeze and sang with the group.

It had been a long time. His throat worked each consonant and spit them out rusty, but Josie didn't seem to care. When the song ended and they'd all spread out on blankets, he found himself plopping down next to Mary.

"Mmm, you smell good. Like cinnamon and roses. Like snickerdoodles."

She blushed beside him. The grin that had taken hold during the song widened. He leaned back, folding his hands behind his head and crossing his ankles. "What's on the menu?"

"Fried chicken, apple dumplings—"

"Snickerdoodles?"

"You know so." She sent him an exasperated look, but he saw laughter in her eyes.

"Where's Josie?"

"I'm right here!" She hopped onto the blanket, spinning, and then dropping down.

"Your dress, Josie."

But the girl didn't hear Mary. She was staring at

a group of kids in the distance. Someone's father, or maybe an older brother, was giving each a turn at being swung in a circle.

"Go over there," he told her.

"She's wearing a dress," said Mary.

Josie sighed heavily, a bit on the melodramatic side. He shook as unexpected laughter bubbled through him. Mary was hiding her own smirk behind tightly pressed lips. He met her eyes and suddenly the laughter dried up.

The chirping of the birds, the sounds of chatter and laughter faded, and all he could see was Mary. Kind, beautiful Mary. Her hair shimmering, her eyes pinned on him, widening when he didn't look away. A strange and almost foreign feeling swept through him. He leaned forward.

"Mister Lou!" Josie tugged on his sleeve. "Will you swing me around like those kids?" She slid between him and Mary, ending what had been an intriguing moment. He shook his head to clear it and then gave Josie a wink.

"I'll swing until you can't stand anymore. Let's go." He followed her to the elm, letting her grip his palm as she skipped beside him. A different feeling filled him, something close to contentment.

When he was gone to Asia, he'd look back and hold these memories dear.

Chapter Eleven

Mary didn't want Lou to sell the ranch.

There. She could admit it to herself. After watching him with Josie yesterday, laughing and relaxed, she realized the life she'd built here wasn't enough. Lou had been right. She needed more than what she had. She was ready for more.

Thoughtful, she pinned a towel on the line, thankful for the sun that dried each piece of laundry. Her mother was in the house with Josie, teaching her to weave baskets. The delicate scents of desert drifted around her and for a moment she closed her eyes as the refrains of yesterday's hymn swept through her heart.

Then sings my soul, my savior God to thee.
How great Thou art, how great Thou art.

Humming, she reached for a shirt and clipped it to the line.

"Mary." Lou's voice rose above her humming.

She turned, shading her eyes from the glare of sunlight, trying to pinpoint his location. She heard him behind her. She whirled, hand to her chest.

"Are you sneaking up on me?"

"Do you have a moment to talk?" He squinted at her.

"I'm almost done. What do you wish to speak of?"

"Plans need to be made," he said gently.

Her spine stiffened. She pinned a bread cloth to the line, avoiding his gaze. "Have you told Gracie and Trevor you're selling the ranch? Don't you need their permission?"

"I have it." He gestured toward the house. "Why don't we go up for lunch and talk a spell."

"Lunch isn't quite ready."

"We'll speak here, then."

She felt his perusal to the marrow of her bones and suppressed a shiver. Lately it seemed as if he'd been looking at her differently, more deeply, as though he truly saw her. She found the interest both intoxicating and terrifying.

Refusing to meet his eyes, she plucked a towel from her basket and stretched it evenly on the line. Lou took a clip from her waist and pinned the cloth.

She wrinkled her nose at him. "If you'd rather do this, I can go prepare lunch. Since you're apparently not busy."

"I'm busy." He shifted closer, and suddenly she became aware of how much larger he was than her, and yet she felt no fear, only an odd fluttering below her ribs that prompted her to step back. She reached for the remaining sock in the basket.

"I can meet you up there." She wanted her voice to remain steady, but it came out wrong, breathy and not at all like her.

Thankfully, Lou turned and paced away, toward the small porch of Trevor's—her—house. Stifling a sigh, she hung the sock and then trudged after him.

Perhaps he wished to speak of the ranch sale or of her mother's presence on this property. Resolve hardened within her and gave life to her steps.

Heart thumping and breath a tad thin, she followed Lou onto the porch. She settled in the chair next to his. Close enough to smell the Wrigley's in his pocket and see the stubble on his chin. "You're in need of a shave."

He cocked his head, catching her gaze with his. "I was going to ask you to do that for me this afternoon."

"Me?" she squeaked.

"Yeah, we're heading out tomorrow morning, early, and I don't have time to get to a barber."

She swallowed her denial. The man needed a shave and a trim, but she'd only given them to James. Rarely had she touched Lou, and now it seemed they were thrown together all the time. It did not bode well for her nerves.

"Josie does not wish to go." She heard the stubborn note in her voice and didn't care.

"I'm gonna be honest with you." Lou peered at her, forehead furrowed. "If we don't take her home, my bosses will be sending someone to do it for us. I've bought as much time as I can but any longer and we're liable to be charged with some kind of wrongdoing."

"That's not right."

"Life isn't about what we feel. You're saying it's not right, but what about Josie's mother? How's she feeling, knowing her daughter never made it safely to relatives?" Lou frowned. "What's gotten into you? I've never known you to be so unreasonable."

Mary recoiled. "It is not I who is unreasonable here. You've wanted to get rid of her since the very beginning."

"I just wanted her to be cared for, out of danger." His eyes were inscrutable.

She stood and paced near the steps, pushing her skirt in front of her knees as she moved back and forth.

Lou stepped in front of her, placing his palms against her shoulders. She stopped, unable to move forward because he'd effectively ended her momentum. Annoyed, she glared at him.

"Remove your hands."

His eyes narrowed. "She's not ours, Mary. You've got to let her go."

No. The word echoed in her heart, a lonely, distant wail that couldn't seem to make it to her lips. She didn't want to let Josie go. She wanted to hold her and love her and raise her. Spin in the sunlight with her a million times more.

His grip loosened, and he crossed his arms across his chest. "This afternoon I need a shave and a trim. Can you do that?"

Numbly, she nodded past the ache that was already spreading through her.

"Good." He paused as though he'd say something more, and his gaze lingered on her face, but she couldn't bear to feel his pity for her.

The alone woman, as he'd said.

She watched as he walked away, his body casting a long, confident shadow against her beloved lands. How many times had she watched him leave? Drive off to fight battles unknown. To rescue those in distress. And never once had she asked him to stay so she wouldn't be alone. It hadn't been her place either, and yet...

This time she was determined to walk first.

Mary rode hard into Burns shortly after hanging the wash. Josie remained with Rose. As for Lou, she planned to cut his hair this evening, but for now she wanted to see about renting rooms somewhere. An idea had blossomed after he left, but she wasn't sure how financially practical opening a bakery might be.

Many are the plans in a man's heart, but the Lord's plan prevails.

The verse resonated within as she hitched up her horse and hurried into the general store.

She found the owner bent beside an old shelf, dusting it.

"Joseph."

"Miss Mary." He stood and shared his ready smile. "Did you bring any winterfat? The ladies wiped me clean within the week."

She shook her head. "I am actually curious to know if you've heard of a storeroom for rent. And if you've advice on how to go about getting some."

"Well, now…" He scratched his chin. "I can't say I've heard a thing about that. Maybe the best one you should be talking to is a solicitor? I bought this place years ago and don't reckon I remember which is the best way to go about finding any places for rent."

Mary pasted a smile to her lips though her heart had sunk to her knees. "Very well. I shall try someone else."

"Are you planning on opening a goods store?"

The too-casual question amused her. "Never fear, I shall only bring my herbs to you."

"I don't care either way." He shrugged, and Mary bit back a smile at the untruth.

She left him and walked the streets of Burns. There were, in fact, several rooms within buildings for sale. But which one would best suit her needs? She peered within dusty windows while pondering the situation.

"Yoo-hoo, Mary!"

Turning, Mary looked for the source of the female calling to her. Across the road a young woman dressed in a frilly garment scooted over, clutching her dress in one hand and a parasol in the other.

Amy. Gracie's friend. She waited as the girl dashed over.

"How nice to see you again." Amy's smile spread wide and fresh.

"And you." Mary inclined her head. "Your dress is lovely."

"Why, thank you. I'm attending a wedding. A Monday wedding, which is rather romantic. This gentleman returned from the war and my friend Sally had waited ever so long for him, but he'd been hurt, you see, and had to recuperate. Well, they're finally marrying and it's the biggest to-do."

"That is very romantic," Mary acknowledged, feeling her own heart wither beneath the girl's innocent, starry outlook. "Young love—"

"Oh, they're not young." Freckles trotted across Amy's features with bold perkiness. Rather like their wearer's voice. "She's been waiting years, ever since school days, and it took his going to war for him to realize that she was the woman for him. It helped that she nursed him back to health, as well."

There seemed to be an underlying message in Amy's eyes, and Mary shifted uncomfortably. "I suppose such a thing could bring about a certain closeness."

"It most certainly can." Amy's grin stretched as she swooped her parasol to point at Mary. "I must be off, but wanted to run over and say hello. Also, I had a bit of news about that murderer."

"You did?"

"Yep." She leaned forward conspiratorially. "Turns out that good-looking stranger has been released. The police have a new suspect. I don't know why or how it all came about." She straightened. "Well, then, care to join me at the wedding?"

"No, thank you." Her mind churned.

"Boy, it's sweltering out here." Up popped the parasol. A vigorous wave and then Amy was off in a different direction.

Mary watched her, feeling a strange intermingling of bewilderment and laughter. When Gracie returned, she probably ought to join her on one of her outings with Amy. She rather liked the girl.

A quick glance in both directions proved the road to be empty. She crossed and moments later knocked on a local deputy's door.

"Hullo?" The elderly man poked his head out. The scent of Colgate shaving cream wafted out and reminded Mary that she needed to get home and help Lou before dusk.

Shrugging off the thought, she straightened her shoulders and gave him a serious look. "Sir, is it true that a murderer has been released from your custody?"

"I highly doubt that." The door widened to reveal his bent structure.

Frowning, she held his gaze. "I've been told the man originally arrested for assault, the man I pointed out to you, is no longer under suspicion."

"Don't know how you heard those details but it's true. Mr. Langdon is no longer considered a suspect. We have a man who came forward and confessed. Is that all you needed today?"

Dumbly, she nodded. She turned and walked down the road, back to her horse, mulling over the deputy's words. It seemed rather convenient that a man confessed. *Too* convenient. And incredibly bothersome.

Did Mr. Langdon know she'd pointed him out as a suspect? She could only guess he did, and of course he knew she worked at Lou's ranch…. A shudder swept through her despite the summer warmth.

Suddenly she had an urge to hurry home, to check on Josie and share with Lou what she'd learned. But perhaps he knew. He was a man who, for all his smiles and carefree words, kept secrets.

She reached her horse and mounted quickly. Casting a look down the road, she felt sure the coast was clear and galloped out of town. She passed the Paiute settlement on the way and waved.

The sight of the dogs, the misplaced tents and the run-down people filled her with sadness. But for her Irish father and renegade mother, she might be weaving baskets for an income and living in a canvas tent that would never be her own.

The horse's even movements lulled her into deep thoughts of the past. She'd been thirteen when her mother dropped her off with Trevor's mom, at the house of ill repute she'd owned.

Although she'd known Trevor since she was a wee one, her mother's constant moving had kept them in sporadic touch. When her da had disappeared and the men in her mother's life had started looking at Mary, she'd dropped her off for safety with Trevor's mom and gone in search of Da.

That choice had forged a loyalty between Mary and Trevor that had kept her safe until she was eighteen.

Until Trevor's mother had grown impatient with Mary's decision to be the house seamstress and nothing more. Until she'd seen the growing bond between her son and her friend's daughter. Until her jealousy had forced her to do the unthinkable....

Mary blinked and urged her horse to move faster, wishing the hot air against her skin could melt the memories that blistered her heart and twisted her stomach. She glanced at the sky. It must be nearing three o'clock. She would go home, make a meal, help Lou, and then she'd have to speak with Josie to explain what must happen soon.

Would the little girl understand?

Mary felt sure she wouldn't. Every day it seemed the pressure on her shoulders grew heavier. It had taken Gracie leaving and Lou being home to make her see how much she longed for family. After her self-induced seclusion of twelve years, the need for family and belonging bludgeoned her senses and as Lou had said, twisted her priorities.

It had been wrong for her to try to keep Josie for so long. A little girl needed her mother and for all she knew, Josie's mother had been frantic with worry. Powerless to change anything since she was ill.

Oh, Lord, forgive me.

Keeping Josie from her mother was the biggest mistake Mary had ever made. How could she have been blind to it for so long? Thinking only of her own desires and not another's?

This must be fixed. Tomorrow she would leave with Lou and do what must be done. It was time to put her trust in the God who had saved her from wicked people, who had filled her with peace.

A hawk swooped ahead, gliding through the sky in search of food. Like that bird, God would care for her and tend to her needs. She must believe it.

And it started with thanks, something she'd sorely neglected since Lou had returned with his injury and since she'd been busy taking care of Josie.

The hawk disappeared from view, its majestic red-tipped wings spread in splendor against the azure sky. Mary lifted her face upward, feeling the graze of sunlight against her skin, and began a song to praise her King.

Her voice echoed, rising and falling, filling the desert around her, reaching, she hoped, the God she loved. As she neared the hidden trail that wound carefully to the ranch's secluded location, her voice tapered with the end of the song and she slowed the mare to a stop.

She took a deep breath. Filled her lungs with the scents of sage and pine, listening to the sounds of summer birds calling to each other across the rugged landscape.

As she sat there, another sound filtered through to her hearing, a different sound. A sound that didn't fit.

She froze, patting her mare to soothe the sudden dance she did with her hooves.

The sound came again. A steady clop, like the muted sounds of covered hooves.

Her breaths shortened as panic began to claw up her breastbone, rising and grabbing her, reaching to her throat and clutching it in an unbreakable vise.

Someone had followed her.

Chapter Twelve

Somehow Mary managed to keep calm and continue onward. She dodged the main, albeit camouflaged, trail and instead guided the horse down a steep embankment into a gnarled, woody area. The steep hills and shrubbery provided decent enough cover if she stayed within shadows and kept to the sides of the range, which in some places rose to over a thousand feet.

The ranch was nestled in a deserted area that was almost like a valley. The Steens Mountains loomed on one side, and the surrounding desert provided natural protection against human intruders. When Trevor had first brought her to the ranch, she'd been in shock from the kidnapping and hardly noticed her surroundings. As months passed, though, the encircling natural formations began to be her peace, to comfort and protect her. But they never did warm the chill in her soul.

It took a special kind of person to do that. She smiled as she navigated a particularly rough patch in her detour. Miss Alma's presence had changed the way Mary looked at life and though it took time, eventually she'd been able to trust others and find joy again.

Fear hadn't been her companion in so long that now when it reappeared, she wasn't sure what to do. Praising God had helped...until she'd heard someone following her.

For the first time in years, her faith was being tested in a large, unanticipated way. She deliberately slowed her breathing, willing her heart rate to follow.

Nothing stood out, though. Just familiar horse noises from her mount. Once she was sure no one had followed her onto this new path, she forged ahead and willed the old memories to stay at bay.

"For God hath not given us a spirit of fear, but of power, love and a sound mind." She uttered the verse beneath her breath. And then she felt strong emotion welling within her, a hot arc of anger that someone dared follow her, that they even dared to make her afraid.

This was *her* home. Josie might be leaving soon, but until tomorrow, she was Mary's responsibility and she *would* keep her safe. Who knew where that stranger had gone who looked for her, but she would not allow him to trespass on her property. If he so much as tried to get in her front door, well...she wouldn't hesitate to use her derringer.

Her jaw set and she lengthened her stride. When she was certain she wasn't being followed anymore, she took a more direct route to the ranch. By the time she reached her home, the sun had dropped to the horizon and a cool breeze scooped and swirled around her.

Josie sat outside the house with her mother, weaving a basket.

Mary rode past, took care of the horse in the stable, then walked home. Josie looked up with a toothy smile. Rose's smile was in her eyes.

"You've been busy," Mary said, grabbing a rocking chair and pulling it near where Josie sat on the porch floor so she could reach and touch the little girl's hair, which glinted in the fading sunlight.

"I have many baskets to sell," Rose answered. Her hands moved steadily.

"You do not have to work anymore."

Her mother's eyes flickered before she looked down at her work. "It is something I've done since I was a small girl at my mother's side. I will pay my way."

Mary wanted to tell her mother that she didn't owe her anything. This home was free. But Josie watched them with bright eyes, and the subject was much too personal to air in front of little ears.

Instead, she shrugged. "My trip to town was fruitful. There are a few store areas that look as though they'd fit my needs." She'd discussed the ranch sale with her mother last night.

"And the cost?"

"I didn't find out yet." She shifted uncomfortably. Though she'd saved quite a bit in the past years, she wasn't sure it would be enough to open a new business, let alone rent a space for a baker. If she was going to own a business, it would be for something she loved to do. Something she knew she could excel at but would also fill a need in the town.

"Building a business often requires money," her mother said.

"I know." Mary sighed and smoothed the top of Josie's hair. "What did you two do today?"

"We made bunches of baskets. I found a little squirrel and almost caught it." Josie beamed up at her and Mary grinned.

"Excuse me…" Lou's deep drawl interrupted them.

She looked up and felt that odd catch in her stomach again. His hair had grown too long since the shooting. It gave him a wild, untamed look. The scruff on his jaw only lent to the dangerous edge he exuded and deepened the blue of his eyes.

"Yes?" She tried to swallow the dryness from her throat. Nerves prickled.

He didn't look at her mother or Josie but focused his gaze upon her, increasing the flame of anxiety that flickered through her body. "Just wanted to verify you'll give me my shave and trim after supper."

No, she wanted to yell. Instead, she found herself stuck nodding a wordless yes.

Every ounce of her felt caught in that magnetic gaze of his.

Finally, he looked away, and she could breathe again.

"Josie, pack your things tonight. We leave at first light," he said.

"Where are we going?"

"Tomorrow we're taking you to your mother." A strange catch in his voice tripped Mary's attention.

Was that pain traveling across his face? The emotion passed too quickly and once again his features settled into a carefree smile.

"Oh." Josie quieted beneath Mary's hand, which still rested on her head.

He shouldn't have broken the news to her like this. Mary frowned and guided Josie to rest her head against her leg. She stroked the little girl's hair. "Don't you want to see your mother?"

"I guess…." Her voice trailed off. "I just don't want to see *him.*"

"We're gonna take you straight to your mother. Only her. And I'm going to make sure you're completely safe before I leave." Lou's eyes darted to Mary before he squatted in front of Josie. "Your mother missed you and thought you were visiting relatives."

"She sent me away," Josie said in a very small voice.

Something bitter and sharp pricked at Mary. She swallowed hard and tucked a hair behind Josie's ear. She felt her mother's gaze.

"I know, sweetheart." Empathy filled Lou's tone. "But she didn't want you to be gone forever, just to visit family. And now that we've found her and I'm better, Miss Mary and I are going to take you home so your mommy won't be sad anymore."

Josie turned her face into Mary's skirt and mumbled something.

"Sometimes a mother makes a very big mistake," Rose said quietly. "It takes a wise little girl to forgive and offer a second chance."

"I'm not gonna go." Josie pulled away, and Mary caught a glimpse of the stubborn glare she aimed toward Lou.

"Mary, please make sure she's packed for tomorrow," he said in a soft voice. He gave Josie a tender smile before looking to Mary. "I'll be ready after supper." He turned on his heel and strode away.

True to her word, Mary showed up after the dishes were done and Rose had taken Josie back to the house for sleep. He watched from the sitting room window as she came up the porch and paused before the front door. She adjusted her skirt and appeared to take a deep breath. Her face looked flushed and her eyes glimmered.

Was she nervous?

Her body language said so.

He stepped away from the window, rubbing the back of his neck. If there was another way to save her this discomfort, he would. Unfortunately, James was busy checking their route for tomorrow and making sure everything was in order while they were gone. He didn't have time to be a barber, too.

The idea of making Mary uncomfortable bothered him deeply, but after spending these weeks here, he realized he'd done wrong in keeping her so isolated. Seeing her with Josie, it had become obvious she loved children. Maybe even wanted a family of her own. Sometimes he worried he'd stolen that from her by keeping her so comfortable at the ranch that she rarely left.

Yes, she'd needed time to heal from her kidnapping, but that didn't seem reason enough now for her isolation. A deep compulsion drove him to do something more, make sure she was okay before he left Harney County for good. But what could he do?

The front door creaked and then there was the click of it closing. Mary appeared in the doorway, her hair neat and shining, her face devoid of emotion. He gestured to the chair near the window where he'd set the supplies. "Have you ever done this?"

"A long time ago."

Her voice wobbled, betraying what her face hid.

A fierce surge of protectiveness shot through him. And uncertainty, because something about him was making her nervous lately. Was she feeling what he was? That could be dangerous for both of them.

The thought soured his positive feelings and turned his voice curt. "Just don't cut me, then. Try to make things even in the back."

"I'll do my best."

He settled into the chair. At least he wouldn't have to see her face, look into her eyes. The deep calm of them had always pulled at him, drawn him in a way he'd hated. But as her fingers combed through his hair, wetting and straightening, he realized that being in this vulnerable position was infinitely worse. Silently groaning, he forced himself to ignore the warm strength of her fingers against his nape.

She worked in silence for several long, torturous minutes. The sound of the scissors snipping took the place of any words they might've shared.

"Have you packed?" he asked at last. Staying quiet seemed worthless when there was something to be said.

"Not yet." Her voice, a lyrical blend of sound, floated over him.

"You should do that. Make sure Josie is ready, too."

"I will." Now she sounded defensive. "She needs time to adjust. We should have given her that."

"She had to know she would go home eventually," he pointed out, despite the guilt twisting his gut.

His head tugged back a little more roughly than normal.

"For some reason, she doesn't want to return home. Don't you find that suspicious?"

"Yep."

"And yet you'll still send her?"

"I told you that I'll be arranging for her protection, but can we talk about this when you're not armed with scissors?" He tilted his head to meet her rather serious gaze. When he winked at her, the color in her face deepened. Yep, definitely not immune to him.

Despite the inconvenience of this unfortunate attraction, he settled back in the chair again with a satisfied feeling. He could handle things. Get Josie out of danger. Find the shooter. Settle James and Mary before he moved on.

Based on that telegram he'd picked up in town, he had a couple of options.

The clink of the knife against the washbowl drew him out of his thoughts. Mary, armed with a towel and shaving cream, hovered in front of him.

"Ready?" she asked.

He nodded and closed his eyes as she dabbed the cool cream across his skin. Then there was the rasp of the razor against his throat. She moved quietly and smoothly, making no conversation. Her scent hovered just beneath the scent of his shaving cream.

As she worked, the unease in his gut spread. Ever since that day he'd seen her in the valley with Josie… This wasn't good. Attractions were best left alone. Then again, sometimes all it took was a kiss to know the woman he'd been mooning over wasn't for him. There'd been a couple like that, women he'd thought might ease his loneliness, maybe help him forget Sarah and Abby.

They never did.

And Mary, well, he didn't even know if she'd ever been kissed. He cracked a lid. Her eyes were focused somewhere around his chin and her brows narrowed in concentration. His mouth twitched. Her attention shifted to him.

Her gaze lingered a little too long before darting away. He shut his eyes but couldn't temper the emotions ricocheting through him, nor the knowledge of what he'd just seen.

Mary felt drawn to him.

Something deeper and more elemental than mere attraction rushed through him. The emotion settled in his chest, patient and alert, waiting for expression.

He forced steady breaths and held perfectly still while Mary continued the shave. His biceps bunched when her skirt brushed against him. Mouth dry, he waited.

For what, he wasn't sure, but suddenly things changed. Moved to a different place. He opened his eyes again. Mary looked at him, soft lips pursed. What would it be like to kiss her? She, who seemed so unreachable?

"Can you turn your head just so?" Her palm cupped his chin.

He reached up and encircled her arm, resting his fingers against the warmth of her inner wrist. Her eyes widened. She began to pull away, but he stood and slid his hand down to hers, lacing his fingers within hers. With his other hand he reached for the towel and roughly brushed it against his lips.

He tossed it to the ground.

"Wh-what are you doing?"

Her stammer did nothing to ease the pulse hammering through him. No, those wide eyes only beckoned him closer. To know exactly what he was dealing with.

"Are you afraid of me?" he rasped.

Her eyes held his, so deep, so full of mystery. "No," she whispered.

His chest tightened and he reached for her, pulling her close to him, drawing her lips to his, searching yet careful, probing yet holding back.

Until he felt her resistance crumble.

When she responded, that band inside his chest snapped and he became voracious, longing, wishing for something that seemed so far beyond his reach. *Home.* The scent of flowers and sage swirled around him in a heady, pulsating rush.

He was the first to pull away. He forced himself to separate from her. Her cheeks were flushed, her eyes burned dark and fathomless.

That kiss had been exquisite. Incredible.

The absolute biggest mistake of his life.

Chapter Thirteen

Mary couldn't stop trembling.

Lou had pulled away and was busy toweling dry the rest of his face and neck. "How much is left to shave?" he asked.

"I completed the task." Her lips burned, but she didn't dare touch them in front of him. Would he see how she shook, how unsettled she felt? She stepped back and bumped against the window.

"Mary… I shouldn't have done that." He faced her and the look of chagrin on his features nearly crumpled her. Was it so bad to have kissed her, then? "We have too much going on to dabble in romantic affections. Why, this place could be sold in a week, and then we'll probably never see each other again." He kept talking, his words swirling through her mind with an odd energy. Each time his lips moved she felt something inside her grow more brittle and finally, when she could stand no more of his pointless ramblings, she stepped away from the window and fixed him a very pointed look.

"*You* kissed me," she said briskly, thankful her voice

did not betray her shakiness. "Do not pull a 'we' into this."

"But you liked it."

At that, her cheeks caught fire. A boldness in his bright blue eyes made her think he wasn't as chagrined as she'd previously thought. "My feelings on the subject are not important."

"Oh, but they are. Tell me, Mary, *did* you like it?"

She wanted to be anywhere but here. If only she could escape, but with her back to the window, there was nowhere to go besides past Lou, and with that curious look on his face, there was no telling what he might do. She squirmed beneath his scrutiny.

"It was…" She paused and then settled on a word. "Enlightening."

His arms crossed his chest as he grinned. "How so?"

"Like s-stumbling on the right recipe for piecrust," she stuttered. The conceited man was still smirking, broad enough to give her a hankering to toss an egg at his face. She wanted to tell him so, but restraint held her lips closed. Instead, she settled for a dark scowl.

He busted into a loud laugh, the kind she hadn't heard from him in too long.

"I'm glad, Mary, real glad you liked it. It worried me a bit that you might be scared and all." Despite the smile, his gaze searched her.

Affronted, she felt her scowl deepening. "I am no longer the young woman brought to you on the threshold of collapse."

"Very true." His gaze dropped to her lips.

She felt that look to the marrow of her bones. Swallowing hard, she fixed her gaze on him. "As a matter of fact, I am looking into opportunities at this very moment. There are several available stores in Burns and I believe I can rent one and run a business."

"What kind of venture are you thinking of?" Lou tossed his towel to the chair. It slipped to the floor.

She bent to pick up at the towel the same time he did.

"I reckon she could do just 'bout anything" came a voice from the doorway.

Hurriedly, Lou straightened, the towel in his hand, and as he did, a folded paper fluttered to the floor. Perhaps from his shirt pocket? She plucked the note off the floor while Lou and James spoke of the trip tomorrow.

The paper between her fingers looked suspiciously official. Could there be more news on who'd shot Lou? Perhaps the perpetrator had been caught. Should she open it? Nibbling her lower lip, she peeked at the men.

They spoke in hushed voices, bodies facing away from her. She turned her back to them and pretended to organize the shaving utensils while an internal war ensued. Unlike Gracie, she didn't go around eavesdropping or telling people what she thought.

She was careful. Considerate... Her nose wrinkled. Boring.

Yes, Gracie was fun and alive and she, Mary, led a very careful, very structured life, with no room for surprises. Not until she'd brought Josie home.

The letter mocked her, its flap open just enough for her to see the typewritten note inside. Biting her lower lip, she cast the men one more look before positioning her body at an angle best designed to hide her sneakiness.

Her heart knocked about wildly in her chest. Quickly she unfolded the paper and scanned its contents. As she did, her pulse ratcheted until she could no longer quite contain her breathing.

How dare he? Throat tight and pained, she very neatly folded the paper, creasing the lines just so. Her fingers shook as she pressed on the paper.

"That right, Mary?"

Startled, she sucked in a lungful and pivoted, the letter clutched in her right hand, which she dropped to her side. "I missed what you said."

"James says you should start a restaurant. I agree. Your baking is superb," said Lou. The rat. The coward.

Betrayer.

All those names, and more, hopscotched through her mind and stuck there. A pounding took up residence in her skull, along with the words of the letter. He'd known. This entire time, he'd known and not said one word. Speechless, she could only stand there as her skin set aflame with anger.

"Well, now—" James scratched his head "—I do believe she's angry."

"About what?" Lou scoffed.

"Iffn' I knew, I'd say so, but women get me all gandered up. I can't tell left from right."

Lou's cheeks bunched. "Nah, Mary only gets angry once a year."

Her eyes stung.

"Hoooeeee, I'm hightailin' it out of here." James gave her a once-over, then his mustache twitched. "Just came by to say things are all set for you leaving tomorrow. I'll take you to the train in the morning and the bureau is getting you some hotel rooms for one night only. Time enough to find Josie's mom and then skedaddle." He edged backward.

Mary fought tears, refusing to show her weakness.

James disappeared from the doorway and Lou turned to her, forehead crinkled in a charmingly deceptive way.

"What's going on? A delayed reaction to the kiss?" He swiped the towel from where it hung around his neck and tossed it to the chair. "It's better to talk now than to hold things inside."

The letter lay in her palm. She could throw it at him in some infantile display of temper. Demand he answer her. But she held back.

"Are you going to give me the silent treatment like you did the first year you were here? I tolerated it then, and even a few years ago when you got mad about your mama, but I certainly won't take it now." He advanced, dangerous intent sizzling in his expression.

Before he could completely crowd her against the wall, she squared her shoulders, summoned self-will and shoved the paper between them. He stopped. Glanced at it, then to her, his face shuttered.

"Where did you get that?"

"Does it matter?" she managed to squeeze out from beneath stiff lips.

"Sure it does." Faster than the pop of bacon in a pan, he snatched it from her fingers and opened the page. He looked at it briefly before returning it to his shirt pocket. His eyes found hers. The intensity of them disturbed her. "Did you read this before or after our kiss?"

She shook her head.

"Before or after?" he repeated.

"After."

"Good." He started to turn away.

"Good?" she said needlessly.

"Yep."

She reached for his shoulder but he kept going. Desperate with rage, she darted in front of him. The door waited behind her.

"How dare you," she said.

"Me?" He had the audacity to look surprised. "It's not against the law to apply for new employment."

"We rely on you. And this letter references your inquiry over two months ago." Suddenly words filled her mouth and she did not dare let them dry up like the desert outside, unsaid, unplanted. "Plans needed to be made, then. How much time do we have now? Have you any clue how long it takes to start a business? The money involved? The time and effort and ingenuity?"

His brows lowered. "I never planned for you to not be taken care of, Mary. And you bought Trevor's house, so I didn't see the problem in selling the ranch. I'm happy to give you whatever money you need."

"Yes, I'm sure you are. So that you may gallivant off to wherever you're going. Asia, correct? And what will you do there?" Her hand flung through the air, narrowly missing his chin. He stepped back, a bewildered expression on his face. She didn't care. "You must realize what sort of position you have put us in. It was unthinking and…and unfair." Her voice caught.

Oh, no, she was going to cry. Swallowing hard, she fought the angry tears.

"Mary, everything is going to be okay. You don't have to worry." He moved as if to hug her, but she put out a hand to stop him.

"I am not worried. I am angry. Very, very angry."

Shaking and not sure how much longer she could hold her inopportune tears, she turned and fled.

Lou's wound pulsed with pain. He pressed on the scarred area with his palm. With his other hand he shoved the letter farther into his pocket, wincing when the front door slammed shut.

Leaving that letter in his pocket hadn't been the smartest thing, but at least today's telegram hadn't fallen out. For a second he'd thought Mary was going to hit him.

Sweet, docile Mary.

Lately the woman acted as though something had been set on fire behind her. Anger and defiance marked everything she said. A natural occurrence as she grew more comfortable expressing herself, but still, it was uncomfortable for him.

Unbidden, the memory of her arms around him crept past his defenses. He blinked, willing the sensation away.

"James," he shouted.

No answer. Shrugging, he gathered up the shaving supplies and stomped out of the sitting room. The hallway gleamed in the darkening evening, thanks to Mary's cleaning skills. She kept up the house better than most.

Shining floors, delicious dinners. She'd make some man a fine wife. His mouth soured at the thought. He put the shaving supplies away, then called for James again.

Still no sound. Had the old man gone home? He lived in a little house down a ways on the property, near the bunkhouse where hands stayed when they'd been doing more ranching. Not anymore.

With the way people were clearing out in this county, the town of Burns might be lucky to survive. Logging seemed to be going well, however, especially with the railroads spreading across the country.

Mary should thank him for pushing her out of the nest, so to speak.

Yet, as he opened the front door and stepped into the approaching dusk, twinges of conscience pinged him. He closed the door and then clomped to the stairs. In the distance, two silhouettes stood against the horizon.

The shadows turned and he noticed the skirts. Mary and her mother? Another problem he wished he could solve for her. If Mary knew her mother had been the one who'd told Mendez where she lived twelve years ago, the one who'd made the kidnapping possible, then she wouldn't let Rose live here. He debated telling Mary about her mother's part but decided against it. What good could come of exposing such a thing? Only more hurt for Mary. Best to just keep an eye on Rose and make sure she didn't put Mary in harm's way.

He went down the porch steps.

Maybe the ladies had seen James. Besides, he needed a reason to look Mary in the eyes again, to reassure himself that her feelings weren't hurt by his dismissal of the kiss.

After all, he had plans. So did she. There was no room for fickle emotions. Heart thumping, he strode toward Mary and her mother. They began running to him. As they neared, his stomach plunged at the expression on their faces.

"What's wrong?" he asked quickly, noting the glazed appearance of Rose's eyes.

"It's Josie." Mary's features were drawn. "She's missing."

Chapter Fourteen

"**M**issing?" A dumbfounded expression slacked Lou's handsome features.

"Yes," Mary snapped. "Mother and I are going to mount up and look for her near the ranch house. She has a fondness for the cows."

"James and I will track her," he asserted, seeming to snap out of his daze.

"He is already looking for her footprints, though darkness will soon make that impossible. Please search the house." She refused to let her voice tremble. Time for that later. "Let's go, Mother."

"Wait." He stopped her with a palm to her shoulder. The intimacy of the touch only served to remind her of what had transpired during his shave. "You and I'll search the property. We know it better. Rose can search inside the house."

"A good plan," she reluctantly admitted, forcing her mind to the present, forcing her lips to stop remembering his kiss.

Lou's hand moved off her shoulder. He gave Rose a stern look. "I'll know if something goes missing."

Mary gasped. "That's a hateful thing to say."

"I am not offended." Rose nodded to him and set off to his house, her shoulders slumped despite her quick pace.

Angry and afraid, Mary whirled away from Lou and ran for the stables. His even breaths behind her told her he kept up easily. Feeling bitter and not liking the words in her heart, she ignored him and kept going.

"You know your mother can't be trusted," he said.

Her chest burned. She bit her lip as a stitch formed in her side. Forced to slow down, she refused to look at the man beside her. The employer who'd been hiding his secrets for two months. What else did he hide? "What does it matter to you? You are leaving, and I choose to keep my mother by my side."

"Regardless of what you may think, I do care for you. Mary—"

"Josie is missing." She whirled. "Until we find her, this conversation can wait."

"That's how it's going to be? Ignoring important things?"

Pulse racing, she glared at him. "Yes. Josie is more important than anything else right now."

A serious look crossed his face. "You're right, but don't think we won't talk." He strode ahead of her and reached the stables first.

Inside, the air was musky and warm. A few horses nickered at their approach. Harnesses jingled and hooves rustled against the straw-strewn floor. She didn't particularly like being in a stable with its overarching odors of hay, manure and mildew, preferring the outdoor air instead, but she'd been in here enough to know which horses she rode the best.

She found a spotted pinto she'd ridden in the past and

led her out of the stall. After tying her up, she went to the tack room for her saddle, a smaller version of Lou's.

"Let me help you." His breath tickled her ear and did nothing to stop the nervous queasiness taking hold of her. Before she could pull the saddle down, he'd reached over and lifted it off its hook.

She followed him back to the pinto, hand pressed against her stomach. The sun's rays were already weak and disappearing. A few more minutes and then darkness. Where was Josie? Mary shuddered. Many dangers existed in the desert. How could a little girl protect herself?

Maybe she wasn't alone, though.

That possibility frightened her even more. She watched Lou saddling her horse, thankful for his calm thoroughness when her hands were shaking so badly. "Do you think…" She trailed off, stomach twisting.

"Think what?" Lou tightened the stirrups and faced her. Deepening light shadowed his face into planes and angles.

"Maybe someone took her. I—I thought someone might be following me this afternoon."

"And you're just now telling me?" His mouth arced downward.

"If that man has her… I need a weapon." She'd left her derringer at home. No more. From now on she'd carry it everywhere.

He studied her silently, then turned and disappeared into the tack room. He emerged moments later, a small sheath-covered knife nestled in his palm. "Take this. Use it if you need to.… In the eyes is where you should aim first, if possible." He paused. "You should have told me about being followed."

She slipped the blade from his hand, thumb smoothing over its fine ivory hilt. "There is a chance it was only imagination."

"Always tell me everything. I'll keep you safe." Sincerity rang in his voice. His eyes shone with it.

Swallowing back the boulder-size lump in her throat, Mary mounted the pinto. "That is a fine thing to say, Lou Riley, but the truth of the matter is that in months you will be gone and then I shall be in charge of protecting myself." She secured the knife in the pocket of her skirt and urged the horse around until she faced the entrance.

A gentle nudge and she soared past Lou and into the deepening twilight, where shadows canvassed the surroundings. Feeling desperate and a little angry, Mary headed toward the east section of the property.

How dare he say that he'd protect her? Fill her with hope and promises when he planned to leave. And to talk that way of her mother… She growled. It felt good, that primal vocal expression reverberating around her. Thankfully, the pinto didn't seem to notice.

Once they were a good ways from the stables, Mary slowed the horse and began scanning the shrubs and dips in the land. She wanted to call for Josie, but if the girl had been abducted, that might alert someone. On the other hand, if Josie was lost, she'd be frightened, and the sound of someone calling would be soothing.

Biting her cheek, she slid off the pinto and walked carefully, heart thudding in her chest. *Please, God, let us find her.*

If only she'd told Lou about the strange sensation of being followed sooner, but the truth was that she'd forgotten. Being near him, cutting his hair, shaving him, that breath-stealing kiss…and now someone might have their sweet little girl.

She fingered the blade and continued searching.

* * *

Lou grumbled as he readied his horse and then cantered to the west, worry over Josie riding his shoulders. He hated that Mary was right. Within a few months he might be gone, sent to Asia on special assignment. Possibly never to return. The thought of that foreign, exotic land of spice and music usually excited him, but at the moment, in the darkening night, searching for a lost little girl, he could only imagine a life without Mary to return to.

Her presence was ingrained in this place.

He slid off the saddle and cupped his hands around his mouth. "Josie!"

Insects and a stiff breeze answered. The unyielding line of mountains fuzzed on the horizon, shimmering with the setting sun.

"Josie," he yelled again.

If she had been kidnapped, his yell might rustle up the kidnappers into making a mistake, maybe some noise. Though, if they were on horses, which was likely, then they were probably long gone. His gut clenched at the thought.

Had someone actually followed Mary? She wasn't one to imagine things like that. Neither hysterical nor prone to fits. Jaw tightening, he strained to see the shrubs around him, looking for odd shapes or movement. His horse jingled beside him.

"Josie, answer if you can hear me." Feeling grim, he trudged ahead. His shoulders bent against the chilly breeze. Now that the sun was down, temperatures dropped quickly in the desert. Josie might be shivering somewhere, alone.

Memories rushed in on him and he bent over, gasping for breath. He wouldn't think of it, not now. Not when he had a different little girl to try to save. Straightening, he gulped deep breaths until he could breathe easier.

Then he continued walking, calling, searching the moonlit horizon. A few times the scurry of a small animal startled him into thinking he'd found the girl, only to watch the form materialize into something not human.

No giving up, he told himself. Hadn't he survived a war and deaths? Perilous conditions that took the best of men? Ears pricked, he stopped and listened for any unnatural sounds.

The slightest wisp of something carried on the wind. Holding his breath, he smoothed his horse's neck as he listened.

There it was again. To the left. Leading the stallion around, Lou went in that direction and continued to call the girl. As he neared, the sound sharpened into staccato sniffles. A relief so profound it nearly buckled his knees rushed through him. Gripping the reins, he hurried to a shrub that looked irregular beneath the moon's iridescent glow.

"Josie." His feet swished through the grasses until he reached the child, who sat hunched over, head buried in her drawn-up knees.

The overwhelming urge to scoop her up and hold her near his heart almost did him in, but he refrained, choosing instead to kneel in front of her.

"We've been looking for you."

She didn't look up. In the silvery light from the moon, he could see her hair matted in places. Her cries cut into the night, unnatural and heartbreaking.

Clearing his throat, Lou tried again. "Josie, honey, it's time to go back. Miss Mary is real worried. She, Rose and Mr. James have been looking all over for you."

The girl mumbled something, then started sobbing as if her best friend had died. Should he just reach out and grab her? Pick her up and carry her?

Throat constricting, he put out a hand to pat her head. She scooted back, out of his reach, faster than he could blink.

Frustration welled up. Frowning, he sat back on his haunches. "Listen. You either come with me now or I'm going to leave you out here. It's getting cold. I bet you're hungry. Is that what you want? To be stuck out in the desert all night long...?"

He cringed as his words trailed off, hollow echoes broken by Josie's quieting cries. He could almost see Mary's disapproving look at his tactics.

He gentled his voice. "Come home, honey. We've got cookies and—"

"You're just trying to get rid of me." The pouty words made his lips twitch. Better than her sobs.

"So you ran away, huh?"

The look she gave him was far too old for a five-year-old, and angry, angrier than he'd anticipated.

"I'm not going back. Ever." She promptly stuck her forehead against her knees again.

Sighing, Lou moved closer. This time when he put his hand on her head, she didn't try to escape. "Your mama misses you. We went over this before."

"Why can't you bring her here, where we'll be safe?" An earnest expression crossed Josie's face.

"Safe from what?" Lou peered at her, instinct rearing. He was missing something. Something important.

Her voice dropped. "You know."

"Josie, you've gotta answer me on this." He turned her shoulders to face him, marveling at how small she was, how tiny. How much would he have given to see his Abby grow up. She'd be thirteen now. His breathing snagged. Almost a woman.

"What, Mister Lou?"

He focused on Josie's eyes, that rare purple the color of a mountain violet. "Who dropped you in the desert? Who left you there?"

Her face scrunched, dirt tear trails zigzagging down her cheeks. "I don't know. Mommy gave me tea and a kiss. Then I woke up all by myself…." She looked away. "I was all alone, and I was so thirsty. I was cold." Her face wrinkled up even more and hurriedly Lou rubbed the top of her head.

"Okay, sweetheart, okay." Someone wanted her dead. But who? Why? He'd get to the bottom of it somehow. "Let's go home."

He got to his feet, then bent and picked her up. She was light and didn't resist as he feared she would. Instead, he felt her cheek against his shoulder, her arms around his neck.

"I'm hungry, Mister Lou."

"That's what happens when you run away." But he patted her back to soften the words.

He walked carefully toward the stallion, who stood patiently for him. Holding her close, he took the reins and started in the direction of the ranch. They'd ride in a bit. The girl was tired, her body boneless in his arms.

"I talked to God," she said suddenly, her voice a mere whisper.

"You did?" His own voice cracked a bit.

"I asked Him to send someone and He did."

"Oh…well, that's good." Nice to know God answered some prayers.

"Do you talk to God ever?" She yawned against his neck.

"Once in a while."

"Miss Mary says He likes it. That He gets lonely and is always waiting to listen. She told me He'd help when I was in trouble. She was telling the truth, right, Mister Lou?"

Funny how a sleepy kid could jabber so much. Might be time to stick her on the horse. He lifted her away from his body and set her in the saddle. "Hold on," he said gruffly.

He mounted behind her, then situated her to be comfortable for the ride back, and safe.

"Was Miss Mary telling the truth?" Her voice drifted upward from where she lounged against him. "Does God hear me?"

Good question. One he couldn't answer honestly.

"Mister Lou. Does God hear us?"

"Uh—"

"Was Miss Mary telling the truth?"

He wished he knew. "Go to sleep, honey."

"But does God hear me?"

"I found you, didn't I?" he said, hoping that would do. Mary filled this child's head with nonsense, the kind of truths he used to hinge his faith on, but he knew better now.

Yet tonight…on all these acres of land, he'd found Josie. Scared but unharmed. What did that mean? And if God cared enough to save her not once, but twice, then where had He been when Lou's family was dying? Why hadn't He saved them?

Heart weighted with questions and arms heavy with a snoring bundle of warmth, he headed home.

Chapter Fifteen

"**Y**ou're traveling *alone?*" Miss Alma readjusted her colorful feathered hat. "Are you sure that's wise, Mary?"

It was early morning. Lou waited in the wagon with Josie who, despite the bumpy ride into town, remained fast asleep. The poor girl was no doubt exhausted from last night's antics. James had needed to go to the post office before he took them to the train and she'd decided to stop in at the dry-goods store for thimbles. Mary encountered Miss Alma by the pincushions. There were only two, and the sweet lady appeared to be debating over them until she noticed Mary behind her.

It took only moments for her to discover Mary's plans and now she studied her with a suspicious look in her bright eyes.

"Not really alone," Mary amended. She scanned the shelves above the cushions for some durable thimbles. She'd forgotten hers at home. "Josie will be with us."

"And on your way home?"

Her cheeks heated. She avoided Miss Alma's gaze.

"Really, Mary." Miss Alma bustled closer and laid

a gentle hand on Mary's arm. Her voice lowered. "You must be more careful with your reputation. I only say that out of concern."

Mary met her friend's gaze. "Thank you, but there really is no other way." She'd thought about asking her mother to chaperone but had decided against that. Especially after Lou had practically accused Rose of stealing. And James was needed at the ranch.

There was no one else.

She patted Miss Alma's hand. "Please don't worry. I hardly think my reputation could be more tarnished than it is."

"Oh, pishposh." Her elderly friend let out an unladylike snort. The hand that had been on Mary's shoulder flapped, dodging through the air, waving away Mary's comment as if a pesky fly. "People here love you. We appreciate your goods at our events, your gentle spirit and the herbs you bring to the store. I am simply thinking of your future good. I wasn't going to say anything but—" she leaned forward conspiratorially "—a certain young man has been asking for you."

Mary felt the blood drain from her face and gripped the shelf. "Does he...does he have strangely colored eyes?"

"Oh, my, no. Brown as a log." Miss Alma tittered. "I won't say who he is but he's well respected and a kind young man."

"I'm getting quite old. Rather on the shelf." Mary pulled a wry face, which made Miss Alma giggle.

"Now, don't you worry. Every man is young to me. He'd do well by you. Come to our summer picnic, my dear. Bring your goodies. Something chocolate."

Mary smiled. She adored chocolate, but it was expensive to buy. However, if chocolate made her merry and soft like Miss Alma, then perhaps she should experiment a wee bit with some new recipes.

"Miss Mary? Time to go." James's gruff voice broke her thoughts. He came around the dry goods and stopped suddenly. A look of horror crossed his face.

She stepped forward. "Are you okay?"

"James." A high-pitched note, more akin to a squeal, escaped Miss Alma's lips.

Surprised, Mary looked at her friend. A becoming blush colored her cheeks.

"I've been waiting for you to come by my house and repair my sink. I fixed a special pie for you just this morning." Miss Alma bustled between James and her. "Mary, darling, take care. I shall be praying fervently for you and that sweet little girl." Miss Alma hooked James by the elbow and led him toward the spooled thread.

Mary stood dumbfounded for a moment, and then she laughed. Well, she hadn't seen this coming, but Miss Alma looked perfect on James's arm. Or rather, he on her arm. Chuckling, she scooped up a thimble for herself and then searched until she found a child's size.

The trip would be long and arduous for Josie. Perhaps a stitched doily might turn Josie's attention and leave her with a keepsake. She palmed the thimbles and headed for the counter.

After picking out penny treats and paying for everything, she stepped into the early-morning sunshine. Wispy clouds drifted across the surface of the sky, rippling the sunbeams and providing snatches of cover from summer rays. A brisk wind picked up dirt and swirled it around her skirt. Covering her eyes, she spied

Lou's wagon across the road. Lou lounged in the front, hat pulled over his face, most likely sleeping.

Once at the train station, they'd board the Union Pacific short line. It had been years since she'd ridden on a train. Prickles bumped across her skin. She did not relish the close quarters she would share with strangers.

Returning Josie was a necessity, though. Her heart quailed at the thought and the thimbles dug into her palms. Not only must she part with the sweet girl who'd become entrenched in her heart, but she must suffer riding with Lou.

The ride to town had proved easy enough. Lou and James discussed matters of all sorts, from selling the ranch to the government's plans regarding prohibition. As they spoke, Mary kept finding herself torn between staring at Josie, memorizing her sleep-peaceful features, to watching Lou and the movements of his mouth…. Had he really kissed her?

Her fingers moved to her lips.

It hadn't been her first kiss, but it had been the only one she'd enjoyed. Sleep had eluded her last night, for memories had risen unbidden to the surface of her subconscious. They'd invaded her sleep, dreams from long ago. From childhood. And then nightmares.

She should have expected those. After all, the only kisses she'd ever experienced had been forced upon her by rough and ungodly men. Though they had not assaulted her, for it would have diminished her worth, they'd nevertheless taken liberties no man should take with a woman. One week of terror when she'd been kidnapped…. It had ruined her image of men for life. Or so she'd thought.

The past years had been healing, but not until yesterday, when Lou had kissed her, had she realized that maybe she could move on from what had happened so long ago. Perhaps the evils Mendez and his cohorts had perpetrated upon her no longer had the power to bind her spirit.

For that knowledge alone, she should thank Lou. And yet she felt as though he'd betrayed her somehow. As if he'd offered the most delectable dessert, waved it beneath her nose, then snatched it back.

Her throat closed and she glanced away from Lou's wagon, down the street, watching as the town awoke. Mrs. Hartley swept the walk outside her fabric store. Others drove or rode past, on their way to various employments.

This was her home.

No matter what happened with the ranch, this place remained hers. God had brought her to this town, and it had been here where she'd found healing. Inhaling deeply, she relished the scents of the restaurant next door and the sage always present in her beloved desert.

"Let's git on with it." James burst out of the store, Miss Alma on his heels.

"But won't you come pick up your pie, at least?"

"I don't want nothin' to do with it." He spun around, right in the middle of the road, and pointed a finger at Miss Alma. Right at her nose actually, effectively stopping her in her tracks. "You leave me alone…you…you confounded woman." He threw his hands up in the air and stomped off toward the wagon.

Lou leaned forward, elbows on his knees, and squinted at them. Mary looked both ways and then hustled to the center of the road, where Miss Alma still stood.

Gently she laid a hand on Miss Alma's shoulder. "Are you okay?"

"Oh, me?" She turned and patted Mary's hand. "Don't worry, my dear. He'll come around." Her hand went to her heart, and she let out what could only be described as a lovelorn sigh. "He's a handsome fellow."

Mary tried not to gape.

"Well, then." Miss Alma patted Mary's hand again and then removed it from her shoulder, where it had lingered, paralyzed by Miss Alma's frightening proclamation. She dropped her arm, trying to assess this odd situation that had seemingly appeared out of nowhere.

"He will come around, no doubt," repeated Miss Alma with brisk optimism. "You take care and don't let that Lou Riley ruin your reputation."

With a swish of her skirts, she left Mary in the middle of the road and bustled back to the walkway.

The trip to Portland was torturous. Worse than the time Lou had been captured during the Great War and thrown into a dank dungeon for weeks. He'd chosen to travel by train because he hadn't wanted to run his tin lizzie over the highways. His Model T was relatively close to the ground and it was too easy for rocks and other debris to lodge up underneath it. That was why he'd insisted they take the UP's short line. He didn't normally mind riding the railroad. He knew all the switches they'd need to make, and at which towns, but traveling with a little girl and a woman proved disastrous for his peace of mind.

For one, Josie didn't stop talking. And she wanted to sit by the window. Being it was the last time he'd see her, he obliged, but that forced him next to Mary.

Somehow she managed to still smell like flowers and sage, despite the cramped quarters and dusty stops. She wouldn't look him in the eye and every time he thought about making conversation, he changed his mind.

He was planning on leaving. Mary deserved better, someone who could offer the home she wanted, the love she needed. Sometimes he thought she felt something for him, maybe even love. But he wasn't sure and not knowing could take a man down perilous mental routes.

He hid his uncomfortable, traitorous feelings by doing paperwork. Mary stayed busy sewing all sorts of things. He'd see her fingers flying and find himself intrigued by the motion.

There was a grace to her movements, a slender fragility in her hands that belied the briskness of her stitches. She urged Josie to sew, even offering a fancy little doodad for her finger, but the little girl alternated between sleeping, yapping and sitting in stony silence.

Finally, after the uncomfortable sleeping arrangements and smells and noises, they arrived at Portland's Union Station.

"*Ewww,* what's that smell?" Josie wrinkled her nose.

Lou hooked a finger into the collar of her dress to keep her close by. "You should be used to it."

"The odor is strong," Mary remarked, moving closer as passengers jostled around her. She clutched her luggage to her chest.

"Here, let me take that." Before she could protest, he hefted her suitcase from her arms and tilted Josie toward her. "You hold the boy's hand."

Josie giggled. "I'm a girl."

"You are?" He waggled his brows at her, enjoying

the mood of the city with all its quick pace and noise. Various smells permeated the air.

Musky river odors dominated the brisk breeze, padded with other scents that weren't altogether unpleasant. Sounds reverberated all around, talking, clanging from streetcars, horns from automobiles…the city at last. Smiling, Lou gestured to a spot on the sidewalk near the Romanesque clock tower, the depot's glory piece.

"We'll go over there to talk," he yelled. Ushering them ahead of him, he guided them through the crowd to a quiet spot against the wall of the building.

Mary's eyes were wary. "It's changed."

"How long since you've been here?"

"Since I was a wee girl. Perhaps twenty years?" Her brow furrowed.

"Back then, the roads used to turn to mud from all the rain. They had to build wooden sidewalks to get out of the mess. Now look at it." He waved at the busyness around them. "Electric streetcars are the way to travel now."

"I like the red ones," Josie chimed in, beaming a smile at him.

He couldn't resist smiling back, though there was the slightest pain to it. In a very short time, this charming sprite would leave them for good. He knelt down in front of her. "Did you take a lot of red cars?"

"My mommy likes them, when she feels good. We went up really, really high." She leaned toward him, eyes wide and bright. "I wanted to touch the sky."

She obviously meant the Council Crest streetcar. It was a popular attraction, taking people from Portland into the highest parts of the hills around them. He knew the feeling of wanting to reach too high. And the rip of the spiral downward.

Throat tight, he touched her face briefly. Then he stood and scanned the station and the roads leading out of it.

"What next?" Mary asked.

He noted her knuckles white on the handle of her luggage. "We've got to get Josie home. That's first on the list. Then I have a meeting with the head agent on my case this evening at the Portland Hotel. The bureau has reserved rooms for us. Did you bring a dress?"

"N-no," she sputtered. "I did not realize—" she cast a look at Josie "—that we'd be staying the night."

"You'll go home in the morning."

"You're staying?"

"I've got to keep an eye on Josie and her mama." He shifted on the heels of his feet, not liking the look on her face. "I've been out of commission for weeks. There's paperwork, unsolved cases, interrogations, not to mention catching the sap who shot me."

Was it his imagination or did something spark in that dark gaze of hers?

"Do I have to go back?" Josie interrupted them and for once, Lou was glad for it.

He avoided Mary's frown, turning to Josie instead. "Your mommy needs you, but I'm going to personally make sure that no one hurts you again, okay?"

Her bottom lip quivered and suddenly Lou's good mood deserted him. Two upset females was more than any sane man could handle. He fixed them both with a stern look despite the pain in his heart. "Look here, girls, I've got work to finish up and don't have time to cart you around Portland."

Josie burst into tears. Lou tripped trying to back up, but righted himself against the wall of the station. Horrified, he watched as the girl sobbed as though her heart were breaking.

And maybe it was.

An unwelcome spear of conscience poked him. Even though he'd arranged for bureau protection, that wouldn't start until tomorrow. For today, what was he returning her to? He'd asked a junior agent to poke around in the girl's mother's background, but his agent found nothing problematic. The family came from money, the father was deceased and they lived in a good part of town.

If he could, he'd never take the girl back, but the threat of a lawsuit was a very real problem he couldn't ignore.

But why did Josie insist on staying with Mary and him? A nagging pressure in his chest distracted him. He rubbed his heart, watching as Mary scooped Josie close, cradling her. Much as he had when he carried Josie to the ranch on his horse.

Frowning, he rubbed harder, but the ache refused to lessen. More and more, Abby came to memory. Her chubby smile. The scent of her skin, soft as a foundling's feathers. How he'd felt when he watched Sarah hold her… Something pricked his eyes and he blinked hard.

Enough of this.

Setting his jaw, he strode forward and snatched up their luggage. "Let's go, ladies."

He felt the fume in Mary's glare but chose to ignore it. Tension filled the space between them all the way to the neighborhood where Josie's mother resided. He glanced at the telegram in his hand, then flicked a look at Mary.

Her face was stone. Several people had given her curious looks. Some more disdainful than curious. Oregon's population was mostly Caucasian, and racial barriers rose high and impenetrable. The usual victims of the whites' prejudice were the Asian immigrants who worked in the lumber mills for next to nothing in pay.

But Mary, with her exotic features and dark eyes, qualified for being too different and thus drew attention. Lou knew the feeling, having visited China and being the only blue-eyed man in a sea of dark-eyed faces.

Their streetcar shuddered to a stop. People rose to exit and Lou looked over at Mary. "This is it."

Eyes blank, she handed him the luggage and took Josie's hand. He was determined not to look at the little girl anymore, for her tear-stained face was starting to give him heartburn.

It seemed he couldn't win no matter what he wanted. Mary refused to show her emotions, and Josie was all feeling. Setting his jaw, he led them out of the streetcar, and as a resolute trio, they found the address listed on his telegram.

Josie's mother. Mrs. Lauren Silver. He unlatched the gate and ushered Mary and Josie ahead of him. The house loomed before them, tall and freshly painted. The fumes permeated the humid summer air. A set of steps led to an ornate door. Baskets and pots of flowers surrounded the porch, and their floral scents became more apparent as they neared the front door.

"I don't like this house," Josie muttered, her little legs lifting high to manage the stairs.

"You live here a long time?" Lou inquired carefully.

Everything inside roared for him to snatch the ladies and run. He couldn't do it, though. That was a sure ticket to jail, and then how would he protect them?

"Nope. I liked my other house better. It was by the ocean."

Interesting. She'd recently moved and then somehow ended up in the desert where Rose had found her. While finding his shooter, he'd also figure out why someone had done that to Josie.

In fact, he might question the mother a bit. He rubbed at his chin, thinking.

Mary was first to the door. He saw her back rigid, her shoulders set as she stepped to the side to allow him to knock. Josie huddled next to her, forehead furrowed and fingers twisting in her skirt.

He cleared his throat, set the luggage down and rapped on the door.

It swung open, revealing an ancient-looking man whose shock of white hair hung precariously over a furry set of eyebrows. "May I help you?" he croaked.

"We're here to see Mrs. Silver. Very special delivery." He winked at Josie, but the little girl didn't smile. He held his own smile in place, even though it felt broken. Could he do this to Josie? God knew, he didn't want to. God knew, if it was in his power, he'd keep Josie safe with Mary. But the situation was out of his hands. He could only do now what he'd been ordered to do, or risk more danger to the little girl by being completely cut out of her life if he resisted the law.

"Mrs. Silver isn't here." The man sniffed, then peered at Josie. He lifted rheumatic eyes to Lou. "I see you brought the troublemaker. You can keep her."

The door slammed in their faces.

Chapter Sixteen

"That ol' Baggs." Josie sniffed. "I never liked him."

"Josie," Mary gasped while fighting a smile. "That's not a nice thing to say."

"It's his name," Josie replied pertly, "and I always tell him he looks older than a bag of bones. He should trim his nose hairs."

Mary's jaw dropped. Had no one taught the girl manners, or did she say whatever she felt, regardless of consequences? It must be pleasant to be so unencumbered by niceties.

"That's enough," Lou said firmly. "We'll wait here until your mother returns."

"Fine." Josie trudged to a swing set in the far corner of the porch. Looking glum and very pouty, the she sat and rocked, using her toes to push herself.

Poor darling. Mary sighed deeply and tried to ignore the pressure at the base of her skull that could quickly turn into a headache. What a stressful situation, only to be compounded by a mother who obviously didn't care about seeing her daughter. "Where do you think Mrs. Silver is?" she asked Lou, careful to keep her voice low.

He shrugged. "I sent a telegram saying we'd arrive today, but there wasn't a time given. Could be she's at the doctor's or something."

"Maybe we should ask… Mr. Baggs…if he knows her whereabouts. Surely he could direct us to her."

Lou's brow rose. "Could try that, I suppose. If he answers."

A low hum interrupted their conversation. They looked in Josie's direction. She'd gotten to her knees, facing outward to a mass of flowers that peeked over the porch rail. Her voice quivered as she sang. Her fingers gently stroked flower petals and sun spilled over her head, a dumped bucket of gold that washed her in light.

Mary's breath caught, suspended as a slow knot formed in her belly. She didn't want to leave this precious child here, alone with a sickly mother and odd circumstances. She glanced at Lou, prepared to beg, or to at least see what options they might have, but his gaze remained fastened on Josie. His eyes looked shadowed in the dimness of the porch, pained, even.

She traced the shape of his face with her glance, giving herself free rein to stare while he was so occupied. His strong nose and jaw, the wild hair she'd kept a tad too long yet remaining fashionable.

In this moment, she realized how dear he was to her. How safe and kind. Sure, now, he had frustrating qualities. Stubborn, flippant, never anchoring anywhere for long…yet somehow she'd become attached to him.

Uneasy, she forced herself to look away, to the road where a fancy, newer-model Ford chugged to a stop in front of the house. A man emerged from the passenger door, tipping his hat to them before moving to the rear door.

Lou moved beside Mary. She caught a whiff of Wrigley's and felt the warmth of his arm near hers. Focusing on the people in front of her, she watched as the man scooped a lady from the rear seat of the automobile.

The man carried the woman up the steps, his face young and unlined. Brown eyes met hers in passing, then traveled behind her, to where Josie still hummed on the swing. Lou rushed to the front door, opening it without knocking first.

The man nodded his thanks and disappeared inside.

"Come on." Lou slid into the house.

He expected her to follow, but she hung back, startling when a hand slipped into hers. She looked down into Josie's wide eyes.

"I don't want to stay," Josie whispered.

Mary tried to ask why but her throat was closing up. This was it. After weeks of caring for Josie, she must say goodbye. She could feel her heart cracking apart inside, sending pulsating waves of emotional pain through her body. Blinking quickly, she knelt to face the girl.

"Do you know how much I love you?" She smoothed a curl from Josie's eyes. "You are special and a joy. Never forget that."

"But I don't want you to leave." Her lip trembled and those beautiful eyes turned shiny.

"Friends are forever, sweet girl." Mary pulled her into a hug, inhaling her scent, enveloping her in her arms and trying to memorize every moment to hold on to.

"You said God heard me. I told Him I wanted to stay with you and Mister Lou...." The girl's voice was as trembly as her lips.

"He heard you, honey."

"Then why am I here? My mommy can go with us. I don't want to be here, never, ever. I never wanted to come back."

That knot in Mary's stomach grew. Drawing in a deep breath, she pulled back and looked Josie in the eye. "Mister Lou is going to make sure you're safe because your mommy needs you here with her. Do you still have that thimble?"

Josie nodded.

"Whenever you're lonely or scared, hold the thimble and remember that I'm always praying for you. And that God is looking out for you and loves you dearly."

Josie sniffled and a lonely tear seeped from the corner of her eye. It rolled down her cheek unchecked. Mary swallowed hard, gave her one last hug and then, hands held, they went into the house.

Mary barely remembered the trip back to the hotel. Leaving Josie had been horrendous. The girl had sobbed, and Baggs had held her tightly when Lou and Mary exited the house. The sound had tormented Mary on the streetcar. She couldn't speak.

When Lou stopped at his office to drop off paperwork and make arrangements for who knew what, she sat on a bench outside. Clouds drifted over the sun, and before long it started raining, but she hadn't even noticed until Lou reappeared, picking up her luggage and leading her to a waiting streetcar.

They arrived at the Seward Hotel in the afternoon, dodging through the rain to the entrance. The massive building loomed before her. Elegant. Expensive.

Blinking back raindrops, she tried not to gape as she followed Lou inside.

She discovered the lobby was gapeworthy, however. A bell motif rounded the interior. Sparkling and clean, people of obvious wealth studded its landscape. Fur stoles, shining shoes... She huddled in a corner of the lobby while Lou checked them in, feeling out of place and wanting to disappear. A shiver coursed through her, and belatedly she realized her clothes were sopping wet.

What was Josie doing right now? Her mother was barely capable of speaking, she was so sick. She'd seemed kind, though, her eyes a paler shade of Josie's, her smile soft yet weak. Tuberculosis was what was killing her, she'd said, speaking past her face mask. A rare strain, the doctors told her. One they had trouble treating. It seemed the Great War, coupled with the disastrous influenza pandemic, had increased tuberculosis cases. Or perhaps made them worse.

Either way, what would happen to Josie when her mother passed away? Who would care for her? The worry nibbled at Mary incessantly. She clutched her luggage closer as another shiver vibrated through her.

Lou stalked toward her, his lips still and serious. "Ready to go up?"

She nodded and followed him to an elaborate staircase. Its surface shone and she wondered how long it had taken the staff to make it look that way. How often must they clean it? She gingerly stepped up.

Lou turned to her. "Let me help you with your bags."

"I can handle them."

"I want to help you. Please." His voice was sober, so she relented. "Now, our rooms are side by side. We have a dinner to attend this evening and I've left you something in your room. A fellow agent picked it out, in case you don't have anything to wear."

"I'm supposed to dress up?" She frowned.

Lou shrugged and slipped her a quick look. "You don't have to, but we'll be eating in the hotel's dining area. It's exquisite, I've heard. There's music, candles…" He trailed off and looked straight ahead.

"Why such a fancy dinner?" They reached the top of the stairs and Mary followed him to the right.

"It's been a hard day. A soothing dinner will be relaxing, don't you think?" He shot her a half smile that faded when he saw her face. "I thought you would like it."

Mary shook her head. "Why? Why would you think that?" Her voice sounded high-pitched, even to her ears. "This is too much…too much noise, and people. A restaurant will be filled with those who stare." She swallowed and made her voice calmer. "I can't help thinking of what Josie is doing right now, if she's still crying. What will happen when her mother dies? What if that man looking for her is really her father? Or some relative who wants to hurt her?"

Lou stopped in front of a door. His jaw was clenched. She saw a muscle work in his neck. "There's already an undercover agent that has been hired on in the house. He'll be there tomorrow. I'm doing the best I can, Mary. Leave it be."

"I can't," she insisted.

He turned slowly toward her, the key dangling from his finger. "It's out of our hands. Your mother found a little girl and didn't report it to the authorities. Josie's mama has been frantic with worry and was ready to take legal steps." A sheen crept into his eyes before he blinked it away. "Take a nap, get ready for dinner, and tonight I'll outline how I plan to protect them."

Hope fluttered for a moment, then spiraled to a crash. "I'm never going to see Josie again, am I?"

His gaze closed. He held out the key to her. She took it. He set her suitcase near the door. His hand came up, near her face, and she almost flinched. Some instincts couldn't be undone.

But he moved softly and the next thing she knew,

his hand was cupping her chin. Warm. Gentle. His eyes were tender.

"If it were possible, I'd make sure Josie could stay with you forever."

Her breath caught, suspended by the unfolding of rare and beautiful feelings inside. It was as though a thousand butterflies had taken flight within her rib cage, fluttering, no, pounding to be let out. This man who'd protected her, who looked at her with such *seeing*... Her pulse thrummed with strange and heady emotions.

Lips dry, she wet them with the tip of her tongue.

Lou blinked and the moment ended. His hand dropped to his side. "I'll meet you in the dining room at seven." With that, he pivoted and left her alone at her door, the imprint of his touch still sizzling against her cheek.

It took her a moment to recover, but when she did, she let herself into her room. The spacious interior welcomed her with warmth. A package lay on the bed, but rather than opening it, she flopped onto her back and stared at the ceiling.

So many feelings ricocheted through her that catching her breath, let alone resting, proved impossible. Thoughts of Josie intermingled with memories of The Kiss. Both tangled her nerves. After an hour of futile search for sleep, she sat up and opened her traveling case. Taking out her brush, she went to the private bath, washed her face and then combed her hair. The snarls made her wince, but she persisted until her locks fell in waves against her back.

She glanced at the package, a simple white box, which remained unopened.

"Oh, Lord, I don't know what to do," she whispered. Life's even road had just become twisty and uneven. To find her footing required a wisdom she wasn't sure she possessed. Inhaling deeply, she went to the box and lifted the lid.

She gasped. With careful fingers, she lifted out a dress more lovely than she'd ever touched. She'd seen beautiful fabrics. French silks, velvets and chiffons. But this… The fabric fell through her fingers, a wispy garment the color of a desert sunset.

She nibbled her bottom lip and surveyed the tiny glass beads across the hem, the swirls of deep reds that dashed across the bodice.

She couldn't wear this.

She couldn't.

And yet the simple dress she'd traveled in hardly qualified for a refined dinner.

But this dress was audacious. Every head would turn. Stare. She shuddered and dropped the silky thing to the bed. Why would Lou do this to her?

He didn't pick it out, she reminded herself. Taking steadying breaths, she paced the length of her room. A rose sachet sat upon the dresser, but she missed the scent of her sagebrush land. She glanced at the clock on the wall.

Six o'clock.

There was time to spend praying or reading the Bible. Perhaps the Proverbs. They'd always been her comfort in times of need or stress.

When she finished chapter one, she moved to chapter two and kept going until six-thirty. Feeling more calm and as though her fears were minuscule, she put her Bible to the side and changed into the dress.

How the agent knew her size, she'd never guess. She wasn't a tall woman, smaller than most, actually, but the dress fit perfectly. The seams stitched even and small at the hem. The narrow shoulder straps exposed more skin than Mary thought she'd ever shown in her life.

Thank goodness she'd brought her black shawl.

Now for her hair. She twisted and pinned and when a knock sounded at her door, she was ready.

She snagged her shawl and opened the door. Lou faced the opposite way, his head bent as though reading something. She closed the door behind her, hearing a subtle click.

Lou rotated toward her and his face went slack.

"What?" She touched the collar of the dress. "Did I wear the wrong thing?" She patted her hair, but everything felt tidy.

"You are…" He trailed off. Was his face turning splotchy? She stepped closer.

"Are you all right?" She'd never seen him look so… so flustered. At a loss for words. Despite the riotous emotions of the day, an overwhelming urge to laugh bubbled through her.

She covered her mouth as Lou's jaw worked but no sound emerged.

"Resplendent," he finally said. He stuffed the paper he held into the breast pocket of his sleek jacket and advanced toward her. Yes, his face colored pinker than normal, but his charming grin was firmly in place.

The giggle bubbled out, perhaps exacerbated by nerves and exhaustion. His smile stretched to show a hint of teeth. "May I have your arm?"

"You may." Nerves quivering, she offered it to him.

His grasp filled her with warmth. He pressed her arm firmly to his side, effectively encasing her in his cologne and security. They matched steps. Down the stairs. Through the lobby. Into another area that served as the restaurant.

She felt eyes on her, the way they followed and perused, but the tingly apprehension she so often suffered failed to materialize. Hardly daring to breathe, let alone talk, she allowed Lou to lead her to a table.

Dinner passed in an odd mixture of unexplained excitement and lingering sadness over Josie's absence. She'd gotten used to the girl's energy and uncontained words. And yet the candlelight on the table, the sound of violins and clinking forks led her back to a reality in which her employer sat across from her, handsome, alive and very, very interested.

At least it felt that way.

Self-conscious, she smoothed her dress, watching as his eyes traced her movements. Heat crept through her. "Thank you for the meal, Lou."

"It's nice to see you enjoying yourself."

"Good food is worth celebrating," she returned, feeling a tug at the corners of her mouth.

"Indeed. I agree." He lifted his glass. "And so is good company."

Feeling flushed, she nodded. They finished their food and before she knew it, they were ready to leave. His eyes sparkled beneath the glow of the chandeliers.

"Care for an evening stroll?"

Why not? She might never visit this place again, and would she even see him after this? She pulled her shawl more snugly around her shoulders and smiled at him. "I'd love one."

They meandered out of the hotel, away from the perfumes and into a different type of atmosphere. She clutched her shawl closer as a chilly breeze brushed by. She glanced at Lou. He looked completely relaxed, the planes of his face smooth. He'd gotten a shave somewhere, and the shadowed line of his jaw was strong beneath the street lamps. He walked as though he knew this place well.

Which, of course, he must, having the bureau's field office here.

"It's odd being alone together, don't you think?" she asked.

He gave her a funny look. "Not odd to me. It's... nice," he finished. "Do you miss Harney County?"

"This place is so different, so many people. But what I miss more is my kitchen. My hands itch to bake."

"Really? A literal itching?"

She smiled at him, lifting her hands. "Do you not see the rash?"

He peered at them.

She giggled and dropped her hands. "I'm teasing you, Lou."

"Oh." Then he cracked a smile that split through her defenses. "Mary the jokester. I like it. And what did you think of your meal tonight? You know, your cooking is tastier." At her doubtful look, he held up a hand. "No, really. I've been around the world, Mary O'Roarke, and your meals rival any fine-dining experience."

What did a girl say to that? They kept walking, and then Lou cleared his throat. Never a good sign. "I don't know how else to say this, but tonight I was brought a telegram. We've got an offer on the ranch."

Chapter Seventeen

"**D**id you hear me?" Lou paused beneath a streetlamp.

Mary nodded, though her heart felt as though it had lodged painfully in her sternum.

"Well, say something," he said, his tone strained.

But she couldn't speak. The words remained bottled inside, not yet fully formed. What could she say? It was his ranch. She'd been blessed to stay there. She blinked to ward off any unwelcome tears.

"I wish you'd say something. Tell me how you feel." He swiped a hand through his hair. It hung in lop-sided angles, tangled by his regret. "This wasn't how I planned things to happen. The sale was expected to take months. Then, if you didn't want to stay on with the new owners, you'd have time to get a new job and place. Independence is within your grasp."

She swallowed hard. "I *should* want such a thing."

"What?"

"Independence. I am thirty years old. Unmarried. I should want to have my own home, shouldn't I?" What was wrong with her that she didn't? No, she wanted things to continue as they had. Peaceful. Secure.

Lou looked away. "Everyone wants different things, Mary. I'm sorry for uprooting you, but it needs to be done."

She exhaled a shaky breath. "Why? For what reasons must you sell?"

He looked at her then and his eyes pierced her. "It's never been my home. Ever. It's been a place to sleep and a place to eat. That's it."

His answer cut her to the core. "Never? All those times we ate and laughed?" There'd been many times she sewed by the fire while he shared an adventure he'd just been on. It had been cozy. Familial, even. "You never felt…home?"

He sighed heavily. "Home is not something I expect to ever feel again. That's just the way of it, and I don't want to talk about it anymore."

"Perhaps I do not own the ranch and am nothing more than an employee, one you've conveniently cast aside for new employment, but I have feelings. You don't want to talk about it, but the longer I stand here, the angrier I get." There, she'd told him. There had been a knot of anger growing in her belly, maybe ever since she'd found that letter after his kiss. "And furthermore, how dare you kiss me knowing you have no intention of returning?"

Yes, anger was coursing through her now, heating her blood and pouring rash words into her mouth.

"Now, Mary, hold on a minute. That kiss was completely unexpected."

"Was it?" she challenged, and was surprised to see a furrow appear at the ridge of his brow.

"I just needed to…"

"To what?" The wind picked up, whipping hair

around his face. The lamplight surrounded him and she felt as though she must be standing in darkness. Could he see her anger? How he'd hurt her with his indifference?

Shivering, she glared at him.

He nudged his coat from his shoulders and draped it over her before sighing deeply, heavily. "I don't know, Mary, and I'm sorry for that. I got carried away with emotion and it wasn't the right thing to do."

His apology irked her, though wasn't it what she wanted? The scent of his jacket surrounded her, filled her senses and warmed her.

"Someday," he continued, "a fine man in town will take to courting you. All this will be in the past."

"Do you mean forgettable? The way you've conveniently forgotten Josie? You handed her off like a package to be delivered." Her voice broke.

"Don't bring her into this. She doesn't belong to you or me." Lou's voice lifted, causing passersby to glance their way. "And our kiss wasn't forgettable. If you don't understand my meaning, I can show you right now."

To her surprise he moved nearer, out of the circle of light and into the shadows between them. Energy sizzled through the air, tension emanated from his body, and a quiver unrelated to cold shuddered through her.

"I think not," she said coolly, and moved opposite him so that she now stood closer to the lamppost. Her pulse hammered. "I have had enough of your kisses to last a lifetime."

"You didn't complain about them before," he said tightly.

Confident, carefree Lou was gone. Where he went, she didn't know, but before her stood the real man.

Edgy. Determined. And for some odd reason, angry. All because she'd brought up Josie. Again she thought of secrets. He possessed them, and in abundance.

She nodded at him slowly. "You are a practiced kisser. It was a fine experience."

"A fine experience," he mimicked, then let out a bark of laughter empty of joy.

"It was also disruptive," she said gently. She must tread softly, for mentioning God in the past had often upset him. "Kissing did nothing but stir up a mess for both of us." In truth, she hadn't stopped remembering that kiss and doubted she ever would.

"Perhaps it was something that needed stirring." His confident voice conflicted with the turmoil she saw in his eyes.

Unsettled, she shook her head. "That is unlikely. Romance is not what will make me happy, Lou. I don't need a man's kisses or even his love. God has given me so much—" She stopped because his brows lowered and, in the darkness, it almost seemed as though his eyes flashed.

"So no marriage in your future? You think you can live without baking for anyone ever again?"

"If I open a restaurant, I shall bake for many," she inserted, trying to follow the train of his thoughts, why he'd jumped to marriage.

"And do you deny the way you felt caring for—for Josie?"

"No," she whispered.

"Well, you need a husband to have a family."

She whipped back as though he'd slapped her. "Perhaps I'd have someone to take care of if you'd looked into Josie's family a little more. You *know* something is wrong. Someone in that family is dangerous. Don't you care?" A surprising boldness took hold of her and she stepped right up to him, nose to chest due to her shortness, but it would have to do. He'd see her eyes and realize she wanted answers.

"Tell me, why do you avoid children? Why do you run from the ranch as often as you can?" A thought occurred to her as the realization of a pattern emerged. "And your stays at the ranch… You've always cut them short after we spent time together in the evenings. What are you afraid of?"

His glare deepened and he took her arms in his hands, pulling her closer than she'd ever been to him, save for that kiss.

"You don't know what you're saying, woman."

"I know exactly what I'm saying. You're afraid—"

"No," he hissed. His grip tightened. "That's enough. No more."

"Then tell me," she pleaded. When he tried to look away, she cupped his face and forced him to look down at her. "Help me understand why you dropped Josie with her mother like a hot ember in your hand. Does it hurt so much?"

She saw it now, the pain that tightened his mouth and crowded his eyes.

His throat moved, and then his head was resting in the crook of her neck. He groaned, and the sound caused hairs to stand on her skin. He let her go. She stumbled back, rubbing at her arms where his hands had clenched her.

"It doesn't hurt," he said at last. His gaze lifted. She stifled her gasp at the rawness of his expression. "It burns. It's a searing ache that never leaves."

Yes, she knew that kind of pain. "It can heal, if you let it."

"How, with God?" That broken laugh of his echoed off the sidewalk. "Don't you see? *God* did this to me. He killed my wife and Abby."

Lou shoved his hands through his hair again, wishing he could wipe away the pain as easily. Mary's eyes were shiny and he couldn't tell if tears glistened or if the lamplight played tricks. He wanted to say something, but his throat hurt with the strain of containing his emotions.

Groaning, he pivoted and started back for the hotel. She walked quietly beside him. Every so often a hint of her perfume teased him. He could feel the questions burning in her. She expected an explanation. *Who is Abby? You were married?*

As though his thoughts had been spoken, she said, "You do not have to explain anything to me, but if you ever feel the need to speak of this again, I will be here."

"Thank you," he managed to say. At least his vocal cords had shrugged off their temporary paralysis. He held the door to the hotel for her and she glided inside.

Near the stairs, she stopped. "Thank you for dinner."

He inclined his head, glad the rush of pain had drained away. "You're welcome."

"Are there specific plans for tomorrow?"

"Yeah, about that." He tapped the railing of the stairs. "An agent will pick you up at your room at nine o'clock and escort you back to Burns."

"I see."

"Don't give me that look, Mary."

"What look?" But the obstinate disapproval on her face didn't change. Or was it hurt?

He couldn't tell, and the gut-spilling earlier had exhausted him. "Just be ready. Your breakfast and room will be taken care of."

Her gaze lifted and she searched his face. "Will I ever see you again?"

"Sure. I've got to come back and handle this sale. I want to see you and James safely settled and—"

Her lips made a funny movement, as though she was holding back a smile.

"What?" he asked.

"I was just remembering how Miss Alma chased him out of the store. If she has her way, I believe James shall be quite all right." Her smile lit up her face and unexpectedly, Lou felt the strangest wish that Mary would chase him into the road, too.

He shook his head. Focus. She wasn't in the plans. Not even close. "James doesn't know what hit him," he said lightly. "I don't think he's ever settled down with a woman, and she seems pretty determined to snag him."

He grunted. This conversation opened old wounds and he didn't plan to let it continue. "Like I was saying, I've got to get things settled. I'll be back."

She bit her lip, studying him intently. Then her gaze skittered away.

He touched her arm. "Until next time, then?"

"Yes," she said, backing away. The dress she wore glittered with her movements, and the attraction he tried to hold at bay surged again.

"Goodbye," he said.

"Goodbye," she answered.

And then she was gone, moving through the late-night guests, up the stairs and disappearing around the corner. Sighing, he settled at the side of the wall and waited.

He had work to do. All this internal caterwauling over the past, Josie, that kiss… It made a man's head spin. He remembered Trevor getting all worked up over Gracie. They'd lived at the ranch as a married couple before traipsing off to California for fun, and Trevor seemed happier than Lou had ever seen him. Now that they'd been married a bit, Trevor seemed better.

Marriage wasn't for Lou, though. No way, no how.

He scanned the guests, looking for one in particular. Mary might accuse him of not caring, but it wasn't the truth. No matter his past, he didn't stand by and watch children get hurt. Women, either. Josie's mama might be dying and frail, but some low-down, evil one had handled her roughly. He'd seen the faint purple smudges on her wrists when she'd hugged Josie.

It only took a call to find out Mrs. Silver was a widow, but she had a brother who happened to have been busy traveling recently. Who happened to be staying in this very hotel tonight. And his last name happened to be Langdon. It was pretty obvious this fellow was the same guy who'd been lurking in Burns.

Why the man hadn't stayed with his sister, he didn't know, but he aimed to find out. So he waited, checking his watch every few minutes. The brother had been described as tall, brown-haired, strange blue eyes that bordered on purple. He matched the description of the man who'd come to the ranch.

And the man who'd recently been accused of murder in Burns.

He needed to know what this man did for a living,

but above all, he needed to make sure Josie and Mary were safe from him.

"Sir?" A young man addressed him from his right.

"Yes?"

"I'm Special Agent Smith."

Smith. The name clicked. "You'll be escorting Miss O'Roarke tomorrow?"

"Reporting in. We'll be leaving at nine o'clock and our expected arrival time is—"

"Have you ever done this before, Agent Smith?" Lou cut him off. He looked far too young to be protecting Mary.

"I served in the war effort." Agent Smith gave him a level look. "Appearances can be deceiving. I'm well equipped to take care of your lady."

"She's not my lady," he said by rote, breaking their visual standoff to scan the lobby again.

"I beg your pardon, sir, but I saw you at dinner."

He cocked a brow, meeting Smith's look square on, hiding his surprise. "And what did you see?"

The agent shrugged. "It wasn't business, that's all."

Lou grimaced. No, their dinner hadn't been. This one might do after all. He hadn't noticed him once, and that ability to blend would aid in keeping Mary safe, should the need arise. Lou gave him a curt nod. "Very well. Telephone headquarters when she's safely home."

"Will do." A quick nod and Smith left.

Lou pulled out a stick of Wrigley's and continued his surveillance. Chewing thoughtfully, he crossed his ankles and waited several more hours. Langdon never showed up.

Or he'd missed him, just as he'd missed Agent Smith at dinner.

Heading upstairs to bed, tiredness riding his back, the realization that he'd lost his mark plagued him. He was too caught up in emotions. Could only see Mary.

His attention had been on her—not a good thing, but he didn't know how to stop it. And then she'd had the nerve to bring up God.

He turned the corner and entered the corridor. *God.*

Did he really blame God for losing Sarah and Abby? In the haze of anger and pain, yes. But then he thought of Mary, a woman who hadn't known Jesus growing up. Who'd been abducted and mistreated, deeply so, and yet somehow still managed to find peace in the way he no longer traveled. How was that possible?

Yep. This job was messing with his head and causing him to lose focus. The sooner he sold the ranch, the better he could work and forget all this malarkey.

He ticked off his goals in his head as he walked.

Tomorrow he'd find Langdon at breakfast, have a little word with the upstart, then he'd finish up his work at headquarters. Track down the shooter, cuff him, maybe get some more information from him before heading home. Sell the ranch. Start a new job, far away.

The list was supposed to reassure, but as he let himself into his empty hotel room, he didn't feel anything at all.

Chapter Eighteen

Mary woke before the sun. She enjoyed the silence of morning, nothing but the birds and their early songs. Normally she felt refreshed, but today, the morning she'd be heading back to the ranch, unease beset her.

Lou had been *married*. And begotten a child. How could she not have known? He'd kept this secret from everyone. Were Trevor and James aware of this? Was she the only one in the dark? No wonder he didn't care to hear of God. No wonder the sight of Josie pained him.

Feeling a tad sick to her stomach, she swung her legs out of bed. Quickly she packed her meager belongings, made her bed, took care of toiletries and then glanced at the clock. Still too early. She had many hours until the agent arrived at her door.

And what then? Go home and search for a new job? Try to get that loan at the bank so she'd have the capital to open a business with? She could stay at the ranch with the new owners, but was that what she really wanted?

Gripping the handle of her suitcase, she opened her door and slipped into the hall. Perhaps they'd be serving breakfast. She could do with a strong pot of coffee.

The lobby was empty when she entered it, though the heady scent of maple syrup permeated the air. Her mouth watered at the thought of pancakes.

Josie loved them.

What would Josie eat this morning? And with whom? Alone perhaps, since her mother was ill. She paused as an idea so beguiling, so dangerous she could hardly believe it, flirted with her thoughts. Her suitcase grew heavy as she stood and pondered the burgeoning plan.

Lou would be furious with her and yet...he had no charge over her decisions any longer. Swallowing hard, a disconcerting excitement building, she marched through the lobby, left a note for Lou and then burst outside, just in time to catch the streetcar.

Odd looks followed her, but she ignored them and focused on remembering the way back to the Silvers'. By the time she stood at Josie's gate, the sun peeked a sleepy eye over the horizon.

She gnawed her cheek, staring at the wrought iron. Yesterday felt far away. Was she really ready to do this? She thought of the note she left to be delivered to Lou first thing. If he tried to stop her, well, that would be too much. Too invasive.

Perhaps he'd shared a dark and sad past, and perhaps he'd opened his home to her, but he did not control her and any claim he made to her time must end with his sale of the ranch.

A vehicle cranked up behind her, startling her and urging her to open the gate. It groaned but gave way. She started up the walk, up the stairs, but before she could knock on the door, it opened.

Baggs glowered at her. His eyebrows were just as

furry today as they'd been yesterday. Mary remembered Josie's comment and a reluctant smile tugged at her lips.

"You again?" he muttered.

"Yes, it is Miss O'Roarke. May I speak with Mrs. Silver?"

"She has not risen yet."

"Oh." She blinked. "I can come back later."

"You may wait. She'll be about soon." The butler, or whoever he was, swung the door open in a reluctant fashion, but Mary was too determined and set in her path to care.

She stepped into the ornate home. A hint of perfume reached her. Baggs led her into the same room they'd met Mrs. Silver in yesterday. She took a seat on the brocade couch.

"Anything to drink? Tea, perhaps?"

"That is kind of you to offer, Mr. Baggs. I would very much like tea."

He shuffled out of the room, closing the door behind him. She studied the great portraits about the room. Studious and elegant, they dominated the walls and lent the room a somber air. Soon Josie's painting would rest with those of her ancestors, if she was related to these people. No doubt she was related somehow to the man looking for her.

Langdon, the sheriff had called him.

She did not wish to remember how it felt for him to be standing in her home, her sanctuary.... Stifling the remembrance, she felt through her bag until she found her knitting needles and newest project. A wedding gift for Miss Alma, who no doubt would find James by her side very soon.

The door opened, and Baggs brought in a platter

with steaming tea. He situated it, and Mary thanked him, preferring to pour her own. "Do you not have a maid?" she asked in a gentle tone.

"Left us last week," he grumbled.

When he left, she sipped the strong brew and worked on Miss Alma's gift. The wait felt interminable. She kept straining to hear Josie's happy voice. The patter of footsteps even, but nothing broke the muted silence.

After almost an hour, the door opened again. Baggs wheeled Mrs. Silver in. She did not wear a face mask today. The faded state of her eyes and pallor of her skin sent prickles across Mary's body. She tucked her knitting back into her bag. An air of death cloaked Mrs. Silver. It hovered over her and as she neared, the odor of it filled the room.

Mary blanched and then schooled her features to blankness, though inside, her heart pounded against her chest. What would happen to Josie when her mother passed? Surely she wouldn't be left with that horrid Mr. Langdon.

"You wish to see me?" Mrs. Silver's voice did not pass a whisper.

Mary nodded, putting her hands in her lap. "I thought perhaps you might…" *Courage, don't fail me now.* She wet her lips and tried again. "With your illness, I hoped you might be in need of a nanny for Josie."

Mrs. Silver's lids fluttered.

"Your daughter is spirited and bright and I have grown quite fond of her. I can provide schooling in many areas—"

"She will attend a private school," Mrs. Silver murmured. She studied Mary, though it seemed to drain the energy from her features.

"I see." Hope seeped away, but she did not allow herself to slump. "Perhaps you might be looking for a housekeeper? Or a parlor maid?"

"You are so desperate to see my Josephine?"

"Not desperate, but I am in search of employment and I care deeply for your daughter. I would like to help."

Mrs. Silver's fingers tapped the arms of her wheelchair. "It fills my heart with gladness to see your love for my daughter, but I must refuse."

Mary's fingers tightened on her satchel.

"You see, her uncle shall be in charge of any plans for Josie. She is at the age where she would benefit from the structure of such a pla—" A harsh cough ripped the rest of the words from her. She hunched over, body racked with the cough of tuberculosis. She pressed a hankie against her pale lips.

Mary watched sadly, knowing she should return to the hotel now. This had been a shallow hope with little chance of success, but she'd needed to try.

"I apologize," Mrs. Silver said when the fit passed. Baggs handed her a glass of water and she sipped it gratefully.

"There is no need for apologies." Mary rose. "Thank you for taking the time to meet with me. I would love to see Josie but do not want to unduly upset her. Please, may I leave my address with you? I've included the hotel I'm staying at, though I won't be there after today." She handed Mrs. Silver the paper she'd scribbled on earlier. "If you or Josie are ever in need of anything, write to me and I shall come."

"Thank you…what is your name?"

"Mary O'Roarke, and you're quite welcome." She

gestured to the door, the bag heavier than ever. "I shall let myself out."

Mrs. Silver inclined her head and Mary headed to the doorway, eager to escape before her burning cheeks gave away her angst. She reached the door frame.

A shadow passed in front of the opening. Mr. Langdon appeared before her, his disturbing eyes fixed on her face.

She skidded to a stop, bumping a fragile table near the wall. The vase on it shuddered and she reached over to steady it. She breathed shallowly and tried to slow her quick breaths before she panicked.

An evil-looking smile lifted the corners of his lips. He appraised her and she hauled her bag in front of her.

"We have a visitor?" he asked.

Mrs. Silver's wheelchair appeared beside Mary. "Yes, this is Mary. She brought our Josie back last night. She was just leaving." Another cough seized Mrs. Silver, but Mary did not dare look away from Mr. Langdon.

No, she could not for fear of what might happen. Mrs. Silver and Baggs were no match for him. He frowned at his sister, then turned that unblinking gaze on Mary.

"You're leaving so soon? Might we have a word?"

Before she could react, he caught her arm in a painful grip and propelled her out the door and into the hallway.

"Brother," Mrs. Silver gasped, but he yanked the door behind them. It pounded shut and then they were alone in the hallway.

His gaze bore into her, as deep and painful as his grip on her arm. The look on his face was menacing in its lack of emotion. "Forgive me, but I overheard your conversation. You must know my sister is very ill. Dying."

He said this last word as though he relished the thought.

Mary's skin prickled all over.

"Therefore, as custodian of her estate, and of my niece, I feel it's in Josie's best interest to be at home during the last days of her mother's life. I will personally pay for you to stay on and teach Josie for one year. When my sister passes, I will relinquish the guardianship of Josie to you."

It sounded too good to be true. That alone made her pause. Be employed by this man to take care of Josie and eventually become her legal guardian? Both elation and terror filled Mary, two opposite emotions that tangled her senses. She blinked. Swallowed. "And if I do not accept?"

Now he smiled, if the baring of his teeth could be called such a thing. "Her mother will think she's been sent off to school. That won't be the case. There are plenty of orphanages for girls like her…or other places."

A sick feeling rushed through Mary so quickly her vision wavered. She knew what he was suggesting, knew his plans for Josie, should she decline his offer, were evil, but this? No, it could not happen.

Still, one thing she'd learned from Lou and Trevor was caution in bargaining with wicked men. Forcing a calm look to her face, refusing to let him see that his threat had already won him what he wanted, she met his gaze.

"I will consider your proposal."

Lou woke in a surly mood. Everything got worse when he found the note on the floor outside his door.

Dear Lou,

As I am not sure how I'd like to be employed in
the future, I have gone to see about another opportunity. I appreciate the agent you're sending to
escort me home but am unable to pass up the job
I have in mind. Please give the agent my regards
and I do apologize if I have complicated the situation. I shall be fine on my own. Thank you for
all you have done.

Mary

Where could she have gone? Groaning, he passed
his palms over his face. Stubble grazed his skin. There
wasn't time to track down a stubborn woman today,
let alone shave. He had a ten o'clock meeting and before that he was determined to find Langdon. He also
wanted to meet the undercover agent assigned to protect
Mrs. Silver and Josie. If he could see the guy for himself, his gut would let him know whether Josie would
be safe or not in his care.

Lou snatched the note, folded it, and then slid it into
a pocket. After tossing on blue jeans and a respectable
shirt, he stalked out of the hotel room. He grabbed a
slice of banana bread on the way out of the hotel.

The ride to the Silvers' seemed to take forever. He
scanned the case files he'd been handed yesterday, a
few reports, but his brain insisted on taking him back
to how Mary looked last night. What he'd told her…
His chest pinched.

Worst of all, he'd exposed something he hadn't meant
to—the root of his anger at God and everything reli-
gion represented. He felt like a fool. He pressed his

head against the wall of the streetcar, glad no one tried to make conversation with him.

He was lousy at that type of thing.

Mary would be better off without him. An attraction didn't guarantee a good marriage. Let alone their differing religious beliefs. He cringed at what had sneaked into his thoughts.

Marriage.

Rolling his eyes, he straightened and began pressing the paperwork back into his satchel, listening as it crumpled into place.

Marriage.

He'd been so young with Sarah. Naive and in love. He thought he knew all the answers. He worked a job with the military that required long hours. Applied for a place in the new unit known as the Bureau of Investigation. He left Sarah at home and worked hard. She waited. He visited.

They had Abby. A tic tugged at his eyelid. He blinked. So many mistakes he could never take back, and now his thoughts had wandered to marriage. Absolutely unthinkable. He couldn't even blame the detour on a single kiss, because he'd kissed others and never had he felt what he did when he embraced Mary. It was a cruel realization that over the course of twelve years, Mary and her quiet presence had worked itself into his soul beneath the guise of friendship.

His only recourse remained backing off. Leaving town and letting the figurative dust settle. If Mary opened a store, she'd surely meet a nice fellow to create a home with.

The tic pulled his eyelid again. He blinked and held on as the streetcar slowed to its next stop. The Silver place loomed across the street. Lou got off with a few others and separated from them.

Time to don his "agent" hat and get to work. Worrying about where Mary might be could wait for later. But as he made his way up the walk, opening the gate, and taking the stairs two at a time, his stomach clenched.

"Focus," he muttered, then rapped quick and hard on the front door.

Almost immediately it swung open. A man with eyes bordering on purple faced him. His hair was slicked in the fashion of the day. He wore a neatly pressed suit and his face was clean-shaven.

Lou disliked him immediately.

"Langdon, I presume?"

Langdon's brows rose, but he quickly recovered and stepped outside, closing the door behind him. "What can I do for you?"

He flipped his badge open. "Special Agent Lou Riley with the Bureau of Investigation." He put the badge away. "Would you mind going to my office to answer a few questions?" His tone brooked no argument.

Langdon bared his teeth. "I've business to attend to."

"We can talk here." Lou gave him a look designed to get his point across.

"I really must go, but here is my card. You may call me." The man's voice was slicker than a politician's on election day.

Lou scowled and closed the gap between them. They stood head-to-head. His instincts roared that something was wrong. "What were you doing in Burns?"

"Business." Langdon's cheeks bunched in a mocking manner. "I stopped by your place."

"I heard." This guy didn't get to own the conversation. "Also heard you murdered someone."

Langdon's eyes flickered. "Really? How odd." He moved back and bumped the front door. "Isn't that business for the police, though? I thought the bureau dealt with other, more important, things?"

"You saying you did it?"

"I'm saying the sheriff has himself the murderer. Go talk to him." Langdon pulled out a pocket watch and made a point of looking at it before stuffing it back into his overpressed suit. "I really must say goodbye."

"Don't think so." Lou cocked him a smile that froze most men. He propped a hand against the door and leaned forward. "You see, Langdon, I'm here unofficially. Your trail… Let's just say it's putting off an odor." He narrowed his eyes. "I'm going to fix that. You might think you're slick, but I'm onto you. With the murder and with your niece. You won't get away with anything."

Langdon inclined his head, a smirk plastered to his lips. He casually brushed off his right shoulder, as if Lou's words had landed there and stuck. "Since you're here unofficially, I believe I might have something that belongs to you."

"That a fact?" Unease skittered up his spine.

Langdon turned and opened the front door. "Someone's here for you. Come, come, don't be frightened." He cast Lou a smile that chilled him to the core. "I'm afraid I might have been a little too…harsh with her."

Confused, Lou's gaze darted to the entryway. Movement, and then Mary emerged, eyes wide and lips pale.

Lou snarled and yanked Langdon up by the sleeve. The man's cologne reeked. "What did you do to her?"

Chapter Nineteen

Langdon tried to shrug out of Lou's grasp, but he tightened his grip and jerked him against the wall of the house. Mary gasped, but Lou ignored her. His pulse hammered through him, and his fingers moved to the scoundrel's collar.

Langdon made a choking sound but didn't try again to get out of Lou's hold. Rather, his lips tilted. "You should take better care of your property."

Lou released him abruptly and turned to Mary, who edged through the doorway in a pained way. A sound like a train filled his ears and his vision blurred. Whirling, he pushed Langdon up against the door.

"You better talk, and fast," he said.

"Release me or I'll have the police arrest you for assault."

Lou's jaw hurt. He ground his teeth and forced his fingers to unlock from Langdon's arms. "You're done for. Don't forget it."

Langdon sniffed and readjusted his shirt. "Have a pleasant life, Special Agent Riley." He turned and pushed into the house. Silence ensued.

Mary gazed off the porch, her face unreadable. A bird twittered. Streetcars rumbled past, casting long shadows against the street. He stalked to Mary.

"Are you okay?" he asked.

She nodded but didn't look at him. He couldn't help himself. He touched her shoulders, gently moving his hands down her arms, looking for any bruising or indication that Langdon had physically mistreated her.

She didn't flinch.

"Are you sure you're okay? Absolutely sure?" He grasped her shoulders, searching her eyes for something, anything, to take away the worry that was cleaving into him.

"I'm sure." Her smile was calm as she backed out of his grip.

Clearing his throat, shoving his hands into his pockets, he asked, "Do you want to walk back to the hotel?"

"That's quite the walk," she murmured.

"I have an appointment at ten." He glanced at his watch. "That's in forty-five minutes. We can be to the office by then and you can wait. The agent in charge of escorting you has been reassigned, so it looks like—"

"I don't need an escort, Lou." She looked at him, her eyes earnest. "I'm a grown woman, quite capable of traveling home."

"I wish that was true, but times are troubled." He thought of the papers in his briefcase.

"They seem fine to me. Prohibition has things a bit topsy-turvy, but the war is over, our economy is recovering… What do you find to be the problem?"

"Let's walk," he suggested as he debated how much to tell her. She held her head high beside him, and if she noticed the stares of those they passed, she didn't let on. He rubbed the back of his neck for a moment and then gave in to his gut. "Our office has received some disturbing information. The Ku Klux Klan is re-organizing. Strategizing. We're expecting to see some integration of their policies and beliefs in the coming year, we're just not sure where or how much they'll be able to infiltrate the public psyche."

Mary's stride didn't slow. "I haven't heard such a thing."

"But you feel the stares, don't you? People look at you and see someone different than them. There's distrust here in Oregon of foreigners. Our office found disturbing evidence that the Klan will prey on people's fears. Especially with the influx of Chinese migrant workers."

"This is nothing new to me, Lou."

"It could influence laws," he said gravely.

"That may be so, but I believe they've already been influenced since the beginning of the country. You're a white man, Lou. Blond hair, blue eyes." She stopped walking and turned to pin him with those bottomless eyes of hers. "For you, life in America has been fair. It has not been so for others." She held up her arm, darker than his, and Lou found his gaze traveling the length of her bone structure, up to her shoulder, then across her dress, which he just now realized fit her perfectly.

He couldn't recall seeing her in this outfit before and abruptly noticed how the dress tapered off at her knees, exposing her legs and ankles. Heat rose to his neck. He yanked his eyes back up to meet hers.

Her mouth was parted, and suddenly he was filled with remembrance of the kiss they'd shared. He blinked, jerked the direction of his gaze to the road and began walking. "Every day we're making strides, though. The Klan is a dangerous group of people and the worst thing is, people in positions of authority are involved. I don't want you traveling alone. Not just because of your heritage, but because you're a beautiful woman."

There, he'd said it. A lump clogged his windpipe. He peeked at Mary. A sober expression rested on her features. The wind stirred up her dark hair, and again he thought of their kiss.

"Many have called me beautiful," she said quietly and without pride.

"You don't like it?"

"Beauty brings challenges...." She trailed off.

"Life brings challenges to everyone." He took her arm and they crossed to the other side of the road. "We're almost to my office. After I deliver these papers, we'll figure out what to do with you."

"Excuse me?" She popped out of his grasp. "I have my ticket. Your twelve years of baby watching has finished."

He halted, gaping, while she strode ahead. "Wait..."

Her hand fluttered up, waving through the air as if dismissing him. He set his jaw and forged ahead.

"Now, stop just a moment," he said, grabbing her shoulders and stopping her. She felt fragile beneath his fingers and he loosened his hold. "You've been caring for us, Mary, not the other way around."

Her gaze flickered. "Either way, that time has passed. We're moving in different directions now."

True, and yet the knowledge pained him. He studied her, taking in the faint flush in her cheeks and her dewy eyes. A stray hair fluttered across her cheek. Using the tip of his finger, he drew it back over her ear. She released a soft breath that brought him full circle, right back to their kiss.

"Please don't look at me like that," she whispered.

"Like what?"

"Like you plan to kiss me again."

He couldn't help the smile tugging his lips. "And if I do?"

"This can't work. You know that. Do you plan to quit your job? Stop traveling to foreign places and saving lives?"

He shook his head.

"I didn't think so," she said. "Quit worrying about me and live your life. I'm thankful for the shelter you provided, but that season is over."

"We're here." He gestured to the building in front of them with his briefcase, glad to stop this conversation in its endless tracks. "Come in and let's work this out. Then we're going to have an early supper and you can tell me what Langdon said to you in that hallway."

A few hours later, Mary chewed her bottom lip, watching as Lou spoke with the waiter at the hotel's restaurant. They'd returned to check out. A cramp tried to work its way through her toes, which she'd stuck into heels to try to look nice for Mrs. Silver.

And maybe for Lou.

It was the last day she'd see him after all. She fiddled with a button on her dress, wondering how he'd remember her. What would supper bring? More arguing? Surely so, if she told him what Langdon had said to her. He was to call her at the hotel, she'd told him, and she'd give him an answer.

There was only one answer to give.

Shuddering, she turned away from Lou's direction. While she'd waited at his work, she debated her possible courses of action. She could tell him the truth at supper and see if he'd help her or offer a different solution. Or she could go home, ignore Langdon's plan and look into getting a loan and opening a business.

"We're ready." Lou appeared beside her, his arm on her elbow and his breath minty. He brought her to the table. After they were given glasses of water, Lou gestured to the menu. "Order anything you want. My treat." His eyes sparkled.

She'd been drawn in by those eyes for too long. Could she forget how he'd sold the ranch beneath her feet? Even though he'd arranged for her to stay, his action had felt like a betrayal of sorts. No, she could not trust that sparkle as much as she longed to.

It was a longing she must deny herself.

Ordering was brief. The waiter took their menus, and then quiet followed. Lou folded a napkin across his lap and leaned back in his seat, hands lightly clasped on the starched tablecloth.

"I finished some work at the office today," he finally said.

She sipped her water. "Have they caught the man who shot you?"

"No, but we will. I'm on his trail. After supper today, I'm going to drop you at the train station, where a special agent will meet you and escort you home." At her look, he grinned. "You really think I'm going to let you traipse off all by yourself? I wouldn't let any woman do that."

"The point is that you're not in charge."

"Once you're safe," he continued without missing a breath, "I'm hunting this fellow down. I didn't see his face, but there was another man I caught a good look at. Talked to, even. A few visits to some unsavory places, and I'm thinking I'll find my shooter and maybe even a crime to tie him to."

"Besides shooting you?" Mary asked drily.

"Exactly." Lou gave her a slow wink, obviously pleased with all his plans.

The cad. He both infuriated her and made her smile. This back-and-forth was exhausting, though.

"Tell me," she said, aligning her knife with the edge of her napkin. "What will you do when I'm not at the ranch when you return?"

His ego appeared to trip along with his grin. "Why wouldn't you be there?"

"I can think of a few reasons."

"I'm not gone yet. The buyers have agreed to keep you on as housekeeper. This sale… It's an offer, but that doesn't mean it's final. I wired Trevor the information yesterday, and he and Gracie are going to talk things through. He never needed the home he sold you, but Gracie's partial to the ranch. In fact, they'll be meeting me here tomorrow or the day after to talk things through."

The fact that he was trying to look out for her should have comforted her, but it didn't.

She let out an exasperated breath. "Do you not hear yourself? Why are you selling if Gracie and Trevor don't want to? Why bother? Can you not travel as you've always done? And things may remain the same."

The grin slid from his face. He leaned forward and pulled her hands toward him in a heated grip. His grasp was decidedly larger than hers, and she had to tear her eyes from their entwined palms to focus on his next words.

"Is that really what you want? To live out your days on secluded property?" His gaze probed her. The way his hands enveloped hers felt so right…. Her tongue tied within her mouth, and she could only look at him.

"I know you want more. You're made for more, Mary." He hesitated and then said quietly, "God has given you talents. Don't hide them on a ranch. Don't waste them on people who aren't around to appreciate what you have to offer."

He spoke of God. She blinked and pulled her hands free from his.

"I have never considered myself wasting away there. The meals I made, the clothes I darned and ironed, the prayers I prayed… It was healing. Not one second of my time there has been a waste." She had to work hard to keep her voice from shaking. "I am sorry your perspective is so very different than mine."

He started to speak and she held up a hand.

"Either way, what I do with my life is not up to you. Your plans for tomorrow are all well and good, but you have given no consideration to what I want. Did you plan to ask? Or do you plan to do whatever you want and then expect me to be there?"

His eyes widened. "I'm sorry—"

"Excuse me, miss. There's a telephone call for you." The waiter pointed to the lobby's desk, visible through the restaurant's entrance.

Lou's gaze narrowed. Mary ignored him, though a trembling had taken up residence in her stomach. "Thank you. I shall be there in a moment."

"Is there something you need to tell me?" Lou stood and walked around the table to her. "What did Langdon say to you?"

Sitting left her at a disadvantage and so she also stood, though it did little good with her small stature. Nevertheless, it must do for now. Lou and his authoritative ways must stop. She placed a hand on his chest and gave him a little nudge.

"This is a telephone call for me."

"Mary." His voice sharpened. "You're playing with a criminal. If there's something you need to say, say so now, because I'm not having my employee involved with the likes of him."

"Don't you think I know what he is?" She nudged him harder, but he refused to move. Well, she'd just go around him, then. But as she stepped to the side, he mirrored her. She hissed and glared up at him.

"Kindly move."

"Not until you tell me what's going on." His eyes were blue steel.

Very well. A surprising burst of anger popped through her. She threw her head up and gave him the sternest look she could muster.

"I know criminals, Lou Riley. You forget, I spent a week with them. It might've been twelve years ago, but I haven't lost my senses. My mind works just fine and I know exactly what I'm doing." Maybe not *exactly,* but at this moment she thought things were quite clear. "Move yourself before I make a scene."

The threat sent hotness to the back of her neck. She prayed he did not force her to do such a dreadful thing. His jaw worked, and his hands went to his narrow hips. He studied her, and she was torn between the irresistible urge to allow him to kiss her again or to scurry past and pick up the telephone.

He seemed to come to some internal decision. His jaw hardened. "Nope. No employee of mine is carousing with criminal types. I've said my piece. Now sit back down."

"Why you...you overbearing oaf." An unbelievable heat swept through her body and pooled in her belly. Her hands clenched. She ignored his raised eyebrows and sputtered, "F-fine, then. If you choose to be this way. Then. I. Quit."

His hands slid off his hips. She took advantage of his slack jaw to skirt around him, hustling to the telephone as fast as she could and hoping he didn't beat her to it.

This was the moment her life would change forever.

Chapter Twenty

Mary couldn't quit.

Lou was tempted to follow her, but her last words had punched a hole in his steady breathing. He opted to keep his distance and reassess the situation when she returned. Moments passed, filled with the sounds of conversation around him, clinking silverware, the aromas of food, and then she turned from the counter.

Her head was tilted down. Shoulders slumped. He frowned. Thoughts ricocheted through him, knotting his gut. He tapped his knuckles against the table.

The indecision twisting through him was unexpected. He didn't like the feeling, but stopping it was another matter.

She'd actually had the audacity to quit.

That wasn't like her. Did she mean her words? The look on her face… He'd never seen it there before. He'd wanted her to be independent, to be okay so he could leave this place for good, but now that she'd flung her independence in his face, well, what could a man make of that?

He rapped the table again, thinking. Plans were going

well. Exactly how he'd thought he wanted months ago when he'd set things in motion. Even with the unforeseen shooting. It hadn't changed his plans, but it had affected him personally. Somehow getting shot and being stuck at the ranch with Josie and Mary had changed him, but he wasn't sure how, and even if he figured it out, he was pretty certain he wouldn't like what he found.

His own father had been trapped at home raising two sons alone after his mother died. And his brother, Gracie's dad, was held beneath the sway of his wife. He'd even cut off contact with Lou for almost twenty years because his wife disapproved of Lou's career choices.

No, he'd seen what a man leashed by hearth and home became. When he was young, he hadn't worried too much on it, but losing Sarah and Abby had reinforced his instincts and for twelve years he'd been just fine, footloose and fancy-free.

Until now.

Mary's independence threatened his own. That much he was sure about. After so long looking out for her, did he really want her gone from his life? *No.* But being hog-tied to one place gave him the urge to draw his gun and target practice.

At least he might get to do that soon. This morning a junior agent had shared some fascinating intelligence. He and another agent had linked Lou's shooter to an international ring that was smuggling alcohol from Canada by way of Oregon ports. Given international waters were involved, the smuggling became a federal crime and he'd been given free rein to bring his shooter in. If he could just find a name…

Mary neared, cutting off his thoughts. A flush

stained her cheekbones. He put his hands on his hips and battled the urge to apologize. And for what? Trying to protect her? It was an illogical, insensible reaction.

Scowling, he sat in his chair. She followed suit, sitting across from him and fiddling with her silverware again. Busy fingers meant nervousness. He eyed her, but she wouldn't meet his gaze.

"Your food, sir." The waiter set their plates down.

"Thank you." He ate, but the food was tasteless. Mary picked at her potatoes. "You might as well tell me what that call was about. I'm going to find out eventually."

"I know. And that is what upsets me." She lifted her eyes.

"So let the cat out of the bag." He shrugged, though he felt anything but nonchalant. After all this time, it was as though she didn't trust him. The thought rubbed him wrong.

"I've been offered a deal of sorts. Employment in exchange for something." Her eyes dropped.

Lou's throat clenched and for the second time that day, a red haze crept into his vision. Fingers curling into fists, he took deep, even breaths. When he thought he could speak without yelling, or worse, scaring her, he said, "What's the exchange?"

She shook her head. "It's between us. Regardless, I'm in need of employment, and though I'd like to open my own shop someday, I think this will work better for now. It is a good thing for me to quit now rather than later. My future is secure, and you need not worry about me or my mother."

He scoffed, if only to let out the tension tightening every muscle in his body. "I'm not worried about her."

Mary frowned. "Despite how you feel, my mother

will be in my life. I suppose it's also good you plan to leave."

Fighting words. He should be alarmed, but they eased his tension a little. Whatever plan she'd agreed to couldn't be permanent or she wouldn't be talking about keeping her ma in her life.

"A good thing, huh?" He flashed a little teeth and leaned forward.

"Don't try to charm me, Lou Riley. Your distaste for my mother is upsetting." She pushed her dish to the side. "I wish you would try to see her side of things. Forgive her, even."

"Sorry, but I have a hard time forgiving anyone who hurt you the way she did. That's just the fact of the matter."

"I see."

"I don't think you do."

She glanced to the right, where a clock perched against the wall. "It is time for me to leave."

Panic knotted the base of his neck. He had to fix things, and quick. "Look, I'm sorry for bossing you around earlier. What say you stay and give me the low-down on the situation? Maybe I can help with this trade you're doing?" He kept his smile in place.

She shook her head. "I'm the only one who can fulfill the terms of the agreement."

"That so?" he drawled. His chest burned with the effort of staying calm.

"I'll be back to the house in a year or so. We shall meet again, I'm sure. Are you okay? You look…red."

He felt it. Drawing a heavy breath, he said, "This agreement isn't illicit, is it? Tell me it's not, Mary. Tell me you haven't sold yourself to protect that little girl."

She gasped. Then her face darkened as she shot up from her seat. "How could you think such a thing?" Her mouth worked.

He stood, too, but she was already reaching for her luggage. She rushed past him, leaving the restaurant in a flurry of movement. He groaned and tossed money on the table to cover the food. He'd really bungled this.

Maybe she wasn't planning a liaison, but he'd seen Langdon look at her. He'd seen her paleness. Didn't take a genius to put two and two together. She might not plan to give in to Langdon's advances, but Lou had met his type before.

If someone didn't step in, Langdon would try to force himself on Mary, and she would never be the same.

Lou spun on his heel and stalked out of the restaurant. Yes, he had a shooter to catch and a ranch to sell and a new employment opportunity, but Mary meant more to him than material things. And so did Josie.

This so-called deal put them in danger, and he would do whatever it took to stop it.

The nerve of that man!

Mary strode the streets, brushing past people as she worked to clear the steam from her head. How could he think such a thing of her? Did he really believe she'd ever put herself in that position? Perhaps this plan could use some finessing and it might require a bit of dodging, but she hoped for the optimum.

To raise Josie as her own.

A breeze rustled up against her and waltzed with her skirt. She should have brought a sweater of some sort. Oregon's personality was moody, and chill bumps rose on her arms in reaction to the cool wind.

Or maybe it was the thought of having a family. Though her heart ached for Josie, knowing the child's mother might pass soon, Mr. Langdon had assured her that there were no living relatives, no one to claim Josie. Without him, she would be put into an orphanage. Mary couldn't abide such a thought. Perhaps her own childhood had been unstable. Constantly moving, a father who was in and out of her life physically, a mother who was emotionally in and out, but there'd been many times of love. There'd been food and clean clothes.

She'd seen orphanages, but worse, she'd heard tales of them. Many of the prostitutes her mother worked with came from these places. Many had been more girl than woman.

A shudder swept through her.

No. Mr. Langdon and the orphanages wouldn't get her sweet girl. His plans for Josie were vile enough to let her know that when Josie's mother died, the girl would be in harm's way. Mr. Langdon's wicked plan *had* to be an answer to prayer. God could use evil and turn it to good. Perhaps that was His plan for her.

She stopped at the corner and waited for the coming streetcar. She wrapped her arms firmly around her ribs. A year or less. If she could make it through that, then both she and Josie would be okay.

She'd agreed to show up in the morning for the job, which meant she should find somewhere to sleep this evening.

"Mary!"

She whirled to see Lou sprinting toward her. His broad frame filled her with a restless longing, an unfair yearning. She closed her eyes, pressing them to block out his image.

He reached her, his breaths short and shallow. Perhaps his scar still ached.

"You shouldn't be running," she said, opening her eyes.

"I'm fine. Look—" he swiped a hand through his hair "—I really am sorry. I've got no business telling you what to do. The past few weeks have been crazy for me. Getting shot, seeing Josie, which brings back all sorts of memories… Let's just say I'm trying to make things right and I feel like I'm failing." The words sounded strained as he said them.

A streetcar rumbled to a stop in front of them. She stepped onto it, and Lou followed. They held the railings as it picked up speed. What could she answer him? Seconds turned into minutes. He let her think, for which she was grateful.

Finally, she turned to him. He still wore that pained, uncomfortable expression. It pulled at the creases of his eyes and made him quite attractive. Stifling a smile, she said softly, "I suppose you're not used to apologies."

His lips tilted. "I'm used to being in charge. Giving orders and having people obey."

"Perhaps there was a time for that in my life, but being by myself so much at the ranch has taught me to make my own way." She hesitated, then reached out and touched one of his hands. His skin was tanned and scarred, rough beneath her fingers. "Your desire to protect me is noble, but I must be free to make my own choices. To control someone is not loving."

His throat worked. His eyes were such a clear blue, penetrating and serious. "The last thing I want is to hurt you or treat you less than what you deserve. I'm going to try to trust your judgment, but I need you to trust me, too."

"When it comes to my life, I reserve trust for myself."

"What about God?" he countered.

The jab stung a bit. "Perhaps my trust in Him is not perfect, but I'm working on it."

"I guess that's the most anyone can do." The streetcar jolted to a stop. They shifted closer to allow a woman laden with bags to squeeze past. Lou's cologne and minty scent enveloped Mary. She was so close she could feel the warmth of his breath on her hair.

As soon as the woman passed, she shifted away, ignoring every impulse to stay near him. The car started up again.

"So…truce?" Lou asked.

She faced him, taking in his sober look. "I suppose so."

"Great. Let me help you, then. What's the plan? What can I do? I have resources you can only dream of." He gave her a lopsided grin.

She reciprocated, thankful the tension between them had ebbed. "For now I must find a hotel to stay at. Tomorrow I will begin my new job."

"Your ma know yet?"

"I'll send a telegram once I'm settled."

"You don't think she'll worry?"

Mary quirked a brow. "Do you?"

"A little." He rubbed at the light stubble at his chin. "Truth is, she's a hard one to pin down, but I can usually see when someone is up to no good. She's about spent all her no-goodness, I think."

"I'm not sure whether you just complimented her or if that was an insult."

"Call it the truth." He winked at her, then his face went stiff. His eyes narrowed. "Don't move," he said softly.

"What?" She turned to look where his gaze had fastened, but he was already shifting, putting his body between hers and whatever he saw. She swallowed. Holding still this way made her more aware of the rapid pump of her pulse and the dryness of her mouth.

"There's a hotel at the next corner. Small but nice. You mind staying there?" He swung her a quick glance, questioning.

"No, no, that's fine." She swallowed hard. "Is everything okay?"

He hesitated.

Suddenly the need to know overwhelmed her. The need for him to share with her more than the curious oddities or the amazing inventions he'd seen on his travels. She wanted to share in his struggles and perhaps even his adventures. An unfamiliar prickle crawled across her skin.

"Please tell me," she said quietly.

He looked around and then bent his head forward, blocking her view of everything but him. "The man behind me sought me out to parlay information right before I was shot. I believe he followed me onto this streetcar, or maybe it's just chance, but I've got to talk to him."

"But first you need to see me settled?"

"Yes." His eyes searched hers.

"That's not necessary. I can do it myself."

He was already shaking his head. "No. Not in this city, not at night."

The streetcar shuddered to another stop.

"Really, I'll be fine. Surely a reputable hotel like you've suggested will be a safe place."

"Maybe so, but it's a risk I'm not willing to take."

And there it was again, that urge to wrap herself in his arms and to never let go. The feeling struck her with such force that she couldn't speak, could only lose herself in the intensity of the moment.

Movement grabbed her attention. Bowler Hat disappeared out the door. She pointed.

Lou blinked, spun around. He grabbed her wrist. "Will you come with me? It's dark, dangerous… I'll try to keep you safe, but you'll need to trust me."

Indecision rooted her feet and each second passed in agonizing slowness. The engine's gears ground, propelling her into action.

She moved forward. Slipped her hand into his and let him lead her into the night, after the mysterious man.

Chapter Twenty-One

Their breathing melded with the sounds of evening as they dropped from the streetcar to the cobbled road. Lou's hand tightened around Mary's smaller one. He couldn't believe she'd come with him, that he was actually going to bring her with while he interrogated this guy.

Her hand was warm in his as they stepped near a brick building. The light was waning, turning into a smoky dusk. He searched for the bowler hat. People still lingered outside, some going to work, others leaving after a hard day.

Businesses lined this street. Women clicked down the sidewalk in heels. Men in suits and eyeglasses who'd stayed longer than expected locked their offices for the night. Still no hat. The man reached medium height. He'd blend in well.

Lou groaned. Mary's fingers flexed in his.

"He went that way," she whispered. Her chin nudged to the right.

He followed the direction of her gaze and spotted a dark alley ahead, hidden between two narrow buildings. He strode forward, releasing her hand. When they reached the crevice, he turned to her.

"Stay here."

"I should go with you." Her eyes shone black in the encroaching night.

"Nothing can happen to you." That knowledge resounded through him. No matter what, she had to stay safe. "You can keep an eye out. Stay here, in the shadows." He moved her inside the alley, up against the wall. "No one will see you, but you'll see them."

Gut tight, he left her there, clutching her dress and looking nervous. It couldn't be helped, though. The man waiting at the end of the alley had something to impart. He wouldn't have followed Lou otherwise.

He edged against the wall, reaching for his revolver. Nothing stirred in the alley. The light from the street only reached so far. A dank, putrid smell pervaded his senses. He blocked it, focusing on the barely discernible shadow at the end of the alley.

Flattening his back, he peeked at Mary. He could barely see her. That was good. He whipped his gaze the other way.

"You wanted to talk," he asked, keeping his voice low, letting the natural echoes carry his words to the other party.

A clatter punctuated the stillness. Then rustling. Finally, Lou's eyes adjusted and he could see the outline of a hat as the man moved near. He adjusted his gun, keeping it low at his hip and aimed lower. His trigger finger flexed against the revolver's hilt.

"Took you long enough." The Irish lilt in Bowler Hat's words confirmed Lou's thoughts on his identity.

The guy sidled up, hands in the air. "I'm not armed, so you can lower your weapon. I just need to talk."

Lou kept his revolver aimed. "Come closer."

"I'm coming, mister." Scuffling ensued, and then the man stood opposite him. The odor of fish guts clung to him. Dusk had settled long ago, marking the way for darkness to creep in. Lou wanted to see his face, but the crescent moon left a lot to be desired for light.

"That your woman over there?" the man asked.

"Who wants to know?" Lou countered.

"No sirree, I'm not stupid enough to give my name. I just wanted to pass on some information and I've heard you're to be trusted. You don't take bribes."

"Go on." Things were getting interesting, and not in a good way.

"There's been talk about shady characters in the bureau. It's been a few weeks, but I didn't have anyone else to give my information to."

"Why me? Besides all your jabber and flattery, you've got no need to pass this on." Besides, Lou had one use for the guy. "Tell me who shot me, and you can go your way."

The man let out a short laugh. "If I knew that, I wouldn't say. I've my reasons for singling you out, and they don't include a shooter. When I tried talking to you last month—"

"You got me shot," Lou interrupted, feeling his patience grow thin. "If you've something important to say, then let's go down to the station and write it down legal-like."

"I told you, mister, there're eyes. This is for you and only you." The man scuffled again and then moved to the center of the alley. "Wasn't my fault what happened last time. I'm telling you the truth. This time I was careful, though. Followed you and made sure we wouldn't be interrupted." He took a step toward Lou. "I'm handing you the correspondence, and you can decide what to do with it. As for me, I'm leaving town and don't want you searching me out."

Lou swallowed his scoff. As if he'd really let this bootlegger slide through his fingers.

The man swept the bowler off his head, closed the distance between them and handed it to Lou. "The information is in the seam. Before I go, I need to know this lady friend of yours isn't going to be in the way. Distractions get a man killed real easy. Even when it's just the messenger."

Lou grabbed the hat, his blood thundering through him at the guy's proximity to Mary. Messenger or not, he didn't know who this man was or what he was capable of. His number-one priority right now was to protect Mary. He placed the hat on his head and stepped into the light.

"Whoa, mister…" The man backed up, hands in surrender.

"The lady means nothing to me." He jerked his head to the alley opening. "Make sure whoever sent you knows I'll take care of the situation. No distractions." He waved his gun. "Now, scram."

"What a disappointment," Lou muttered.

Mary flinched when he took her by the arm. The mysterious man had faded out of the alley and disappeared onto the street, but her limbs still felt paralyzed both by the situation and the words exchanged. Somehow she set into motion next to Lou, her lips like cotton and her heart pattering an uneven rhythm.

They found a streetcar still operating and settled in a corner. The people around her looked tired and bedraggled, no doubt from a long day's work. They would never guess the drama that had just transpired.

Bribes in high places. Strange stalkers. Unknown assailants. She almost wished she hadn't followed Lou off the streetcar, and yet the experience had given her a different perspective of her former employer. That carefree smile he wore masked so very much. In the alley he'd sounded completely in control, powerful. Not lighthearted in the least.

How many times had he faced such danger? She chanced a glance at him and the hat upon his head, which supposedly contained the secret missive.

Gracie would find this all very exciting, but Mary was only conscious of exhaustion. She longed to be home, kneading bread, breathing in the delicious aroma of yeast and flour and milk. She wished to listen to Josie's chatter and to feel the sage-scented breeze upon her brow, not to ride a loud streetcar filled with odors and stares. Adventure wasn't for her.

Home and hearth. Family. Those filled her heart.

"Are you okay?" Lou's brow crinkled, and Mary flushed. He'd caught her daydreaming while still looking at him. Did he think she'd been ogling? The thought quivered through her.

"I am fine," she said.

"You look shaken," he persisted.

"Really, all is well. I am simply tired." And heart worn. Not only had the experience been exhausting, but

Lou's words still echoed in her head. *The lady means nothing to me.*

"We'll get you to the hotel, then. Are you sure you want to go through with tomorrow? I don't trust Langdon."

The one thing she felt for certain was that she didn't feel like arguing. Tiredness weighted her very bones. "You shouldn't spend time worrying about him when it sounds as though you have something wrong with your Bureau of Investigation."

He snorted. "I doubt that."

"Why so certain? The government has a long history of deceit and underhanded methods." She'd heard the stories of her maternal grandmother and grandfather. How they'd been forced to march. Offered land only to have it rescinded. And more tales of blood and lies. No, Lou might do much good, but that didn't mean all men in government were like him.

"You're right about that, but in this case, I have a different feeling."

"Feelings are not a solid guidepost for life." She crossed her arms.

"Right again, but the gut never lies."

She grimaced, and he laughed.

"Instinct and feelings are two different animals," he continued. "One to be trusted, the other to be wary of."

"At last we agree." She felt the corners of her lips lift unexpectedly.

They arrived at the hotel too soon. After situating her in a room, Lou said an unnervingly brisk good-night, and she shut her door.

Alone at last.

The room smelled a little of mildew, but she trusted

the bed to be clean. The space looked sparse, filled with only a dresser, a bed and one nightstand. A lone lamp stood in a corner. She set her bag beside the bed, and then went to check the tub. The hotel had running water, thank goodness.

She cleaned up and even rinsed her dress, hoping it would dry by morning. Sending it down to be laundered seemed a waste of money when she must leave in the morning. As she worked, Lou's words revolved in her head.

The lady means nothing to me.

Deep down, she knew she meant something to him. Something more than a friend. But to hear him so casually dismiss their relationship to the bowler-hat man sent apprehension through her. The words had left his mouth without effort. Whatever he felt for her, it wouldn't impede his job or change his life.

And did she want it to? The memory of his kiss tingled her lips. She rubbed at them and climbed into bed.

No, she had never wanted a husband. Kisses were one thing, but everything after could only stir memories she'd long healed from. Or at least suppressed. The thought nagged at her. She pulled the blankets up and rolled to her side, staring at the wall.

Hadn't Miss Alma helped her? Years ago she'd told the kind lady everything that had transpired when Trevor's mother had arranged for her to be kidnapped by a gang of evil men. They'd planned to sell her, and though there'd been rough talk, handling that still gave her chills, and countless leers, no one had assaulted her.

The emotional impact had still been traumatic.

Memories traipsed through her mind, rolling silently like one of those new films they showed in theaters lately. Only her memories were in both color and sound, and she couldn't turn them off with a flick of the reel.

Restless, she rolled to the other side and plumped her pillow. Things that had happened so long ago shouldn't keep hurting, but they did. Granted, the fear had subsided and now she felt only an uncomfortable knot of tension.

Why was she thinking of marriage in conjunction with Lou, and what would he do about the attraction between them? And if he did do something, how would she respond?

Marriage might bring it all back, stir up too many issues. Despite Miss Alma's assurances, the thought of being trapped, powerless, in a permanent contract with a man, closed her throat in a panic.

Even if the contract was with Lou.

His kiss, his many kindnesses throughout the years, shouldn't drag her thoughts in this direction. Why had being with him these past weeks make her think of marriage? Perhaps Miss Alma's hint in the store about a young man sparking for her was what had sent her mind down the path. Or it could've been the way Lou interacted with Josie. In so many ways he reminded her of her own departed father. When he'd been in the beginning stages of drink, he'd been quite affectionate and loving. Though his mood had often turned to moroseness followed by oblivion, she'd treasured the first hour of attention he gave her. Children needed that. Lou didn't drink, but he had that same playfulness when dealing with Josie.

And that was why future thoughts of Lou must halt, because any path they took together could only lead to a dead end.

Besides, there was no way she'd leave Josie. Mr. Langdon had made quite clear what he *thought* might happen to the girl when her mother passed away, and though Mary longed to turn him in for the evil he'd suggested, she doubted any official would take her word against a wealthy businessman like Mr. Langdon. She couldn't prove his words, and he'd done nothing illegal that she knew of.

One year. She'd give one year or less, just until Mrs. Silver passed away, and then Langdon had promised to give her guardianship of Josie. She would press to adopt the girl, though she had little to bargain with.

She probably should have told Lou what Langdon had threatened.

She squeezed her eyes closed, longing for sleep to take these burdens away. Her eyelids burned with exhaustion, but worry kept her awake.

If she hadn't accepted Langdon's employment, Josie would be in harm's way. There had been no other choice, she tried to reassure herself.

Yet she kept thinking of the way he stared at her. The predatory quality to his look. She couldn't escape the feeling that she was walking into a trap.

She shifted again in the bed before rolling out and digging through her luggage until she felt the small Bible Miss Alma had given her years ago. After clicking on the lamp, she leafed through it until she found Psalms.

Her finger followed chapter 69, to verse 16.

Hear me, O Lord, for Your lovingkindness is good; turn to me according to the multitude of Your tender mercies. And do not hide Your face from Your servant. For I am in trouble...

Prickles scattered across her skin at the words.

Hear me speedily. Draw near to my soul and redeem it; deliver me because of my enemies.

She read to the last verse and into the next chapter. She read until her soul felt settled and her thoughts calm. No matter what occurred in the next year, she could trust God to be near, to be her help in time of need. She closed the book, laid it beside her pillow and crawled back beneath the sheets.

The sound of a door closing nearby made the walls shake.

Was Lou leaving? For a second, the preposterous urge to follow him swept through her, but then logic intervened. Traipsing all over Portland because of curiosity wasn't something she could afford to do. She must be rested and feeling well for tomorrow.

The last thing she wanted was for Mr. Langdon to change his mind.

With thoughts of Josie and Lou crowding her mind, images of them playing at the picnic, riding on the train, she finally slept.

Chapter Twenty-Two

It wasn't hard to find his mark, even in a city the size of Portland. The bloke's eyes and coloring, combined with his accent and odor, brought Lou to the Willamette River's docks. He'd left the hotel long before sunrise to get a head start on the dockworkers.

He wanted to see who showed up. The man claimed to be leaving town, but experience had taught him that people usually stayed with the familiar, even at their own risk. Unless he was in immediate peril, Lou doubted the man would just give up his job and leave the state.

Water lapped at the dock, dank and noisy. A heavy mist coated the air and made him glad he'd worn his coat. He watched the sun slowly start its trek upward. A hazy orange that brought new hope to some, new despair to others.

He shook the maudlin thoughts away. He was a man of action, seeking out criminals, pursuing justice, not pondering the mistakes he might've made. Or the people he'd hurt.

He hadn't missed that look on Mary's face last night

when they'd exited the alley. There'd been a fraction of a second where her calm facade slipped and he'd seen hurt...but from what? Maybe he'd misinterpreted things. Still, when he'd dropped her at the hotel door, guilt had turned him into a brusque person, and he'd skedaddled before she could stir his emotions up any more.

Things had been better when she'd kept house while he'd traveled. Whenever he went home and life started feeling too cozy, he headed out. She'd been right about that unconscious pattern.

Frowning, he watched as mist dissipated simultaneously with the arrival of men. Heavy boots clomped down the docks. English was the primary language spoken, but every so often he'd hear some Mandarin or Gaelic.

Such diversity. As a young man, he'd thought God was incredible and brilliant. One of the things that had attracted him to Sarah was her artwork. His wife had used wild colors in her paintings, scattering them across the canvas, her thick brushstrokes laying claim to the proof of God's beauty with her talent.

He'd loved her so much.

She'd been a vibrant fire, and their Abby was just like her. Alive and beautiful.

And then snuffed out before their lives had barely begun.

He blinked hard and studied the men. Most were small framed and sinewy like the man he'd met, but no one shared his towheadedness. Of course, the guy could've gotten a new hat to cover his blondness, but Lou doubted that. This kind of work was too physical. A hat might fall in the water and waste someone's hard-earned money.

These men worked long hours. He worked hard, too, but in a different way. Sarah had appreciated him, but she'd wanted him to come home. To be always home for her.

Just like Mary.

And yet they were different. Sarah had been a flame, hot and exciting with a quick temper and ready tongue. She'd challenged him defiantly…and he'd loved it.

Mary wasn't like that. She reminded him of a steady warmth, careful and secure, but no less exciting. Her flame was like that deep blue kind, the color beneath the bright oranges, the kind you needed to keep a stove cooking.

He grimaced at the mental analogy and decided to keep his focus on scoping out dockworkers, not beguiling beauties who had no trust for men and no taste for travel.

Forty minutes later he located his quarry.

Clamping his jaw, he strode toward him. Raucous laughs filled the air; grunts and the sounds of things hitting various spots filled the previous silence.

Lou dodged people and continued stalking his man. A foot away, the guy spotted him and took off at a run.

Just great.

Uttering a groan, he sprinted after him. His feet pounded against the uneven wood of the dock. Faces blurred as he raced past. He managed to jump an outstretched foot and couldn't resist whipping a grin at the offender. He paid for that, though, when his right foot connected with a bucket. It flew forward, landing to his right.

"Hey," the guy next to it sputtered. Lou ignored him and kept going, hopping over a pile of salmon, never taking his sights off the man in front of him. The docks shuddered under his gait, but his breath stayed easy. Good news for the old wound.

Sucking in another lungful of fish-scented air, he rounded a corner in time to see the bootlegger duck into an old brick building. The place looked unsteady, but Lou followed. At the door, he drew his gun and edged in.

"I'm not going to hurt you, I just have a few questions," he called out.

A clatter echoed through the room in front of him. Filthy windows allowed little sun to cut through the dimness of the place. It appeared to be a dilapidated warehouse, no longer used. Sliding forward, he moved behind a metallic-looking contraption and then peered around it.

Shafts of light hit the wooden floor, highlighting dust motes that danced in lazy abandon. Undisturbed. He couldn't see the floor well enough to track prints. He'd just have to convince the guy of his intentions.

"I'm going to step into the light," he said. His words carried well. Unless the man had slipped out, he had to hear him. "My gun is in the holster. I just have some questions about that hat I bought from you."

Sweat tickled the back of his neck and his scar burned. It was step out in faith or do nothing. But faith in what?

Banishing the thought, he forced his limbs into motion. Slowly and carefully, he inched onto the floor while holstering his weapon. His ears strained for the slightest indication that someone aimed to shoot him.

Planning to dodge a bullet put an ache in a man's gut, that was for sure.

He made it out in the middle just fine, though. He exhaled a long breath. And waited.

The guy didn't make him wait long. A shuffle and a stirring of air, then the man who'd given him the bowler hat appeared in his peripherals, hands up.

Lou's neck relaxed a tad, but he kept his hands at the ready. He turned slowly. "We need to talk." Carefully, he gestured at the empty space surrounding them. "This place safe?"

"Yeah." The man appeared conflicted, edgy. His gaze shot around before his posture shifted to a more relaxed shape. He walked forward and held out his hand. "The name's O'Leary. I've been undercover, working the smugglers, trying to get a lead on which boats are bringing the hooch into Oregon. A few weeks ago I heard some blokes talking about a hit. It was put out you were going to die."

"Almost," Lou muttered.

"So I started digging because I recognized your name from a few years back. You helped take down that kidnapper, Mendez. It was a real coup. I've been in the bureau for a while now and I remember how he kept giving us the slip."

Lou gave O'Leary a look and his throat bobbed.

"Anyway," he hurried, "I tried to meet up with you, give you a tip, but I was there at the wrong time, too late."

"You risked your cover to keep me from dying? That's a dangerous move."

"Not quite. I'd had a hunch the smuggler in charge of this operation was nearby. I wanted to get a look at those arrested. I saw you by chance and recognized your likeness from a bureau photograph. I felt like God was prompting me to give you a heads-up."

"God?"

"Yeah, you know the Big Guy who loves us?"

"Don't tell me you're religious."

"Me and the Big Guy, we talk a bit. So I went to find you, but I guess someone was tailing me, or maybe lying in wait for you...." O'Leary's mouth twisted. "These bootleggers, they're talking about big money getting dished out. Well, people around here with big money include politicians and smugglers. I listened closer and found out you bumped off someone's cousin, and that someone has had a contract out on you for over a year."

"That long?"

O'Leary grinned, his teeth flashing in the muted light. "Your reputation doesn't do you justice. You're like a shadow, which is why it took me so long to get to you. People know you have a hideout, but no one knows where it is. If the higher-ups have any idea, they're not saying."

"Why didn't you take this information to them?" Lou reached in his pocket and drew out the paper that had been hidden in the bowler.

Fear flashed across O'Leary's face. He backed up. "Why'd you bring that?" His glance swiveled across the room.

"Relax." He tucked the hat away. "I figured it would be safer on me than in any hiding place." Lou studied O'Leary. "Are you sure the information in it is correct?"

"Pretty sure. I jotted things down as I heard them.... Your lady... I don't know her name, but you should keep a watch on her. Keep her near. They have spies everywhere."

"Who? I need names. More than what you gave me."

"Look, I've done more than I should. If anyone hears, I'm a goner."

Probably true. Lou rubbed the back of his neck. Mary was by herself right now at the hotel. No one knew where they were, but maybe he should have brought her with him.

No. The docks were no place for a lady.

"I appreciate this, O'Leary, but I have to ask again. Why didn't you take it to my supervisor? He could have safely relayed the information to me."

"I didn't even know you were still alive until I saw you by chance at that hotel restaurant. And then…well, I told you, sir, ears and eyes, everywhere." O'Leary blinked, looked around, then held out his hand again. "It's an honor to meet you."

Lou gave a curt nod and shook his hand. "And you. Thank you for your service to our country. You're a real credit to the bureau."

O'Leary acknowledged the compliment with a flush and tilt of his chin, then he swiveled and melded back into the shadows. Lou backed up, too, until he knew he was no longer discernible.

The paper burned against his thigh. O'Leary had given him the name of the smuggler he thought wanted him dead. It wouldn't take much to find out if he was related to Mendez.

His gut told him if he found the smuggler, he'd find his shooter.

The man had messed him up good, not just laying him up for weeks, but putting him through a bunch of emotional weirdness he wanted no part of. He had his plans, and they didn't include a beautiful woman, a sweet kid or a God he'd stopped trusting long ago.

Mary's head throbbed when she woke up.

The lady means nothing to me.

Perfect. Now Lou's words were following her into the morning. There really was no reason for them to still be in her head. Of course he hadn't meant them. She rolled out of bed, went to the water room and splashed her face clean. A clean towel at the side of the sink felt like bliss against the headache pounding her skull.

If only she were home, baking. Sinking her knuckles into floured dough, creating nutritious perfection. Inhaling the warm aroma of cinnamon and yeast. And when she took this job, she might be given the opportunity to work in the kitchen.

Drawing in a deep, cleansing breath, she prayed for wisdom and set about getting ready for the day. She left the hotel, head slightly clearer and walk brisk. Morning fog hugged the streets. Her luggage felt heavy without Lou to help her.

But he hadn't been in his room. Not in the lobby. And she was through relying on him. Through being the poor girl who'd been kidnapped. Sleep and reading the Bible had refreshed her spirit. She no longer wished to be taken care of but to step out and take care of others.

Determined, she asked someone for directions to a post office. After sending a telegram to her mother explaining the situation, she hopped aboard a streetcar and began her journey to Mrs. Silver's.

Closing her eyes, she leaned against her seat and thought of Josie's smile and endless chatter. Such a stubborn, sweet little girl. Her arms ached to hold her. Then Lou's smile invaded her thoughts. Her eyes shot open. The car shuddered to a stop and she realized she was near Mrs. Silver's home.

By the time she walked to the house, the mist had receded, but clouds rolling overhead warned of coming rain. The heavy scent of it filled the air. She let herself into the gate and moments later, faced a sour-looking Mr. Baggs.

"I'm here for employment," she said, the words wobbling out of her. She'd never applied for a job before. She forced her shoulders back. "Mr. Langdon told me to come this morning."

Mr. Baggs's eyebrows lowered. "Servants go to the back." He shut the door in her face.

Oh. She frowned. Perhaps she should have known that. She hefted her luggage and found her way to the back. Mr. Baggs opened the door as she neared. He must have been watching for her.

Lord, give me strength.

Her nerves thrummed a frantic tune as he let her in. The walls closed in on her. She followed him down a narrow, gray hallway. An odd smell permeated the place, and it was so very quiet.

Finally, they climbed stairs and then passed through a door that opened into a spacious room with pleasing blue wallpaper and regal furniture, and at last she felt she could breathe.

"Mr. Langdon will be right with you. Have a seat." Mr. Baggs gave her an odd look, his brows crinkling together like fuzzy caterpillars. The unexpected image caused her to smile, which prompted a disapproving grunt from the butler.

"Wait here." The door closed behind him with a grim finality.

Mary clutched her luggage to her chest. Was she doing the right thing? The enormity of this choice settled on her shoulders like extra weight. She sank onto a couch someone had positioned against the wall.

Pain in her knuckles caught her attention. She looked at her hands. White and strained. Her breaths quickened. This would be different, so different than anything she'd known. Her eyes prickled and she blinked rapidly.

She'd agree to work for Mr. Langdon, but wanted nothing to do with the man except for him to fulfill his part of the bargain. He'd promised to pull up a contract. Perhaps she should have involved Lou after all.

But what could he do? This was employment. Yes, Mr. Langdon scared her, but that did not mean he'd breach the contract or try anything inappropriate. Especially in his sister's house.

"Miss O'Roarke." The subject of her thoughts sailed into the room and held out his hand.

Out of habit, Mary stood, leaving her luggage on the floor, but she did not offer her own hand in return.

His features remained placid even as his hand lowered, but his eyes… She repressed a shudder. "Good morning, Mr. Langdon. Have you brought the contract?"

"Ah, yes, the contract." His lips stretched into an alarming half circle. "Unfortunately, circumstances have changed, and we will need to renegotiate terms."

Mary froze and a trembling started in her stomach, working through her body until her knees ached.

"You see—" his brows quirked up and he tapped his finger against his chin "—this morning I experienced a most unsettling and inconvenient loss. Quite unexpectedly my sister decided to die, thus ruining my plans for…" He flashed his teeth at her. "Well…for you, my dear."

Mary couldn't breathe. A paralysis had hold of her.

"I see you're afraid. Very good." His eyes slit. He moved toward her and his fingers pressed roughly against her neck. "Your pulse is jumping. Rather like a little rabbit leaping away. That's quite exciting…. May I call you Mary?"

She couldn't move. Fright had rooted her to the floor and every muscle in her body locked into place. This had been a colossal mistake. What had she done? "Where's Josie?" she managed to say through lips that felt heavy and numb.

"Josie is the least of your worries," he whispered, bringing his face close to hers. His eyes glowed with an unnatural fervor. "Mmm, your vein is pulsing."

His fingers dug into her neck and his thumb crept to the other side. He squeezed. Mary wanted to gag, to shut her eyes, to melt through the floor and disappear.

He released her and backed away. She sucked in air, too much, and her vision wavered.

"Don't faint, my dear girl. That wouldn't do. Terror is good for you. It speeds blood flow, increases awareness… Shall we talk a bit?" The door behind him opened and he turned to Baggs. "Send someone in with tea, would you? The news of my sister's demise has greatly upset our newest employee."

The door shut and Mr. Langdon turned back to her. "Have a seat. Rest your legs and take some steady breaths. I have a new proposition for you."

Chapter Twenty-Three

"Since my sister has passed away, my proposal of yesterday has become void. Furthermore, my needs have changed. I'm aware of your mother's reputation. Have you ever considered following in her footsteps? That's what I'm offering you now." A smug smile stretched his lips, as though he believed he'd already won. "A steady job at my side, seeing to my needs, in exchange for Josie. You'll have the full care of her, should you accept this offer."

Mary felt even more faint. His gaze burrowed into her, intrusive and cold.

She sank onto the couch, wishing to disappear within its confines. Never would she accept what he offered.

Never.

Could she bolt for the servants' hallway? What would happen if he followed? Her derringer was in her luggage, but dare she use it? She cut her eyes in his direction. He studied her as though she was a trifle to be bought in a store.

Her mind whirled. Mrs. Silver...dead. What about Josie? Was she safe? If she didn't accept this plan, who would protect Josie? She desperately wanted to be brave and stand up to Mr. Langdon, but the present seemed to be colliding with the past. She looked at him and saw Mendez.

She blinked. His features did resemble her late captor's, though his complexion was much lighter.

"Yes, you're putting it together, aren't you?" The smile on his lips chilled her. "Do you really think I stumbled onto that ranch house by accident? It's nestled in a valley and blends so well that none of my men have been able to find the place. It took me, the one with brains, to follow my cousin's directions accurately."

Her breath caught. It couldn't be…could it?

"Getting Josie to you was a small feat. You see, I've had plans for a long time now, and they've been foiled by ignorant men. Success took a woman's help, whether she realized it or not." He walked forward and sat beside her. The couch sank and she pulled back, away.

His breath, rank and sour, puffed over her. "I don't mean to bore you with the details, only to let you know you're rather stuck. You see, my plans have been in place since my cousin was ruthlessly murdered by that employer of yours."

He thought Lou killed Mendez? She met Mr. Langdon's crazy eyes and finally felt as if she could breathe. The adrenaline rush was fading, leaving a tiredness she must shake off if she was to survive this.

"Lou didn't kill Mendez," she told him shakily.

"Oh, he surely did."

"Mendez was poisoned. I saw him myself."

"Do you think I care how it happened or who caused it? My cousin was assigned a simple job. Find Striker and bring you back to me. I couldn't allow his obses-

sion for Striker to stand in the way of what I wanted
. He died trying to fulfill his duty. Don't you think I
know who was in charge at that hideaway? You must
understand, Mendez was my favorite cousin. We shared
certain…qualities."

"I—I don't understand…. Why did you want me?"

"You don't remember?" His brows pulled together
and his lips tightened. "My father visited your mother
often. He brought me when I was twelve, and that's
when I first saw you."

A rush of sickness rose in her stomach. She remembered him now. A young boy who had stared so much
she felt uncomfortable and never met his gaze. She
couldn't recall his eye color, perhaps because she'd
avoided him so much. Months later, she and her mother
left in search of her father, and then her mother had
dropped her off at Trevor's.

"How did you find me?"

"By chance, as it were. I saw your mother on a business trip when I was a young man. She was frantic,
searching for your father, and I realized we could help
each other."

"You bribed her."

"It didn't take much. Women are emotional creatures, and your mother's loyalty is commendable. Too
bad your father died before she could reach him."

Mary pressed her fingertips against her forehead,
willing the ache to recede. All this time she'd blamed
Trevor's mother for selling her, but it had been her
mother who'd led the villains straight to her door.

Lord, help me. The prayer rose in her heart and
crossed her lips.

Mr. Langdon uttered a harsh noise that masqueraded

as a laugh. "God isn't anywhere near you. In fact, I'm quite certain He abandoned you long ago, right about the time your father left."

She flinched.

"That's right. I know all about him. Your mother, too. Like I said, she's quite loyal for a woman. Back to my proposition. In a moment, Baggs will be bringing your tea and some special paperwork regarding my newest offer. Don't look so disgusted. You worked at Julia's brothel, did you not? The one your mother left you at to chase down her foolish husband, the place where I found you."

"I was a seamstress, nothing more." The words sounded weak, even to her ears. She kept thinking of Lou's *the lady means nothing to me,* and now Mr. Langdon's assertion God was nowhere near. Had God left her again? Would He allow a repeat of the past? She could not bear such a thing, and yet it seemed certain to occur.

"You could have been more than—" his hand fluttered toward her "—this. You *are* more." He placed his hand on her knee and squeezed painfully. "Stay here, with me. You'll have your Josie then."

A knock sounded on the door.

"Come in." Mr. Langdon slithered to the other side of the couch.

Mary swallowed hard. She could make it to the door, but how would she escape this house?

Silverware clinked as Mr. Baggs shuffled into the room. Pattering steps followed Baggs and then Josie burst into the room, her eyes pink and tear-stained.

"Miss Mary," she cried and launched herself at the couch.

Mary caught her, pulled her close and buried her face

in Josie's hair. *My little girl.* The thought didn't startle her, but rather strengthened her. She would do almost anything to save Josie. She'd wait for the opportunity and then be gone from this place.

And Josie would go with her.

That's kidnapping, prodded a voice from inside.

But what other option did she have?

"How did she get out?" Langdon's voice bit into the room. He grabbed Josie's arm, but Mary smacked his hand and he withdrew, brows narrowing into angry arrows. "You will pay for that."

"I apologize, sir, but there's a gentleman at the door for you. It won't wait. You might want to see him out quickly." Mr. Baggs inclined his head and whatever that meant, it propelled Mr. Langdon to his feet.

"Do you want me to take the girl?" asked Mr. Baggs.

Josie's uncle looked at them, a calculating gleam in his eye. "No, let her stay. She shall encourage Miss O'Roarke in her decision, no doubt. Just keep an eye on them, Baggs."

Mr. Langdon swished out of the room. Josie pulled away from Mary, tears spilling over her cheeks. "My mommy is dead."

"I know, sweetheart." She smoothed an errant strand out of Josie's eyes as her thoughts raced. This was their one opportunity, but could she do it? Could she get them out? She glanced at Baggs. Her only option was to overpower him somehow, but the thought rattled her. Hitting an old man did not seem the right thing to do.

Mr. Baggs cleared his throat. He blinked and held out a hand to Josie. "I might miss your chatter. That's all I have to say."

"Why, Baggs, I shall miss you, too!" Josie didn't take

his hand but instead moved out of Mary's embrace. As she beckoned Baggs closer, Mary stood and reached for the teapot.

Josie leaned up and planted a little kiss on the man's weathered cheek. His eyes met Mary's as she raised the pitcher. Her stomach churned.

"Do it," he said, "or it's my life on the line. There's a door there." He pointed.

"That's my hideaway." Josie hopped over and tugged open the door Mr. Baggs had brought Mary through earlier.

"Wait for me in the hallway," said Mary, but Josie had already disappeared behind the door. She swallowed hard. "I am truly sorry, Mr. Baggs, and hope I do not hurt you."

He gave her a curt nod. Drawing a deep breath, she brought the pitcher down upon his head. He groaned and crumpled to the floor. A line of blood appeared on the right side of his forehead.

Mary held in her sob and set the pitcher down. She dug in her luggage, retrieved her derringer and bullets and slid them in the pocket of her skirt. There was no Lou or Trevor here today. The onus rested upon her, and she'd do whatever necessary to save Josie. She raced to the door, spotted Josie near the stairs and ran toward their escape.

Lou paced the library, twirling his hat in his hands, as he waited for Mrs. Silver to appear. After his meeting this morning with O'Leary, he'd gone straight to the hotel to fetch Mary, only to find her room empty. While staring at the neatly made bed, he couldn't remember the last time he'd felt fear. True, bloodcurdling fear.

Despite its paralyzing hold, he forced himself to go to his office and make a telephone call to the director himself. After relaying the smuggler's name and the suspected boat carrying Canadian whiskey, Lou hightailed it out of there and headed to the Silvers'.

Where he'd found nothing of Mary.

Something was wrong.

She should have been here by now. Where else could she have gone? He perused the hangings on the walls, impatiently tapping his hat against his thigh. Dusty antiques. Family photographs. Langdon looked supremely arrogant in his still shot.

"Mr. Riley. To what do I owe this visit?" Langdon appeared in the doorway, a smirk marring his even features. Smart man kept his distance, though.

"I'm here to speak with Mrs. Silver."

"Ah." His smirk grew. "She has unfortunately passed on, negating your need to see her. I shall show you to the door."

Lou's fingers clenched the brim of his hat. "Where's Josie?"

"That's none of your business, officer of the law or no. She's my ward. Now, if you'll excuse me, I have funeral arrangements to attend to."

He took a deep breath and settled into the kind of calm that gave a man an edge over his opponent. And Langdon was worse than an opponent. He stalked toward him. The man faltered for a moment but didn't budge.

"I smell…something." Lou sniffed. If this guy was a bootlegger, and based on O'Leary's notes, Lou felt certain he was, there should be a kind of hint somewhere.

"Perfume from the arrangements. My sister's favorite."

"Indeed." He took another breath and realized it was true, he did smell something floral, and not the prohibited whiskey he'd been ready to accuse Langdon of importing. "Funeral flowers aren't a pleasant smell on you, but I suppose it works well to mask the odor from your day job…. You know I work for the Bureau of Investigation, right?"

"You flashed your badge in my face."

"You're a smart man. Maybe coming into money soon?" Lou gestured around him, watching Langdon's face closely.

His lids flickered. "The terms of the will have yet to be disclosed."

"Maybe you've got your own money?"

"Maybe it's time for you to leave, Special Agent."

"Yeah, because your heart is real broken by your sister's death." Lou moved closer still, frowning when he whiffed that scent again. Something unforgettable… Mary.

His jaw clamped. Deliberately he loosened his jaw and bestowed a predatory smile on Langdon. "Heard you're a rich man. In fact, I have a source who tells me your income is swimmingly large. You own a boat, right?"

"Are you trying to accuse me of something? You're in my house, on my property—"

"You mean your sister's?"

Langdon's face settled into stubborn lines. "Get out of this house."

Lou held up his hands. "Relax. I'm just here to pick up Mary."

"Who?" But Langdon's eyes flickered with recognition.

"Your new employee," he said smoothly. "She asked me to meet her here."

"Oh, yes, the nanny. She left moments before you arrived."

"Really?" He leaned forward, anger a frigid weight in his chest. "I smell her."

Langdon chuckled. "She's very, how shall I put it? Friendly."

Lou's gaze snapped up to meet Langdon's hard eyes. He had to play this smart. "Which way did she go?"

"The same way her type always goes. Now kindly leave this house or I'll have you escorted out."

"Thanks for your…help." Lou flashed his teeth. "I'll be back, though, and next time you might want to be more convincing."

He spun and headed toward the door. He felt Langdon behind him and his rage grew. Fine way God took care of Mary. Bringing her to this place, putting her right into the hands of danger. They stepped into the hall and that was when Lou heard what had been covered by the carpeted study.

An uneven tap behind him. A sound that resonated in his memory. He stopped abruptly and faced Langdon. His gaze dropped to Langdon's boots. Shiny, definitely expensive and outfitted with spurs. A vision of a dark alley crept through him. Moonlight. A gunshot and pain…

"Problem?"

Lou tucked his thoughts away and forced a grim smile. "Nope. Just admiring your shoes."

"Some say vanity is an evil thing, but it's served me

well. I call these my lucky spurs. When I wear them, great things happen." Langdon's eyes flashed, belying his amused tone.

"Looks like I need a pair of those." Lou pulled on his hat, tipped it and scooted out of the house. Once down the porch, he walked the block, turned a corner and hurried across the street. Sliding into the shadows of a different house, he removed his hat, untucked his shirt, slicked his hair back and stuck a piece of gum in his mouth.

The disguise would have to do for now. He bent the rim of his hat upward on the sides. It would ruin the fit and the leather, but circumstances called for it. He could always buy a new one. Adjusting his gait, he meandered down the sidewalk until he passed the Silvers' place. One house down, he found a hiding spot near a newer home's expansive porch.

No gate and the perfect spot to blend in.

From here he could see everyone entering and leaving the front of the Silvers'. The servants' quarters looked to be on the side of the house, and he thought he could see a gate exit near the backyard. This was the optimum vantage point.

He settled into the corner where the stairs met the house and waited. Heavy clouds warned of impending rain. There was a definite bite to the air. He hoped Mary was safe.

She might be in the house, but without a warrant, he couldn't force his way in there. She should have stayed at the hotel and never taken this deal. Trusted him to take care of Josie. He chewed his gum, hoping for inspiration to kick in.

He could leave and get some men to follow Langdon. Now that he knew who his shooter was, it made more sense to personally follow him, but who'd take care of Mary? She couldn't wander Portland for long by herself. She didn't have any money that he knew of for a ticket home.

And he was sure she wouldn't leave Josie.

He couldn't, either. For all he knew, the will stipulated Josie be sent to relatives, but if it called for her to be left with Langdon… He mashed his gum. Not good.

This was the problem in getting involved with people. He liked his job of catching criminals. Investigating crimes. He didn't like getting close because it worried him, and a worried man couldn't accomplish anything.

Look at his past.

He'd held Sarah in his arms after Abby died. Instead of running for the doctor, he'd worried and fretted. Rocked her tenderly, but she'd lost the will to live and, letting the pneumonia have its way, slipped away quietly the same night.

O'Leary thought God had led him to Lou, but after losing his family that way, Lou had trouble believing God cared.

Yet Josie believed God had used him to find her in the desert. He swallowed hard now, feeling the rough wood of the house against his bare arm. It was solid and real.

Why couldn't he feel God that way? Had he ever?

Watching the Silver place for movement, he let his mind stew on the thought. Maybe he hadn't felt God the same way he felt this house at his side, but he sure felt some kind of presence when he'd gone to that church picnic with Mary.

Years ago, Sarah and he used to pray together, and

there'd been a certainty inside that the God he talked to was real and cared about him. Thoughts jumbling, he blinked at the emotion encircling his chest. How could he have been so wrong then if things had felt so right?

And did that mean he was wrong now, despite how he felt?

He glanced at the sky for an answer. Swollen clouds greeted him. Back in the desert the air would be dry, ripe with the scents of rock and sage. He missed that. Selling the ranch had seemed like a good idea months ago, but suddenly it felt like the wrong move.

He scoffed at himself.

Dwelling on feelings changed nothing. They shifted like the clouds above, always at the whim of change. Just as he'd moved on...away from God, from faith.

The thought hit him square on.

He'd left God. Said goodbye and refused to let Him near.

An automobile moved into his line of vision. Classy high-end car. Black. He noted the rims and distinctive chug of the engine as it drew to a stop outside the Silvers' gate. Arrogant Langdon was on the move, but how was he supposed to follow him?

Hissing between his teeth, he rose from his position and sauntered onto the sidewalk. He couldn't follow, but he could intimidate. Langdon rushed out the front door. Lou stuck two fingers in his mouth and let out a piercing whistle.

Langdon jutted to a stop and, despite the distance, Lou saw anger in his movements. He waved, throwing his hand up and letting it flow casually above him.

"See you at the docks," he called out.

Chapter Twenty-Four

Escapes surely put a cramp in Mary's stomach. She bent against the neighbor's manicured, thorny bushes, Josie at her side.

"See you at the docks" a voice called out. Lou? She peeked through the leaves and saw a man waving at a fancy automobile as it sped past. Then the man put a quick pace to his steps and started up the sidewalk. Definitely Lou. She'd know that swagger anywhere.

"It's Mister Lou," Josie whispered excitedly. "Let's go get him."

"No." Mary shushed her, thoughts racing. She could do this. She could rescue herself and Josie without a man's help.

The lady means nothing to me.

Her mouth tightened. He'd proved that and more. Selling the ranch out from beneath everyone. Always following his job wherever it took him. She had no right to be miffed, and she really didn't want to be, but at the same time, thinking about his actions gave clearer insight to his character.

He didn't want chains. He didn't want commitment.

But now she knew she did, and that changed everything.

Chin up, she beckoned Josie to stand. "Let's go. Your uncle left in that vehicle, so we should be safe for a while."

"Where are we going?"

They stepped onto the sidewalk, Josie's hand fitting snugly within hers. She wanted to smile and reassure her, but her lips refused to relax. "I'm not sure, sweetheart."

She could go to the police, but what would she tell them? *Please help me save this little girl. Her uncle is a rich ogre who has had an obsession with me.* Or perhaps they could disappear and she could find work elsewhere?

A solid plan, but could she break the law that way? Maybe Langdon had lied to her about Josie's family. What if she had loving relatives who wished to take her in? The idea stabbed Mary's heart, but she must face the fact that she wasn't the only one who wanted Josie.

She might as well admit the only one who could help her now was on his way to the ports. Her best recourse was to follow him. Josie couldn't go with her, though. Maybe waiting at the hotel might prove a better solution.

Yes.

She'd do that.

Feeling more secure in her decision, she smiled at Josie and hummed a little ditty she'd learned as a child. Josie picked it up and together they walked to where she knew a streetcar passed. The money she'd brought from home helped immensely. She might even have enough to bring both herself and Josie back to the ranch...although that presented a new set of problems. Namely, kidnapping charges.

Right now she could defend her actions as a rescue. Possibly. She frowned. Things were altogether confusing.

"Excuse me, ma'am?" An automobile pulled up beside them. A man leaned out the passenger door. His scruffy features sent a frisson of apprehension through her, prickling the skin of her palms.

She stopped reluctantly, placing Josie behind her. A fat droplet of rain splashed against the shiny hood. "Yes?"

"Thought you might need a lift. You and that young-'un."

"No, thank you, we're quite fine."

"Well, now, we weren't asking."

The flurries in her stomach took flight and Mary pivoted forward, causing Josie to emit a squeak as she strode away from the vehicle. The bushes beside her seemed too thick to dodge across and the next house sported a forbidding wrought iron fence.

From behind, a hand clamped on her arm and spun her around, jerking her toward the car. "You'll be coming with us, Miss Mary."

"Let the girl go," she gasped, her arm aching beneath the force of the man's grip.

"Nah, we'll be taking her, too. Langdon has plans, and I'm not fool enough to interrupt them."

The driver opened the back door, and her captor shoved her in. Josie came next, Mary's body breaking her momentum and cushioning her against the side of the vehicle. She hugged the girl close, pulling her onto her lap. Josie buried her face in Mary's shoulder, and she felt the trembles rippling through her.

Fright filled her, too. She tightened her hold on Josie.

The scruffy man hopped into the front of the vehicle.

"Let's go," he told the driver. "Looks like it's about to rain, and I don't fancy getting wet."

The ride took forever, a confusing maze of twists and turns. She kept eyeing the latch on the door, but the way the driver sped through the streets disabused her of the notion to jump out. She'd never forgive herself if Josie was hurt.

But they had to get away somehow.

"Excuse me," she shouted above the noise of the engine and whip of the wind. This type of automobile had a roof that only covered the backseat. She hoped it rained on her captors. Served them right.

The men in front ignored her. Worrying her bottom lip, she peeked out her side. Vehicles swerved around her, proving a jump out that side would be foolish. She shifted and glanced toward the passenger side. The sidewalk had disappeared when they'd left the residential neighborhood.

The air felt thicker, laden with the odors of water and fish. Would anyone at the docks help her? Knowing the rough elements as she did, possibly. Many men working in these conditions were honest and didn't care to see a child come to harm. Then again, many drank too much and had allowed their morality to emulate the tide, coming and going as it pleased.

The driver finally swerved to a stop on a street hugged by ramshackle warehouses. The man in the passenger seat jumped out to open their door. "Slowly now," he warned. "I've no patience for uppity women."

Despite the fear curdling her stomach, she stifled a snort and the tart reply she wished to give him. Josie refused to move off her lap, so she scooted across to the passenger door. "Tell the girl to get down," the man ordered.

"I shall hold her," she said, daring to meet his eyes.

He shrugged, a leer on his lips. "Your choice. I'm just the deliveryman."

As she moved over, the driver made an odd sound. She whipped him a glance. He'd removed his cap and she had to swallow her surprise. His blue eyes were familiar. The bowler-hat man from the alley? He met her look and winked so quickly she almost missed it. "All will be well, miss," he said with his familiar brogue. "Follow directions, okay?"

She nodded and continued out of the automobile, trying to keep her balance on the broken sidewalk. Josie clung to her but she managed to hold her steady enough. Bowler-hat man pulled the automobile away, and she was left with the scruffy man.

Her first instinct prompted her to run, even with Josie in her arms. Her captor must have seen the impulse on her face because he grabbed her arm and propelled her toward a large, nondescript building. The road steeply declined toward the Willamette, whose muddy waters lapped lazily against the docks. Dockworkers rushed from boat to boat, making her dizzy.

Or maybe it was panic at this man's manhandling. He stopped at a building only feet from the river and thrust her through a narrow doorway. It took several seconds for her eyes to adjust. The sound of the port dulled in this place, replaced with a muffled stillness that swathed the shadows. No movement. If she could reach her pocket, then things would be solved quite neatly. She'd have to put Josie down, though, and make her move quickly.

"Come on," the man growled behind her. His grip dug into her arm as he plowed ahead. If she was going to run, she must do so now. She yanked her arm back, causing the man to let out a startled oath. "What're you playing at? Let's get moving."

"We are not going with you." She yanked again, and he was so shocked by her words that her arm slid from his fingertips, albeit painfully.

"I'll not be having any of this," he snarled. He reached for her, but she dodged his hand and backed up.

"We must run," she whispered into Josie's ear. The little girl's head moved imperceptibly in a nod before she wiggled out of Mary's grasp.

The man reached for her again, but she whirled away, dragging Josie with her. The door behind them had shut and so she opted for scuttling near the wall. Darkness closed around them as they moved farther into the shadows of a corner.

The man's heavy breathing filled the space, combining with the dank odors of mold and rotted wood. As far as she could tell, he wasn't following them. And how could he? The lack of light served her well. She ran her fingers down Josie's cheek before grabbing her hand again.

"I'm going to find you," their captor said suddenly, his voice grating in the silence. "And when I do, it won't be pretty."

They crouched in the darkness, every breath seeming a siren to her, but still, no movement to be heard. After an interminable wait, a scraping to her right made her catch her breath. One hand gripping Josie's, she used her other to slide the derringer out of her skirt pocket.

The metal fit coolly into her palm, comfortably. Just imagine he's a target, she told herself. A wooden target, like the kind she and James practiced with. Drawing a steady breath, she willed her heartbeat to slow.

She'd just achieved a sort of eerie calm when something flew into the room, startling her. Her captor as well, for he made a noise, followed by the loud pop of his weapon. The sound echoed through the room, filling her ears. And then out of the shadows, he lunged toward them. All she saw was his shape before instinct took over and pulled the trigger.

Lou arrived at the docks minutes after Langdon. He'd been fortunate in that Portland traffic's heaviness slowed the man's automobile enough for him to hop a streetcar headed in the same direction. If Langdon saw him, he gave no indication.

Now he stalked to the port, weapon at the ready. He spotted O'Leary pulling away from the curb near an old, broken-down building. Careful to be inconspicuous, he gave O'Leary quick eye contact, only to be surprised by the undercover agent's swift chin jerk toward the building before speeding away.

Hmm. Lou tapped the pockets of his blue jeans. He probably should have stopped in at the office and set up some sort of operation. For now he would just observe. Hopefully, he'd see enough to get a warrant later. Plan in place, he edged up against the building. Filth covered the panes of glass.

He peered in anyway, but saw nothing. Moving forward, he kept his back to the building and his eye on the docks. Only feet away, workers bustled and moved. No sign of Langdon, but the name of his vessel should be obvious soon enough.

The rough wood of the building behind him scraped at his shirt. A man pushing a wheelbarrow toward him gave him a wary look. Stifling a groan, he jammed his hat more firmly in place. People in these places had no use for authorities.

Looking like a policeman closed more mouths than if

he waltzed in with his badge flashing. Maybe he should lose the hat. At the least.

He took it off his head and inched toward the door to the building. He pressed it open and poked his head in. Met nothing but stink. Perfect. He whipped his hat into the dark room and then stiffened when a muffled *oomph* issued from the depths.

Before he could draw his weapon, a volley of gunfire blasted out. He dropped to his stomach, revolver at the ready.

The noise ended abruptly.

He drew his knees up under his stomach and held still, listening. Someone groaned from inside.

"Bureau of Investigation. Hold your fire," he shouted into the room. A crowd was gathering across the street, but he ignored them.

The sound came again, and then a scuffling sound… or was it sniffling? Crying? He rose to his feet slowly. "Come out, weapons down, by order of Lou Riley, special agent to the Bureau of Investigation."

"Lou?"

It felt as if his gut dropped to his feet when he heard Mary's voice. She appeared in the doorway, Josie in her arms and a small Remington derringer clutched in her fingers. She blinked as she came out of the dark.

The sound of police drawing near scattered the crowd, most of them having no desire to be seen in this vicinity.

Lou couldn't take his eyes off Mary.

Her eyes were huge, shocked. Filmy spiderwebs clung to the mussed strands of her hair. Josie was nestled in her arms, her shoulders shaking with the force of her fear. He swallowed, his throat tight and dry. Carefully, he reached for Mary's hand, prying the pistol from her cold fingers.

Her eyes met his. "I shot him," she whispered.

Local police pulled up behind him. Taking his gaze from her, he flashed his badge, introduced himself and gave them the details. He put his arm around her shoulders and steered her and Josie to the side, away from the open door and closer to the end of the building.

She felt tiny and frail beneath his hands. What had happened in there? How had she come into possession of a pistol? He had a million questions, but seeing the look on her face stilled them all.

No tears. Just a blank heaviness.

He knew exactly what that felt like.

He tucked his fingers beneath Josie's ribs, but she wouldn't let go of Mary.

"I'm okay," Mary said, her voice quiet and flat. "You should check that man...." Her voice trailed off and her gaze dropped.

Lou pulled her to him, pressing her hair against his chest, dropping his lips to her and Josie's heads, cradling them and warming them. This shouldn't have happened. Just like before. Just like Sarah and Abby. He'd been too busy working.

He should have been here for them.

And where had God been?

Absent, as usual.

A hot anger started in his stomach and spread through his chest. He tightened his grip on them as a vow worked through his blood. Langdon would pay.

No matter what.

He would pay.

Chapter Twenty-Five

Mary had killed a man.

Feeling numb, she watched Lou pace a few feet away, engaged in discussion with a man in a wrinkled suit, maybe his superior. The crowded, busy office of the bureau wasn't what she'd expected. The rooms bustled with business. Telephones rang and rang, adding to the flow of conversation and creating an atmosphere of bare walls and cacophony.

She and Josie waited on a hard bench while Lou tried to straighten out their situation. Beside her, Josie sipped hot chocolate a kind man had brought for them a few minutes ago. Her legs swung in a pendulum rhythm and she didn't smile.

Mary gripped her own cup of chocolate, an immense pressure compressing her heart. This was her fault. If only she hadn't taken Josie from that house. She should never have tried to do things her way. If only she'd prayed for wisdom this afternoon instead of going with her instincts…

Because of her foolishness, someone lay dead. Not only that, but Langdon was missing and a little girl had been through far too much. The blame for Josie's fright rested solely on her shoulders, and that knowledge crept through her like a slow poison. She swirled her hot chocolate, watching the curves in the liquid disappear and then reappear.

If onlys never changed anything. She wished they could.

Movement at the corner of her vision drew her attention from the cup to the center of the room. Lou threw his hands in the air and stalked away from the man he spoke to. His agitation shook Mary even more. She blinked hard, her lids burning and gritty. How had this happened?

But she knew exactly how.

Thinking she should manage things on her own. Leaving no room for help, not even from her Savior.

Where could she go from here? How could she escape this disgrace? This guilt? For it tore at her, shredding her tattered confidence, leaving her protected by nothing but a rag not worth stitching back together.

"Mary." Lou stood before her, drawn and unsmiling. "Can I talk to you alone?"

She cast a look at Josie, who blew bubbles in her hot chocolate.

"An agent friend's wife will be here in a moment to sit with her," he said softly.

She touched Josie's shoulders. An unforced smile came to her lips when the little girl glanced up, her mouth rimmed in chocolate. "I'm going with Mister Lou for a moment, but I'll be right back."

"You're not gonna leave me, right?" Josie's voice quivered, and Mary's stomach clenched.

"No, sweetheart. I'll be right over there." She pointed outward, not really sure where Lou planned to take her.

"In that room there," said Lou. He dropped in front

of Josie and pulled a peppermint stick from his pocket. "These are good for stirring. By the time this is gone, we'll be back. A nice lady will come and sit with you, okay?"

She nodded and reached for the stick. "It's going to be gone fast," she told him gravely.

A grin cracked his tired features, and a surge of emotion vaulted through Mary at his smile. "We'll hurry then, my sweet girl. Stay here." He patted her knee.

Mary followed him to a door that opened into a tiny room.

"Interrogations," he explained, noticing her look. "Were you okay with yours?"

"Yes." It had been terribly exhausting to explain how she'd ended up in the warehouse. Then the hardest part had come, describing the *oomph* of noise into the dim room, which she'd later found out was Lou's hat, and then the lunge as her captor appeared right in front of her, his pistol at her nose.

She'd shot him without thinking. An immediate reaction. He hadn't expected that she'd have a weapon. He'd dropped his gun, falling backward, clutching his belly. Gut shot. That's what the detective told her it was called. Most often fatal.

"Hey. Come back to me."

A feather brushed her cheek. No, Lou's finger. He was touching her, close, his eyes so very blue and serious. "It's going to be okay, I promise. There was nothing you could do."

"I had to protect us." She faltered, her voice abandoning her.

"You did good. None of this is your fault."

"Have you found Langdon?" she asked.

"Not yet. Let's talk privately." He applied a soft pressure to her shoulder, moving her farther into the room.

Lou tucked his hands in his pockets and studied her. "We have a situation with Langdon and Josie regarding custody. I've a man bringing in the family attorney right now to figure out where Josie needs to go."

"And me?"

"You're not being charged with anything. The shooting was clearly self-defense and we have a witness who saw him force you and Josie into the automobile." He cocked his head. "How'd you get a pistol anyway? Let alone know how to shoot it."

"James taught me years ago. I bought the derringer one year after a scare with wolves."

"Where was I?"

"Working."

An odd grimace crossed his face. Did it bother him that he hadn't been there? Surely not…and yet a hard little knot began to grow in her stomach.

"What about the driver…the man?" She stumbled over the words, her tongue feeling thick and unwieldy. "The one who gave you the hat?"

"Don't worry about him. I'm taking care of things."

Exhaustion weighted every limb. "Where do I go from here?"

"Gracie and Trevor are on their way. They're going to take you back to the ranch." He paused. "I've decided not to sell it— Look at me, Mary." He tipped her chin, his fingers warm against her skin, and she met his eyes. "I'm *not* going to sell the ranch. Our place is rich in history. I don't want to lose that. While here in Portland, I realized it's home to me in a way other places can never be."

She blinked at his words, an onslaught of emotions rushing through her. Fear, happiness, everything coalesced into a giant wave of feeling that engulfed her and left her speechless. She touched his cheek. His unshaved skin scraped against her fingers as she cupped his jaw and held his gaze.

"I'm happy you're keeping the ranch. You have been my hero in so many ways," she began. "And yet I feel as though my hand is still being held." He started to shake his head, but she stopped him with a bit of pressure from her fingers.

A rueful smile crept across his lips.

She smiled back, her riotous emotions blending together, harmonizing into a single feeling that spread through her in rich pulses of energy. "I am not going to be your housekeeper anymore. I am going to open a business and thrive."

He reached for her hand, removed it and laced his fingers through hers. So gentle. He drew their entwined fingers against his chest.

"You are free to be whomever you want. To choose your way. I only want you happy." His fervent words touched a place deep inside her, bringing to life a longing she finally felt free to embrace.

Without hesitating, she placed her free hand on his back, pushed upward on her toes and kissed him. Their lips met in a union of warmth that blazed into a blistering heat, burning away any reservations she may have held. His mouth slanted against hers, minty and firm. He pressed her against the wall, and she melted beneath his love.

For that was what she felt. Love radiating from him. Care. Her own blood lit with a passionate joy she hadn't expected to ever experience.

And then everything ended. He pulled away, his breath ragged, his head hanging so she couldn't see his face.

But that was okay. She smiled despite her own uneven breathing and the rapid pounding of her heart. She stroked the top of his head, relishing the strands beneath her fingers. It had taken twelve years, but her heart had finally healed enough for her to accept the truth.

"I love you," she said. The words came out clear. Grinning, she said it again. "I love you, Lou Riley."

"I know," he groaned.

She stopped stroking his hair, her fingers lingering in a painful pause. *He knew?* And then it came to her that she had been foolish. Laying out her affections, thinking he returned them. Her heart strangled beneath her breastbone. She chose not to speak. She dropped her hands to her sides and waited.

He lifted his head, his eyes piercing. "I haven't done you right, Mary. I don't deserve your love."

She shook her head, surprised at his words. "But of course you do—"

"No." He gripped her shoulders. "I should have been there for you. Protected you."

"But you did." She touched his cheek again, amazed by the contrast of masculinity and vulnerability on his face. "God led you to us."

He shook his head, but she stopped him from speaking by holding up a palm. "I doubted God, you know. Words can do that, dig deep holes that are not easily filled. God seemed to forsake me. Now, when I needed Him with Langdon, and so long ago, when Mendez came for me. But then you showed up. Both times, you have been there. If you hadn't tossed your hat into that building, you may have continued past. I may have huddled with Josie in a corner until that man found us. I can't deny how God has used you to protect me."

"I don't know if I can believe that." A grimace passed

across his face. "He wasn't there with Sarah and Abby. He could have spared them, but He didn't."

She tried to hide her flinch. "I am truly sorry for your loss."

Perhaps he saw something in her face that she hadn't successfully hidden, for his features softened. "I'm not saying I'm not glad you were spared. I am, more than you can believe. You and Josie are... You're special. I guess I'm just struggling with why God helps some but not others."

She had no answer for him and perhaps it would be unwise to speak anyway, because her emotions tangled within and skewed her perspective. She'd confessed her love, and he'd ignored that, even bringing up his wife and daughter. She'd thought what stood between them was his job, but too late she saw she'd been wrong.

It was so much more. What she'd felt in his kiss hadn't been love, it had been a normal, physical attraction. Her face burned at her naïveté.

He released her shoulders and took a step back. His face shuttered. "You deserve more than a washed-up agent who can't get over the fact God gets to make all the rules. If God cares, He'll give you someone wonderful to love."

He already has, but the man is too stubborn to realize it. She swallowed her reply. "Will you still be going to Asia?"

"In two weeks."

"And Langdon?"

"I'll track him before then."

So he planned to find Langdon after all. Frustration welled. "Shouldn't you let objective agents look for him?"

"No, this is too important." He cast a fervent look to

the door, then leaned close to her. "The man put out a contract on me. He wants me dead, and I don't aim to give him that pleasure. I haven't worked out why yet, but that's not important."

"He and Mendez were cousins." She watched as shock etched slackness across his features.

"Who told you that?"

"He took pride in sharing that information with me, but I also noticed a resemblance in their bone structure." It was hard to speak over the pain of Lou's rejection, but she forced a calm facade. "From what I can piece together, Langdon was behind Mendez's obsession with me. The man worked for him and carried out his orders."

"Did he tell you anything else?"

"A little more." Only that because of her mother's part in this drama, she'd been kidnapped for one week and the course of her life had been forever altered. "Langdon met me when I was a child. I remember him as a boy who stared too much. I suppose I had reason to be wary of him."

"He discovered you lived with Trevor's mother and sought you out."

She nodded slowly. "Yes."

"That…" Lou sucked in a deep breath, his eyes angry and bright. "Go home and rest peacefully, knowing he'll pay for what he did to you."

"Please don't take revenge," she said quietly.

"I don't get revenge, sweetheart. I get justice."

Two hours passed before the lawyer arrived. Trevor and Gracie followed close behind.

"Mary! Lou telephoned our hotel. I'm so sorry." Gracie rushed forward, arms enveloping her in a gentle embrace that brought tears to her eyes. It had been too long since she'd seen her exuberant friend. Gracie had cut her hair short in a stylish bob, and her beaded dress swirled around her knees.

Mary's smile wobbled as she extricated herself from Gracie's grasp.

Trevor hugged her next, and she felt the support from her childhood friend in the firm pressure of his hands. He stepped back and put his arm around his wife's shoulders. They fit well together, and his face held a peacefulness that hadn't been there when he and Mary were growing up.

Warmth at her side brought her attention to Josie.

"This is Josie," she told them, patting the little girl's shoulder. She'd been too quiet today.

"A pleasure to meet you," Gracie said in her bubbly way.

Mary glanced at the lawyer behind Trevor, a lean man with a tired air to his sunken features. A chill rippled through her—this might be the last time she saw Josie.

Lou stalked toward them. She averted her gaze. She could not bear to look at him, not after their disastrous conversation.

"Are you okay?" Gracie peered at her, eyes wide, and Mary realized she'd missed something.

"I'm sorry. Just thinking."

"No, I shouldn't be chatting your ear off. They're going in for the meeting, though. I will wait out here for you. Shall I watch Josie?"

"Are you okay with that?" she asked the girl at her side. Josie's head moved slightly and though it pained her to leave Josie again, she took her hand and brought it to Gracie's.

"We're going to have great fun. I know a wonderful game...." Gracie's voice faded as Mary swiveled and headed toward the same interrogation room where Lou had kissed her. Her lips burned with the memory. Her heart ached.

He'd shot down her profession of love so easily.... Had she misread him this entire time? But surely he did not feel only brotherly things for her. No, he was a man in flux and there was nothing she could do about that. Feeling grim, she squeezed into the room.

The lawyer hadn't bothered sitting at the little table with its scrawny chairs. Instead, the men crowded into the small space, filling it with the scent of cologne and rustling suits. Lou's blue jeans were out of place and yet he still managed to look more comfortable than everyone else.

Even Trevor waited near the wall, his eyes sympathetic. She flashed him a weak smile and took a spot in the corner. Another man stood near Lou, perhaps a fellow agent? She huddled against the wall, feeling its bareness at her back.

The lawyer cleared his throat. "This is a highly unusual situation. Unforeseen, actually. The will is binding and unchangeable." His eyes skittered to Mary. Did he feel her fear? She blinked and looked away.

She found Lou staring at her. His face was unreadable, his thumbs hooked into the pockets of his jeans, and yet she thought she detected regret on his face. Or maybe she imagined it. With difficulty she pulled her attention from him and focused on the lawyer who held the rest of her dreams in his hands.

Mentally she shook herself. No. God held her dreams. She must trust Him because she had nothing left, no one left, to turn to.

The lawyer held up the packet, which looked cumbersome to her. "Are all parties ready for the reading of the will?" he asked.

Chapter Twenty-Six

God worked amazing wonders.

Mary watched passengers board the train in front of her. People milled around her, their voices melding with the sound of brakes and steam. Dirt and perfume mingled in the air, stirred by the excitement of those whose lives would change with a train ride, if only temporarily.

"When do we get to go on?" Josie tugged the hem of Mary's dress, her eagerness palpable.

Mary grinned at her and pulled her close. "As soon as Trevor returns."

They'd stayed in Portland a few days longer, going to the funeral and making arrangements for Josie's home, which Josie had inherited in the will. It had become obvious why Mr. Langdon wanted Josie out of the picture. She was a wealthy little girl now, but if she died, the money went to Mr. Langdon as next of kin. The lawyer had pronounced Mary, of all people, to be Josie's legal guardian. Apparently Mrs. Silver had changed her will at the last moment. Not only was Mary the named guardian, but she was also in charge of funds for the child's care.

They spent the nights at the hotel, and Josie slept in Mary's room with her. Though joy filled her at the thought of taking care of her precious girl, at being a mother, she hadn't been able to sleep well.

Her thoughts always returned to Lou.

Beside her, Gracie bobbed up and down on antsy feet. "It's been so long since I was home. Has anything changed?"

"Not quite. I had planned to paint the sitting room but someone spilled the bucket." Mary winked at Josie, whose smile widened in the burgeoning dawn light. "Maybe we can try again."

"Ooh, I'd love to help paint," Gracie gushed. "A passionate purple. Or maybe a subdued pear. It will be just the thing, except... Well, I must be careful of the fumes."

Fumes? Mary looked at her friend and saw the secret smile playing about her lips. Gracie's fingers splayed across her belly and knowledge sunk in. "You must be very careful, indeed. No ladders, either," she said.

They smiled at each other, the moment bonded by friendship.

"Can I get on the ladder? I won't fall," Josie added, a determined look in her sparkling eyes.

"We'll see," Mary said.

"That means no." A pout curved Josie's lips.

"Let's go." Trevor pushed through the crowd and beckoned them.

Josie's hand in hers, Mary followed Gracie and Trevor to the edge of the train. She was just about to board when a hand on her shoulder stopped her.

She turned to see Lou, mouth tight, eyes shadowed, his hat lying at a crooked angle on his head.

"Can we talk?" he asked.

"Now?"

The train whistled, signaling a warning. Mary looked up. Gracie gave her a thumbs-up and put her hand on Josie's shoulder, who was looking everywhere and hopping on one foot. Biting her lip, Mary moved away from the train, Lou right behind her.

He had filled her every waking moment. His smile. His kiss. The way she could talk to him, or even yell at him, and he didn't hurt for it. He didn't reject her.

Until she'd offered love.

"What do you need?" she asked now, more curt than necessary.

He studied her, gaze serious. "I need to know we're still friends."

Friends? She wanted to slap him at that moment. It was a shocking urge, so surprising that she clasped her fingers to keep from acting on it. Was it his fault that he still loved his wife? Could she fault a man for such loyalty? No, and yet her heart was splintering within her chest.

The lady means nothing to me.

He'd meant it more than she'd realized.

"Mary, I'm serious. I value your friendship and the way you've served our makeshift family. I know that lately I've been bossy. Demanding. But I did it for your own good." He doffed his hat and placed it against his chest. "I know I was wrong, though. That you're an adult capable of taking care of not only herself, but a little girl. She's something, isn't she?" A wistful look crossed his face, so at odds with the jut of his strong jawline and determined eyes.

Mary swallowed. "She is. And you and I are friends,

always." Much as it hurt to say, she could never deny him that.

"You've always had such loyalty. I envy it. My own family refused to speak to me for years because of my work with the bureau, and it's tough for me to forgive them. But I look at how you treat your ma, I see the love of God in your actions...." He trailed off before saying, "The way you live encourages me to live better."

She shifted, uncomfortable with his praise. With the entire situation, really. If he only knew. She looked at him and saw how he gazed at her, his eyes like sapphires in the sun. She wanted to remember this moment forever. Wanted to memorize the lines of his face, to touch them and carve them into the tips of her fingers, to hold on to always.

"I'm not perfect," she blurted. "Langdon said my mother led him to me. All she cared about was finding my father. If not for her, I would have never been kidnapped. I might be married, with a family. Emotionally whole." Her voice caught and she couldn't continue.

Her throat felt tight and raw. She waited for Lou's shock, but it didn't come. Instead, he winced. The minuscule movement stunned her. It was a physical blow. She staggered back, the pulse of her blood surging and then slowing, her lungs constricting until she thought she might never breathe again.

And yet she did. A deep, oxygen-filled inhalation borne of necessity.

"You knew," she whispered on her exhale.

"I knew." His eyes met hers. Apologetic.

Her hand shot out and connected with his cheek. He didn't move, not even when the mark from her hand suffused an angry red. She swallowed hard, her whole body aflame, her palm smarting. He'd known…for how long? How many secrets did he hold? How much more did he keep from her? She'd been very wrong to trust him.

"Secrets do not make a friendship," she said coldly. His face was blank, as if unaffected by her anger. So be it. She was done with this man, with everything. Never again would she allow herself to dream of him, to relive his recent kisses and his tender words over the years.

Shaking, she whirled and forced her trembling knees to march to the train, just as it let out another ear-splitting whistle.

Let Lou seek his revenge. Let him ignore the God who cared for him. Let him reject the woman who would have given him her all.

She was done with him and everything he represented.

Her eyes burned as she stepped onto the train and searched the seats for a familiar face. She had Josie, and she was going home.

She would have a family, with or without Lou Riley.

The heart was the biggest betrayer of all.

Mary discovered that unfortunate tidbit when she couldn't stop dreaming about Lou during the journey home. She'd see him stretching out his hand, asking for help, but her pride kept her heart far from him.

No.

Her broken feelings were the culprit, not pride, for even seeing him in her dreams caused her to wake with dried tears upon her cheek.

The bright spot in her life was Josie. Between her and Gracie's excited chatter, there was little time during the days' travel to pine over Lou. Only at night did he steal her sleep.

Finally, weary and dirty, they arrived at the ranch. Josie pounded up the steps, yelling for James. Gracie bounced around in excitement before grabbing Trevor for a long kiss. He embraced her, the quiet smile on his face testament to his love for his young bride.

God had changed him so deeply.... Could He do the same for Mary? Give her peace with how things had ended with Lou?

Feeling unsettled and scattered, Mary stepped out of the neighbor's wagon. James had been unable to meet their train due to ranch duties, and so Mr. Horn had come to fetch them.

"Don't forget the potluck next month," he said from his perch on the wagon seat. "It's our last meeting with food before the cold weather shows up. We've got a special afternoon of preaching and then supper and music. Miss Alma has everything planned out."

"We'll be there," Mary said feebly.

Mr. Horn inclined his head and then took off, his team of horses digging up the road and clouding the air with desert dirt. Summer in Harney County was dry and sunny. The climate remained the same. Not like her feelings, which had been flung about in a tornado of change.

Everyone had gone into the house, but she stayed outside, longing for freedom from the cage she'd put herself in. Not only did she feel guilty for saying what she had to Lou, but she dreaded seeing her mother.

It had been easy to forgive her when she'd understood a woman's need to find her husband. It was much harder now, knowing the nightmare of her past could have been prevented if only her mother had kept quiet. Examined more deeply Langdon's inquiry. Anything but flippantly giving out her daughter's whereabouts in exchange for her husband's.

She gripped her luggage and slowly walked to her house, leaving the ranch house behind. She must face her mother at some point. Now, with no audience, seemed best.

And yet her feet dragged. Knowing Trevor's mother had sold her hurt, but she'd been aware of Julia's character and hadn't been surprised. What her mother had done was a different matter.

A strong wind blew at her hair. How she wished it would also blow away this knowledge of her mother's unwitting betrayal.

Eventually she reached the house. Her mother stood near the gate, hair unplaited, eyes the deep black of the Paiute. Grimness painted her face into grooves and shadows. Her skirt whipped around her ankles and familiarity washed over Mary.

She'd wanted her mother here. Longed to see her restored to the laughing, beautiful woman of her youth. Maybe somehow she'd thought this would do the same for her, that if her mother was healed of her past, then she could be, also.

Did that mean she'd only been thinking of herself? That her motives had always been more selfish than she'd realized?

She stepped forward, eyes on her mother, a frown niggling at her lips.

"My daughter." Rose spoke quietly, and the breeze diluted her words into a faint sound of pleading.

She couldn't do this. She couldn't face her or accuse her. Better to leave things in the past.

"This morning James brought me a telegram from Lou," said Rose without blinking. "He wrote that you know what I never wished to confess. Do you understand his hatred for me now? Can you see why I hesitated to intrude in your home?"

Mary's mouth was so dry she could taste the desert upon her tongue.

"I have packed my bags and stayed only to tell you one thing—I am sorry, with the deepest regret a human can feel. This sorrow is a wound within my soul that does not heal. Nor should it. I have prayed to the spirits that you may have a good life. A blessed life with strong loves and much goodness." Rose blinked and a single tear edged from beneath her lashes. "You deserved more than what I gave you."

"Mother…" Mary dipped her head, hiding from the pain on her mother's face. She wanted to comfort her somehow, to ease her pain. *God help me.*

Seventy times seven.

The scripture reverberated through her. Like a seedling on the wind, dropped into the soil of her heart, and with her acceptance of His words, a new feeling spread through her. She lifted her head, feeling different, alive, helped. She stepped forward and before her mother could respond, embraced her.

She hugged her tightly for several moments, inhaling the wind in her mother's hair and the cedar scent that clung to her skin from her basket weaving.

When she felt able to speak, she pulled back and looked her mother in the eyes. "You speak of spirits and blessing. I am blessed and healed by One, my mother.

The One who created me. He also created you, and loves you. Though my life has had pain, it has not lacked comfort."

Rose nodded slowly, her lips trembling. "I have seen the peace on your face and wondered at it."

"Yes." Mary felt the smile start in her heart and work to her face. "My Bible says God is our comfort so that we can be a comfort to others."

"The white man's God is trouble." Her mother frowned.

Mary's smile wavered. "No. He has been my peace. And now, in His name, I offer you forgiveness."

Rose shivered as though the parched breath of desert wind sliced through her very bones.

"Please stay and live with me," Mary continued, feeling the wobble in her voice. "I love you, and though what you did hurts, I know we can be healed."

"How can you forgive me?" Her mother's eyes welled with tears. They dripped down her cheeks, filling the grooves like flooded riverbeds.

"Because…no one is perfect. Not one person but Christ Himself. I choose this path, Mother. Please walk it with me." Mary held out her hand, afraid, hoping her mother would take it, that she would pass from the shadowlands where she'd lived for too long.

After what seemed an interminable wait, her mother reached for her and burst into tears. Taken aback but feeling weepy herself, Mary allowed her mother to gather her into her arms.

She hadn't known she would forgive her mother, not until she'd seen that pain upon her face. Forgiveness was the right thing to do, and she hoped she would have done it anyway, whether or not her mother felt regret. But she did, and it was as though a piece of Mary's heart finally felt respite.

She rested her cheek against her mother's shoulder, and her thoughts turned to Lou. She hoped he'd find Mr. Langdon, because she had no doubt Josie's uncle would come looking for them at the ranch—it was only a matter of time.

Then perhaps Lou would run to Asia again. Maybe stay there this time, because to face his sorrows, to forgive God for the pain in his life, had proved too hard for him.

She hoped the best for him, she really did. But she also hoped for herself, because there was one part of her heart, a large portion, that might never be free unless she could let him go.

And right now, letting go wasn't even something she could imagine.

Chapter Twenty-Seven

A sea of ebony stretched before Lou. The image altered. A woman, small and gently curved, stood at the door. Glossy strands of her hair glistened beneath a milky moon. Her face… He couldn't see her face. He moved closer, his pulse thumping through him in quick, steady beats.

If only he could see her somehow. It wasn't Sarah. Her hair was blond. And she was gone, wasn't she? Gone forever. He waited for the familiar ache to surge through him, but it didn't arrive. Instead, he drew closer to the woman before him, the one whose expression he couldn't see. But he wanted to. He wanted to touch her skin, to see laughter light her eyes.

Moonlight flowed over her slight shoulders, undulating into the room where he stayed. He moved quickly, needing to reach her, but the moment his hand connected to her sleeve, she vanished and he awoke. He blinked, his eyes gritty and his feelings raw.

Mary's face swam before him, the way she'd looked when he'd kissed her that second time. Soft and dewy. In love.

And she'd said it, too. Said that she loved him, with luminous eyes and trust in her voice. Idiot that he was, he'd thrown her feelings in her face. Remembering how he'd mentioned Sarah, he groaned and pressed his palms against his eyes.

Enough whining. He'd made his bed and it was the best one for him. Common sense told him Mary needed a good man with a whole heart and a spiritual bent. What could he offer her? A house. That was about it.

You make her smile.

Okay, so he could give her some good stories. So what?

She trusts you.

Not anymore. Not since she found out he'd known her mother exposed her whereabouts to Langdon.

Muttering, he sat up and threw the flimsy blanket off his legs. He had a criminal to hunt down, and today was his last day to find him before shipping out for Hong Kong. If he didn't arrest Langdon today, he'd have to leave the duty to his team, and that wasn't going to happen.

This was his man and he'd get him no matter what.

He hurried out of bed, dressed and went in search of his junior agents.

"You're sure he's here?" Lou gazed dubiously at the rickety house in front of them. The structure seemed barely capable of standing against such a steep wind.

"Yep. I've been here several times in the past few years. They let the hooch sit here a spell after the drop-offs and then slowly move it out." O'Leary shaded his forehead against the sunset. "Langdon doesn't usually do the dirty work, but with heat on him, he's probably hiding out here. We've taken down his other spots and put the word out that we're done with the search. He's an arrogant fellow, usually handles the money and the politics. He doesn't suppose we'll keep looking for him now that we've got some success on the table."

"I'll take your word for it," said Lou grimly. Getting Langdon would be a real coup, not just professionally but personally, too. And if they couldn't get him on the shooting charge, they'd have a smuggling charge to put him away for a while.

He eyed the house. "Best way in?"

O'Leary, whom he'd specifically requested work at his side, gestured to the right. "Around back there's a cellar door. We'll drop in there and work our way up."

"Let's go." Lou and the four other men who made up their team followed O'Leary to the back. He located a heavy door set into the incline leading up to the abandoned house. The moan of the wind disguised the hinge's whine when O'Leary and Lou opened the cellar.

"It's not padlocked because the men use it routinely, and they don't expect theft in this place."

Lou glanced over his shoulder as the agents filed in. No other lights were visible on this rugged portion of Oregon landscape. Even the roads didn't come this far. They'd hiked a jagged path to reach the house. O'Leary had done his work well. Lou planned on making sure he received a commendation for it.

He dropped down after the last agent, leaving the cellar door open. The cold damp hit him square in the face and he suppressed a shiver. They followed O'Leary up the stairs quietly, and listened for sounds.

Nothing.

The lights had been on in the upper parts of the

house. O'Leary nudged the door open and Lou slid through first, revolver ready, back against the wall. He eased into what looked like the kitchen in the waning light. He cocked his head, listening, but only heard the shushed sound of the other men filtering into the room. They spread out in a tactical offense formation.

Lou used his gun to gesture upward. O'Leary nodded. He gave the other men the sign to scope out the rest of the house while he and Lou made their way to the next set of stairs. Positioned in the living room, the narrow staircase had obviously been built for much smaller people.

Lou semisquatted his way up the stairs, keeping O'Leary behind him. He didn't like casualties on his watch. Knew they happened, but not when he could help it. As they touched the top step, the crackle of a radio reached their hearing. He craned his head around the corner.

Unbelievable.

A short hiss escaped his lips, lost beneath the soft jazz emanating from the room. Langdon sat in a chair, head between his hands… Alone. No one else present that Lou could tell. The closet was open. A single window.

Wait, there might be a hallway…. He shifted a bit forward. Yes. An open door to Langdon's right looked like a hallway leading to other rooms. He'd go around, then, and leave O'Leary here.

He pulled back, motioned for the agent to stay put and went to the right. The narrow hall creaked with every step. He kept his gun ready, his eyes open until he reached a doorway on his left. Peeking in, he caught a glimpse of shaggy brown hair and blankets. Langdon's guard asleep on the bed.

That made things easy. He zipped into the bedroom and took care of the guard. He'd sleep for a few hours and wake up with a headache.

Satisfied, he stalked to the door that led to Langdon's room. He paused in the entry, aimed his gun and said softly, "I didn't take you for stupid."

Langdon startled, whipping his head up and looking wildly around. His eyes were bloodshot, his chin whiskered. Dirty light filtered in from the small window behind him.

"Had a tough time lately?" Lou goaded. "Lost your girl, business is shut down, times are hard all around. Where're your goons? The one sleeping in the bed was easy to take care of. I expected more from you." He showed his teeth in what might pass as a smile to some. "Stand up."

Langdon glared at him but did as he said. "I hope you have a warrant." His sneer was filled with arrogance.

"Got it and more. You're facing quite a bit of time, you know. Your cohorts are snitches, every one of them. Got no loyalty to you."

"You have nothing."

"I've an eyewitness to attempted murder."

"Who?" he scoffed.

Lou's lips twitched. "Me."

Langdon's face visibly paled. His eyes darted. "Says who? I want my lawyer."

"You'll get him. Make no mistake about that. In the meantime, why don't we have a little chat. Off the record." Lou used his shoe to flip the door behind him closed. He stepped into the room, keeping his revolver trained on his quarry. No doubt Langdon had some kind of pistol stored on his person.

"I'm not talking."

"Sure you are. We'll just have a nice little chat about Mary." Lou looked down the barrel of his .38. "She's a special lady. You've had your eye on her for a long time, and the way I figure things, your time is about up. In fact, it's been up."

"I don't know what you're talking about," Langdon said stiffly. His fingers clenched at his side, inching toward a pocket.

"Wouldn't do that if I were you. At this range, there's no way I'd miss that pretty face of yours. I don't think you'd like that."

Langdon's fingers wavered, then slowly moved into a more relaxed position.

"That's a good smuggler," Lou murmured. "Here's the thing—you'll be done following Mary. You'll leave her alone and never set foot in Harney County again."

"Or what?"

The silky arrogance of his voice set Lou's teeth on edge. He just wanted to shoot this guy, get rid of him forever. He could feel the anger burning through his veins.

"You don't want to find out. I expect you'll be put away for a long, long time."

Langdon's face twisted suddenly. All the smoothness left it, the spoiled surety wiped away by a bitterness Lou hadn't expected to see.

"You think you know everything." Langdon spat on the floorboards. "Mary's nothing to me, but I plan to ruin her just like her mother ruined my father."

Well, this was new. Lou narrowed his eyes. "You're out for revenge?"

"Justice, the kind the law doesn't mete out. The kind God forgets to give. Mary thinks God is watching out for her, but she's wrong. He looks out for no man. Her mother destroyed my father. Stole his money, broke his heart and left him a withered, whupped old man. He killed himself a year later. I was sixteen. Mary's mother, *Rose*—" he said her name with vitriol, his face marred by angry lines "—will pay for what she did to me. God doesn't hand out justice, but I do."

"Why are you telling me all this?" Lou asked in a deliberately bored tone.

"Because I want you to know that I will never, ever give up. Mary is my revenge, and it doesn't hurt that she has a face a man doesn't forget. This will never be over until Rose feels the torture my family experienced. You can put me away—" Langdon's voice lowered to a hiss "—but you will never stop me."

Lou's finger itched to stroke the trigger. A bit of pressure. That was all it would take to make this mess go away.

And then he'd be no better than Langdon. Using his power to get what he wanted. Believing God had no place in his actions, that God didn't care. Lou swallowed, his throat tight.

Right now, with the mustiness of the room in his nose, the impaired light that washed Langdon into shadows, Lou felt as if his soul was being tested. As if his decision at this moment would affect the rest of his life.

He looked at Langdon and saw himself. The anger over his past. Everything that had gone wrong, things he had no control over, things he'd believed God should control. He'd read enough of the Bible as a kid to know it said God gave each person a free will to make his or her own choices.

But Sarah and Abby hadn't chosen to get sick. They hadn't chosen death. It had chosen them.

His stomach clenched, but his aim didn't waver. Langdon watched him carefully, his entire being poised in stillness. Whether they had chosen sickness or not, he didn't want to be like Langdon, letting his bitterness over the past poison him until there was nothing left but evil. Maybe Langdon had been born this way; maybe there was something off with his mind that had nothing to do with his childhood.

Nevertheless, Lou felt as if he'd come to some kind of crossroads. A place to make a choice and to change the course of his life. He looked at Langdon and felt anger and pity. Setting his jaw, he repositioned his weapon and gave Langdon a hard stare.

He knew what he had to do.

"Got a telegram from Lou," James announced, coming into the kitchen where Mary had laid out four pies, a cake and a platter of snickerdoodles.

Despite the delicious scents permeating her kitchen, Mary's stomach roiled. Six weeks later and the mention of Lou's name still unsettled her so badly she couldn't eat. She covered her apple pie with a cloth, noticing how her fingers trembled.

"He's left the Orient. Done with special agent stuff," James added when Mary didn't respond.

She didn't know what to say. She could feel James's gaze on her and ignored him in favor of covering the rest of her dishes. They'd have to hold them tight to keep them from being smashed in the wagon.

"You riding with me to the church picnic?" he asked.

She nodded and handed him her snickerdoodles. "Hold that very carefully."

He balanced the cookies in one hand. "Your ma is staying home, ya know."

While Mary and Rose had gone far in mending their relationship, her mother still felt uncomfortable in church-like settings. Mary hoped someday she'd feel good about joining them, but for now it was a blessing she'd stayed.

"Josie might feel badly that Mother isn't going," she said, stacking a pie gently into a Pyrex storage container.

"Nah." James snickered. "That girl is running all over the place, and Gracie thinks it's fun joining her. I've got the feeling Josie'll be riding with Trevor and Gracie to the picnic. You and me will ride in the wagon. We've got to get a move on to make it in time. Alma don't like it when I'm late." A funny smile crossed his face, and Mary paused with her fiddling.

Was he in love?

He caught her glance, but the mooning look didn't leave his face. "Sometimes it takes an old man time to figure out the important things in life." He winked at her and left, carrying the snickerdoodles with him.

She continued filling her pie holder, but her emotions threatened to overflow. She blinked hard and picked up the carrier. The wagon was parked just outside the front door. Carefully she maneuvered through the kitchen door, traipsed down the hall and let herself out into the warm August weather.

The sun chose to shine today. It was neither hot nor chilly. Perfect for a picnic. She heard Josie's squeals and watched her balance atop a horse, Trevor and Gracie on either side of the saddle.

Smiling, Mary loaded the food onto the wagon and then climbed in. James had thoughtfully left a hat for her on the seat. He must have snagged it from her living room. She arranged it on her head, trying to feel happy about the picnic.

After all, God had heard her prayers. He'd given her a family. Brought her mother back to her, given her a daughter to love. Even James felt like a father to her. With Trevor and Gracie staying at the ranch, she should have felt content with their big family dinners and the long walks they took together.

She didn't, though. There was always this nagging awareness of something missing. When she went to town, her eyes caught on every blond man she saw. She paused at the sound of a man's low tones. Everywhere she went, she thought she saw Lou. She hoped to feel his hand on her shoulder, to see the sparkle in his eyes or the way his lips turned at the corners when he smiled. His ready laugh followed her.

James heaved himself into the wagon beside her. The horses pranced, ready for their jaunt. Their manes wavered in front of Mary, blurring as an unwelcome stinging filled her eyes. She blinked again, harder this time.

"You okay, Mary girl?" James patted her shoulder, his palms an awkward pressure on her blouse.

"I'll be fine." She tried to quiet her sniffle, but it came out loud and unattractive.

"Anything you want to talk about?" His voice was gruff but kind.

He hated emotional outbursts. She knew that, but wanted nothing more than to cry and ask him why a man kissed a woman, listened to her pain, gave her advice and then left her for a job across the ocean. Why couldn't a man say goodbye to a family he no longer had, to welcome a new family? He didn't even have to say goodbye, she wouldn't expect that. She just wanted him to be willing to be open to a new season in his life. To change.

But evidently that was too much for Lou. Frowning, she picked at a piece of linen sticking out from one of her pies. "Let's just go, James. There's nothing to change what is."

"Now, now, you never know what's around the corner. Miss Alma surely took me by surprise." He let out a crackly laugh that tilted Mary's lips a bit.

"I'm sure you must have seen her coming," she pointed out. "Miss Alma is not a subtle person."

"What I didn't see coming were my own feelings. When I fixed that pipe at her house while you were making mischief in Portland, why, I stood up, caught a sniff of something baking in the oven and that fancy perfume she wears, and I just felt like I'd gone home. Like there was something missing out of my life and she held that missing piece, right there in her bathroom."

Mary bit her bottom lip, torn between happiness for James and sadness for herself. "So that's how she snagged you, food and perfume?"

"Nope. It was that home feeling." He cracked the reins and the horses set off. Mary gripped her pies. "Not that you haven't provided a home, my girl, but I always knew I was an employee."

"Oh, no." She turned to him. "You've been…like a father to me. In so many ways."

His cheeks flushed. "Well, I'm right glad to hear that." He cleared his throat. "Mark my words, Mary girl. If Lou don't get himself home soon, if he don't make right whatever's wrong between you two, then he's a bigger fool than I thought. You deserve better. My Alma told me she's got a surprise for you at this picnic."

Mary stifled her groan. "Don't tell me it's a man."

"Well, now, I didn't say that. I don't want her thinking I ruined your surprise."

"Here's the thing, James." She took a deep breath and suddenly found she believed it. "I miss Lou and hope he'll come home, but I am blessed and filled by the family I have. I don't need a man to make me whole or to give me purpose."

"Nah. I know that." He shot her a grin. "But love, not a man, surely makes a person's life more full."

She looked forward and exhaled her pent-up breath. That might very well be, but she wouldn't put her life on hold, hadn't, in fact, waiting for a love that might never come.

For a love that almost was.

Chapter Twenty-Eight

❧

Lou came home to an empty ranch.

Dropping his luggage in the hallway, he meandered around the empty house before stepping back outside. It was a nice August day, perfect for an outing. Maybe that was where everyone had gone.

Fatigue pulled at his eyelids. He shook his head, ran fingers through hair that hadn't been trimmed in a while. He circled the house and headed toward Mary's home. Flowers bloomed outside her door.

He knocked, and Mary's mother answered. She looked happier than he'd ever seen her, a smile playing on her lips and knitting needles in her hand.

"You are here for my daughter?"

He nodded.

Rose studied him carefully. He couldn't read her dark eyes but somehow felt her disapproval. "They went to Horn's," she said finally. She touched the door, beginning to swing it closed, but he stopped her.

"I've got something to get off my chest," he said. Taking a deep breath, he kept her gaze. "I treated you wrongly. Will you forgive me?"

This time she blinked and it seemed as though her features softened. Then her lips curved again. "*Besa soobeda*. This is a good thing," she said quietly. "You are forgiven. Find my daughter and make things right."

The door shut. Grinning, he pivoted and went to get a horse.

He supposed he could wait for them to get home, but he didn't want to. Mary's mother was right. He hadn't traveled for so long to come home to emptiness.

He was back to do what he should have six weeks ago. No, what he should have done months ago. It had only taken seeing an old friend with his new family for him to realize that he'd made a huge mistake. Interspersed in all his traveling was some Bible reading and serious soul searching.

He readied a horse and within minutes was galloping toward the Horn place. It didn't take long to find the huge picnic in progress. The scents reached him before he could even distinguish faces.

He patted the rump of his roan and tied her up next to the other horses. He spotted Trevor's truck parked next to the few other vehicles some had dared to drive over the challenging roadways.

Sparse grasses flowed with the direction of the breeze. A bird twittered in the oak beside him. He took a steadying breath, surprised by the tightness of his gut. He'd faced down professional killers and never felt this nervous.

Wiping his hands against his jeans, he set off toward the picnic. Children shrieked with delight as a small dog ran in circles around them, yapping and wagging its tail. Other kids were climbing Horn's maple. They'd have skinned shins, no doubt, by the end of the picnic.

He grinned, thinking of his own childhood and all its adventures.

"Mister Lou!" The high-pitched scream barely reached him before Josie smacked into his leg. He chuckled, reached under her arms and threw her into the air. Her squeal almost shattered his eardrums.

Laughing, he brought her close and hugged her.

"I missed you so much," she said into his ear, her arms a vise around his neck.

His smile quivered, and he hugged her tighter. "I missed you, too."

She pulled back and gave him a serious look. Her purple ribbon hung over one eye. "Are you leaving again? Because I don't think Miss Mary will like that very much."

"What about you?" he teased, tweaking her nose. "Don't you want me to stay?"

Her eyes rounded and her whole body tensed. "Are you teasing me?"

He winked at her. "Let's just say I plan on sticking around, if Miss Mary will have me."

Her face lit up and she wiggled to get free. "Okay, I'm going to get her right now and tell her you have to stay."

"Wait, wait," he said, laughing and putting her down. "Let me surprise her."

"Ooh, I like surprises!"

"Shh." He rubbed her head and she leaned into his touch, beaming at him with such wide-eyed openness that his chest clenched with emotion. "I love you, little Josie. Do you know that?"

She nodded, a very solemn look crossing her face. "I know, Mister Lou. I love you, too, ya know."

Smiling, he fixed her ribbon. "Come back in a bit and I'll get you some chocolate cake."

"Miss Mary said I had to eat my broccoli first. I hate broccoli!" She scampered off before he could respond, which was all well and good because at that moment he glimpsed the shine of black hair moving through the crowd of people.

He moved toward her, his heart racing, his stomach churning. He'd wondered how he'd feel when he saw her again, and the emotions roaring through him proved to be more powerful than he expected.

He stepped over a bush and followed Mary to the dessert table. Of course that was where she'd be. Checking out the goods, arranging them just so. She'd always be a homemaker.

She was quiet and deep, like a refreshing lake in the middle of a forest. Fresh and sweet to the taste, offering sustenance to all those who visited. He'd missed this stillness of hers, the ability she had of setting anyone at ease with her gentle smile.

Even her movements were soft and contained…and yet he remembered her in his arms. Full of passion and energy, giving all of herself to him in the way only a woman in love can do. His throat felt hot and tight as he watched her rearrange snickerdoodles on a plate. Her hair was up in some kind of doodad. Its glossiness beckoned to him. He wanted to pull it down, let the waves flow wild in the breeze, let them weave through his fingers with abandon.

He wanted her in his arms.

His hands ached to hold her, to feel the love she offered. But was he enough? Could he make her happy?

Swallowing hard, he stepped behind her. He saw the moment she felt his presence. Her back stiffened. There was the slightest intake of air, almost indiscernible beneath the noise of the picnic.

* * *

Mary swiveled around, her hand against her heart.

Lou grinned at her, his lips curving in that familiar way, smile lines fanning out from his eyes, and her breath caught so hard she choked.

Coughing, she put her hand against her mouth. He was immediately near her, rubbing her back, asking if she was okay.

She nodded, face hot. It wasn't fair how he made her feel, these emotions he'd brought alive in her.

"You're back," she managed to croak. Not the most attractive speaking she'd ever done. Her neck felt on fire.

"I'm back." His mouth twisted into a rueful smile. "China wasn't quite what I wanted."

"Oh?" she breathed. Words were forsaking her and she did not appreciate their absence.

"It looks like you've been doing well without me." His hand waved in the air. "You even talked James into attending a church picnic. Impressive."

She swallowed, willing herself to breathe normally when every nerve ending tingled with unspoken anticipation. "That was Miss Alma's doing."

"Ah. Somehow I'm not surprised." Lou's eyes twinkled and he moved closer, edging into her space. "And you? Now that I'm not your employer, how have you been surviving?"

"My mother is with me. She sells her baskets."

"No need to be defensive. I'm sorry about what happened with her, but if you can look past it, I can." His finger came out to touch her cheek.

She shivered.

His gaze probed and she couldn't look away from the intensity in the blueness of his eyes. "What I want to know is how *you* are doing," he repeated in a low tone.

She wet her lips, unnerved and yet strangely alert to his attention. "I'm fine. Besides my selling herbs to him, Joseph at the general store likes me to bring in baked goods two or three times a week. The town ladies enjoy getting fresh, ready-made food. It is enough money for something I enjoy doing."

"Sounds like you're handling things just fine, then. Not needing me, I suppose?"

What did he mean by that? She studied him, her voice coming out stiffer than she expected. "I am content."

"Well," he said, his fingers rubbing through his hair and sending it in all sorts of directions, "wish I could say the same about myself."

Her brows lifted.

"See, this here's the thing. I'm not doing good at all. In fact, I'm miserable." The smile left his face. "I had a girl once, a long time ago, who I loved. She was carefree and opinionated. She was a bright fire that burned out too quickly. And I thought I'd never survive when she took our baby with her."

Mary's heart pounded beneath her sternum, an unsteady beat that matched the pace of her breathing.

"I thought I'd never feel whole again. But when I was shot, things began to change. So before I left Oregon for China, I put in for a different job." He shrugged, a thoughtful look on his face. "And then I traveled to Hong Kong, lots on my mind. I thought I'd left God in the dust, but He's been pursuing me. He's in my thoughts all the time. I think of you and I see Him. So I popped open the Bible and pretty soon I started feeling this change. This remembrance." His gaze turned very solemn. "I never told you this, but Sarah and I were churchgoing folk. I believed in Jesus and followed Him. When she died—"

"I'm sorry, Lou." Mary couldn't help it, the words slipped past her lips and broke his confession.

"But I don't want you to be sorry." His eyes crinkled. "I reached China, and the man who met me was an old agent friend. He'd lost so much, like me, but when he met me at the port, he had a wife and child with him. He'd moved on, and I realized so had I."

Mary glanced around at the picnic. She saw people watching them surreptitiously. James had his arms around a very satisfied-looking Miss Alma. Gracie was giving her a thumbs-up.

Lou gripped her shoulders, forcing her attention to him. His hands were gentle, his fingers rotating in a comforting movement against her blouse. "I visited Sarah's and Abby's graves."

She felt her eyes widen at his words.

"And I was okay. As I knelt there, I thought of how I'd loved them but then I thought about how I love Josie. And—" he trailed off, his eyes softening "—how I love you."

She sucked in air, suddenly feeling fear spread through her. Biting her lower lip, she pulled from his grasp. "But your job—"

"Is nothing without a home to come home to. What I realized is that God is giving me what I've missed for so long. He's been trying for a long time, but I was too dumb to realize it. You're the home for my heart, Mary." He crowded her again, backing her against the dessert table, but somehow she didn't feel encroached upon. Rather, she felt enveloped, hugged…safe. "Whenever I come home from a trip, I look for you. It's been like that for years, but I chalked it up to brotherly feelings.

To friendship. What you said weeks ago, about us not being friends, you were right. I don't want friendship."

"You don't?" she whispered. Her whole body trembled. She could hardly think.

His hand reached up and touched her hair, then slid down to cup her cheek. His palm was firm and strong. "I love you so much it hurts to breathe. I want to hold you and be with you, to inhale the scent of your hair while you bake, to watch your fingers works as you knit, to go to sleep with you and wake in the morning, your hand in mine. When I think of you, I think of heat and strength and goodness. I don't ever want to let you go."

Mary pressed her lips together, hardly daring to believe what he was saying, and yet her pulse sped with the honesty in his voice. "Your job?" she ventured carefully.

He chuckled. "You're awfully worried about that, aren't you? Langdon is going to be locked away for a long time. We've got more witnesses against him. I put in for a position with the Harney County Sheriff's Office and was accepted. Turns out they think I'll be good at the job, with a little training. Any more questions?"

She shook her head, wondering in a very scattered way if this was the moment where they'd kiss. Her lips tingled at the thought.

"Good, because I have one more question for you, and I'm going to need a direct answer." His smile spread lopsided across his face and his eyes sparkled. He dropped down on one knee. There was a collective silence, and Mary felt every picnicker's eye upon them.

"Mary O'Roarke, woman I love, the one lady I want to spend the rest of my life with, will you marry me?" He held up a ring. The light caught the planed surfaces of a modest diamond, splaying rainbow glints.

"Of course she will," Josie piped up from beside her.

She hadn't even felt the little girl's presence, but here she was, her back straight and stoic, her tone firmer than a mama with a naughty little boy. Mary couldn't hold back her smile; her lips curved and wouldn't straighten.

"You think so?" Lou asked her, his own lips playing tag with his cheeks.

"I know so," Josie asserted, but there was the slightest tremble to her words.

"In that case, let me present you with your ring," said Lou. He pulled out a tiny diamond solitaire.

Josie gasped. "For me?"

"Yep. It's a symbol of our devotion."

"I'm going to wear it forever! Look, James." She ran off and Lou stood, the ring still in his hand. "What do you say, Mary?" An uncertain look entered his eyes.

Taking a deep breath, smile unwavering, she held out her fingers. "I'd say I'd like to see how it fits."

Laughing, he slid the ring onto her finger and pulled her close. His lips met hers and she felt his smile against hers, and then they were heart to heart, fingers entwined.

When the kiss ended, when the cheers and whoops from onlookers quieted, Lou pressed his cheek against hers and whispered in her ear, "What God has brought together, let no man tear asunder. Here's to our new family."

She giggled and kissed him again. When she felt sufficiently dizzy and slack limbed, she pulled back and winked at him. "To our family on the range."

* * * * *

**IF YOU ENJOYED THIS BOOK
WE THINK YOU WILL ALSO LOVE**

LOVE INSPIRED
INSPIRATIONAL ROMANCE

Uplifting stories of faith, forgiveness and hope.

Fall in love with stories where faith helps
guide you through life's challenges, and discover
the promise of a new beginning.

6 NEW BOOKS AVAILABLE EVERY MONTH!

LOVE INSPIRED

INSPIRATIONAL ROMANCE

UPLIFTING STORIES OF FAITH, FORGIVENESS AND HOPE.

———————————

Join our social communities to connect with other readers who share your love!

Sign up for the Love Inspired newsletter at **LoveInspired.com** to be the first to find out about upcoming titles, special promotions and exclusive content.

———————————

CONNECT WITH US AT:

f Facebook.com/LoveInspiredBooks

🐦 Twitter.com/LoveInspiredBks

Facebook.com/groups/HarlequinConnection

Get 4 FREE REWARDS!

We'll send you 2 FREE Books plus 2 FREE Mystery Gifts.

Love Inspired books feature uplifting stories where faith helps guide you through life's challenges and discover the promise of a new beginning.

FREE
Value Over
$20

YES! Please send me 2 FREE Love Inspired Romance novels and my 2 FREE mystery gifts (gifts are worth about $10 retail). After receiving them, if I don't wish to receive any more books, I can return the shipping statement marked "cancel." If I don't cancel, I will receive 6 brand-new novels every month and be billed just $5.24 each for the regular-print edition or $5.99 each for the larger-print edition in the U.S., or $5.74 each for the regular-print edition or $6.24 each for the larger-print edition in Canada. That's a savings of at least 13% off the cover price. It's quite a bargain! Shipping and handling is just 50¢ per book in the U.S. and $1.25 per book in Canada.* I understand that accepting the 2 free books and gifts places me under no obligation to buy anything. I can always return a shipment and cancel at any time. The free books and gifts are mine to keep no matter what I decide.

Choose one: ☐ **Love Inspired Romance**
Regular-Print
(105/305 IDN GNWC)

☐ **Love Inspired Romance**
Larger-Print
(122/322 IDN GNWC)

Name (please print)

Address   Apt. #

City   State/Province   Zip/Postal Code

Email: Please check this box ☐ if you would like to receive newsletters and promotional emails from Harlequin Enterprises ULC and its affiliates. You can unsubscribe anytime.

Mail to the **Harlequin Reader Service:**
IN U.S.A.: P.O. Box 1341, Buffalo, NY 14240-8531
IN CANADA: P.O. Box 603, Fort Erie, Ontario L2A 5X3

Want to try 2 free books from another series! Call 1-800-873-8635 or visit www.ReaderService.com.

---

*Terms and prices subject to change without notice. Prices do not include sales taxes, which will be charged (if applicable) based on your state or country of residence. Canadian residents will be charged applicable taxes. Offer not valid in Quebec. This offer is limited to one order per household. Books received may not be as shown. Not valid for current subscribers to Love Inspired Romance books. All orders subject to approval. Credit or debit balances in a customer's account(s) may be offset by any other outstanding balance owed by or to the customer. Please allow 4 to 6 weeks for delivery. Offer available while quantities last.

Your Privacy—Your information is being collected by Harlequin Enterprises ULC, operating as Harlequin Reader Service. For a complete summary of the information we collect, how we use this information and to whom it is disclosed, please visit our privacy notice located at corporate.harlequin.com/privacy-notice. From time to time we may also exchange your personal information with reputable third parties. If you wish to opt out of this sharing of your personal information, please visit readerservice.com/consumerschoice or call 1-800-873-8635. **Notice to California Residents**—Under California law, you have specific rights to control and access your data. For more information on these rights and how to exercise them, visit corporate.harlequin.com/california-privacy.   LIR21R